If Only
She Knew

Derville Murphy

POOLBEG

Published 2021
by Poolbeg Press Ltd
123 Grange Hill, Baldoyle,
Dublin 13, Ireland
Email: poolbeg@poolbeg.com

A catalogue record for this book is available from the British Library.

ISBN 978178199-4177

www.poolbeg.com

About the Author

Derville Murphy practised for many years as an architect and art curator before completing an M Phil, Irish Art History, TCD, and subsequently a PhD in Art and Architecture, UCD. In 2008 she founded art@work art consultancy. As an artist, she has exhibited widely, with solo exhibitions in 2005 and 2007 in the RIAI – her paintings are in several public art collections. As an academic, she has written articles for journals including the *Irish Art Review* and *Architecture Ireland.*

If She Only Knew is her second novel. Her debut novel *The Art Collector's Daughter* was published by Poolbeg in 2019.

Dedicated to Brendan Murphy

Acknowledgements

They say everyone has a book in them – I feel that this is my book. It was the bridge between academic and creative writing – a big leap of faith, particularly for an art historian. "She's written a bodice-ripper," I imagine – with a certain amount of paranoia – them saying. But when I finished this novel, I realised that writing historical fiction enabled me to understand people and real-life events in a way that the cold facts of history seldom did.

At the beginning of this journey, Dr Philip McEvansoneya and Dr Rachel Moss from Trinity College Dublin, and Art Historian Éimear O'Connor, ignited my interest in Margaret Allen, Victorian Art, and overlooked Irish women artists generally.

To unlearn academic writing, a skill that had been a struggle to acquire in the first place, and for teaching me how to write a novel, my heartfelt thanks are due to the inspiring and generous author and educator Patricia O'Reilly, who runs the UCD adult-learning, creative-writing course. Patricia's classes were a warm, friendly and safe place for me and many other aspiring writers to craft our novel-writing skills.

Once the book was written, early beta-readers were Deirdre Grant, Ger Canavan and Mary Byrne, literary PR consultant, all of whom gave me enormous encouragement which, at the time, was really important to me. Also, thanks to Jonathan Williams, Literary Agent, for his helpful advice, and Vanessa Fox O'Loughlin for facilitating 'Date with an Agent', and her ongoing support for Irish authors on the writing.ie website.

Thanks, as always, to my book-club buddies, Marguerite Hanratty and Yvonne and Mavis Donnelly, for their constant encouragement and, sometimes, therapy. Likewise, to my writing group: Elaine Banfield, Carol Hayden, Tricia Holbrook, Elizabeth McGillion, Ger Whelan and Monica Whelan.

Once more, the team at Poolbeg have been a joy to work with. I would like to thank the wonderful, multiskilled Paula Campbell, Publisher, for making all this possible, and Gaye Shortland, whose editing skills have greatly enhanced the final product.

Finally, thank you to my lovely husband Brendan who always supports me in everything I do.

Author's Note

This novel describes fictional characters and events, inspired by my research into the life and times of Margaret Allen HRHA (1832-1914) who, in 1878, became the first female artist to become an honorary member of the Royal Hibernian Academy. I would also like to acknowledge Christy Campbell's fascinating historical research in *Fenian Fire* (Harper Collins Publishers, 2003) into Fenian and British Government activity during the Irish Home Rule debate which inspired aspects of the plot. However, although several historical figures are featured, such as the republicans John Devoy and Jeremiah O'Donovan Rossa, the dynamite plot at the Botanical Gardens, Manchester, is entirely fictional.

Derville Murphy

Prologue

Water surrounded them. It was high tide, the marsh was flooded, and the wooden bridge seemed to be endless. It was as if they were walking out into the middle of the bay. People, dressed in their Sunday best, smiled as they passed by – she knew they made a handsome couple. Eventually, when they reached the island, they started the long walk along the empty beach, as a quarrelsome horde of seagulls squawked overhead. A sea breeze brushed across her skin, speckling it with fine grains of sand. She adjusted her bonnet which had become loose, her chignon askew. Her other arm was beginning to ache from the weight of the lunch things in the basket. Carrying the bag with their paints, brushes and the two folios of watercolour paper, he walked slowly beside her, so she could keep up with his long stride. But the going was heavy and as the sand got softer, less travelled, she could feel grains of it in her boots. To add to her discomfort, the shiny layers of her mourning costume absorbed the sun's rays, making her hot and irritable. She felt like a wounded magpie, or a crow, trapped and unable to escape. She regretted agreeing to come.

Eventually they stopped. He looked out to sea.

"The view is perfect here," he observed.

In the distance the Hill of Howth glistened as if it were floating on the horizon – a seascape, like aqueous moire silk, shimmering and pulsating in the midday sun.

They turned westward and headed into the dunes. Wild rabbits scurried ahead of them between sea pinks and tufted shards of seagrass only to disappear as others, appearing out of nowhere, replaced them. Finally, they reached the island's marshy edge where only the seabirds ventured.

There, the taste of salt on her tongue, he lay her on the coarse woollen blanket and carefully unhooked her bodice. As he lifted her skirt, her heart racing, she felt the strange sensation of the heat of the midday sun caressing her skin.

Part One

꙳ꙮ꙳

Chapter 1

14 Westland Row, Dublin
24th May 1872

Her sister was late. They say, some things never change. But after today, she thought, everything, even Julia, would have to change, and change irrevocably. Harriet looked out of the window at the busy street below to see if she could catch sight of her as musical chimes marked the hour from the carriage clock on the bureau. At this stage, lunchtime traffic was building up with people coming and going from the railway station. Travellers were laden down with portmanteaus, holdalls, and bags of all shapes and sizes clutched to their chests or thrown over their shoulders, military style. And at the road's edge, horse-drawn cabs lined up to collect the wealthier passengers who had just arrived from the seaside towns of south County Dublin and were discharging into Westland Row. Whilst between the carriages, street urchins lurked, nonchalant, poised to fleece the gullible.

Harriet returned to her seat, breathing in slowly. Her mother, who appeared to have shrunk since the onset of widowhood, sat beside her. On the other side of the wide mahogany desk sat Mr Octavius Roe. The room was airless and stuffy. Her mother's gardenia perfume was overpowering and competed with the pungent, old-man smells of tobacco and unwashed linen emanating from the greasy solicitor. She wondered why the old goat did not open the window. She coughed delicately into her lace-edged handkerchief.

With a flicker, Mr Roe drew his own white-linen handkerchief from his waistcoat pocket and blew his bulbous nose loudly. Then, even though the funeral had occurred two years previously, he began to drone on about the remarkable respect shown by the good people of Dublin who had attended St Mark's in their droves. Also, the virtue of the graveside oration in Mount Jerome by Reverend Charles Benson. With his slightly shortened upper lip pulled back into a grimace, intending to project respectful sorrow, Roe displayed teeth that were long and yellow like a donkey's.

Harriet thought with grim amusement how she would describe the scene to Edward later.

A door could be heard opening below at street level, and Bridget the housekeeper greeting Julia who had just arrived.

"How are yeh, Miss Benson. Himself is waiting upstairs with your mother and sister. Go on up, miss, no need to announce yeh."

Julia appeared at the door of the room.

"So sorry I am late, Mama and Harriet. Apologies, Mr Roe. I was so absorbed in my painting I did not realise the time."

"The artistic spirit," mumbled Roe as he visually devoured Julia, who, slightly dishevelled, unceremoniously entered the room.

6

"My dear Julia," her mother sighed, patting the empty chair beside her.

"Could we get this rather unpleasant business over, Mr Roe, if you would be so kind," said Harriet, sitting on the edge of her chair.

"Of course, Miss Harriet."

Roe examined the document in his hand and coughed for effect. "This is the Last Will and Testament of Mr Mark Benson of 14 Westland Row –"

"Mr Roe, could you cut to the chase, please?" said Harriet. "I have to get back over to Gardiner's Row for a lesson at two o'clock."

"Of course, Miss Harriet, so sorry." He continued, "I, Mark Benson, leave all my worldly goods and effects, amounting to four hundred and fifty pounds, including Mark Benson and Co. printing and lithographic business, the lease on 14 Westland Row, bank shares and other sundry funds to my daughter Miss Harriet Benson of 14 Westland Row, who is to be the principal beneficiary of my estate." He paused and looked up at the three women.

There was a stunned silence as Harriet's mother and sister exchanged horrified glances.

"There must be some mistake," said Mrs Benson.

"Yes, I am the eldest daughter by two years," said Julia.

"No, there is no mistake. Is that not so, Miss Harriet? Your father left quite explicit instructions. All his worldly goods – other than your late grandfather's books and a silver cup and salver donated to him by the artists of Dublin which are left to Julia – are bequeathed to you."

Harriet rose to leave, avoiding her sister's eyes.

"Thank you, Mr Roe. We will be in touch shortly no doubt. Mama, Julia, we must not detain Mr Roe any longer. Maybe it would be better if we talked about this at home."

Mama, instantly energised, pulled herself up from the chair and stormed out of the room. Julia, glaring at Harriet, followed in quick succession. As she reached the door, she turned to her sister, her face contorted with rage.

"*You won't get away with this!*" she shouted furiously as she banged the door shut with unnecessary force.

"This was never going to be easy, Mr Roe," Harriet said apologetically to the solicitor.

"Indeed, Miss Harriet. Indeed," he responded, as Harriet offered him her hand.

A painful hour spent with the practically tone-deaf Miss Lynott at the Misses Allens' School of Music, trying to teach her one of Moore's melodies – so that she at least had sufficient skill not to embarrass her mother at social events – had exacerbated Harriet's pounding headache. She decided not to take a hansom cab – a growler – although she was supposed to. She had declined the younger Miss Allen's usual offer to let her girl, Ruby, accompany her home. If Papa were still alive, he would have insisted on it. Instead, she would walk. She would save the sixpence fare and the exercise might clear her head. She needed to be alone to think after the morning's meeting.

The afternoon sky was clear, although it had rained earlier, and the low sun cast long shadows on wet pavements. As she walked briskly down Sackville Street, towards the lower end where it was all hustle and bustle, she did not tarry. She passed by the colourful awnings of Findlaters, and the Gresham Hotel, and for once she was blind to the lure of this season's costumes in the plate-glass windows of Delany's store. On the far side of the wide street, near Nelson's Column, fruit-sellers were displaying their wares under the colonnaded portico of the GPO. The cacophony of sounds – the incomprehensible shouts of the hawkers, and the grating of steel wheels on cobblestone – all made her head ache even more. Trying to blank out the noise, she pushed ahead as swarms of scantily clad children ran barefoot amongst the mud and filth of the streets. "*Miss, could yeh spare a penny for a starvin' chiuld?*" one wretch shouted. Another tried to climb up on the backboard of a cab to catch a free ride, before the jarvey's whip sliced through the air, making walking a better option. Today, Harriet dismissed them all with a sideways swipe of her umbrella.

She was tired, "ready for the clay", as their housekeeper Molly would say. The last few months had taken their toll, running between the School of Music and Westland Row. She wondered if Papa was watching over her. Was he in some sort of ethereal no man's land, a restless spirit, waiting for tensions to be resolved and hovering between this world and the next? She shivered, pulling her cloak around her neck. Breathing deeply, she placed her handkerchief over her mouth and, increasing her pace, crossed Carlisle Bridge over the stinking waters of the River Liffey and headed towards Warburgh Street and Westland Row.

By the time Harriet entered the drawing room on the first floor of Number 14, her mother's anger had dissipated, and she was lying prostrate on the chaise longue whilst Julia paced the room.

"*You absolute sliveen, you snakey vixen!*" Julia spat.

9

"How could you? After all I have done for you over the years. For God's sake, Harriet, how could you?"

Harriet, her face paler than usual, stood in front of the fireplace, her hands behind her back so they could not see them shaking, and addressed her sister. "Can we talk about this reasonably, Julia, and of course you too, Mother? I am so sorry that this has come as such a surprise. Or that I was not able to tell you of Papa's plans, but that was his wish. In any event, now probate has been granted, at least we know how we stand, and can plan for the future." She sat down in the wing chair beside her mother. "Father did not make these arrangements lightly, you know. He gave it a great deal of thought. He was concerned about your health, Mama, and he did not want to burden you with the worry of sorting out this business."

"And what about me?" demanded Julia. "How could he have so disregarded me, his eldest child? After all, I am the one who has shown initiative. I bought the new camera and converted the print shop into a proper studio and hired Pierre. If left up to you, we would have continued to eke out a meagre living selling artists' supplies and lithographic prints. It would only be a matter of time before Papa's gentlemen chums went elsewhere, once they discovered that the business was being run by a pack of women. Oh, in the name of God, Harriet, what do you propose we do?"

Julia sat down on a chair beside her mother and started to sob noisily. Her mother tried to console her while Harriet watched, her face set in grim determination.

Eventually, her tears spent, Julia wiped away the black powder she used to enhance her eyelashes, now smudged and running in rivulets down her face. She turned to her sister.

"I cannot believe Papa would do this to me. Why?" Without waiting for Harriet to reply, she continued, "Are you going to tell me that he didn't want to distract me from my painting? I would have thought he would have been glad of the opportunity. He never paid me any attention, not ever. You were always the favourite child."

"Julia, don't be so melodramatic – let's try to be rational about this. Papa simply thought that I was the most practical. He knew I had a head for figures. And, let's be honest, he worried about your moral welfare and impulsive nature."

Julia sat upright on the edge of her chair, her face contorted with anger.

Harriet continued, exasperated. "Your association with Donal has brought this family nothing but grief and shame. You have given no thought to our standing in the community, or the fact that it took Papa years to build his reputation in this city." She paused. "Look, we need to sit down and talk. I need to plan for my future. I have put my marriage to Edward on hold for long enough. Time is running out for me – I am thirty-two years of age and I want to marry and start a family of my own. Please be reasonable, Julia, it has been my salary from teaching that has paid most of the bills. And it was I who nursed Papa through his final illness. You made your choices, Julia. Staying loyal to Donal, with all the risk and uncertainty that entails, was your choice. You have pursued your dreams on all fronts: painting, photography. What is more, you have made a spectacle of yourself in front of our friends with your strange clothes and revolutionary ideas. I am surprised that Edward still wishes to marry me at all." She paused, and then, drawing on some inner strength, continued resolutely. "I have been the one who has made all the sacrifices, Julia. After Papa died, I picked up the pieces and kept our family together. The investment in the camera and Pierre may, or may not, pay off in time. But meanwhile, Julia, we have some tough decisions to make."

"What is to become of us?" said her mother. She blessed herself and then slowly and painfully got up from the chaise longue and left the room.

Julia blew her nose and wiped her eyes, still furious. She breathed in slowly and looked up at her sister.

"I see now what I have refused to acknowledge before: you have always been jealous of my success. You are a cold and calculating young woman. Edward and you are well suited. This has been a shock. But, Harriet, rest assured I will never, *ever*, forgive you for this."

Later that evening, on her way out, Harriet closed the front door gently. Earlier, her mother had retired to her room on the second floor with the curtains drawn and had not stirred, even when Harriet had called her for supper. Julia had also remained in the bedroom that she shared with her sister. Lying on the bed pretending to sleep, she had kept her back to Harriet as she grappled with her stays. Although Julia – much to their mother's dismay – refused to wear them, she usually gave Harriet a hand with hers. Harriet had changed into her barathea skirt and satin appliqued jacket to go out to meet Edward. She had been afraid to light a candle. She hoped she looked presentable – she had fumbled in the half-light with her face powder and to refix her hairpins to keep her hair in place.

As she walked the short distance up Westland Row towards the hotel, memories of her childhood drifted through her mind. As a child, she used to hide under the stairs when Julia, two years older than her, had tantrums, or when she engaged in frequent arguments with their father. She had always been difficult. Worse still, Julia had treated her as a personal maid, always there for her entertainment, and to run her errands. But as she grew up, music had given her confidence – a passion she shared with her father – she sang beautifully and had passed all her pianoforte exams with distinction. She knew she was her father's favourite. But, despite their different personalities, the sisters had always managed to maintain a close friendship. In the black of night, back to back, under soft woollen blankets, they had talked for hours. Harriet had whispered her childish fears to her elder sister and Julia would blow them away, one by one. They laughed together at the small comedies of the day: Mama's carrying on, the neighbours' antics. But mostly they talked of their dreams. Whereas Julia wanted to go to France and study art, and one day hoped to become a famous artist, Harriet's aspirations were more modest. All she ever wanted was to be a music teacher, to marry a handsome man and be a good wife and mother. Although she had achieved her goal to be a teacher, romance had eluded her until now. Harriet knew that she was not unattractive, but she was shy and sensed the young men they met at church socials found her serious nature off-putting. She usually relied on Julia to keep the conversation going.

There was also a question mark over her dowry, as she discovered to her cost at the age of eighteen. She had formed an attachment to the son of a well-to-do fruit importer – they sang in the choir together in St Mark's. She had been so in love with him, and he with her. He even brought her red roses from his mother's garden. Until one day, without warning, he ceased all contact and avoided her after church service. A few weeks later, Harriet saw him on a warm summer's evening in the Phoenix Park, in a phaeton, with the greasy Mr Tyndall, the butcher on North Brunswick Street, and his red-faced daughter. "Plain as a pork chop," as Mama cruelly described her afterwards. And over the years the various young men, deemed suitable by her parents, who had shown her any interest, had turned their attention elsewhere once the meagreness of her dowry was established – until Edward came along.

"It was worse than I expected it was going to be," she said to Edward half an hour later, as she sipped a glass of sherry in the foyer of the Royal Hotel at the top of Westland Row. There was a hullabaloo coming from the adjacent public bar where an accordion played a lively Irish ballad. A flushed gentleman bumbled out through the bar door, pulling his scarf around his neck, and fastening his greatcoat before heading out into the night, no doubt to catch the last train to the suburbs. Harriet imagined a patient wife at home, children bathed and scrubbed waiting for their lord and master to return. She shivered and took another sip of the warming liquid. She did not normally drink mid-week, but this evening she'd felt she needed one.

Edward looked tired but smiled reassuringly at her.

"Well, the worst part is over, my dear. It's been a long road for us both. Did Roe bear up?"

"Oh, he played his part alright."

"It is for the best. If Julia had been left in control, she would never have agreed to you leaving and going with me to Manchester. Frankly, without the money we would not have been be able to manage. Harriet, we can finally be together." Grasping both her hands in his, he pulled her closer.

"Don't, Edward, not now – I feel guilty," she said, withdrawing her hands and crossing them on her lap.

"But why should you? Julia will manage, she always does. She has made her own bed, and now she can lie in it. Her high-handed decisions when your father died were unforgivable. She refused to take my brotherly advice – instead she listened to your Uncle Charles – a buffoon, even if he is a man of the cloth. In fact, she was downright condescending when I recommended continuing the existing business. To spend whatever cash was left in the coffers on alterations, and a new camera, and to fire your father's assistant with all his knowledge of the business, and then to take on Pierre is beyond belief. Her plan to capture the passengers from Bray and Greystones has not worked out – she is still competing with established names. As far as I can see, she has already missed the boat. People are no longer satisfied with *cartes de viste* – now they all want these newfangled, larger format 'cabinet' photographs. Why throw good money after bad, I say. Anyway, from now on she can run the business whatever way she pleases. I can come over every few months or so and check the books – make sure that we get our share of the profits. If there are any, that is. And when the business falls flat on its face, as it will eventually, we can lease the building to professionals, doctors and the like, and earn good rental income. Julia will always have her painting. I reckon she made about two hundred pounds last year. She must have received fifty pounds alone for the portraits of the Colville children that she showed in the Royal Hibernian Academy. I must say the sooner I can put the Irish Sea between your headstrong sister and me the better. How you two are related is difficult to comprehend. You are quite the opposite – so kind, and so modest –"

"Mama took it worse than I had anticipated," Harriet said. "I thought she would see the wisdom of it, be happy for me, but then underneath it all she is as selfish as Julia and would want me to stay to wait on her hand and foot."

"Harriet, I will take you away from all this. In the beginning it won't be easy – as you know, the house I rent is modest. But in a few years, once I am qualified, we can move somewhere more substantial. And then, if your mother wishes, she can visit – we will always find room for her."

"I suppose, Edward, if things don't work out here with Julia, Mama could always come and live with us."

"Harriet, we have talked about this – your mother is not an easy woman. Visit, yes – live, no – that is out of the question, I am afraid. Now enough of these maudlin thoughts. Let us raise a glass to us. To Harriet and Edward – to the future Mr and Mrs Williams!"

When the last student had been collected, Julia's friend Louisa sat down at the small card table in the corner of the studio beside the stove.

Julia took two china cups that she kept for special

visitors down from the shelf and wet the tea before turning to her friend.

"One lump or two?"

"None for me, I'm afraid. I have just finished reading Harriet Martineau's accounts of her travels in America, the evils of slavery and a black woman called Mum Bett. Thank God they stopped that barbaric practice. It really makes you realise how morally wrong it is for one human being to own another. After I read it, I had a fight with Papa about smoking Cuban cigars. He told me he would stop, but only if I gave up using sugar – completely! Of course, I agreed, but I will miss it dreadfully in my tea."

Julia smiled and tried to appear interested, but she was tired and not in the mood for her friend's proselytising.

"That wiped the smile off his face, I can tell you." Louisa pushed her spectacles back up her long nose. "Anyway, I shan't be able to afford sugar in my tea when we go to Paris. A friend of mine, Olive Eaton –" she leant forward conspiratorially, "do you remember her? Your Molly used to say, rather cruelly, that she had a face like a flounder – a stout girl, her father was an engineer for the Northern Railway Company. Well, she worked in Paris as a governess a few years ago, a horrible family, the husband kept pestering her. They kept lapdogs who wore jewel-encrusted collars, and they made poor Olive clean up after them in restaurants. Well, she gave me the name of a very respectable pension where we can stay. It's only ten minutes' walk from the Académie des Beaux-Arts. We will have to share a room, which will be a new experience for me, but I knew you wouldn't mind."

Julia's heart sank.

"Just think of it, Julia, to be in Paris, the heart of the

art world, to study the work of Ingres, Manet, and Pissarro! And to rub shoulders with Renoir and Degas. I really want to see what all the fuss is about, their use of colour and the flattening of their images. Not that I want to paint in their style. Not that I could! Courbet and Millet are more to my taste with their honest attempts to depict real people going about their daily lives. What is it about France, I wonder, that makes them produce such exciting artists? Maybe it's their hot summers, seeing things through a heat haze. And, of course, their Gallic passion," she added dreamily. She picked up the discarded art journal they had been discussing earlier with the students. "It is hard to imagine the paintings described here through eyes accustomed to soft Irish weather." She paused, contemplating the matter, then continued enthusiastically. "Oh, I cannot wait to go there, to eat snails and croissants, although not together, I hope. Just imagine what it will be like to sit outside at a boulevard café on a sunny afternoon, to watch the world go by. Maybe we could take a few days in Fontainebleau and paint *en plein air*, unchaperoned! Just to be free, Julia, to wander at will without a Mary or a Molly to mind us, following us about everywhere like we were pedigree puppies about to be ravished by a Great Dane."

"I think you mean ravaged," Julia said, smiling wistfully.

Louisa finally noticed her friend's lack of enthusiasm.

"Well, have you told Donal yet?" she said sharply, her mouth set in grim determination.

"No, not exactly – I will see him later in the week." Julia put her cup gently down on the table. "To be honest, Donal is the last thing on my mind. We had the reading of my father's will since I saw you last."

"And?"

"He left Harriet everything, other than a few of Grandpapa's things – art books and the like. But Harriet got everything else."

"I don't believe you!"

"Unfortunately, it's true – it has taken me a few days to come to terms with it."

"Julia, I am so sorry, how awful for you! Can you contest it?"

"I don't know, I haven't thought that far ahead. But I must admit I am devastated. All the plans that I have made – we have made – are now impossible."

"You mean you – we – cannot go to France next summer?"

"No, not next summer, Louisa – not any time soon, the way things are."

"Is it the money?" Louisa looked like she was going to burst into tears. "I am sure Papa –"

"No, it's not only the money, although that is part of it. The fact is, Louisa, all we have is the business, and the house which is on a long lease. Harriet wants to marry Edward and go and live in Manchester, and I am to stay and run things at home."

"Well, will that not give you a certain freedom, and income for that matter?"

"Some income – yes – but freedom – no. I will be more tied than ever. Edward pointed out my Christian duty, as a daughter and a sister. He told me in no uncertain terms that I must play my part if the family is to survive. I will have to run the business and mind Mama while Edward will mind the purse-strings. I cannot see him letting me swan off to Paris for six months."

"But we have been planning this for years!" Louisa pleaded.

"My circumstances have changed, Louisa – my duty is now to my family."

"Even though your father treated you so shabbily?"

"Maybe that was his intention, to make me conform, be responsible." Julia had decided not to confide in her friend about her suspicion of Harriet's involvement, the fact that she would even think it reflected on them both so badly.

"What does Donal say about all this?"

"When I found out, and I explained the situation to him, he assured me that my lack of income changed nothing between us. You know Donal – he is well intentioned – but our relationship is still as uncertain as ever. I would say his family might have an entirely different attitude – as a younger son they would expect him to marry into money. Anyway, marriage is the furthest thing from my mind right now." She looked away from Louisa, afraid that she would see the tears welling in her eyes. "I cannot live independently on what I make from my painting, so I am dependent on them, and, for the moment, they are dependent on me."

"Of course your duty is to your family, but that is so disappointing … poor you … poor me," said her friend, deflated.

Julia sighed. "I am so sorry, Louisa."

She looked at the portrait of her pretty young cousin hanging on the studio wall, varnished and ready to be collected. She had worked so hard to get where she was today. She had given up so much, and now when her paintings were finally being regularly accepted by the

Academy, and she was mature enough to be allowed a modicum of freedom, she was trapped more than ever. Papa's death had not been the blessed release she had dreamt of – instead, it had presented shackles of duty and obligation from which there seemed to be no escape. She was no better off than one of Harriet Martineau's slaves, she thought bitterly.

꧁꧂

Chapter 2

Near Campile,
County Wexford

September 1872

Hidden from view in the trees, he could smell the wild garlic on the damp morning air. They had held their position at the hollow on the New Line Road since five o'clock that morning. At this stage, Donal's feet were numb with the cold. A horsefly had bitten him on the leg, and he was resisting the urge to scratch it. Crouched beside him was the commanding officer, Matt Synott. The older man's breathing was laboured, but a sharp intake of breath alerted Donal to the sound of wheels climbing the hill on the Duncannon side.

Matt stood upright, hands on hips to stretch his back before crouching down again. He whistled and signalled to Seamus Dillon who was positioned on the far side of the road with Pat Roche and young Tommy Duffin, the son of a local fisherman.

Seconds later, the coach appeared through the mists on the horizon like a ghostly galleon rising out of the sea. And as Matt started counting, it commenced its creaking descent towards them.

"Ready, men – at the count of ten."

By the time Matt reached five, Donal could see the face of the driver.

"Fire!"

Simultaneously, Matt and Seamus jumped to their positions in the middle of the road and shot their rifles in the air.

"Throw down your guns on the ground where we can see them and dismount. Do as we say if ye value your lives!" Matt roared.

The horses reared, snorting in frenzy, their eyes flickering with terror. Pat approached and ordered the driver to hand over the reins, and then proceeded to calm the horses.

But as the driver and the two soldiers standing at the backboard reluctantly jumped down, a single shot came from inside the coach and young Tommy crumpled and fell to the ground. Donal felt bile rising in his throat.

A second shot was fired, and a bullet exploded on the side of Donal's face. I am dead, he thought. But the throbbing pain that erupted and the blood that blurred the vision in his right eye indicated that he was still very much alive.

Matt Synott aimed at the coach door. Three shots reverberated in the still morning air – and then, silence. They waited for a few minutes … it seemed like an eternity … then Seamus and Donal gingerly approached the coach. As Seamus opened the door, a young soldier fell out, still breathing, half-hanging from the seat like a rag doll, a bloodied hole in his face.

Donal turned back, pulled down the scarf that was

masking his face, and vomited at the side of the road. Wiping his mouth on his sleeve, he raised his head. Amongst the trees, drawn by the scent of fresh blood, he glimpsed an emaciated hound with amber eyes, standing motionless and staring at him accusingly. Donal froze, his sense of time suspended – seconds later the creature fled, gone as suddenly as it had appeared.

"Wake up, O'Keefe, what are yeh waiting for? Tie up these bastards!" Matt shouted.

Donal and Seamus made the three terrified, but compliant, young soldiers kneel at the side of the road. They bound their hands behind their backs and attached them with rope to their ankles then proceeded to wrap bandages around their mouths. Though, Donal thought, who the hell would hear them here?

Seamus was trying to rouse young Tommy. He had turned him over, and was slapping his face, but Donal could see a puddle of blood from his chest gathering in between the stone chippings of the road's surface.

"Jesus feckin' Christ, he's dead. The bastards killed him." Tears ran down the older man's face as he closed the boy's eyes then blessed himself.

Matt watching, grey-faced, shook his head slowly and made the Sign of the Cross.

"God have mercy on his soul," he whispered. He turned to Donal. "You alright, O'Keefe?"

"Yes, just a surface wound."

The screeching of steel wheels on stone and horses' hooves, faster this time, signalled the arrival of the back-up at the top of the hill. After a few minutes, the cart drew alongside them.

"A coach full of Snyders – keep the boys busy for

months. But the British bastards shot young Tommy dead," Matt said by way of greeting to the cart's driver and his companion. He turned to the others. "Use the other door, lads – load the rifles and the ammunition into the cart. We'll meet you later in New Ross."

Matt, wiping his forehead, turned away from the slaughtered boy and approached the coach. He lifted the groaning, wounded soldier, pushed him back on the seat, and closed the door behind him.

"What about the other boyos?" said Seamus.

"Leave them. By the time some kind soul releases them, we'll be long gone."

A muffled cry was heard from one of the tied and gagged soldiers.

Seamus hit him across the back of the head with the butt of his gun and he fell forward, blood seeping through the bandage. "Shut up, will yeh? If yeh don't want yer head blown off."

They finished unloading the boxes of rifles.

"*Pat, turn the coach around!*" Seamus shouted. "*I'd say these fine horses know their way home!*"

With the dexterity of a seasoned jockey, Pat turned the horses, jumped down and gave them a few slaps on the rumps, and they trotted slowly back up the hill towards the armoury in Duncannon.

"Pat, you get our horses – Seamus and I will take Tommy to the priest," Matt said, "and, Donal, you had better go and tell his poor mother. We'll bring the body to her later after we have cleaned him up."

In the dining room overlooking the landscaped back gardens of the Georgian house in Fitzwilliam Square,

25

Donal stared at the food, pushing the kidneys and bacon around with his fork. The smell made him nauseous. He pushed the plate away.

The hound, which turned out to be Tommy's, had followed Donal's horse to the boy's home, a smoky shebeen in Arthurstown.

"He died for Ireland," he had told the boy's mother. He knew it was not enough – just as he knew it was for others to console her. He couldn't shake the memory from his mind. The amber eyes of the hound, its haunted howl, and the primeval wail of the mother's keening had stayed with him and kept him from sleeping for the last two nights.

"Really, Donal, you need to look after yourself," his sister Bea remonstrated. "Do you think he should go to the police, Eoin?"

Her brother put down the newspaper he was reading and, looking at Donal, considered the question.

"These men that attacked you, would you recognise them again?"

"No, not really, it was dark, and the streetlights were not working on that side of the Green, so I didn't really see their faces at all."

"You should report it anyway," his sister said.

"I'd rather leave it, Bea. Look, I'm fine," he said, stroking his bandaged cheek. "Anyway, I have paperwork to prepare for a case in the Four Courts tomorrow. I really don't have the time to deal with their archaic formalities."

"*Mm*, yes, probably a waste of time in the circumstances," Eoin said.

"Well, Eoin, you know best," said Bea, "but this city is overrun with thugs and common criminals. I don't even feel safe in my bed anymore. And did you see in the *Times* that a military coach was attacked in Wexford on Tuesday? Fenians, of course. One of the soldiers was severely injured and a consignment of rifles stolen."

The Fenian Brotherhood was, in fact, the American sister organisation to the Irish Republican Brotherhood and had been succeeded after 1867 by Clan na Gael. However, members of all three organisations were commonly known as "Fenians".

"Yes, I did, Bea, dreadful news," said Eoin. "By all accounts the militia walked straight into an ambush." He sipped his tea and then replaced the china cup carefully on the saucer.

"I know where your sympathies lie, Donal," said Bea with resignation. "But where will all this end, I would like to know?"

Eoin wiped his mouth with his napkin.

"Now you two must excuse me," said Bea, getting up from the table. "I have an appointment to take Lydia to the dressmaker's to be measured for some summer dresses. Your daughter seems to be getting taller by the day, Eoin."

"Well, don't let her cajole you into spending all my money, Bea," said Eoin.

"Oh, don't worry, I am well used to her wheedling ways."

"Thank you, Bea. What would we do without you?" He smiled gratefully.

After she left the room, Eoin turned to his brother, all good humour gone, his face now grim and one eyebrow raised sardonically.

"You were in the south-east, down that way, on Tuesday, I believe."

"Yes, I was in New Ross. I had a meeting with Kennedy's – you know, the bread people. A boundary dispute with a neighbour."

Eoin glared at Donal. "You are a bloody fool if you were involved in that skirmish and want to waste your life fighting a doomed cause, and I will not let you bring disgrace on this family. I won't stand for it, do you hear?"

"Perfectly, Eoin. But, you know, it really is none of your business," Donal replied politely.

"Actually, it *is* my business, and you are an employee. For the moment anyway." He threw his napkin on the table and rose to leave the room.

Donal sat back in his chair, rubbing the lint dressing on his cheek. He disliked fighting with his older, and somewhat formidable, brother. He loved him dearly and, when he was a child, he used to follow him around like a spaniel. But they were cut from different cloth. Bea and Eoin's mother had been a Huguenot from the wealthy Trench family. She died from consumption when Eoin was only five years old. His father had told him he had married his mother, his second wife, for love, and to comfort him in his old age. And though he was well rewarded in his first aspiration, he was badly served in the second.

Donal smiled, thinking about her and sipping tea from one of her opal-coloured china cups. They always reminded him of her. She too had died early, in childbirth, when he was fifteen. Her father had been the local magistrate on the Inishowen peninsula. However, to the dismay of her staunchly Unionist husband, he had discovered that the shy and charming young girl, with her soft Donegal accent, was a passionate supporter of Irish Nationalism.

On long journeys, from Dublin to Donegal, she had whispered stories into her young son's ears of the adventures of Cú Chulainn, the ancient Gaelic warrior, a giant of a man gifted with superhuman strength and skill. As a child, driving through Inishowen, those ancient tales seemed possible – as mists, like tumbled clouds, rolled down the sides of mountains, and glided across the deep veridian waters of Lough Swilly, out towards the open sea and the wild Atlantic Ocean. A land where pockets of turf lay like chequered cloths on rugged terrain, and tenant farmers on smallholdings eked out a meagre living. In the safety of the carriage he listened, enchanted, wrapped in blankets with warmed bricks at his feet, tucked in beside his mother, while his father slept off the Magistrate's brandy of the night before. She told him tales of the daring battles of Fionn mac Cumhaill, who had eaten from the Salmon of Knowledge, and the Fianna his loyal band of warriors. These stories, etched on his soul, were poignantly vivified by sights of starving families aimlessly traipsing the roads of the peninsula – poor creatures unable to pay their rent, evicted from their homes by absentee British landlords. These were the dispossessed, the walking dead of the Great Famine, spectral figures that pervaded the breathtakingly beautiful and desolate landscape.

His mother explained how, for centuries, the English had plundered their country, and had tried to steal its Gaelic heritage by imposing their wooden tongue and soulless Saxon ways. But she promised him passionately, repeatedly, that one day in his lifetime, Ireland would be free.

Dreams of these journeys still haunted him, and he frequently woke in the middle of the night in a cold sweat, fearful and with a terrible sense of loss. Whereas Eoin, who had been sent to school in England after his mother died, had different nightmares. No, Donal thought sadly, no matter how many times he tried to explain to his brother, he would never understand.

Chapter 3

14 Westland Row

November 1872

It had not been a productive day. Julia looked at the dark-blue outline she had painted on the canvas. She had found it hard to capture the likeness of the child. Although she had posed for her, the young and myopic Miss Maunsell was clearly uncomfortable without her glasses. As a result, she had continuously fidgeted, despite her mother's requests to refrain from doing so. It was impossible with small children. Tomorrow she would have to resort to using the photographs she had taken to try to get some semblance of a likeness.

Julia took her paintbrushes over to the sink in the corner of the room where she cleaned them in turpentine, reshaping their heads and leaving them to dry in the chinoiserie jug on the dresser. She pulled the blue smock she wore for painting over her head and checked her dress for paint splatters. Fortunately, there were none – it was one of her better costumes in a jade satin with black lace trimmings and covered buttons. She knew it suited her auburn colouring. Loosening her hair from the plaited coils at the sides of her head, she fixed the curly mop at the back into a simple knot. A dab of powder, a touch of rouge on her cheeks and lips and she was ready for her guests.

Outside it was already dark. She drew the wool curtains over the large window that faced out onto the garden separating the studio from the main house, and double-locked and bolted the garden door. Methodically she set about preparing the room for the evening's meeting. First, with some effort, she pushed her large studio easel to the alcove at the end of the room and pulled across the linen drape to hide it from view. Then she unstacked the wooden chairs, normally used by the drawing students, and arranged them in a semicircle. Finally, she filled the kettle on the wood-burning stove and arranged twelve enamelled tin cups on a tray. Julia had told her mother, who had taken to her bed earlier in the week with a cold that refused to shift, that she was hosting a discussion about Irish Poetry amongst her fellow painters. Conveniently, Harriet was attending choral practice around the corner in St Mark's. Molly had been warned that Julia did not want to be disturbed.

The first knock on the back door facing onto the lane at the back of Westland Row came at about half past six o'clock. Probably the early birds from Healey's brass works which was just around the corner on Great Brunswick Street. Looking through the spyhole, Julia saw three faces she recognised, and she opened the door and let the men in. A waft of hops from the Guinness Brewery was carried in with them on the cold evening air. Greetings were exchanged. Huddled together, they gravitated towards the cast-iron stove at the other end of the studio. The men were well wrapped up, but they took off their hats out of respect for her presence, keeping their greatcoats on for warmth while vigorously rubbing woollen-gloved hands.

Diarmuid, whom she recognised from previous meetings, took a packet of cigarette-papers out of his pocket.

"We will have none of that here," she said cheerfully. "We have white spirits and chemicals about that we use in photography, and a fire would be difficult to explain."

"Sorry, Miss Benson – of course," he said, returning the papers to his pocket. "Are yeh expecting many this evening?"

"Well, Finbarr said there would be about twelve."

"And how about Donal, miss? Will he be here?"

"I have no idea," replied Julia curtly, and turned to answer another soft knock on the door.

There were eleven men present when Donal eventually appeared at seven o'clock.

Donal O'Keefe was in his mid-thirties, of medium height, with a shock of brown wavy hair which he wore to one side. Dressed in the garb of an office worker, with a stiff collar and tie visible under his greatcoat, his handsome face was set with his usual amiable smile. He cut a striking figure. Immediately, he headed over to where Julia stood apart from the others.

"Ah, Julia, how are you? You're looking well," he whispered in his gentle voice.

"Your face is almost healed. Does it still hurt?"

"No, only my heart for want of seeing you," he said, smiling affectionately and looking into her grey-blue eyes. "I have missed you. It seems ages since we were together. We will talk when the others are gone."

Julia flushed slightly. It was not that she was unused to receiving compliments, because she did so on a daily basis – mostly unwelcome – but something inside her was stirred by this man. She knew he was scorned by her father and sister. But his charm and kindly intelligence were so unlike the stoic reserve characteristic of her extended family that good sense seemed to fly out the window when he was around. There was also the not inconsequential fact that she had done the unforgivable. On a summer's day beneath a cloudless blue sky – on a blanket of golden sand, accompanied by the sound of seagulls – they had made love. She was not sorry – she would do it again. In fact, every nerve in her body tingled at the thought of that day, of his hands on her skin caressing her body. A body that, till then, had been hidden from the world, unexplored, encased in cages of corsetry, silk and lace – a body that had never been pleasured by normal acts of human intimacy.

"Later, Donal," she said, moving away to hide her confusion.

"Right, men, let's get down to business!" said Finbarr – or Sergeant Duffy as he was referred to – as he strode over to the centre of the room.

The men took their seats and the meeting began. "Well, men, another successful initiative by our brothers in the south-east, masterminded by one of our own, no less." Nods of approval and a wolf whistle were directed at Donal by the men. "However, this unexpected largesse means that the pressure is on to recruit and train new men. But, just for now, until the dust settles, we will keep our heads down and our powder dry. So, with that in mind, tonight we have a new member for our Irish Poetry Reading Group!"

Guffaws and more wolf whistles followed.

Julia knew this young man must have taken the secret oath of allegiance to the Irish Republican Brotherhood, witnessed only by his recruiter. He stepped forward to a round of enthusiastic, but muted, clapping of gloved hands.

Donal had recited the oath some months earlier to Julia and she had committed the words to memory: "*In the presence of God, I do solemnly swear that I will do my utmost to establish the national independence of Ireland, and that I will bear true allegiance to the Supreme Council of the Irish Republic and government of the Irish Republic, and implicitly obey the will and preserve inviolate the secrets of the organisation.*"

After the recruit was welcomed, sundry items were discussed. The meeting took a little over thirty minutes and was followed by a quick cup of tea, prepared and distributed by Julia. The men did not tarry. Most of them anxious to get home for their suppers, they dispersed into the night.

Donal was the last to leave.

"Julia, I cannot thank you enough for this. It's very brave of you. I realise what a risk it is."

"It's not so bad now since Papa died, and at least Edward is in Manchester. However, the way things are, if Harriet found out, I'm afraid she might get me committed to the Richmond Asylum."

Donal smiled sympathetically. "Things are still difficult with your sister then?"

"I am afraid so. I cannot believe that Papa could have done this to me. I am convinced that in some way she and Edward persuaded him to change his will. But I have no proof."

"Well, I must admit it is hard to understand. But your father was a principled man and must have thought that this arrangement was in your best interests, misguided though you think he might have been. Look, why don't you go and talk to my brother Eoin. I probably could look at it myself, but he is the expert, and he has the advantage that he's not directly involved." He took her hands gently. "He would quickly be able to establish if there are grounds for contesting it or not."

"Thank you, Donal – I think I would like to do that. I am visiting Uncle Charles on Monday to talk to him as well. But, yes, I will arrange to visit your brother."

"Julia, you just need to be patient. Look, regardless of the outcome, things will sort themselves out in time. Once they have both gone to Manchester, you will no longer have to worry about Edward, or Harriet, interfering with your life."

"I would like to think so. But Edward is adopting this paternalistic attitude towards me that I find infuriating. I am too used to my own independence to revert to an outmoded concept of womanhood based on the puritan ideals admired by Edward."

"God forbid that should ever happen," said Donal and he pulled her to him, wrapping his arms around her, his mouth gently forcing her lips apart.

Julia moved the struggling aspidistra, to hide the stain on the oilcloth-covered floor where Pierre had spilled chemicals the day before. The first client was due at ten o'clock. She looked at the ochre visiting card which read, *Mr Cecil Brown, Ceylon*. Probably a tea importer, she thought. He had called a few days earlier to make the appointment for sixty *cartes de visite*. A good order, thought Julia, about one guinea's worth – it would help to pay some outstanding bills.

She smoothed her black, bombazine costume which was tighter than normal. She was still smarting from Harriet's comments after their father died. Since then, she had been making a conscious effort to dress with more care, and more conservatively than she used to. Artists were naturally a bohemian lot, and she loved the freedom of the unstructured clothes favoured by her friends. They wore them proudly as a mark of defiance against the inequality that was a woman's lot. And although recent events had exacerbated this frustration and made her feel even more powerless, in her new role as a businesswoman she supposed it was in her own interests to try to look a little more professional.

The camera was covered in a protective cloth. To the rear wall behind the sitter's chair, she had pinned a classical scene that she had painted on a large canvas sheet. It showed steps flanked by an ornate balustrade leading to the portico of a Greek temple. She liked the overall effect, and it usually drew admiring comments from the customers. She checked her appointments book – she had three clients this morning and one in the afternoon. If there were not many impulse callers, then maybe she would get some painting done later.

Upstairs she could hear the muffled sounds of Molly shouting at Padraic. It was early in the day for them to be fighting. She walked into the hall and, standing at the end of the stairs, she called, "*Molly, I am expecting a customer in ten minutes and he will probably hear you shouting like a fishwife from the gates of Trinity College!*"

Molly's reddened face, looking truculent, appeared at the top of the stairs.

"Sorry, Miss Julia."

Really, Molly should know better, she thought, returning to the studio. Harriet was obviously not around – she was probably upstairs with Mama at this stage. Giving her a lecture no doubt, possibly a continuation of the one Julia had endured earlier. Harriet had taken it upon herself to continue Papa's morning ritual whereby family and servants gathered in the first-floor dining room and said a brief prayer before breakfast. Papa had done this out of duty, and to provide moral guidance to the staff. They had all attended: Molly, who had minded the girls since they were babies, her husband Padraic who did all the heavy work, Mrs Cunningham the cook, Tilly the housemaid, and the boy, Billy, who used to mind Papa's horse, but now did odd jobs. Initially Pierre had joined them, but after a week or so he had endured enough. He had informed Julia that he would breakfast at his lodgings. He also promised to say his morning prayers in St Andrew's across the road before starting work. He was a Catholic, after all, not an Anglican, so Harriet could not reasonably object to his request.

No one had asked Harriet to become moral guardian of the Benson household after their father died, Julia thought. She had just assumed it was her place to act in his. Initially Julia had considered nipping it in the bud and leading the prayers herself. But the thought of carrying out the sorry ceremony every morning was just too tedious to bear, so she let her sister continue. However, recently Harriet had taken to adding homilies after the prayers, and these were becoming increasingly moralistic. She was losing the run of herself. Edward's influence no doubt. That morning she had droned on about the evils of drink in response to Pierre's fondness for Irish whiskey which he sampled most evenings in the local hostelry. Unfortunately, his path crossed frequently with Harriet's while he was on the way home and she was heading out for evening prayer or choral practice in St Mark's. I don't know why she bothers, thought Julia. Pierre is no more intoxicated now than he was when he first arrived from Paris. She hoped Harriet's self-righteous indignation would not drive him away. The young Frenchman had been a godsend. He was a skilled photographer, and he would find no problem getting work elsewhere from the growing numbers of commercial photographers in the city. She needed him. It was not feasible for a respectable woman to be seen in that role – for a woman of Julia's class it simply would not do. Nor would it do Julia's reputation any good with conservative members of the Academy. She had to admit she had learnt a lot from Pierre, though she was still getting to grips with some of the finer nuances of the process, like the right balance of chemicals, and the precise timings involved in developing the glass plates.

Her thoughts were interrupted by the sound of Molly's leather boots on her way out to the ashpit in the yard, followed by her sister's more delicate tread coming down the stairs from the bedrooms two floors above. Harriet's head eventually appeared around the door.

"Julia, Mama has taken a turn for the worse. I am sending Billy for Doctor Whyte. She has a high temperature, and her breathing is heavy and laboured. I know you are expecting a customer at ten o'clock, but could you come up and sit with her afterwards? I have to be over in the Academy at eleven o'clock."

"Of course. Poor Mama. I will come up directly after he leaves. Pierre can manage without me."

"Thank you, Julia," said Harriet, tight-lipped, as she closed the door behind her.

Mr Brown arrived on time, was photographed by Pierre and dispatched by Julia in just under an hour. It had taken some time to coax the gentleman into a natural-looking pose.

"Some men just don't know how to stand properly – they don't have the bearing that comes with military training," she remarked to Pierre afterwards. "He was quite stooped – you would think he had been picking the tea leaves himself."

"Or else he too has been beaten down by strong women." Pierre laughed and then headed out to develop the silver bromide, collodion-coated plates, in the darkroom adjacent to Julia's studio at the back of the house.

Julia gingerly entered her mother's bedroom on the first floor. The curtains were open. It was a cold but bright winter day, and the window looked out onto Trinity College Park where students could be seen in the distance playing rugby football. Julia was not sure whether her mother was awake, but she was immediately alarmed when she heard the older woman's rasping breath. The doctor had come and gone. He suspected that her chest infection had turned into pneumonia. He had left medicine for her to take, advising that a basin with boiling water and oil of cloves be prepared and left in the room to help her breathing. But really, Doctor Whyte had said, her condition was poor. Pneumonia was a serious condition, and with her mother's delicate constitution it was even more of a risk.

Julia moved to her mother's side where she lay in the four-poster bed, encased in rugs and blankets, and reached for her hand which was clammy and cold. Her face underneath her linen mobcap was waxy. Oh my God, she looks dead already, thought Julia, feeling an overwhelming sadness engulf her. Lying before her, this once-vibrant woman was now so small, shrunken and vulnerable.

Meg Benson had not had an easy life. Uncle Charles had often told Julia that her mother had been a beauty when she was a young woman, her looks and vivacious character persuading his brother to overlook her less desirable social status. In fact, he had married against his father's wishes – Grandpapa had thought that his son could have done better. Knowing this, Meg had constantly aped the behaviour of her betters, and her 'carrying on,' as they had called it, had amused the family for years. But Julia remembered her warm arms enfolding her as a child, remembered her being always there to wipe away her tears with a kind, encouraging word. Yes, she was dramatic – yes, she was needy – but Julia simply could not imagine life without her. There was no doubt she had struggled since Papa's death – she was not a modern woman by any means. And the chill atmosphere between herself and Harriet had been difficult. Julia knew she was torn between supporting her wilful elder daughter, who was entertaining but completely unreliable, and her equally headstrong younger daughter who was faultlessly dutiful, but who she also suspected had influenced her husband to alter his will.

Meg opened her eyes, "Julia, my dear, I feel absolutely awful … can you pass me some water?"

Julia poured water for her mother into a glass from the jug on the bedside table.

"Dr Whyte says I have pneumonia," Meg said weakly.

"Yes, Mama, you need to rest. Don't talk, just try and get some sleep."

"Julia, my dear, I think this is the end – it's time for me to meet my Maker and join your poor father. I dreamt about him last night, you know."

"Hush, Mama, don't be foolish. You will be up again in no time. Don't forget you promised we would go and see that new play that's on in the Theatre Royal next week."

"Julia, before I go, I want you to do one thing for me."

"Mother, you really are being quite dramatic."

"Just one thing. Promise me, Julia."

Julia sighed. "Yes, Mother, what is it?"

"I want you to make up with your sister. She will be all you have once I am gone and whatever happened – or did not happen – you may never know. In any case it is done and dusted, and maybe it was for the best. Harriet has kept us on the straight and narrow. Although I don't know why she made such a fuss when I bought that lovely emerald dress ring. It was only a trifle – we cannot be that badly off." She paused, coughing and spluttering, before she continued. "Anyway, she is your sister after all, your own flesh and blood. I hope she will have the family she so desperately wants with Edward. Although he is such a serious young man. He seems to lack charm completely. But no doubt even he will want children – and then Harriet will need you – and you will need her." She paused again to catch her breath. "Everyone needs to be part of a family. Particularly a single woman like you. I won't say *spinster*, Julia, I do hate that word. But, my darling girl, you need to forget that Donal O'Keefe – he is nothing but bad news. And let us face it, my dear – you are unlikely, despite your good looks, to get married at this stage."

"Mama –" Julia started but her mother's eyes had closed, feigning sleep.

Not wanting to fight with her, Julia dutifully kissed her clammy cheek and left the room.

In the rectory just off Brighton Square, the Reverend Charles Benson sat behind his desk in the booklined dining room he used as a study. On one side of the room were leatherbound medical books in pristine condition – on the other side were tomes on theology – and in the middle, with finger-patinated and well-worn leather spines, were some of his father's old art books. A Catholic collection for an Anglican clergyman, he thought with some amusement.

In the garden, silver birch trees swayed in a gentle breeze and bay-leafed hedges glistened from the recent rain. He watched the blue tits fight over stale bread on the bird table – while overhead a seagull hovered menacingly, waiting to swoop and plunder any bounty the small birds dislodged. Young Bridie, barely ten, was reaching up with chilblained fingers to hang out starched white sheets and pillowslips – the Monday wash – in a neat row. Like an army lookout, the maid kept glancing upwards, checking the sky for advancing rainclouds.

The Reverend sipped from a glass of water containing a small amount of laudanum. He reckoned he needed to calm himself before his niece's morning visit. He clenched and unclenched his long waxy fingers, concentrating on controlling the involuntary tics that beset his ageing body. Putting his boots up on the desk with long legs crossed, he tilted back precipitously in his chair and, taking off his round wireframed glasses, closed his eyes.

He smiled to himself. Julia was the daughter he never had, and it had given him no end of pleasure over the years to encourage her artistic talent and enquiring mind. If the truth be told, he also enjoyed taunting his staid and conventional older brother by encouraging his nieces to think independently – a value that often conflicted with the feminine values of modesty and sacrifice to others that his brother tried to instil in his daughters. It had been a pleasurable task for Charles to be Mark's foil, to encourage where he condemned. But, with his brother's death, Charles felt obliged to take a more responsible approach in his relationship with his headstrong niece.

It was an unfortunate business. Charles had been disturbed when he had first heard of the contents of the will, and the subsequent turn of events. Although Julia's emotional response was a natural one, in fairness the arrangement was a rational solution. Mark's wife Meg had the sense of a small child. As for Julia, although he loved her dearly, she was wilful and sometimes misguided, and liable to bring them all to the brink of social disgrace and financial ruin. So, there was some logic in putting sensible and practical Harriet in charge. Furthermore, this would give Harriet enough money for a dowry. To marry without one would bring dishonour to the family. Also, Edward would provide important male guidance to the sisters. Even though he did not entirely approve of Edward – there was something about him that he could not put his finger on – he knew in his heart that he represented the best offer Harriet was likely to get.

Despite recent changes to the property laws, once married, in effect, Edward would own all that was Harriet's, although she would be entitled to profit from the business. In reality, she would be dependent on Edward's generosity. Still, he seemed a sensible, if somewhat dull, sort of chap.

Julia, on the other hand, was left in a very difficult situation. Although entitled to own her own property, she had none, and was now entirely beholden to her prospective brother-in-law. Money that she earned from her painting and drawing lessons was insufficient to allow her any reasonable independence. But the fact of the matter, reasoned Charles, was that it was now a 'fait accompli', and they all simply had to move on.

Charles thought carefully about how he would handle this situation. He would have to appeal strategically to his niece to persuade her to accept her lot, regardless of how unfair the circumstances.

"Reverend, Miss Julia is here – will I show her in?" Kitty the housekeeper, a handsome woman, kindly, with a twinkle in her eye, stuck her mobcapped head around the door.

Charles hastily took his feet off the desk, tidied his stiff neckcloth, and pulled down his waistcoat and jacket.

"Thank you, Kitty – yes, show her in. Some tea would be nice and, Kitty, if you have any of those madeleines left over from yesterday, I am sure Miss Julia would enjoy one of them."

When Kitty ushered Julia in, Charles noted that his niece was dressed more conventionally than usual. A definite improvement.

"Uncle Charles, how are you? Praying for me, I hope? I think I need at the very least a cathedral-full of intentions for my soul if I am to sort out my current difficulties."

"Disrespectful child! Sit down here beside me. Things are rarely as bad as they seem."

"People usually only say that, Uncle Charles, when things are really desperate."

Charles twitched uncontrollably, his mouth momentarily contorted and his head shaking in a jerking movement.

Julia sat down in a chair opposite him. Averting her eyes, she waited for the spasm to pass.

"It is not good, I must admit," he said then.

"Well, Uncle, I have been turning this business over and over in my mind. In fact, I have not slept since the reading of the will. The implications for me are quite dismal. You know I told you I was planning to go to France next year with Louisa, to paint?"

"Finally," said Charles kindly.

"Well, that is impossible now. I have to mind Mama when Harriet leaves for Manchester." She paused and arranged her black satin skirt. "Her plan is selfish in the extreme. Although I love my mother with all my heart, you know she is not an easy woman. And, to leave me to manage the photographic studio and the business as well, is downright cruel. I will have no life whatsoever. I will be little more than a slave."

Charles looked through his glasses at his niece and pressed the tips of his long fingers together.

"There are other options, Julia. You could apply for a

46

job as a governess. You might even enjoy that, in a good home, with a good family, a roof over your head and a modest annual income. Possibly in Dublin, so that you could still keep an eye on your mother and continue to meet up with your art colleagues."

Julia looked, grim-faced, at him.

Charles took a deep breath and, with a wooden smile, continued valiantly, "Or, if you prefer, you could both come and live with me and you could be my housekeeper. I could pay you a small stipend from my living. Of course, you would have to do some parish work, visiting the sick and dying, organising church social meetings, that sort of thing. But I think we could all rub along relatively well together." He paused and then said somewhat whimsically, "Do you bake, Julia? You know I am rather partial to Kitty's madeleines?"

"Your housekeeper – you cannot be serious, Uncle!" exclaimed Julia, ignoring the facetious comment. "Although I appreciate your offer, I cannot see myself as either a governess or – God forbid – a vicar's housekeeper. Believe me, I have thought long and hard about the different options."

"There is one other option." Charles paused. "You could find yourself a husband." Before she could interrupt, he raised his hand, indicating that she should listen. "It might not be so bad, you know. There are plenty of widowers in the parish. Maybe, and provided that you restrain from voicing your political opinions, I could find one who could afford to support you in reasonable style and allow you some level of independence to pursue your painting. A marriage of convenience, as they say."

"Uncle Charles, that is never going to happen," Julia

47

replied passionately. "Harriet has agreed to marry Edward, a decision I hope she does not live to regret. She is now nothing more than her husband's chattel, doomed to a life of subservience and boredom. I could never accept that, regardless of my circumstances. No, I would rather die."

She got up from her chair and paced around the room.

"I cannot believe Papa would do this to me." She stopped and addressed Charles directly. "In fact, I refuse to accept it. I am going to see if I can contest the will, and I have made an appointment with Eoin O'Keefe to get a second legal opinion. Grandfather always spoke highly of him."

"More sensible, I hope, than that rascal of a brother of his with whom you are so friendly. But if —" Another involuntary spasm jerked his body, preventing him from finishing the sentence.

Swiftly moving across the room, Julia stood behind him, and placed her hands firmly on his shoulders until the tremors passed. Once he became still, she returned to her seat and passed him a glass of water.

"Are you alright now, Uncle?" she enquired gently.

"Yes, my dear, it has passed."

Julia looked at him, her head tilted. "Right now, it is my only hope. The atmosphere in Westland Row is unbearable. Mama is still very poorly, and Harriet is already throwing her weight around with the staff and has become even more prim and self-righteous than before, if that is possible. For some reason that I cannot fathom, she also believes she is the victim here. She really needs to get down off that cross, as Molly would say."

"At least the happy couple will be in Manchester,"

Charles responded with a smile. "Things will get better, my child."

Kitty opened the door and brought in a tray with china teacups and a plate of madeleines.

"Kitty, you are an angel, you do spoil me. I should be so very sorry to lose you."

"Thank you, but I am not going anywhere, Reverend," said Kitty dismissively.

"No, Kitty, hopefully not."

Julia looked witheringly at her uncle.

From its elevated position, the strident peal of the great bells of Christchurch rang out across the city, their mellifluous sounds dominating all the other bells in the circus that was the midday chorus. In the shadow of the cathedral, on the north side of the river, Julia sat with Molly in the narrow hall of the solicitor's office, waiting to be called. She wondered where Donal worked – was his room on the floor above? Her thoughts were interrupted as a door from an anteroom was opened by a young clerk. He looked barely thirteen, greased hair slathered to one side, his collar too big for him and accentuating a weak, hairless chin.

"Mr Trench-O'Keefe will see you now," he said in a shrill voice, somewhat officiously.

Julia nodded at Molly. "Shan't be too long." She carefully lifted her skirt, and reached for her tapestry handbag, then followed him to Eoin's office. It was a first-floor room with a large window overlooking Capel Street and, despite a pervasive musky smell, she noticed that that the windows were firmly closed. Unlike the clutter of Octavius Roe's office, here there was a sparsity of furniture and military-style order, with leatherbound books and ledgers neatly arranged according to height and colour in a mahogany bookcase which filled one wall.

"Miss Benson, good morning. It's been a long time, I think." He came out from behind his desk and shook her hand firmly. His brown eyes were lidded.

"It has indeed, Mr Trench-O'Keefe."

"O'Keefe is sufficient," he replied with a polite smile. "Please sit down."

Donal had explained to Julia that his brother used the double-barrelled name for business reasons, as Trench, despite its French origins, sounded more Anglo-Irish than O'Keefe and reassured his customers of his political affiliations. Although, according to Donal, his brother was not beyond espousing the Nationalist cause when it suited him.

You would not think they were brothers, she thought. Eoin was taller and olive-skinned with black hair combed flat on his head, but she noticed his sideburns had a ginger tinge. He was a handsome man.

"I don't think we have met since I was a young girl in my grandfather's shop, and you visited with your grandfather."

"Actually, we have met since then. I was introduced to you a few years ago at one of the Academy open nights. You were exhibiting a portrait as I recall."

"Oh, yes. Yes, of course," she said, although the memory evaded her.

"I believe that you are also acquainted with my brother Donal. He told me you were coming to see me today."

"Yes, I know him well – we share similar interests."

"Indeed."

"In art," she emphasised, smiling.

"Well, enough pleasantries. What can I do for you, Miss Benson?"

"Oh, that's a pity." She had been looking forward to meeting him and was disappointed with his abruptness. "I think you can only really get to know a person when they are exchanging foolish pleasantries."

Eoin smiled perfunctorily but did not respond to her comment. He then coughed slightly into his clenched fist and opened the file on his desk.

"The papers you sent over to me regarding your father's will – I have studied them carefully. What exactly can I do for you, Miss Benson?"

"If you have read the papers, then I should have thought it was obvious," she said amiably. "As you can see, I have been harshly treated. My father has left his entire estate to my younger sister. With the intention that she should take financial care of my mother and me."

"Yes, I believe that is correct."

"It is so unfair, don't you think? I feel I have no alternative but to contest the will."

"On what grounds, might I ask?"

"Well, my father was not well the week before he died. He was rambling, not in his full senses. He had a stroke. His death was quite unexpected. Initially, our family solicitor, Mr Octavius Roe, could not find the will, but it eventually turned up some weeks later in the Bank of Ireland's vaults in College Green. However, the executors had not been named, so my sister had to apply for Letters of Administration to the Court. At the time she told me that we were both beneficiaries. I had assumed that we would be equal. I had no idea that I was only getting grandfather's books and some silver items of sentimental value. My sister kept the details very quiet. Her fiancé, Edward Williams, was no doubt pulling the strings. Maybe, if I had known earlier, I could have done something about it."

"But this was drawn up three years ago. Have you found any later will?"

"No."

"Was Mr Roe aware of any other document?"

"I don't believe so, no."

"Can you get a doctor to state that your father was in an unfit state of mind when the will was signed and witnessed by Roe, and two independent witnesses?"

"No – he was quite fit when the will was made – as I told you, he was only rambling for the last week."

"Do you have any proof, or reasonable grounds, for suspecting that this will was forged, or signed under duress?"

"Well, only that it is so unfair, and I cannot understand –"

"So, it is the unfairness of the will as it pertains to your interests that you object to, if I understand your reasoning?"

"Yes. As it is, I am completely beholden to my sister and her fiancé."

"Yes, I know Mr Williams." He paused, choosing his words carefully. "Fairness does not always equate to justice, or legal entitlement, Miss Benson. The law takes a logical approach to business affairs rather than an emotional one. From what I can see, we must accept the fact that the testator made this will in a sound state of mind, since we cannot prove otherwise. And – despite your view to the contrary – any reasonable person would consider your father's actions to be entirely responsible in the circumstances."

"What exactly do you mean, Mr O'Keefe?" she said coldly.

"I mean that although you are the elder daughter, you are a spinster. Whereas your sister is engaged to be married to a respectable man of good standing in the community."

Julia stiffened in her chair.

"You are also an artist and, if I might speak directly, I believe from what I hear that you have certain political affiliations that your father would have considered less than desirable. Once these facts are made known, any reasonable judge would find it hard to contest the logic of your father's actions." He paused and then said in a kinder tone, "As a single woman, Miss Benson, society would also consider that you deserve to have the benefit of male protection and guidance. And Mr Williams, from what I know of him, is certainly a sensible man. So, I am afraid, Miss Benson, unless you can produce another, more recent will, your attempts at contesting this one would be entirely futile." He pressed the tips of his fingers together and tilted his head to one side. "My advice to you, Miss Benson, is to use all of your considerable energy to build on the advantages that this will gives you, and don't waste it on attempting to change things that you simply cannot undo."

"What advantages?" she said in frustration. "I cannot for the life of me see any."

"Well, firstly you can still live in your family home, a fine house by all accounts. I understand that your sister, once married, intends to move to Manchester. And from the arrangements you sent me, proposed by Mr Williams, you can keep a share of whatever profits arise from the business once the expenses are met."

"It is not just about the money," she said, exasperated. "It is about independence. I don't need the guidance of any male figure, Mr O'Keefe. I am perfectly capable of managing my own affairs."

"That's as may be, Miss Benson, but society and the legal system that represents it consider otherwise. Now, Miss Benson," he took his watch from his pocket, "unfortunately I have another appointment. My clerk will show you to a cab."

He got up from his desk, went to the door and opened it.

"Next time, I hope we will have more time for pleasantries, Miss Benson," he said, an amused smile animating his brown eyes. "Freddy, could you show Miss Benson and her servant out, please?"

"Thank you, Mr O'Keefe," said Julia. "but I doubt there will be a next time."

"My misfortune," he replied, bowing his head briefly in acknowledgement and then he shut the door.

Still fuming after her morning meeting with Donal's brother, Julia was working in the room behind the photographic studio that they called the shop. It was where they kept the artists' supplies, lithographic and fine art prints, and photographs of famous people imported from London. They were running out of *cartes de visite* of Queen Victoria – she and her late husband Prince Albert were keen collectors of photographs, having commissioned a series of their entire family. Now that her father was dead, Julia would not be ordering any more of those.

The room was laid out like a chemist's shop, lined on two walls with bottles of chemicals, tubes of paint, and various pots and potions. Over the fireplace was a painting of her paternal grandfather William Benson and, in front of this, a mahogany desk that had come from his original premises in Dame Street. However, the dour representation in the painting did not reflect her family's recollection of him as a larger-than-life character. His shop was always chock-a-block with paintings, prints, maps and curios. Her uncles told her that when he was alive a constant stream of visitors, artists and patrons called in to browse or discuss art and the politics of the day – or simply just to gossip with this charismatic, charming man. Uncle Charles had certainly inherited his personality. But, importantly, despite their best endeavours, her father and his brothers, Henry and John, lacked his passion for art and his business acumen. After he died, they had sold the original shop and gone their separate ways.

Grandpapa had invested in lithography early, believing that this would bring famous artworks to the masses, to be enjoyed by all. He had also been a staunch supporter of the Royal Dublin Society Drawing School, and the Irish art scene generally. He had passed this love on to his youngest son Charles. Julia remembered how her uncle's eyes used to light up as he showed her paintings by Irish artists such as James Arthur O'Connor and Francis Danby – and how they used light and scale in landscapes to make you feel awed by the majesty of nature. This was what was meant by 'sublime', he told her. It was Charles who had first encouraged her to paint and, having no children of his own, he had paid for various private tutors to come to her home. Because, despite their family's associations with the Society, Julia's father would not countenance a girl from a respectable Protestant family attending lessons in their school.

Apart from art, Julia shared another interest with her Uncle Charles and the grandfather whom she had never met. A desire to see the day that Ireland would be a nation in her own right, free from British control. Charles Benson had supported the petition to the King, to save the lives of the Fenian prisoners following the failed Irish uprising of 1867. Julia shivered at the memory of that time. Over in England, armed Fenians attempted to rescue their leader, Colonel T.J. Kelly and Captain Timothy Deasy, as they were being brought to prison in Manchester. A shot was fired through the ventilator of the van killing Brett, a guard. Although the prisoners escaped, three men were charged, amongst them young Philip Allen, accused of firing the fatal shot. And, although they expressed regret for the man's death, the three men were subsequently hanged. The event had shaken the country badly. These 'Manchester Martyrs' were the first Irishmen since Robert Emmet to be hanged for political action. She would never forget Philip's poor mother's grief at the ceremony in Glasnevin cemetery. A ceremony in name only, with not even his body to mourn.

Julia tried to put these thoughts out of her head. There had been a delivery that morning, and there was work to be done. She unpacked the chemicals first, which were highly flammable – she would ask Billy to take them to the darkroom store at the back of the house.

Looking up at the painting of her grandfather, she wondered what he would do. What advice would he give her? Her meeting with Eoin O'Keefe had been disappointing. But, as well as being angry, she was also worried. It had been one thing running the photographic studio when Harriet was there to do all the bookkeeping – Julia herself was useless at numbers – but to be here on her own trying to manage the day-to-day running of the house and the business would undoubtedly be a strain. She looked at her grandfather and breathed in deeply.

"I am being pathetic," she said out loud in the empty room. "I don't need a man to lean on. I am well capable of doing this."

She unpacked the remaining boxes of brushes from Winsor and Newton in London and set them out in the display cabinets, and then tidied the leatherbound volumes of lithographic prints. It was five o'clock, there would be no more customers that day. Pierre was in the darkroom developing the images of Mr Brown, whom she had correctly guessed was a visiting tea importer.

She sat down at her grandfather's desk to gather her thoughts. Since the reading of the will, the atmosphere had been awful. She had barely spoken to Harriet – usually only in front of their mother and the servants and, even then, only when strictly required to do so. What had happened to bring them to this? On one level she despised her sister's need to be married, but on another she understood. The last few years had been a struggle. Harriet had constantly worried about their financial situation as their father's health deteriorated. The business had suffered badly which had come with a loss of social prestige amongst their church-going community.

In the years before his death, despite the continuous economies they had made to save face, the family had struggled to keep up appearances. Regularly, the women had to resort to refashioning their bonnets with new ribbons, and their dresses and cloaks were noticeably shabby.

The Christmas before he died had been the worst. It was hard for them to remain cheerful while the rest of the city celebrated. Shop windows, filled with baubles and finery, were decorated with fake snow and fairy candles, as Dublin's wealthier citizenry tripped around with arms full of ribbon-wrapped gift boxes. It was the first time that they had not had the traditional goose – they had rabbit instead.

She shivered at the memory of that New Year's Eve. During the small hours of the morning, the two sisters could not sleep due to the racket on Westland Row. Then suddenly they had been distracted by the sound of a bottle shattering on the granite steps below. They had looked out through the curtains to see a figure sprawled on their doorstep. A poor wraith of a young woman, down on her luck, drowning her sorrows with cheap gin. Although they both knew their duty as Christians was to help one of God's fallen creatures, she was only one of thousands – poverty was everywhere in the city. Instead, they went back to bed, wrapping the blankets around themselves, snuggling into one another for comfort and hoping the poor creature would be gone by morning.

The incident seemed to crystallise their positions. They both knew that, despite the fine words, a sudden change in their circumstances would mean that the elegant doors on the street would be kindly, but firmly, closed in their faces. Although their relatives, Uncle Charles or his sister Aunt Sarah, might help for a while, the sisters would ultimately be faced with a life serving others. Or, in the worst scenario, they would end up in the workhouse – a living death – a disgrace that anyone in their right mind would want desperately to avoid. Then out of the blue, Edward, who had seemed keen on Harriet for some time but was slow to declare his interest, to everyone's surprise including Harriet's suddenly proposed.

After Papa died, they were unable to access his money in the bank. But the delay with getting the letters of administration had given Julia time to develop the studio. Although, she remembered, they had fought viciously as Harriet tried hard to stop her from using the money left in Papa's safe, but Julia's determination had prevailed in the end.

When she had been told of her sister's engagement, Julia had suppressed her dislike of Edward and had been genuinely pleased for Harriet – she was finally getting her wish. But the reading of the will had changed everything. She was convinced that Harriet had influenced her father. There was no excuse – what she had done was unforgivable. She still could not fully believe her sister was capable of such an act. But there was simply no other explanation. For despite her arguments with her father, she could not believe that he would treat her so badly. It was as if he had accepted that her getting married was not even a possibility. He had fashioned a future of dependency for her, and this had hurt her to the core. Although she felt that, for her, marriage was still a possibility, being a mother was unlikely to happen. The hairs rose on her neck at the very thought of it. She could feel her body come out in a cold sweat as she remembered how quickly fear had superseded passion during the days after

Dollymount Strand. She had caught Molly looking at her with concern in unguarded moments – she had been a few days late – but fortunately to her intense relief her monthlies returned. It was not that she did not like children, but she was not prepared to give up her life, her art, to motherhood. Then there were also the memories of Mama's terrified screams, as if her body was being rent apart, and then the silent whispers that followed for weeks after her frequent miscarriages. Julia shivered. No, it was not for her. She got up from the desk and smoothed down her dress. It was time to talk to her sister.

"Harriet." Julia opened the door to their bedroom where Harriet was getting ready to go to her music lesson.

She was sitting at the dressing table brushing her hair, which was a lighter shade of red than Julia's, and usually described as 'strawberry blonde'. Her sister's cheeks were freckled despite constant application of lemon juice to fade the unwanted blemishes. Unlike Julia's blue-grey eyes, Harriet's were pale blue, like their mother's.

"Julia." Harriet nodded but continued to brush her hair, addressing Julia's reflection through the mirror.

"How is Mama?" Julia asked.

"I have just met with Doctor Whyte and he is still worried about her."

"Hopefully she will pull through after a few more days of bedrest. However, with Mama's failing health, I think we need to talk about the future. Have you and Edward set a date yet?"

Harriet turned slowly, eyes lowered. "Not exactly … while he is studying for his exams, we decided that we will try to save money. Although he is getting paid at the clinic attached to the college, it is not enough to support me also. So, we don't intend to marry for another year."

"I see. And how did Edward get the money to pay for his fees at the Royal College of Surgeons?"

"Oh, his father gave him the money." Harriet glared defiantly at Julia.

"He is obviously a more successful silk merchant than we gave him credit for. How very lucky Edward is – and to have met you, of course."

"Look, Julia," Harriet stood up, exasperated, and faced her sister, "I know you are deeply unhappy about the will. But can't you see that Papa was trying to protect us both? He was concerned that what little income we have would be managed properly and that there would be provision for Mama. And, Julia, you know Papa wanted me to have a decent dowry. Whereas he felt that you …"

Julia could see her mind working, trying to find the right words.

"He would have thought it improbable that you would marry. You must admit, it is unlikely to work out with Donal, and in any case with no dowry you know his family would not approve. Anyway, I am not sure you have the disposition to be married, which requires compromise and obedience, two qualities that you seem to completely disregard."

"Harriet, you really are an insufferable prig. If you want to marry that dry old curmudgeon, good luck to you. I would rather be a spinster than share my bed with that pontificating stick-insect. I hope you do not live to regret it!"

"Regret it, oh no!" came her sister's heated response. "*You're* the one who has made foolish choices. Edward is a good man, a Christian man. Whereas the fact that you have devoted the best years of your life to – not one – but two lost causes, is beyond belief. Donal O'Keefe and the Fenians will be your undoing, dear sister, wait and see."

Her pent-up energy spent, Harriet sat down again at the dressing table and clasped both her hands together, head bent.

"Julia, you are so strong, so confident – you make people laugh – effortlessly. And you are also so attractive – everyone loves you. It's been hard being your little sister." She looked up at Julia. But her sister's face was still thunderous. "Sometimes when we are out with friends, I think that if I stay quiet long enough, I could just slip out of the room and no one will notice. At home it was different. I think Papa found my quietness soothing, and there was my music of course. And, if the truth be known, he himself was not as strong as you are. It was always easier to give in to your demands, especially when Uncle Charles spoilt you so."

Julia could see that she was shaking.

"But, Julia, this is my only chance. Time is running out if I am to have children and a family of my own. If you have remained unmarried, it is because you have chosen to do so. It is not for want of admirers." She looked at Julia with tearful pleading eyes. "Julia, please, I don't want to fight with you. I need you to be happy for me. I want you to be a part of my new life. Please, Julia."

"Did you persuade Papa to change his will?"

"No, Julia – how many times do I need to tell you? I swear I did nothing, and said nothing, to make him change it. If it ever was changed, that is. Can you not see, knowing Papa as you do, that it was entirely his decision? He thought he was doing the right thing, what was best for us all."

"Do you swear to Almighty God, Harriet?"

"Yes! Yes, I do! I did not persuade him to change his will. I only found out what it contained when Roe showed it to me and told me of Papa's wishes. I should have told you then, but Roe persuaded me not to upset you until it was official." Tears ran down her freckled cheeks.

"Edward too, no doubt."

Harriet said nothing, her answer written on her face. But now Julia was certain her sister was telling the truth about the will. She did not have it in her to lie so convincingly.

Molly's head appeared around the door.

"Ye better come quickly – yer poor ma is slipping away!

~~~~~

Chapter 4

Fitzwilliam Square

April 1873

Roses, their mother's favourites, had filled St Mark's the previous November, their sensuous smell at odds with the sight of the corpse in the open coffin in front of the altar. After the ceremony, the hearse had travelled along the River Liffey Quays to Mount Jerome, drawn by six black horses each festooned with long black feather plumes. Behind it, the carriages of the Benson family and friends followed. Although the crowd was smaller than had attended their father's funeral, the mourners had been rewarded with Meg Benson's meticulously planned production. Even the Reverend Charles, for once, had stuck to the script. The event had also marked the start of an uneasy truce between the two sisters.

Today, five months later, the roses were serving another purpose. They had been picked fresh from the O'Keefe's garden to the rear of their house on Fitzwilliam Square.

"Look at what you are trying to draw, Lydia, look closely. Can you see the shape of the leaves on the rose, how they are delicately crinkled and how the light catches each petal in different ways? So that the deep-pink colour where the petal is in shade has undertones of purple, and of coral where it is in full sunlight. And look how it is a paler pink at the diaphanous edges."

Lydia looked at the watercolour painting that she had been struggling with for the past hour. It looked nothing like her teacher's polished example.

"Yes, Miss Benson, I do see, but in my case the seeing and the doing are not necessarily attuned. But I do know what you mean."

Lydia O'Keeffe was fifteen and quite a madam, thought Julia. She had agreed to do these lessons with some reluctance. She had been surprised when Eoin's sister Bea had asked her to teach her niece, particularly after her visit to him and his apparently low opinion of her. She was also concerned that, through this association, he might discover just how friendly she was with his brother. A fact that Donal was anxious, for the time being, to keep from him. Julia suspected that he just wished to put off the inevitable row with his brother and sister that would follow.

"I am afraid I just cannot concentrate, Miss Benson. I am so excited – I am going to my first ball in Dublin Castle this evening. My dress is so beautiful, simple but elegant, in the finest white cambric with pink ribbon pleating on the neckline. And the shoes, Miss Benson, are kidskin pumps, also pink, with tiny glass beading from Venice at the toe."

"Well, I can see why you have no interest in painting flowers, Lydia. Well, it is nearly three o'clock – I think that we have probably had enough for one day."

The door of the music room opened, and Donal walked in.

"Good afternoon, Miss Benson, I am so sorry to disturb you. My sister Bea is anxious that Lydia should start preparing for this evening's ball. She asked me to deliver you to the care of our coachman who will take you home."

Lydia curtsied briefly to Julia, said rather ungratefully, "Thank you so much for rescuing me, Uncle Donal," and dashed out the door.

"I am sorry about that, Julia," said Donal. "She is completely spoiled – being an only child has its disadvantages. Her manners could be much improved."

"Don't worry, Donal, it's a spinster's lot. I am used to being slighted," she said dryly.

"Please don't say that, Julia – you know I wish that things were different. Listen, I can't talk now. Eoin needs to go over some papers with me. But we must meet as soon as possible and discuss the future." He kissed her gently on the lips. "Next Tuesday, at the Academy, I will meet you at noon. Bring your sketchpad and we will draw one of the sculptures. To any onlooker we will be two artists honing their life-drawing skills. I would not imagine Tuesday would be a busy day. See if you can lose Molly, and we can talk privately. Until then, my love …"

And he was gone.

Julia, smiling, picked up the brushes discarded by Lydia and rinsed them in the basin of water. She placed tissue over the watercolour painting, shaking it first to make sure it was completely dry. She then left the room to find the footman to take her to their coach. Donal in his enthusiasm had clearly forgotten his promise to do so.

It was nearly noon. The main exhibition space in the Academy was virtually empty, except for a governess and her two young charges huddled together at the other end of the large room. They were discussing the merits of Edwin Hayes' turbulent seascapes of Dublin Bay. The walls of the gallery, painted a deep burgundy colour, were filled with paintings of all shapes and sizes, each vying for attention. Julia was pleased to see that the portrait of her great-grandmother was in a good location, at eye level, and flanked by smaller portraits in pastel and pencil that did not detract the eye from hers.

"It's very impressive, Miss Julia – you have really captured her likeness," said Molly approvingly.

Young at Heart certainly caught the eye. She had been delighted that the *Irish Times* had singled it out and commented so favourably. They had called it "clever". And it was, thought Julia. It was a showpiece intended to demonstrate her skill to the Academy, and hopefully to attract new students to her drawing classes. Not only had she handled the light reflections and folds on the intricate fabric of the gown very well, but she had also managed to capture the old woman's indomitable spirit. The power and pathos of old age were more difficult qualities to portray than the innocence of youth.

"It's difficult for women, Molly," said Julia, "to develop drawing skills. Although I provide a draped model in my classes, it is simply not the same as drawing from a nude one. It is so unfair that women are not allowed to attend life drawing at the Academy."

"Well, I'm not surprised, Miss Julia! Why would you even think about it? God save yeh from all harm! I mean, Miss Julia – those models are stark naked. Holy God never intended us to be seen naked. If he did, he wouldn't have med us wear clothes, now would he? My Padraic, let me tell you, has never seen me naked. Oh no. He just gets to see the bits of me he needs to see to do his business."

Julia laughed, and looked around to make sure no one was listening.

"Molly, I really don't want to know what you and Padraic do in the privacy of your bedroom. But, you know, artists believe the naked body is something to be celebrated, that it represents God's gift of life to humanity. As an artist you have to understand the naked body to be able to draw clothed ones."

"But –"

"No buts, Molly, I don't intend to have this argument with you here in a public place. I came here to draw this sculpture ..." She gestured towards Thomas Farrell's *Tarpeian Rock*, which depicted two classically modelled figures hewn from the rock – one, an executioner poised with a sword to slay the other, his victim. "So why don't you go down to the tailors in Grafton Street and pick up the satin skirt that you left in for me last week to be altered."

"But that will take me an hour."

"Perfect, just in time for me to do a few sketches."

"Very well, miss. I will see you back here in an hour. But will you be alright here on your own?"

"Of course, Molly, perfectly alright."

When Molly had gone, Julia looked at the sculpture in the centre of the room, at the terror etched on the victim's face, and shivered. She felt like a victim herself, already pierced by the sword. There was an emptiness in her since her father and mother died. It wasn't only grief – or the bitterness that followed between herself and her sister – it was also as if all her dreams of developing as an artist had evaporated, and she would never have the same purpose again. When she was younger, she had fought passionately to be allowed to live in Paris – the centre of the art world – for a year or two. But Papa would not countenance it. Instead, he organised a series of private tutors at home, some better than others. Photography had really helped her, even the negatives where you could differentiate, in reverse, light and shade. She had spent hours copying discarded *cartes de visite*, and the chromolithographs of famous paintings that they sold in the shop. But it was not enough. Over the years a number of her male artist friends had studied at the Académie Julien, a famous Parisian Atelier. Unfortunately, like most other art educational establishments, women were not allowed to attend. However, when she was in her late twenties, and money was tight, Uncle Charles had taken her to Paris for a month and paid for private lessons in the hope that she might learn the skills of the French masters. She had persuaded him it was an investment to enable her to boost attendances at her small drawing and painting school. She longed to return to Paris. And now after all these years, finally, she had hoped to fulfil her dreams of spending time in the French capital visiting the Louvre, then travelling to Antwerp, and finally studying in Rome – aspirations that were now impossible. She remembered how jealous she had been, when she heard that young Sarah Purser – a niece of her aunt's friend – had enrolled in the School of Art in Kildare Street, founded by the RDS, the only art school in Ireland open to women. But then, her father was less strict, and the family's flour business was supposedly in trouble – and soon she too would have to earn her own living.

There was Donal of course. She did love him – yearn

for him. At the thought of his imminent arrival, desire welled deep inside her, spreading in a sensuous wave all over her body. But even as she savoured the sensations, her mind was resisting. What was the future in it? Where would it all end? Her financial independence might have made it possible to brave the social approbation that would surely follow if they married – that is, when he finally got around to asking her, she thought in exasperation. But now, she was more tied than ever, and there was still so much uncertainty about what lay ahead. But one thing was for sure, as a woman she knew things would be harder, not easier. Less help with the tedious everyday labours of living – less time to paint. She would have to make the best use of the time she had left, she thought with determination, before everything changed.

Julia checked her pocket watch. It was ten minutes to noon. She took out charcoal and a sketchpad from her tapestry bag and, pulling over a chair from the side of the room, started drawing the bronze sculpture.

"Evil-looking devil, isn't he?"

"Donal, you are early!" she exclaimed, startled.

"Fortunately, Eoin is in court all week and, apart from young Freddy, the chinless wonder, I have the office to myself."

Julia laughed, her maudlin thoughts forgotten as he pulled over a chair beside her.

Taking a well-worn, leatherbound sketchbook from his case, he started drawing, looking at the artwork intermittently for reference. The room was deserted – the few stragglers had left the main hall and moved into a smaller room that showed parts of the Academy's permanent collection.

"How are you? You are looking as beautiful as ever, despite everything." He paused then continued solicitously, "Are you bearing up? It must be so strange to be without both your parents."

"Thank you, and yes," she replied. "It is hard to get used to. Sometimes I go into Mama's room and take one of her silk scarves out of her dresser just to smell her perfume. They say no one loves you like your mother." Her eyes welled with tears.

"I love you too. But not like your mother." He leant over and kissed the soft skin on the side of her neck.

"Be careful! Anyone might walk in."

"Sorry. It's hard to be so close. I can't get you out of my mind, especially after Bull Island."

"Donal, I wouldn't like you to think ..." She tried to find the right words.

"Think what? That you are brave and honest, and that I love you, and intend you to be my wife?"

Her initial smile of delight quickly faded and was replaced by a look of complete despair.

"Donal, flattered though I am, you know it is impossible," she sighed. "The deaths of my parents have changed nothing – public knowledge of our relationship would be a disaster." She got up from the chair and walked distractedly around the sculpture. "I am forgiven, to some extent at least, for my political opinions because I am an artist – I am expected to be unconventional. But to marry you would be to nail my colours to the mast, in a way that would estrange me from my extended family and friends."

"Julia –"

"I have thought carefully about this, my love," she cut

71

him off gently. "The reality is, I have no dowry, no prospects. I am completely at Edward's mercy. God help me! He has come up with a plan. He intends to marry Harriet in November and to take the boat to Liverpool the next day to start a new life in Manchester. Meanwhile, I must stay here in Dublin with Molly in Westland Row and run the photography business with Pierre. I will continue with the drawing lessons, and hopefully get a few more portrait commissions – this will be my own money – but I must pay Harriet and Edward rent for the privilege of using the space. I also have to earn sufficient to pay the rent on the rest of the house in Westland Row and the wages for the staff."

"But, Julia, that will involve a lot of organisation – a whole level of administration that you are not used to."

"Yes, but Edward and Harriet have thought of that. An acquaintance of Edward's, the snivelling Stephen Spendlove, will do the books, the ordering and invoicing, every evening, after he has finished his clerical job in Trinity. And Edward will come home himself once a month to check up on the business, and me too I suppose. Harriet hopes to start a family. But their long-term plan in Manchester is unclear, except that I am not a part of it. Not that I want to be."

Donal stood up, pulling her gently to him and wrapping his arms around her.

"Oh, ye of little faith – and you think that I am going to leave you like this as Edward and Harriet's indentured slave. That is simply not going to happen." He released her but grasped her hands. "Julia, I have some good news for a change. I will be away in America for the next few months, my darling. An uncle, on my father's side, died recently. Funny old chap, a bachelor, family rarely heard from him. He ran a successful cotton-export business, and I am one of the beneficiaries of his estate. I expect the inheritance to be a reasonable amount – it will be enough for us to marry. Although, I must admit, this is not the only reason for my visit there – after my recent adventures in the South-East the Brothers think I should make myself scarce for a while. At least until things calm down." He gazed into her astonished eyes. "But when I return, if we move to England, no one will know about our circumstances, whether you have a dowry or not. There are so many Irish in England as it is. I can travel between the two countries when necessary. Despite their pious aspirations, what help have your aunts and uncles been during the last year? The Bensons have done very little for you and Harriet, other than drawing-room visits – tea and empty words of cold comfort, as far as I can see. Who do you really care about other than Uncle Charles? And he will always stick by you, no matter what you do."

Julia, mesmerised, hung on his every word.

"Just imagine! We would be together, with no more hiding and prevarication." He paused and looked dreamily off into the distance. "I had thought of Cornwall – the scenery is stunning and there is a well-established artists' colony based around St Ives. I can try and gain employment with a local solicitor."

Julia felt her heart racing and a warm glow spread over her body at the prospect he painted of their future together … then the unwelcome thought occurred to her that this was too good to be true.

"What about Eoin?"

"Oh, at first he won't be happy, but Bea and himself will soon come around – they always do."

In the empty gallery, under the benevolent eye of the portrait of her great-grandmother, he got down on one knee.

"Julia, my love, will you marry me?" he said simply and sincerely.

"Well, I cannot leave yeh for a minute!" said Molly as she bustled breathless into the room, her face red and her brow sweating.

Donal jumped up, startled, nearly falling over in his attempts to regain his balance and composure.

"Molly, that was quick," said Julia, flustered. "Eh … Mr O'Keefe was just picking up the pencil I dropped."

"Lucky I wasn't so long. Looks like I came back just in time! Before he picked up that pencil!" retorted Molly, clearly aware of what had been afoot. She nodded curtly. "Morning, Mr O'Keefe." Without waiting for a response, she turned to Julia. "Your aunt, Miss Anne Benson, passed me in her coach and gave me a lift there and back. Lucky for some, as it turns out." She glared at Donal.

Julia's elation turned to despair as she watched Donal, eyes startled, caught between frustration and embarrassment, bow deeply, gather his briefcase and sketchbook and hastily move towards the door.

"Lovely to talk to you, Miss Benson," he said over his shoulder. "Goodbye Molly." And, as an afterthought, "Miss Benson, I will be in touch in a few days about that commission I mentioned."

When he had gone Molly turned to Julia and said, "Miss Harriet will be waiting for us at home – the dressmaker has an appointment for your final fitting for the bridesmaid's dress. We will be late. I don't know what you see in that rascal, Miss Julia. I will go and ask the porter to call us a cab."

Julia, totally exasperated, watched as Molly bustled off. However, there was no point in reprimanding her. Although Julia was thirty-five years of age and no longer a blushing debutante, to Molly she was still her responsibility. She had minded her since she was a baby. In many ways she was more of a mother to her than her own. But, really, sometimes she went completely beyond what was acceptable. The less said the better, thought Julia. At least Molly would not rat on her to her sister, or to Edward. There was no love lost there.

Julia packed up her things, her heart soaring and her mind trying to process what her darling boy had just said, and how this could change everything. They could be together at last, no more secret meetings and fleeting embraces. To live with him, as man and wife, to wake up beside him every morning, his body cocooned with hers. She never thought she would see this day. If Papa was alive, he certainly would not have allowed it. But could she just leave Harriet to deal with everything? Well, it would serve her right – her sister had no reservations about abandoning her. They had Pierre after all – he could manage – if supervised of course. And now at least she did not have to worry about who would look after Mama. Maybe she could just turn her back on it all? Maybe being a married woman would not be so bad. She could still paint. They would have servants, of course – and Molly could come with her. Her heart lifted at the prospect, as she thought about how much she loved Donal. He was different from all the others – he did not try to control her. In fact, he was the only man she had ever met that she truly respected, his strength of character a match for hers – and he lifted her spirits and made her laugh.

Marriage was not something she had considered seriously, before now. In the beginning, their relationship had started out as a diversion – the danger appealed to her, the intrigue of it all. But then she had allowed him to make love to her. She had persuaded herself that she was in control and that she had not wanted to die a virgin. But, to her surprise, afterwards it was as if she had suffered a trauma, been depleted by a passion that unsettled her very being. From that day forward, she was in a state of constant anxiety – she could not get him out of her mind. And with love also came fear that she might lose him, and that each day might be their last. The path he had chosen was perilous. Every morning when she opened the newspaper, her heart was in her mouth, as she read the frequent articles announcing *'an important arrest has been made,'* thinking – this time it could be him. She shivered apprehensively. She knew that marrying Donal would not be easy. But then life was never easy.

Chapter 5

The Sherman Hotel,
Clarke Street,
Chicago

4th May 1873

Dear Julia,

I arrived safely in Chicago after almost three weeks'
travelling from Cork. The sea crossing was worse than
anything I had ever imagined. We hit a tropical storm
mid-Atlantic with mountainous waves and screeching
winds that lasted for twelve hours and blew us off course,
delaying us by several days. I was so ill after the voyage
that the clothes I left Ireland in are now at least two sizes
too big for me. I had to recuperate in New York before
making the two-day train journey to Chicago.

This country is like nothing you have ever seen

before. On arrival, I was awestruck by New York, and the Brooklyn Bridge, currently being constructed, which spans the East River and will be the longest suspension bridge in the world. Also, the city's cast-iron buildings which are often eight or nine storeys high. But, above all, Julia, you would love the sheer spectacle of the place. There were people from every country on earth: serious-faced Chinamen with long ponytails – black-haired Indians with skin the colour of clay and painted lines on their faces (they carry their infants, in bags called papooses, on their backs) – copper-coloured Mexicans – serious-looking Germans – flirtatious Frenchmen – and of course the Irish, who you can spot a mile off with their bacon-and-cabbage complexions and ginger hair. I would imagine there is a lifetime's inspiration for an artist concerned with the human condition in New York city.

Chicago, on the other hand, is a good deal more sombre. It is also a strange city, built on the swampy lands on the edges of Lake Michigan and rebuilt with incredible speed in the last two years since the Great Fire. Because of this, the city's brash offices and warehouses possess a great sameness. Although it is called the Windy City, it is unseasonably cold here now and I find the freezing temperatures hard to tolerate. I have bought myself a fur hat and fur-lined boots. But, despite these luxuries, the dry cold gets into your bones and you never feel warm – even in front of a roaring fire. And with the prohibition on drink, there is not even a drop of the hard stuff to be had to warm your blood.

Despite these challenges, I have contacted Eoin's friend, a fellow graduate of Trinity, Robert Armstrong, and I am staying at the Sherman Hotel near his office. He will advise me which authorities I need to engage with in order to sort out my uncle's estate. I do not need to tell you how much I miss you, Julia. Every night I say a silent prayer to God to keep you safe. I think about you all the time and keep your handkerchief close to my breast. I can still smell a trace of your perfume and with this sensation memories of your loveliness comfort and inspire me.

Yours always
Donal

* * *

27 Clarke Street,
Chicago,
Illinois

16th Sept 1873

Dear Julia,

As you can see, I have moved from the hotel to new lodgings on Clarke Street. The house is run by an elderly Irishwoman from Donegal, a Mrs Quinn. Unsurprisingly, she spoils me, which has made me most unpopular with my fellow lodgers who bitterly resent my bigger dinner portions, while I grow fat and content with her kindness.

Last night I had my first outing in Chicago society. Mr Arnold Stephenson, a business acquaintance of Eoin's in the mining business, invited me to dinner with his family. It was a most enjoyable evening. I met his daughter, Mrs Georgianna Grace, a widow whose husband died in the Civil War. Her husband's family were Irish. She is very interested in the Irish situation and has promised to make introductions for me to Clan na Gael here in Chicago.

Although my days are busy writing letters of enquiry and visiting banks and institutions to unravel my uncles' affairs, my nights are long and lonely and filled with thoughts of you. The scent has faded from the handkerchief, and now I only have a photograph to sustain me. Oh, how I miss you, and long to wrap my arms around you, and feel your body entwined with mine. My heart beats so hard in my chest that I cannot breathe at the thought of you. You are my beloved, lover, and dearest friend. I am besotted and bereft without you.

Yours only
Donal

Chapter 6

It had been a simple ceremony. Julia had been Matron of Honour, and Edward's five-year-old niece Emma had been a flower girl. Harriet's white lace and Julia's lilac satin dresses signalled to polite society the end of mourning following their double loss. Today was also the beginning of a new life for them both.

Julia looked closely at her younger sister. At thirty-three, Harriet looked almost girlish. Although Julia feared she was making the greatest mistake of her life, she understood her dilemma – Harriet wanted so desperately to have children, and time was running out. Harriet still had a chance. If truth be told, Father and Mother had died just in time for Harriet to live a life of her own. Julia had to acknowledge that without Harriet's inheritance this marriage would not have been possible. From her own perspective, Donal and herself had agreed for the moment to keep their betrothal a secret. Julia did not wish to upset her sister's big day and felt it would be easier to tell Harriet once she had figured out how the business could operate without her. Snivelling Stephen had already started managing the books and the ordering. He had even put new systems in place. They now had appointment books, receipt books and even a petty-cash box. He was not the worst really, just painfully shy and surprisingly nervous of her. Donal had also said nothing to anyone – he had told her that he was anxious to establish the amount of his American inheritance before broaching his intentions with his brother.

Today, thought Julia, Edward was smartly turned out for the occasion in top hat and a smart black dress coat. And although not exactly handsome, he was not unattractive, with dark looks that you often get on the west coast of Ireland. If only he would smile more often, she reflected – his face was transformed on the few occasions when this actually happened.

Looking back, it had been a difficult year for them all. With no hope of contesting the will, Julia had to make some tough decisions. She could not go on fighting indefinitely with her younger sister, and she had to grudgingly accept that the arrangement had been her father's decision, and in these circumstances Harriet and Edward's departure was for the best.

She looked around the dining room. The Waterford glass and the brass were both sparkling. Molly and Tilly the housemaid had been working for days to get the room ready. Molly was in top form, serving sherry and full of chat with the twelve guests. She was wearing a white starched apron, hair tied back tidily for once, the new leather boots Julia had bought her peeping out from under her long black dress.

They were about to enjoy a light wedding breakfast of poached salmon, brisket of beef in the French style, and some roast chicken. Mrs Cunningham had made a wedding cake that was to be served following the dessert. Julia moved over to her sister's side.

"Well, Harriet, are you all packed and ready to leave tomorrow?"

"Well, almost. I still have my toiletries and jewellery to sort out. I will be sad to leave Westland Row – we have had such a happy childhood here."

"Despite all the rows?"

"Despite all the rows, they were mostly good times. You were too like Papa, you know. In many ways that was why you sparked off each other. But, Julia, I don't want you to think that I don't love you dearly, my brave and beautiful sister." She looked at her directly. "Nor do I want you to despise me. You must think I am a desperate coward to choose to marry Edward. But he is a good man, a kind and Christian man and we get on well enough together. Let's face it, Julia, unlike you, there was never a string of suitors knocking down my door."

Julia smiled at her sister. "I don't think you are a coward, Harriet. I hope with all my heart that Edward becomes the husband that you deserve. Promise me you will write often and tell me everything. This new life will be such an adventure for you both."

"I will, of course – hopefully you can come over and visit once we have settled in."

Julia leaned over and was just about to whisper her own news to her sister when a booming voice interrupted them.

"*And how are my two beautiful nieces?*" Uncle Charles

was bearing down on them, his face beaming, and his cheeks flushed from several glasses of sherry. "Manchester, Harriet, has one of the finest art galleries in England – the Royal Manchester Institution in Mosley Street. I simply cannot wait to visit!"

Chapter 7

Butte,
Montana

2nd June 1874

Dear Julia,

My dearest love, as each day goes by without you, I die a little more. Toujours un petit mort. I miss you with all my heart, and I yearn for you with my body and soul. As I write this, I sit here beneath the vast swathe of stars somewhere in the Northern Rocky Mountains near the copper-mining town of Butte, Montana, where we have set up camp for the night. We are a group of twenty or so. After Mrs Grace's kind introduction, I eventually met up with local members of C na G and got on famously with them. They invited me to join them on a fundraising tour to the North Western territories. I was at a loose end in Chicago waiting for one of my uncle's tenants to vacate a property in Baltimore before putting it on the market. So, I accepted their invitation as an opportunity to build contacts here, and at the same time see more of this incredible country. At this stage, we have been on the road for six weeks, and my wanderlust is now satisfied. I am tired and weary and looking forward to returning to some semblance of civilization in Chicago. The frontier towns are godless places. Although the days are torture with the dry heat, constant burning sun and flesh-eating insects – the nights eventually bring some physical respite.

Tonight, above me, I can see Venus, named after the goddess of love and I dare to hope that somewhere, on the other side of the world, that at this moment in time you too, also, are thinking of me. You would laugh at the pathetic image I present, as I clutch to my breast the worn and frayed picture of you – a yellowing aide memoire that in no way reflects your beauty. Oh, quell those modest denials I hear you make, my love!

Not a day goes by that I do not think of you, my darling girl, and at night, alone, I shudder at memories of our lovemaking – the thought of your touch, your soft yielding flesh. So much so that I envy those who pass you daily in the streets whose glance fulfils their momentary desire, while I, abandoned as I am in this wilderness, thirst for such a fleeting glimpse of you.

Hard though our separation has been for us both, my love, the sacrifice for our country's freedom is at last beginning to bear fruit. John Devoy's powerful rhetoric in the New York Herald has swayed the hearts of many of Ireland's banished sons and daughters living here in

America, and the coffers are nearly full. We have toured several mining towns to which many Civil War veterans have gravitated following the end of the action, with dreams of gold in the streets – only to spend their days drinking and gambling in taverns, and often their nights in the gutter. These poor divils' hearts are gladdened with news and talk of home. They hate the British and lust for revenge and are only too happy to support our cause.

Tomorrow we will start our long journey back towards civilization to a C na G rally in the city of Pittsburgh. I hope to return by the autumn, or "the fall" as they call it here.

I trust that you are not too troubled by Edward, and that Stephen is not being over-scrupulous in his accounting practices. Hopefully, you are also managing to get some time to yourself to paint. Please write, my love! Your letters are all that keep me from madness here in this godforsaken place.

Your loving Donal

Chapter 8

6 Shakespeare Street,
Ardwick Green,
Chorlton-on-Medlock,
Manchester

4th June 1874

Dear Julia,

I hope this letter finds you well, I am sorry it has taken so long to write. I caught a chill on the boat to Liverpool and I am only now recovered.

When we arrived first, it was not easy. We did not realise how hard it would be to get set up in Manchester. Although Edward was living here for some time, he did not even own a kettle! He admitted to buying coffee and most of his meals from street vendors.

We are living in Chorlton-on-Medlock, which is on

the outskirts of the city and, like Dublin, is built mostly in brick. But, in contrast to the variety of shades at home, these bricks are dark-red in colour, and the buildings are stained black from the coal burned in the factories and mills. Continuous plumes of black smoke constantly stream from the tall chimneys that dominate the skyline. And when the weather is heavy, the smoke descends on the city like a mantle of grey cloud that sinks to the ground. Sometimes this is so thick that you cannot even see six feet in front of you. As a result, my asthma is playing up a bit. It is all so big and noisy here and even dirtier than Dublin, if you can imagine that.

I don't mean to paint a negative picture – the city has many benefits. Gas lighting is everywhere and some mansions in the city's suburbs even have heating systems with hot water piped to metal heaters in each room, bathrooms with flushing water closets instead of privies, and running water in their sculleries. You would be impressed with the many fine municipal buildings (particularly the art gallery) and so many different churches for denominations that I have never even heard of. There is also every manner of modern contraption, exotic materials, and food to be bought in the shops.

The Irish are everywhere, many of them living in our neighbourhood, although mostly in tenements. Conditions are very bad in those quarters and disease, particularly typhus, is rampant. Unfortunately, the demon drink is also a big problem amongst our countrymen and causes many a brawl on the city streets.

But where we are in Ardwick Green is very nice. However, the house is not nearly as big as Westland Row, or as well appointed, but it suits our needs very well. We have three lodgers: a widow, Mrs Hunt, and her two daughters who live with us. They sleep in two bedrooms and we sleep in the third. You would be very impressed with my newfound housekeeping skills. We have only one servant who does the cleaning, the laundry, and bringing in the water and coal. I have to do some of the housework too, and all of the cooking, so I am working non-stop all day long, and fall into my bed at night. Mrs Beeton's Book of Household Management is constantly at my side. Although it is written for households far grander than ours. Still, despite all the hard work, I am enjoying being a new wife here in Manchester.

I hope you are managing with the bookkeeping and ordering. I am sorry that Edward has not been over to you yet, but I am sure that Stephen is a great support. Edward is pleased with the reports he sends every week.

I still read the Irish Times. I am sure you were delighted with the Home Rule League's success in achieving fifty-nine seats in the general election. There was much celebration here amongst the Irish after Mr Butt's powerful speech supporting Home Rule in parliament. Although we are not allowed discuss the matter. Edward is still staunchly Unionist. I never thought that I would say this, but I do miss the heated debates with you and Papa, even if they usually ended in a thundering row. Maybe it is because I am very conscious of being Irish here. Although Edward is trying hard to become less so. He says it is in our interests as a family to become more Anglicized. As always, I must trust in his better judgement.

As soon as we arrived, we attended service in the

local Anglican church, St Clement's, and I am hoping to get some calling cards made in the new year when we are more settled. It would be good to visit other parishioners and maybe make a few friends.

Julia, bicycles are all the rage here, with cycling clubs set up in all the main cities. The machines are called High Wheelers. They are an odd sight to see, with a saddle and handlebars on top of the front wheel, which is about four feet high. The back wheel is much smaller. Last week, I even saw a woman on a bicycle, although it was a three-wheel variety. She was wearing a skirt with bloomers – they call them knickerbockers – that you could actually see! Imagine! Edward told me not to even look at her, and that she obviously had no father or husband to save her from making a public spectacle of herself! I thought to myself – my brave sister would probably want one of those!

So that there is absolutely no misunderstanding, Julia, I am joking!

Your devoted sister

Harriet

* * *

14 Westland Row

3ʳᵈ January 1875

Dear Harriet,
It was lovely to get your letter. I must admit I was

getting worried when I did not hear from you. Christmas was a sad time here without you. Uncle Charles joined us for Christmas dinner, and we invited the Misses Allen from the Academy of Music. We had a lovely Wicklow goose and all the trimmings. They were all asking for you and hoped that you were still teaching.

We are all well here. Although Molly had a bad chest infection over Christmas, and I had to help out. She is only now back on her feet. Padraic, who was lost without her telling him what to do, has been wandering around the house like a dog who has lost his bark, and Mrs Cunningham is like a rat with all the extra work. Pierre has been missing for most of Christmas – enough said! But from what you say, it sounds as though things are not so different with the problems of drink in Manchester. But I am glad to hear that you are settling in, though I am sorry that you have so much housework to do. Mind your beautiful hands, little sister. Those hands were made for playing Mozart not scrubbing floors! Regarding your comments about bicycles, I actually saw a bicycle in the Phoenix Park last Sunday – the young gentleman kept falling off and people were jeering at him. A Dublin wit shouted out, "Don't shoot your horse just yet, your honour!" I must say, though, I like the idea of a bicycle – it would be great not to have Molly shadowing me all the time. But she would probably get one too, just to keep up with me.

Although I miss you, I too am kept going. I finally feel vindicated, as despite Papa's and Edward's scepticism, our photographic studio has finally taken off. We have been really busy. I am doing particularly well with children. I have painted some more lovely backdrops *of classical scenes. Sailor suits are still all the fashion since Queen Victoria dressed young Prince Albert in one for his portrait some years ago. I even made papier mâché rocks for coastal scenes that are proving to be very popular. And I hand-colour the prints. The mothers love them!*

Unfortunately, prices continue to go down because of the increased competition. However, the demand is also increasing as everyone wants to send likenesses to their families who have emigrated, especially at Christmas when they are dressed in all their finery.

The Christmas season has distracted us briefly from the harsh reality here. This year's poor harvests and high rents have resulted in widespread evictions that continue to fuel emigration. When I was getting customs clearance for chemicals from England last week, I witnessed some harrowing scenes down on the docks. Hundreds of emigrant families were waiting in the bitter north wind, dressed in rags, shivering with the cold, and surrounded by their pitiful belongings. Unfortunately, the heartless absentee landlords in England are still doing nothing to alleviate their condition! But I rant – you know all this, Harriet.

However, because everyone now wants C de V's, I have had very few children's painted portrait commissions, which earned me good money for the last few years. In fact, I have been so busy with the photographic studio that I have not done much painting at all, apart from a portrait and two other paintings that I submitted to the Royal Hibernian Academy summer exhibition.

As you know, Edward insisted I let Pierre go and,

with a heavy heart, reluctantly I did. His drinking meant that he was very unreliable, and Edward advised that we could no longer afford to keep him. I am sure you heard I had a row with your intractable husband about his short-sightedness in this matter. Sadly, I could not make him see sense. Fortunately, Padraic, although he is a bit slow, can help with setting up the camera which is a beast of a thing, and far too heavy for me to manage on my own. He also does all the mixing of chemicals and helps me with the development process. Because of this he has earned new respect from Molly and she now calls him "my Padraic" instead of "yer man". For me, this is long and backbreaking work. Fortunately, my health is good.

My heart on the other hand is heavy. I have had no word from D. He has been gone for over a year and a half at this stage. His uncle's estate took longer to sort out than he initially thought. But then he seemed to have got increasingly involved with C na G. Although he initially wrote to me every week, his letters stopped suddenly last June, and I have not heard from him since. I am worried sick about him. I have asked everyone I know for news of his whereabouts. I even wrote a letter to his friend Finbarr who works in Healy's brassworks to see had he heard anything – but it seems he is also in America. Donal is not the most organised, but surely he must know how worried we are about him? I even questioned Lydia during her painting lesson. The little madam looked at me slyly and commented that she was gratified that Miss Benson had such an interest in her family. The urge to strangle her was overwhelming. Every morning I buy The Nation newspaper at the station to see if there

*is any news coming from America – but nothing. He
seems to have vanished into thin air.*

Your loving sister,

Julia

* * *

*6 Shakespeare Street,
Ardwick Green,
Chorlton-on-Medlock,
Manchester*

15th February 1875

Dear Julia,

*I have not heard from you since New Year, although
Edward keeps in touch with Stephen. But as you know
men fail to capture the important details of life. Any
word from D yet? It has been such a long time. I scour
the papers daily to see if his name is mentioned.*

*Things are hard here too, Julia. The weather, a
constant source of conversation for the English,
continues to be depressing. It has been sunless and
raining most of the time, and there are fears here too of
another poor harvest. Because of all the imported grain
from America, prices are low, and many farmers here
have been unable to pay their rent. (Although, unlike
Ireland, rents are controlled by the government and have
not been raised to supplement landlord's losses.) There*

have also been lay-offs in some of the factories with rising competition from Europe for finished goods. Because of the shorter hours and reduced pay, worker's unions are becoming increasingly agitated. There seems to be groups of disgruntled and semi-starved men at every street corner. This has been hard – the city, already full of Irish immigrants, is now full of country people also looking for work.

Food and basic commodities have become awfully expensive. No one has any spare money. Unless people are in terrible pain, they do not go to the dentist and if they cannot pay they might go to a barber instead, or attend the public hospital.

Unfortunately, we are not living in the right neighbourhood to attract better-off customers, and we cannot afford to move. Hopefully, things will be better next year.

Julia, I am telling you this not to worry you, or put on the poor mouth, but to explain to you why Edward might seem so harsh and constantly demanding money. It is because he needs to, and he is too proud to say why. Forgive us, sister. I know you are working as hard as you can.

That is all for now, except to say I miss you so much, and often think of Westland Row and all of our neighbours and friends. Give my regards to Uncle Charles, the Misses Allen, our neighbours the Gunns and Molly and Padraic of course.

Your loving sister,

Harriet

* * *

14 Westland Row

8th May 1875

Dear Harriet,

I hope you are keeping well. Apologies for my tardy response to your last letter but I have been so annoyed with your dear husband that it has taken me some time to calm down. Edward's constant demands for money are totally unreasonable. To meet the rent and his expectations in profit has meant that I have had to let Mrs Cunningham go, and Molly and I are now cooking as well as trying to run the business. It will be the death of us all! Snivelling Stephen checks every single penny I spend. I feel I cannot even buy garters without his approval! I am so permanently exhausted that I have not even lifted a paintbrush for months. To make matters worse, still no word from D. It is hard to believe that he has been gone for so long. Uncle Charles and I bumped into his niece, the lovely Lydia, last Sunday in the Botanical Gardens in Glasnevin. She said that D was still in America trying to sort out his uncle's estate, and that there were rumours that he was seeing a wealthy young woman there, a Miss Amelia Berkeley whose father is a successful newspaper magnate from Pittsburgh. She prattled on – I cannot even recall any other detail of the conversation.

I feel such a fool, Harriet. What do they say? "There is no fool like an old fool?" I have tried to come to terms with this news. But, as you can imagine, I am devastated. If you have any feeling left for me, dear sister, please burn this letter as the last thing I want is a lecture on morals from Edward.

Love

Julia

***

6 Shakespeare Street,
Ardwick Green,
Chorlton-on-Medlock,
Manchester

12th September 1875

Dear Julia,

I am sorry to hear your news about D. And don't worry – I tell Edward that your letters are full of gossip about the family, the latest fashion, and the art world. Apart from asking about the business, he has absolutely no interest in them.

That is sad news altogether, but it is also a bit odd. Although I do not agree with his politics, I always thought that Donal was a gentleman, a man of his word. Maybe he has formed an attachment and is simply too ashamed to confess this fact to you. Whatever the reason,

Julia, marriage between Donal and you was never going to happen. Although you might have entertained hopes after Father's death, unfortunately now you also must reckon with Edward – and, in many ways, Edward is even more conservative than Papa ever was. But you are not old, Julia, and with your beauty, a respectable match is still not out of the question. Maybe someone of independent means would overlook the absence of a dowry. But, you know, dearest sister, the art and political circles that you move in are unlikely to yield suitable partners!

Why not get more involved with the ladies in St Mark's? Some charity work might be the thing.

I have been unwell for a few weeks with a bilious attack but thank God I am much better now.

Love

Harriet

***

14 Westland Row.

16th February 1876

Dear Harriet,

Sorry it has taken me so long to write. As ever things are busy here. Although the business is ticking over, competition is tough. There are so many photographers between Sackville Street and College Green that they are

calling it the Golden Mile. But being on the ground floor
does have its advantages. Equestrian photographs are
always popular. Also, those going off to join the British
army want to send photos home to their mammies.
Unfortunately, last week we were double-booked: a
British Officer stationed at Dublin Castle and his horse,
and old Mrs Kilbane from Pleasant Street, who wanted
a photograph of her cat. The horse scared the cat who ran
out into Westland Row. It took Padraic an hour to catch
him. Meanwhile the gentleman with the horse rode off
in a huff after the horse left a deposit on the studio floor.
Screaming babies are easier! I have also started painting
again, and I was fortunate to receive a few commissions
for children's portraits through the Royal Hibernian
Academy.

My big news is that I bumped into a friend of Donal
and Finbarr's in Grafton Street. He said that, although
he had not heard from either of them directly, as far as he
knew they were both still in America and heavily
involved with Clan na Gael. There is also a question of
it still not being safe for him to return to Ireland, because
of some incident in Wexford that it is alleged he was
involved in. However, he was surprised that Donal had
not been in contact with me. He also thought Edward
would have heard news of him through his business
dealings with Eoin. Although I am relieved that D is
alive and well, I am still at a loss as to know why he has
not contacted me for all this time.

Really his absence is too long a time to be sustained
by unrequited love and I have finally decided that I am
going to devote my life to my art. Dowry or not,
marriage is not for me. My experience with Edward has

highlighted that I neither want, nor need, any male interference in my life. I find the fact that the Irish Sea is between your husband and me a great comfort. But, despite our disagreements, dear sister, I sincerely hope that you and he are still getting on well together.

Love, always,

Your sister

Julia

***

6 Shakespeare Street,
Ardwick Green,
Chorlton-on-Medlock,
Manchester

5th August 1876

Dear Julia,

How are you? I am so sorry to hear about Donal, but maybe it is for the best, my dear. Now you can get on with your life. He has wasted enough of your time. I hope that my wonderful news will cheer you up. Julia, I am with child. I have managed to hold on to this pregnancy for three months. Although I did not tell you at the time, as I did not want to worry you, I had a failed attempt earlier in the year. Needless to say, Edward is over the moon, and is so solicitous about my welfare, making sure that I eat properly. However, I have suffered from morning sickness and I am exhausted all the time. This also means that Edward feels that he must work harder to provide for our new family. At least business is improving.

Edward still works at the hospital seeing his public patients in the morning. He now has his name over the door in Shakespeare Street and, in the afternoon, he has a few private patients who call to the house.

Regarding Donal, I asked Edward had he heard any news about him. But he claimed to have heard nothing about him for some time. Although he met Eoin with Stephen recently to go over some legal papers.

Irish affairs always seem to be in the news here. Charles Stewart Parnell, the handsome young Home Rule supporter, is causing quite a stir in Westminster and is gaining popular support amongst the Irish with his fighting talk. Most people are fed up with Mr Butt's failure to sway British MP's opinion regarding Irish independence. Parnell's tactics of obstructing parliamentary business has certainly proved to be an effective way of highlighting Ireland's plight.

Julia, you will be surprised to hear that the further I am from home, the more I am inclined to be sympathetic to the Irish cause. Particularly when you see how the English treat us here, and the terrible poverty and hopeless conditions of our country folk. Although, it must be said that many of them are their own worst enemies when it comes to the drink.

Edward is still staunchly Unionist in his outlook and continues to believe that the British will look after their loyal Irish subjects. These days I am not so sure.

Please write with news of Westland Row, of Molly and Padraic. I think of you often and miss you all. Love to Uncle Charles. He wrote asking to visit, but I put him off until after the birth. I am so tired these days and Edward works such long hours. Maybe you and he could come over next year for the baptism.

Your loving sister,

Harriet

Chapter 9

Westland Row

August 1876

The horse portraits were not worth all the trouble. On this occasion, by the time the animal was manoeuvred into the studio and calmed by Julia and its owner – sugar cubes as usual did the trick – they had about ten minutes maximum to arrange the pose and set up the camera. The horse was inevitably nervous with all of the oil lamps and left a mess that had to be cleaned up afterwards. Consequently, Julia was late for the weekly Friday five o'clock meeting with Stephen Spendlove to go through the books.

He was already sitting in her father's chair when she entered the office, a presumption that annoyed her intensely.

Mole-like, with black hair thinly covering his ivory pate and a pallid pockmarked complexion, Stephen was probably the same age as Julia, she reckoned, although he looked ten years older.

He was already inspecting the ledgers with squinty, red-rimmed eyes through roundy glasses. It was quite amazing, thought Julia, how quickly his initial nervousness towards her over the last year had been replaced with a condescending superiority that she found infuriating.

"Ah, Miss Benson, take a seat."

She glared at him and sat down.

"A disappointing week, Miss Benson, if I may say so. Only twenty-six *cartes de visite* were sold – two of which were hand-tinted, and two were equestrian portraits. Lithographic print sales were also poor, three pounds and two shillings in all. It was slightly better with the artists' materials."

"Yes," said Julia, unsmiling. "I spoke to the masters in the RDS Drawing school and offered their students a deal in sketchbooks and pencils. A number of students took up the offer."

"*Mm*, good, good. The cost of the *Irish Times* advertisement for the photographic studios must be deducted from this week's profits, of course, as does the claim for a new oilcloth for the floor. Could that not have been repaired, Miss Benson? Could you not have patched the damaged piece?" He looked over his glasses directly at her. "I am sure with all your other accomplishments that you are an expert needlewoman."

She breathed in deeply. "No, it could not, unfortunately. Between tears from the horses' hooves and chemical spillages it was beyond repair."

"Pity, Miss Benson, pity. As you know we need to reach a certain level of profit in order to meet our outgoings. Although we have managed to do so thus far, the profits over the last three months have been gradually diminishing, and we might have to make some hard decisions in the future. But Mr Williams has agreed – for your sake, Miss Benson – that we can have six months to try to turn this situation around before doing so." He took off his glasses and squinted at her. "There are some ways, if I might respectfully suggest, that we might earn some extra income. How about letting Tilly go, and letting Molly do the cleaning?"

"Absolutely not," retorted Julia. "Molly's back is not able for carrying water or coal up and down the stairs, nor for the heavy laundry work. Besides, the maid costs so little – barely two shillings a week."

"My wife, Miss Benson, despite her frail health –"

"With all due respects, Stephen, I am not interested in your wife's situation. This is not a one-up and one-down tenement. This is a large townhouse and a business premises – there is no comparison. This house simply cannot be run without adequate staff. Now if you have no more questions, I have some negatives that I need to develop."

"I am sorry if I have caused you any offence, Miss Benson. I am merely trying to do my job. Did I mention the idea of making photographer's cheesecakes?"

"No, I don't believe you did."

"Well, if you take all of the yolks left over, after you have removed the albumen you use to coat the photographic paper – and use them to make cheesecakes, it could be quite a lucrative side-line."

"As I said, Stephen," she said contemptuously, ignoring his suggestion completely, "I must go and attend to my work. Goodbye. I shall see you next week."

Julia, without looking back, did not bother to close the door as she left the room.

Julia straightened her hair in the looking-glass over the fireplace, pinched her lips, and then sat down, only to get

106

up again abruptly to stand in front of the window overlooking Fitzwilliam Square. Her back would be to him as he entered the room. A marquee had been set up, and ladies in their colourful summer dresses, bonneted and bustling, were queueing up at the main tent carrying all manner of cakes. Small children were playing tag on the grass, while lines of men and women were testing their prowess at archery. From inside the room, the sounds of a piped band could be heard in the distance. She had always loved the panoramic view of the square from the drawing room of Donal's family home, she thought sadly. She tried to put thoughts of him out of her head, as she had unsuccessfully been trying to do lately. A situation that was not helped by this summons from his brother. She hoped he was not the bearer of bad news. She breathed in deeply to calm herself.

"Good afternoon, Miss Benson. What a pleasure to meet you again," Eoin said cheerfully as he entered the room. "As you can see it is that time of year again, the summer fair. It is always a big event in this house. Mrs Clarke, our cook, is famous for her meringues, she has won the prize for the last three years. We have been eating cold cuts all week while she perfects her techniques."

She remembered that Donal had told her how Eoin's young wife had died tragically giving birth to Lydia and he had never remarried. It seemed to be a family tradition, thought Julia sadly.

Although he spoke with the same easy wit as his brother, there was a coldness about Eoin. She took some satisfaction in the knowledge that her initial unfavourable impression of him was not mistaken. Abruptly, she noticed with amusement, the social niceties were over as

Eoin pulled over a spoon-back chair to sit opposite her.

"Miss Benson, I know my letter to you said I wanted to discuss further drawing lessons for Lydia. You must have wondered why. Particularly after you tactfully advised my sister Bea that painting and drawing, for my daughter, were unlikely to be accomplishments. A pity really – her Uncle Donal is such a talented artist."

Julia squirmed in her chair, but smiled woodenly, waiting to hear what he would say next.

"In fact, it is about my brother that I wish to talk to you today and, after I tell you why, hopefully you will forgive my subterfuge. Firstly, I have recently learnt the nature of your association with my brother. I must be honest and tell you that I cannot approve of his intention to marry you, Julia … if I may call you Julia – I feel have known you since you were a small girl in your grandfather's print shop."

Julia nodded, his reference to her family's involvement in the world of commerce noted.

Their eyes locked.

"Unfortunately, Donal's prospects as you may or may not be aware, are limited. As a second son he was encouraged by my late father to study law, but he was never a good student and failed his matriculation to Trinity, and now he is only a law clerk. And, although he works in the family business, he will never run it. I had hoped that he would marry into money. I admit that I agreed to his request to go to Chicago to sort out our uncle's estate with this intention in mind. Our uncle, Jeremiah O'Keefe, has left Donal a modest sum – not much, but enough if well invested to buy a house in Dublin. I had also made certain social introductions for him in Pittsburgh, in the hope that he might form an alliance with a suitable lady, a Miss Amelia Berkeley with whose family I have associations." Elbows resting on the desk, his long fingers touching at their tips, he looked under lidded eyes at Julia. "They are extremely wealthy – in the newspaper business. Fostering these connections in America also served the purpose of distancing him from his unfortunate political activities here in Dublin." He paused as if to gather his thoughts.

Julia's rage at his impertinence had been building during his speech. At this stage she was furious. How dare he talk to her like this, as if she were of absolutely no consequence? This would not be happening if her father were still alive.

"Mr O'Keefe, enough!" Julia got up and, drawing herself to her full height, she looked down on him scathingly. "Mr O'Keefe, you insult me – I cannot listen to your self-righteous ramblings any longer. I may not be considered a worthy partner for your brother, but you need have no fear. I have not heard from him for over a year. He has clearly got over whatever misguided attraction he had for me. But you – you are possibly one of the most pompous men I have ever met. If you hope to succeed as a solicitor may I suggest that you ask your daughter's governess to help you brush up your manners and social skills."

She turned to leave the room.

Quick as lightning he was at the door, barring her exit. His face was so close to hers that she could almost feel his breath.

"I can see why my brother finds you so attractive, Julia. Such spirit, and such a beauty if I may be so bold to say."

"How dare you, Mr O'Keefe!"

"Julia, I am sorry," he said, instantly contrite, his eyes lidded, his expression controlled once more. "Please forgive me. Sit down. Please, Julia, I have something to tell you."

Reluctantly she returned to her seat.

Eoin paced around the room, his hands behind his back. The brass band outside was playing a military tune and it seemed to accentuate the tension in the room. He did not look at her.

"In August of last year, I was becoming increasingly concerned about my brother. I had been in regular contact with him up until then, mainly about the estate and how the work was progressing. It was a complicated business and involved selling some properties and leasing others. There were also several minor beneficiaries to be dealt with. A slow and tiresome exercise in a different legal jurisdiction. Donal was working with a firm of lawyers based in Chicago. One of the partners, Robert Armstrong – a fellow graduate of mine from Trinity, informed me that Donal had become involved with the American organisation, Clan na Gael, and its leader John Devoy. The damn fool got caught up in a brawl in Chicago following a fund-raising meeting in support of freeing Fenian prisoners from English jails – he ended up himself being thrown in jail. Robert secured his release after paying a hefty fine, and he persuaded him to move to Pittsburgh. I decided that I needed to go there and talk some sense to my errant brother, to try and show him the foolishness of his ways. When I arrived there in October, I found Donal in a sorry state. He had caught an infection in gaol from which he was recovering slowly. Then he told me of his romantic attachment to you. I must admit, I tried to talk him out of it, to make him see sense." He stopped and looked at her directly. "To speak plainly, your attachment is foolish, Julia. It will not do for either of you. You have no fortune, and frankly you are not a young woman."

Julia started to get up again. He put his hand out to stop her.

"Sorry … Anyway, he told me of his plan: to move to the south of England, to become an indentured apprentice to a solicitor, to work his way up through the ranks, and to buy a small house where the two of you could live – on love and fresh air presumably. And then, Julia, he broke down. He was quite inconsolable. He told me that he was concerned about your safety, that he had posted many letters to you since leaving Dublin, but that since June his letters had been unanswered."

Julia stared at him, dumbfounded.

"He asked was there a reason why? Had you formed an attachment with another? Had you emigrated? Were you unwell? He was completely beside himself." He paused, waiting for her to respond.

"But that cannot be true! I have not received any letters from Donal! I have been worried sick about him. I didn't contact you because I didn't think that you knew about us. Donal warned me that you would not approve of our friendship. I have asked just about everyone else who knew him for news of his whereabouts. But the only feedback I received was from Lydia who told me he was just about to be betrothed to Miss Berkeley!"

"No, unfortunately that is not the case," he said with a sigh. "Donal wasn't interested in that particular lady, at least not in that way. He was only interested in writing pro-Fenian articles for her family's newspaper. But her father got wind of his political leanings and put a stop to all of that, and with it any possibility of furthering their acquaintance."

"But why haven't I received his letters if they were sent by post?" she asked in bewilderment.

"Why indeed? It sounds like someone is interfering with your letters. It could be the post boy, but that is unlikely – interfering with Her Majesty's mail is a criminal offence which would result in a hefty prison sentence. It is more likely to be someone in your household."

"I can think of no one in my house who would sink so low."

"Maybe for money, Julia? We all have our price. But that is not the only problem. I returned to Dublin in November of last year and, apart from a card at Christmas I have not heard from my brother since. Robert Armstrong told me that Donal left for Dublin just before Easter, but I am afraid that he never arrived here. In fact, I contacted his friend Finbarr Duffy who returned home last week, but he hasn't heard from him either." He looked at his pocket watch. "Julia, I am afraid that I must leave you. I have a client below in my study and I have already kept him waiting. If you hear any news, anything at all, you must let me know. In the meantime, I wish you well. My footman will show you out."

She stood, and with unnecessary familiarity he took her hand, kissed it, and bowed slightly.

"Goodbye, Mr O'Keefe, and thank you for letting me know."

A loud wail like a banshee was heard from the kitchen two floors below.

Eoin looked with some amusement at Julia.

"I fear Mrs Clarke's meringues have not performed the way she intended. Cold corned beef again for supper, I fear." And with a languid smile he left the room.

Julia rose early the next day, before Tilly had even brought up water for her to wash. She dressed quickly, putting on the same costume she had worn the day before, and quietly crept down the stairs. From the kitchen she could hear Molly making the breakfast. Padraic was in the print room at the back of the house sorting out the glass plates for the day, and Tilly was upstairs clearing out the embers in the sitting-room hearth.

Julia opened the door quietly and entered the photographic studio. She pulled over a chair and sat down beside the door which she opened slightly, giving her a clear view of the entrance hall and the four brocade-covered chairs lined up against the wall, where visitors waited to be called for appointments. In the middle of these was a small table with a brass jug and matching brass plate where the letters were usually left for Julia to collect after breakfast. The post was usually delivered at half past eight.

Julia did not have to wait long. At about eight fifteen, a key turned in the lock of the front door, Stephen appeared in the hall and sat down on one of the chairs, pulling a watch from his pocket to check the time. How did he have a key, Julia thought furiously – he had no right to have a key. Just then she heard the click of the letterbox and the thud of letters falling to the floor. He sprang from the chair and crouched down to pick up the letters.

"*What exactly are you doing?*" said Julia, flinging the studio door open.

113

Startled, Stephen jumped up and back like an alley cat, his pupils dilated, his pockmarked face white with fright.

"Miss Benson. I can explain."

"Yes, that is exactly what you are going to do." She held out her hand. "Give me those letters."

Trembling, he handed them over.

She glanced at them. Nothing from Donal.

"Now come with me," she commanded.

She marched down the hall to the shop and sat down at her grandfather's desk, but this time she sat in his chair and indicated to Stephen that he should sit opposite her.

"Now, would you mind telling me exactly what you think you are doing intercepting my letters? This is a criminal offence, Stephen. What is going on?"

Stephen sat hunched in the chair, wringing his hands, with sweat glistening on his forehead. He was a miserable specimen, thought Julia, his thin black hair greasy and unkempt, and his clerk's jacket worn and dusty.

"Miss Benson, Mr Williams asked me to send on any letters to you from America. He explained to me that they were from someone unsuitable, and that he wanted to protect you and the family from an unfortunate association with this gentleman who he claimed was a criminal. I am so sorry, Miss Benson. I was only doing what the master told me to do. I didn't mean any harm."

Trying to control her temper, Julia said, "Firstly, he is not 'the master' as you call him – at least he is not *my* master. Stephen, you are a pathetic, spineless excuse for a man. There is no reason on God's earth to sink so low as to steal someone's letters. I am not a fool. It is unlikely that my head would be turned, or that I would be bamboozled by anyone. I have a good mind to call the police."

"No, Miss Benson, I am so sorry! Please don't do that – my job in Trinity – I have three small children, and my wife is sick." Tears started to fall down his cheeks.

"Enough, Stephen, you are pathetic. There is no need to use your unfortunate wife as an excuse for your despicable actions. I have had enough of your constant spying on me for Edward. But this has gone too far. Have there been many letters, Stephen?"

"About twelve, Miss Benson, but there have not been any for quite a while."

"And where are they?"

"Mr Williams has them – I posted them on to him. Except for this last one which I seem to have overlooked." Guiltily, he took a letter from his pocket.

Julia, fuming, got up and grabbed the letter from his hand. Stephen sat, head bowed and hands clenched.

"Firstly, hand over the key." She put her hand out.

He withdrew the large brass key from his inner breast pocket and placed it in her hand.

"From now on you have no right to enter this property without an appointment. Secondly, I do not want you to tell Edward that I have discovered your seedy little arrangement. I will deal with him myself. And thirdly, you are never, *ever*, to interfere with my post again, or I will go directly to the police. Now go, Stephen, and I will consider what further action I will take."

As soon as he left, she opened the letter which she noticed with dismay was well-thumbed and greasy.

***

115

Pittsburgh

22nd September 1875

My darling girl,

It has been so long since I have heard from you, I cannot sleep with anxiety. You are constantly on my mind. I keep telling myself that there must be some reasonable explanation why I have not heard from you these past two months. Could it be that the post is being intercepted at the port by the American authorities? Although Fenian activity is tolerated here, amongst the various republican brotherhoods there is fierce in-fighting. This is the only explanation I can think of for your silence. I am so concerned that I have told Eoin about us and asked him to ascertain your wellbeing.

As you can see, I am now staying in Pittsburgh. I caught a chill in Chicago that I am trying to shake off and I long to go home. But it is still not considered safe for me to return. So, despite my frustration, I am trying to put my time to good use. An old college friend of my brother whom he met in Trinity owns the Pittsburgh Times, and Devoy has asked me to use this advantage, and to persuade them to allow me to publish a few articles in support of the cause. They have resisted these requests so far. But, because of my persistence, I have become friendly with the family who have taken it upon themselves to feed me. They fear I have become emaciated after all my travels. I get on quite well with the son, a decent man and well read. We go shooting together on their estate near the lakes. They also have a daughter,

116

Amelia, who is sweet girl, but quite tedious. Fortunately, she is besotted with a dashing young cavalry officer who is stationed nearby.

A day does not go by without my thinking of you, my love. Your smile, your gentle touch. I am lost without your laughter, and physically wilting with the want of you. Only you understand me, sustain me, know what I feel. My heart is yours. If I could rip it from my body, I would give it to you, my love.

Wait for me, Julia. I beg you, do not leave me for another. No one can love you as I do – my love, my lover. Please write to me soon and put me out of my misery.

Your Donal

When she finished reading the letter Julia put her hands over her face as tears ran down her cheeks. She was distraught at the thought of his anguish. She remained sitting at the desk for ten minutes, thinking about what she should do, until eventually she heard the bell. Her grief turning to annoyance, she remembered there would only be tea and toast for breakfast – it was Cheesecake Day. Today Molly would use all of the leftover egg yolks to make cheesecakes to sell to the hotel and the teashop on Westland Row. Another of Stephen's ridiculous economies she had given in to.

Her first appointment that day was not until ten o'clock, so she busied herself sorting out the photographic studio. She tidied up the rolled canvas backdrops and filed the appointment cards with the customers' details. Her next client, a Mr Colm Drennan was looking for twenty-four *cartes de visite*. Thank God it is a man, thought Julia. She was not in the mood to contend with a preening female. Some ladies took so long to fix their hair and powder their faces that an appointment could take up to an hour. Particularly if they wanted to try on period costumes which were currently all the rage. She had learnt to her cost, from painting portraits, that female vanity knew no bounds – women were rarely satisfied with their painted portraits. Initially, several ladies – in their failure to comprehend the photographic process – had argued with her that she had not taken a good likeness. They had even gone so far as to claim that it was not them and had threatened not to pay. At least the men were more straightforward. Their most common conceit was a desire to look taller. So, she had bought a small-scale chair for them to lean against to serve this purpose. And although she did not allude to this fact, the gentlemen were invariably grateful. However, the special chair was not necessary for her next customer who arrived promptly as the clock struck ten o'clock.

"Miss Benson, I presume. How do you do?"

"Good morning, sir – you must be Mr Drennan."

"Yes, nice to meet you." He stretched out his hand to shake hers.

Julia noted the firm handshake. He had pleasant features, neatly cut brown hair and was cleanshaven. He was also lightly tanned and looked like he had recently spent time in foreign parts. But, although he was smiling, the smile did not animate his grey eyes.

"I understand that you are looking for *cartes de visite*."

"Yes, I need to send them to my family in Manchester to assure them that I am taking care of myself – eating properly and such like. Mothers, you know."

"Indeed and I do, Mr Drennan. How would you like the pose – seated or standing?"

"Standing, I think."

"And the background?"

"Something plain, maybe beside a curtain and a desk, something simple."

"Fine. I shall ask Padraic to set that up."

Julia rang a bell and Padraic, who was next door in the shop, came in and started arranging the scene according to Julia's instructions. He then proceeded to load the glass plates into the camera and set up the oil-lights.

Meanwhile Julia invited Mr Drennan to sit down at the desk and proceeded to write his details on the appointment card.

"I have relatives myself in Manchester, in Chorlton-on-Medlock. My sister and brother-in-law moved there last year."

"Yes, Miss Benson, so I believe." Drennan lowered his voice, so that Padraic could not hear. "In fact, Miss Benson I have a confession to make – I have actually met you before."

Julia looked up, surprised. She had an excellent memory for faces, particularly in her line of business, and had not recognised his.

"Really?" she said cautiously.

"Yes, I met you in another studio in this house – at the back of the house, if I remember rightly."

"My painting studio?"

"Yes, so I believe. But I was not there to engage in artistic pursuits if you understand my drift."

"Really, Mr Drennan, I am not sure that I do." She could feel her pulse racing as she listened carefully to what he was saying.

"Oh, I think you do, Miss Benson. I am a friend of a friend of yours, a Mr O'Keefe."

Her heart leapt. "Yes, I know Mr O'Keefe."

"And am I right in saying that you have not seen our mutual friend for some time?"

"No, Mr Drennan, I have not seen him for quite a while."

There was something about him that Julia did not entirely trust. She looked into his eyes and did not sense the sincerity she would have expected, if this was indeed a true friend of Donal's.

"The Brothers, Miss Benson, are trying to help Mr O'Keefe who is in hiding following certain treasonous activities which the authorities discovered he was involved in – in Manchester."

Julia tried to conceal her alarm at this news. "What has this to do with me, Mr Drennan?"

"Well, Miss Benson, the Brothers thought that as you have been such a loyal supporter to the cause that you might be willing to help us to contact Mr O'Keefe. We wish to bring him some relief in his current hazardous situation."

"You are mistaken, Mr Drennan, if you think that I would become engaged in an act of subterfuge, or indeed anything illegal for that matter."

"But have you not already, Miss Benson? Anyway," he continued, not giving her a chance to reply, "think on it. If you ever want to see Donal again you will need to help us. Here is my card." He handed her a card and got up to go.

"What about the *cartes de visite*?"

"Maybe they were not such a good idea after all. There are certain advantages to remaining anonymous, Miss Benson, don't you agree?" With that, smiling, he put on his hat, retrieved his silver-topped walking cane, and left the studio.

At his abrupt departure, Padraic came over to Julia. Although he had not heard their conversation, he saw that Julia looked shaken.

"That's a quare bird, Miss Benson, if ever I saw one, a quare bird indeed."

"I must admit that I thought so too, Padraic," said Julia, trying to regain her composure.

Later that evening Julia lay in the bed that she used to share with Harriet. It had been an unsettling day, and she was having difficulty getting to sleep. The candle spluttered, creating ominous shapes on the ceiling. Outside on Westland Row, horses' hooves and the steel-rimmed wheels of carriages clattered on the cobbled street. It was one of the disadvantages of living on a busy thoroughfare. She could hear late-night revellers leaving the Royal Hotel. For many of them, she thought, the night was still young, full of promise, promiscuity, and more porter in the city's labyrinth of brothels and shebeens. While others, numb to life's daily tragedies, were probably already lying comatose in the gutters, swollen and senseless with drink. She remembered the poor creature from New Year's Eve, who had fallen on their steps, and wondered what had become of her. Here in her virginal bed, she was sheltered from this harsh reality, but only a length of brocade and a sheet of glass separated her world from theirs. She had been reading *Jane Eyre* by Charlotte Bronte, but the bleak images it conjured up of a governess's life had not served to calm her nerves. The stress of constantly trying to save money and drum up more business was relentless. Her mind wandered fretfully – she was worried about Harriet. Although she was delighted that her little sister was pregnant, she was terrified at the same time. Julia was only too aware of the physical hardships and risks to health that pregnancy involved. The physical and emotional toll of her mother's frequent miscarriages had ground her down over the years.

Julia had also noticed a change in the tone of Harriet's letters – recently there had been less self-righteous advice. She sounded humbled if that was possible. At least they were becoming close again. Still, Julia thought, no matter how much it upset Harriet and damaged their new-found peace, she would have to confront Edward about Stephen. He would have to account for his actions. No, she could not live like this anymore. And to deal with the situation by letter would not deliver the full force of impact that she intended, one that would leave him with a clear understanding that she would no longer allow him to control her life.

But, more importantly now, the meeting with Mr Colm Drennan had also shaken her. She was shocked to hear Donal was in Manchester. What if he really was in danger? It would surely explain his lack of communication with Eoin. Maybe she could kill several birds with one stone. See Harriet, deal with Edward, and see if she could find Donal. Also, now she knew he had been trying to contact her, she could no longer do nothing.

There was a light knock and Molly put her head around the door.

"Miss Julia, I could see the light under your door. I was just checkin' that you hadn't fallen asleep and not blowed out yer candle."

122

"No, Molly, I could not sleep – but now that you are here, could you come in for a minute?" Molly, with her own candle, wearing a nightcap with a shawl over her shapeless sleeping robe, shuffled through the door in her brown leather boots and sat down on the edge of the bed.

"Molly, could you and Padraic manage if I went over to visit Harriet in Manchester for a week or two? Just so that I can set my mind at ease that she is alright?"

"Of course, my dear. I worry about her meself now that she is with child. Imagine our little Harriet being a mother! If only your own dear mother were alive." Big, soft Molly wiped a tear from her cheek with the edge of her shawl. "Sure, what else would we be doing, Miss Julia, only lookin' after things here for yeh. And isn't himself an expert now – he's like that Professor Gluckman who used to be in Sackville Street with his fancy studio. I'll have to mind that he doesn't get notions though."

"Thank you, Molly," said Julia gratefully.

"Not at all, dear. Not at all, and now I am knackered, and ready for –"

"I know – ready for the clay."

Molly withdrew, and Julia blew out the candle, pulled the soft patchwork quilt around her and immediately fell asleep.

Chapter 10

2nd September 1876

It had been a stormy passage – autumn crossings were notoriously unreliable. As they reached mid-channel, the ship heaved and creaked in awesome sea-swells as ten-foot-high waves crashed against the bow of the ship.

At least Julia had travelled first class and was able to sit in the cabin for the five-hour journey. The passengers on deck, poor divils, were not so lucky – sea-sick and terrified, they clung on to each other, huddled around the steam-funnels for warmth like saturated sewer rats. They were a sorry sight. She had politely declined an offer from an elderly couple to play cards. Instead, she closed her eyes and, although sleep was not possible, she tried to focus on her destination and the days ahead. Despite her apprehension at the inevitable showdown with Edward, Julia was looking forward to her visit. Her sister's description of the industrial city across the water, where things seemed to be improving for the family, had lifted her spirits. In contrast, the dreariness of Dublin, and the relentless struggle to make ends meet, was wearing her down. It was now eighteen months since Harriet and Edward had left to set up home in England. Julia's arrival would be a great surprise for her sister.

Young Philip Grady, a son of a neighbour, had agreed to accompany Julia and carry her valise. He worked as a shipping clerk and often had to travel between the two countries. The plan was he would accompany her to Liverpool, and then onward by train to Victoria Station in Manchester. From there they would get a tram to Piccadilly and then a cab to Shakespeare Street, which was not far from Ardwick Green. Philip was staying with his sister in the city centre and would bring over her valise the next day.

But later that evening, when they got off the tram at Piccadilly Square, Philip met up with an old friend. On Julia's urging, taking her valise he left her to find a cab. However, once alone, her sense of anticipation quickly disappeared. She was stunned – winded even – by the cacophony of noises that assailed her from all directions: horses neighing, costermongers shouting, steel scraping and clanging, crankshafts ratcheting, and steam squealing from the nearby station. Overwhelmed by this onslaught, she cowered against a wall. It was like nothing she had experienced before. She had imagined it to be a bigger version of College Green in Dublin, but Piccadilly Square was vast in comparison. Larger than life monuments adorned the public space, which young Philip had told her were of Wellington and Peel, and dramatic fountains shot water twelve feet into the air. And in this frenzied milieu, horses, carts, cabs, and phaetons swarmed in all directions.

She pulled herself together and looked at the map that

Philip had drawn for her. Shakespeare Street did not look that far away, and there was at least another hour of daylight left – but the cabbies were leering and staring at her in such a queer way that she decided to walk. Grasping her carpetbag and her cloak close to her body, she determinedly sallied forward. As she left the main thoroughfares, the streets were less clean and not quite so ordered. Everywhere was a hubbub of commercial activity. Timber-framed and brick-built shops, hotels, bars – some three, four, and even five storeys high – surrounded her. She passed factories and mills, like prehistoric beasts with massive brick walls that seemed to throb while their windows vibrated, barely containing the grumbling and squealing pistons within. And everywhere were piles of cinders, like detritus, she thought, from giant imaginary termites that secretly inhabited the underworld of this extraordinary city.

Julia made slow progress as she shook off the beggars who pulled at her skirt, ravaged human beings, scantily clad and starving, many of them looking half-dead. What struck her to her very core was the Irish brogue of these poor creatures. As a way of distracting herself she noted their origins – Limerick, Cork, and Newry – whilst crying "Sorry, sorry, sorry!" repeatedly as she blindly pushed them out of her path.

Increasing her pace, she made her way southward, down London Road and over the River Medlock, where she stopped briefly, aghast, to inspect its extraordinary purple water, which she presumed was stained from local dyeworks. Shops on either side of the street provided every manner of service imaginable: umbrella re-coverer's, corn removers, and snuff-box makers. Street

126

hawkers were selling their wares, offering oranges, matches and beans, one was even selling baths. She was surprised and saddened to see notices on several boarding house doors saying, '**No Irish**,' or '**No Irish need apply**'.

The road narrowed into Downing Street until eventually she arrived at Ardwick Green. Surrounded by railings, it was not a large park – it was long and narrow with a few trees, planted beds, an ornamental pond and a bandstand. Around the park were fine houses, although a little shabby, a church and what looked like a municipal building. This was quite nice, she thought – some greenery, at last. She turned down Stockport Road and turned left into Shakespeare Street.

Once off the main street, the houses were much smaller, red-bricked and stained black as Harriet had described, and quite close together. The cobblestones gave way to compacted mud, with an open drain running down the centre of the street. She could see that the houses were built almost back-to-back with only a narrow lane between. Gaunt women, dressed in little more than shifts and shawls, with wooden clogs on their feet, hung around the doorways, watching, as raggle-taggle barefooted children chased a scrawny dog. Piles of smelly ash were heaped outside the doors and an old man filled a bucket of water at a standpipe. Nauseated and shaken with fear, Julia arrived at Number 7. Her sister had described a modest eight-roomed house. This was a two-up, two-down terrace. There was no name over the door – no sign saying *Edward Williams, Dentist*. The number must be wrong, thought Julia. She stopped a passing matron and asked after the couple.

"Yes, this is where the Williams live."

She pressed the doorbell. But getting no reply, after several minutes, she leaned against the wall of the house and waited. One hour later, thick black evening smog surrounded her that eventually turned into grim darkness. The lamplighter had long gone. Her tears had dried up, she was cold and tired and frightened – she had endured being heckled and jeered at by groups of men returning from work with dirty faces and hungry eyes. Mrs Jackson next door had eventually come out at the sound of the shouting. After hearing about the circumstances of her long journey, and the fact that she was waiting for her sister she had brought her out a cup of weak black tea.

"The' mean no 'arm, missus – it's just yeh look like a stray duchess with yer fancy costume – thems just acting the maggot."

She could not ask her in, she explained, as she was only a servant for the man of the house. "Mrs Hunt is usually here, but she's away at her sister's. Your sister will be home at half past seven from 'er shift at th' mill."

"The mill?"

"Th'mill, yes."

The woman directed her to stand under the single gas lamp a few doors up and promised that, if she did so, no harm would come to her as a policeman lived at the end of the terrace.

An hour or so later, she saw a figure trudging through the black smog. It was Harriet returning home. Harriet burst into tears at the sight of her sister, and the two women embraced joyfully despite the awkwardness of Harriet's swollen belly.

"Julia, I am so pleased to see you. *We* are so pleased to see you, I should say." She patted her bump. "But you shouldn't have come – it's awful here, more awful than your wildest dreams."

Still sobbing, Harriet opened the door, and they climbed the narrow rickety stairs to the two rooms on the first floor where the couple lived.

"The Hunts live downstairs," Julia explained. "Two sisters, Grace and Dora, and their widowed mother Ann – the girls work as mantle-makers. But the mother is quite deaf and even if she was there she would not have heard you knocking."

She opened the door into a small sparsely furnished room where one upholstered chair and two hardbacked chairs were arranged around a cast-iron stove. Julia recognised her mother's sewing table and a few other meagre items that they had brought from Dublin.

Harriet, who had calmed down at this stage, lit a fire with kindling, and once the stove got going, put on the kettle. She took out a japanned tray and placed it on the sewing table, taking two mismatched china cups and saucers from a shelf over a cupboard unit that served as a pantry. Pulling over the two chairs, she indicated to her sister to sit down.

"The servant and the dental surgery were made up so as not to worry you – and you all alone in Dublin. Whatever money you send, we use to pay for rent, food and saving towards next year's fee for the Royal College of Surgeons in Dublin. Without this qualification, it is difficult for Edward to get any work privately. Presently he works for a local dentist for a pittance and puts in a few hours every evening at the Salutations public house

– it's near Owens College on the Oxford Road. He gets home at about eleven o'clock, studies for two hours and then falls into bed exhausted. Times are hard, Julia – Dublin seems like a lifetime away – another world, a dream that I think about – often. And now …" she smiled sadly at her sister, "soon we will have another mouth to feed."

Several hours later Edward returned home. As he opened the door and saw his wife's visitor a mixture of shock and disbelief spread over his grey and careworn face. Julia was struck by how much he appeared to have aged since she had seen him last.

"Julia, this is a surprise! I hope that nothing is wrong?"

Julia got up to shake her brother-in-law's hand. Ignoring her formality but without any great warmth, he took her hands and kissed her fleetingly on the cheek.

"This must seem … Our circumstances are not as we have led you to believe. But rest assured it was with your interests at heart that we were not entirely truthful."

"Really, Edward, really!" Julia tried to control her temper which she felt rising rapidly. "The dental practice, the servant? My sister is living in a hovel, Edward – a hovel! How could you do this! If my poor father could see her now. Look at her. Look at her, Edward – she is skin and bone, exhausted – working in a mill! My sister, a gifted musician, has become a mill girl!" She was now shaking with anger.

"There is no need to be so dramatic, Julia – it is not as bad as it seems." He rubbed a large hand over his thick black hair nervously. "This is only a temporary situation, until I get my licence – then we can afford to move to a more salubrious location."

"Yes, Julia, don't be so hard on Edward – he works morning noon and night – this is only until we get sorted out. Please, Julia, calm down, your concern for me is admirable, but I am fine. And I am so pleased to see you – don't spoil it all – we can explain everything. And, Julia, poor Edward is exhausted – 'ready for the clay'." She said this with a sad smile, "I really must be a good wife and make him some supper."

Although she did not return her sister's smile, Julia relaxed somewhat and sat down, while Edward sat in the one armchair and glared at the two women.

Harriet busied herself heating up vegetable broth, to which she added some cold mutton from a small meat safe that was hung on the wall. After they had finished the modest meal, Julia was still hungry but said nothing. Instead, she opened her carpetbag and pulled out a half bottle of sherry.

"I suppose a small drink wouldn't go astray," she said in an attempt at reconciliation.

As they sipped, Julia told them all the news of Westland Row, of their neighbours the Gunns and of the goings-on of the notorious Wilde family, who used to live on the row but were now living in Merrion Square.

One hour or so later, Edward excused himself to sleep in the other room, and the two women talked on late into the night. Mellowed by the sherry, in a lowered voice Harriet described the true story of her arrival in Manchester and the difficulties they had initially encountered. She told Julia of the weeks she had spent looking for work, walking the streets of Manchester, to shops and mills. She explained that, although preferable, work in a shop was poorly paid and they needed the higher wages paid to millworkers to survive. It was only for a short period. She described how initially the masters were suspicious of her because she looked too well dressed – not sturdy enough – they thought she might be uppity. Until she was so worn down and hungry that she got to look like all the others, and they eventually gave her a job. She told Julia of the long hours in the mill, working on the spinning machines and how her back ached, and her fingers were worn to the bone – how it was hard with no help with cooking and laundry. Eventually, her hands cradling her growing belly, she told Julia with great sadness of her previous miscarriage, a baby that she had carried almost to full term, and the physical toll that this had exacted on her. She described the kindness of the Hunt family downstairs and how they had nursed her and minded her, like she was one of their own. She could never repay them, especially old Mrs Hunt.

At midnight, Harriet signalled her intention to head for her bed. But before doing so, she pulled out folded quilts for Julia to sleep on and laid them down by the fire. She warned her sister she would be up by five o'clock as her shift at the mill started at six.

Harriet need not have worried that she would wake her. The quilts could not ameliorate the hardness of the wooden floor, and after a sleepless night spent tossing and turning, the following morning the discordant clanging of mill and factory bells were a welcome distraction.

Edward fetched ice-cold water from the standpipe in the alley – one bucket of water for them to use to wash, the other for cooking for the day. Harriet cleaned out the stove, relit the fire, and prepared a meagre breakfast of hard bread, cold sausage meat and hot tea. She made a midday meal for the three of them: more cold mutton and oatcakes, a bottle of beer for Edward, and milk for herself and Julia. She left Julia's food on the sewing table.

The couple left with instructions to Julia to go for a walk around Victoria Park. But she was to be sure to return home before dusk and wait for their return. Harriet promised that the next day, Sunday, they would go on an outing to the infamous Belle Vue Botanical Gardens, with its man-made lake and island for firework displays. On the way out, Julia heard Harriet knock on the Hunts' door, telling them of her sister's arrival.

An hour or so later, Julia left the house and headed southward. She felt exhilarated to be walking alone for once. Molly would be shocked. Harriet had told her that circumstances and necessity rendered the social nicety of a chaperon an impractical luxury for a working, middle-class woman in Manchester. But even this freedom, thought Julia, was tainted by the thought that it was used to define her class.

She travelled through congested streets and tenements facing onto narrow courts – everywhere the same blackened red-brick houses. She found it all very depressing. The streets were quieter than they had been the previous evening. Presumably all the able-bodied were already at work, leaving infants to be minded by the old, the feeble and the infirm. People were huddled around doorways, like expectant feral cats, the day's gossip spent, waiting patiently for the breadwinners' return. Gaunt faces stared at Julia, and even though she was still wearing her travel-stained gown and cloak from the previous day, she felt over-dressed and out of place.

Turning right into Upper Brook Street, eventually she reached the toll house that Harriet had warned her about. However, she was surprised somewhat when the keeper gruffly asked to see her handbag. Julia clutched it to her chest in alarm.

"I mun check yer bag, missus, fer dynamite. Blem those Fenian folk if you will."

Reluctantly, but saying nothing in case her accent betrayed her origins, she handed over the commodious bag and he looked through it. When he returned it, she then gave him the penny toll and entered the estate.

Victoria Park was indeed impressive. Edward had told her that the seventy acres of individual houses had been built for Manchester's elite, for wealthy industrialists, artists and professionals. This was a far cry from the Manchester she had experienced so far, the city that Elizabeth Gaskell and Charles Dickens had described. This was heaven. The houses were magnificent, set in landscaped grounds, with neatly trimmed box hedges and planted borders – they were turreted, towered and decorated in a variety of architectural styles, Classical, Italianate, and the Neo-Gothic style made fashionable by the designer William Morris.

Julia watched as uniformed children's nursemaids wheeled large perambulators down the leafy roads – as shop delivery boys unburdened their baskets loaded with fresh fruit, vegetables, and groceries, jumping down from their pony and traps. No hard bread here. It was well for those well-dressed women, with their smart bonnets and costumes, thought Julia. No doubt there was a fleet of Dollys or Daisys at home doing the donkey work, doing the laundry, polishing the brass, and cooking the meals.

She thought of Dublin and how she would bring home presents to Molly and Padraic – she had never appreciated them so much as she did now.

She breathed in the air – it was cleaner here, she noted, built to take advantage of the prevailing westerly winds and avoid the foul-smelling smoke over the rest of the city. Julia had time to think as she strolled around the neighbourhood. She had still not got over her shock on her arrival and had yet to talk to Edward about the reason for her visit. Although, this now seemed less important. After her long talk with her sister the previous evening she had begun to see another side of the couple's present misery.

Edward and Harriet had been unusually accepting of their situation. When Julia had asked if Harriet had tried to teach music, she had replied that she could not teach music without a piano. When she'd asked if she had enquired about getting the use of one, Harriet had excused herself, saying that she had felt unable in her present circumstances to make social overtures to other parishioners, or even neighbours. Everyone was as poor as church mice. Although, looking around Victoria Park, Julia thought that this was clearly not the case. Despite Harriet's hard-work ethic and apparent confidence, she seemed to have become so ground down by their misfortune that she lacked the wherewithal, or motivation, to change her current situation. Edward, despite being as tight-fisted and mean-minded as ever, she grudgingly had to admit was working as hard as he could. But Julia could see it would take several years before things improved for them. She didn't know whether Harriet could physically last that long. Despite the fact that she despised Edward, Harriet was her sister, and she had to rescue her somehow from this intolerable situation – and if that meant making peace with Edward, at least in the short term, then so be it. Slowly, she began to come up with a plan. Until eventually some hours later, tired but resolute, she headed back to Shakespeare Street.

⌒⌒⌒

Chapter 11

Two days later, on Monday morning, she slept through
the mill bells. Tiredness from her long journey had finally
caught up on her – as well as the fact that the day before,
after church service, she had walked for hours around
Bell Vue with Harriet and Edward. The weather had
finally turned, the temperature risen, and it had been such
a beautiful day in the landscaped gardens, where the trees
were sprinkled with early russet-and-golden autumnal
leaves. The zoo was indeed as impressive as Harriet had
promised, with its array of exotic foreign animals. But
what had interested Julia most were the human animals
in the park, the Mancunians, who were also on show.
Families free from the shackles of the factories and mills,
scrubbed clean and shiny and dressed in their Sunday
best, were out for the day. All ages and classes of people
were cavorting with gusto, waltzing in the open air,
dancing to the exuberant strains of Strauss's "Blue
Danube". It was quite a spectacle, as young girls danced

with their bonnets and mobcaps awry, negotiating advances from over-amorous partners with haughty disdain, or a laugh and a playful slap. She had watched the dancers, whirling and swirling in a swarm of continuous motion. Silk and satin skirts brushed against worsted and coarse linen, and for the most part people managed almost miraculously not to collide.

Julia, caught up in the carnival atmosphere, had politely declined Edward's offer – at Harriet's prompting no doubt – to engage in a waltz. Despite this, Edward had been courteous and considerate, and they had all enjoyed a pleasant day. But she couldn't help feeling that they were both wary – like lizards determinedly skirting around one another – alert, senses heightened, waiting for the inevitable attack to occur.

Today, alone, she felt more relaxed. Philip had brought over her valise the previous evening, and she was wearing a fresh costume in dark-grey taffeta edged with black lace and a matching pelisse in a light merino wool. The sun had come out again, and Manchester seemed to sparkle with life. The street urchins who had terrified her on her first day she now saw as cheeky versions of Dicken's Artful Dodger, and, once she had a handle on their accent, as witty as their Dublin counterparts.

As Julia moved northward, she had a chance to admire the architecture of many of the city's fine institutional buildings. She was heading towards Mosley Street to the Royal Manchester Institution. She had been looking forward with anticipation to visit this centre of the Manchester art world.

In the entrance hall of the impressive neoclassical building, a young woman with an open, friendly face, and a mass of curly brown hair greeted her. Smiling, Julia noticed she had a slight gap between her two front teeth.

"Unfortunately, madam, I will have to charge you two shillings for the entrance ticket, but at least you will have the place to yourself. It was like Bedlam here yesterday. Sundays are always a nightmare. You can't hear yourself think, let alone get near a picture. The main gallery, showing the Academy's collection, is through there. Would you like a catalogue?"

"Thank you. Yes, a catalogue would be very useful."

"Another shilling, I am afraid."

"That's fine," said Julia, handing over the coins.

"Would you like to sign the visitor's book?"

Julia signed her name, giving Westland Row, Dublin, as her address. The young woman watched her write.

"Oh, I see you are from Dublin. I have a good friend who is working there at the moment, a Mr Erskine Nicol. Do you know him by any chance?"

"Oh yes, I do indeed! I know him quite well – in fact, he gave me lessons some years ago. He's a wonderful painter and also a dear friend."

"Oh, what a coincidence! It's such a small world. I'm Isabel Susan Dacre. I'm so pleased to meet you, Miss …"

"Julia Benson."

"Oh, Miss Benson, we were expecting you. I have two letters for you. One of them I know is from the Academy of Fine Art, because I recognise the envelope. The other one a gentleman left in for you a few days ago. He said you would be visiting. I'll just go and fetch them from the office."

Julia anxiously waited. The Academy? She had been expecting a reply from them, good or bad, since she submitted a painting to them for possible exhibition. But a gentleman? She couldn't help but think of Donal – was it possible he had found out she was here? Through Eoin perhaps?

Isabel returned with the letters and handed them to Julia who glanced at them before putting them in her reticule. Neither was from Donal.

"Thank you, Miss Dacre."

"You are very welcome, Miss Benson. It was a rather unusual request – I was at the desk myself when the gentleman visited. I must say he was extremely charming. We were delighted in this instance to help a visiting artist. Provided, of course, that you both do not make a habit of it." She laughed, with a knowing look. "I am also a painter, Miss Benson, but I am working here today to support the Royal Manchester Institution. It's hard to keep these things going, as you can imagine, and although the Manchester Academy of Fine Art has the use of this magnificent building, it is so expensive to run. Well, I mustn't natter on. I do hope you enjoy the exhibition. I'll be dying to hear how we measure up to Dublin." She said this all at speed, with a broad friendly smile that lit up her expressive, dark-brown eyes.

Although Julia was dying to open the envelope from the unknown gentleman, she resisted, deciding it would be prudent to do so away from Miss Dacre's inquisitive gaze. So she set about inspecting the exhibition. She moved around the room, slowly examining each painting. It was the usual mixture of idyllic countryside scenes and history paintings with classical themes. This could almost be a Royal Hibernian Academy exhibition in Dublin except for the portraits of dour Manchester industrialists. He who pays the piper calls the tune, thought Julia. A few works caught her attention, those that managed to distil the essence of this extraordinary city, with its stark contrasts between its industrial achievements and the pitiful lifestyles of many of those who lived there. These artists captured life on the streets, like John Haughton Hague's, *The Chadderton Taxidermist*, an emotive depiction of a local eccentric with his collection of stuffed birds.

Even though she did not paint landscapes herself, she did admire the attempts of others and examined these closely. Portraiture had always been easier for her. She did not have a carriage at her disposal to transport her painting equipment to different locations on a whim. And, like most women of her class, the need to be chaperoned presented other difficulties.

In Dublin, landscape was not something that she thought of as representing a place apart as the landscape mingled with the fabric of the city – the shabby gentility of Dublin's architecture lay loosely between the mountains and the sea. But these Lancashire landscapes, inspired by the work of Turner and Constable, transported the viewer to another place entirely, where life was slower, closer to nature. Ironically, she thought with some amusement, these rural idylls were the very places from which most of the citizens of Manchester had only recently escaped and had no intention of returning to. She wondered, if she had grown up in this city, would she have been more attracted to this genre?

Paintings by Joseph Knight also stood out, executed in the realistic style popularised by Corot and Millet who painted real people working and going about their daily lives, their use of light and colour imbuing the experience of being in a place. But the strong daylight colours of the

Barbizon painters were not in evidence here. Instead, a grey greenness captured English summer rain on morning hills. These artists had turned their back on this industrial city.

She noted with some satisfaction that there were quite a few women artists' work on display – a few landscapes, the ubiquitous flower paintings, children's portraits, and some rather unusual fairy paintings.

"What do you think of these? Are they not exquisite?"

Julia, lost in thought, had not heard Isabel Dacre approaching her.

"Well, yes," said Julia somewhat hesitantly. "They are intriguing. I must say – they are quite explicit."

"Yes, shocking, is it not? Undraped nudes really, of young girls. The artist calls them fairies and suddenly they are acceptable to the academicians and the critics. Not my cup of tea, I must say. Although they are very pretty. And you, Miss Benson, what is your cup of tea?"

"Well, I paint portraits mostly, in oil and pastel. I also work as a photographer in Dublin. I took over my father's business when he died. Fortunately, I am able to combine the two activities rather well."

"Oh, how exciting! Will you be here for long?"

"Just for a few more days – my sister has moved here – but I hope to be spending more time here in the future. I must say I find it encouraging that there are so many women painters represented here."

"Yes, there are quite a number of professional female artists in Manchester, mostly working as portrait painters. But this year, through a process of constant cajoling and bullying, for the first time nine ladies were admitted as members of the Academy. I myself am one of those honoured. We are called 'lady exhibitors', if you don't mind. Although we still cannot join the Academy's life drawing lessons, which is rather annoying for many of the women. For me it is of no importance. I am currently working and studying with my friend Miss Robinson in Rome where there are quite a few opportunities for life drawing. And then of course the light there is wonderful, as is the classical architecture, and the sculpture. But you know all of this, I am sure. So, you see, like you, I am only here on holiday. What's it like in Dublin?"

"From an artist's perspective, much the same I am afraid, but women are not admitted as Academy members."

"Oh dear, but I am sure it will come there too, in time." Isabel turned to Emily Gertrude Thomson's fairy painting. "I, for one, refuse to paint flowers, or fairies for that matter." A large wall-mounted clock chimed the hour and Isabel turned back to Julia. "And now, Miss Benson, I am afraid I am going to have to close the gallery for lunch. I have enjoyed our conversation so much. Here is my card. If you have the time over the next few days, do call into my studio – it's over the Ducie Arms in Strangeways, where my mother is the landlady. I paint there most afternoons between two and five. There is usually somebody interesting to talk to. Lydia is often there – Lydia Becker, the writer – a great supporter of votes for women, and all of that. Have you heard of her?"

"Yes, indeed I have. I have read with interest her articles in the *Women's Suffrage Journal*."

"Wonderful! Maybe we can continue our discussion on the vicissitudes of lady painters."

"Thank you, Miss Dacre, I would like that very much."

Out on Mosley Street Julia opened the letter and saw it was from Drennan.

Dear Miss Benson,

Further to our conversation in Dublin the situation with D is now critical. A lady known as Mrs Wilson will make herself known to you over the next few days and she will assist you in your endeavours. I will be in contact again shortly.

Respectfully, CD.

Julia felt a fluttering in her stomach. All this subterfuge was somewhat alarming. Still, if Donal needed her help, she would simply have to do what was necessary.

The second letter, however, lifted her spirits. Her painting *Farewell to Ireland* had been accepted by the Academy of Fine Art in Manchester for the autumn exhibition, which was in a few weeks' time. This was wonderful news, sadly now diluted by her anxiety for both Donal and Harriet.

Disturbing her reverie, a newspaper boy shouted, *"Fenian escapees arrive in New York – read all about it!"*

She bought a paper and, as she walked, read of the arrival of the 'Fremantle Six' in New York to a crowd of thousands of supporters. The article described how six Fenians had been rescued from an Australian prison by sea some four months earlier, in a ship named the *Catalpa*. Instigated by Clan na Gael's John Devoy in America, and masterminded and executed by three men, the paper claimed that the dramatic escape had captured the world's attention. The writer suggested that the coup had also emboldened the Irish Republican Brotherhood after the failed rebellion of 1867 when informers had alerted the British authorities in Dublin Castle.

Julia thought of the brothers and sons of all of those she knew who had been imprisoned following that fiasco – and of young Philip Allen, one of the Manchester Martyrs. Their courage, and the courage of those involved in the *Catalpa* strengthened her resolve. Still, she would not share her plans or all of the day's events with Harriet and Edward. And as she approached the junction of Shakespeare Street with Stockport Road, she threw the newspaper into a rubbish bin.

That evening, after Harriet had gone to bed, Edward was reading *The Times* newspaper.

"Madness, the whole thing. What has it achieved? Nothing. Thousands of pounds sending a whiting boat halfway around the world to capture six condemned men, scoundrels probably, about whom everyone has forgotten. They would have been better off sending the money to the starving families in Ireland." His face was black with hatred. "It's difficult enough to be accepted here in the city by the English. To make them see that we are decent, hardworking people, loyal to queen and country, without having to contend with this kind of tomfoolery."

He glared at Julia, daring her to contradict him.

Instead, she raised her eyes from the stocking she was mending and looked at him directly.

"Edward, we need to talk."

He rose to check the fire, avoiding her eyes. Stooping slightly, he seemed almost too big for the room. His large, calloused hands shovelled coal into the stove to revive the dying embers.

"Were we not talking all evening? What's more to be said?"

145

"I know about Stephen, that he has been intercepting my letters from Donal."

Caught off guard, he looked up at her directly, shoulders squared.

"You have no right being involved with the likes of him."

"No right, Edward? It is *you* who have no right."

"It was for your own good, yours and Harriet's."

She could see beads of perspiration on his forehead.

"Where are they?"

"*Burnt*," he said belligerently. "It beggars belief how a grown man could write such drivel."

Furious at the thought of him reading what was meant for her eyes only, she looked away so he wouldn't see the tears springing to her eyes. But then, breathing in deeply and releasing her clenched fists, she smoothed her skirt. Then she turned to him.

"What you did was despicable, Edward," she said slowly and carefully, "cowardly even. And although you are married to my sister, you will have no control over me. Look at the results of your moral guidance and superiority, look at what my sister has been reduced to." She looked disparagingly around the room. "This is a hovel, Edward – my sister is living in a hovel."

He followed her gaze grudgingly. "Your scorn does you no service, Julia. We have had a series of bad luck. But things will get better."

"Not soon enough, Edward – not soon enough for my sister. The child – your child – will be born in a few months."

She saw fear briefly in his eyes, but quickly his implacable expression returned.

"We could always sell the lease on Westland Row –

146

that would solve our problems immediately," he said. "There's no point in you living like Lady Muck over in Dublin, if you are so concerned about your sister."

She controlled her rising temper. "That would only be an answer in the short term. Tell me, Edward, where is all Papa's money gone? How did you manage to go through four hundred and fifty pounds in less than two years?"

"After we paid the solicitor, and for your father and mother's funerals, and discharged the outstanding debts, there was only three hundred pounds left. Since coming here, with all the expense that has involved, Harriet had a miscarriage as she told you. She was ill and weak afterwards. Between the doctors' bills and medicine … and then she couldn't work for a month …" He paused. "What she didn't tell you, out of loyalty to me, is that I am not paid by the dentist – I am apprenticed – *I* have to pay *him*. And I only get a pittance from working as a barman in the pub. With mostly students as customers there is not much in the way of tips. We rely heavily on the money you send us from Westland Row. There is only a hundred pounds or so left of your father's money. I have been keeping that for emergencies, for Harriet's confinement … if she goes full term, that is."

"How long will it take for you to get your licence?"

"Three more years. But God will give us strength to see this through."

"God's help may not be enough," said Julia tartly.

"I have talked to Harriet about the Westland Row lease, but she was reluctant to sell – for your sake. But her reluctance will eventually be superseded by necessity when we have another mouth to feed. Then I must make hard decisions, Julia. My income from Dublin – that is, mine and Harriet's – is insufficient for our expenses. There doesn't seem to have been any serious attempt on your part to increase the business or reduce ongoing costs."

Julia, trying to stay calm, was silent. She sipped the sherry she had brought – it was the end of the bottle. After a few minutes, she looked at Edward.

"I am genuinely very sorry for the hardship that you have both had to suffer, but I am not a child and you should have told me about your circumstances sooner."

"Well, you were never good with money, and you were so angry about the will."

"Yes, and I am still angry, but I cannot change that now. Nor can I forgive you for interfering in my personal affairs." She smiled grimly at the unintended pun. Edward, however, remained implacable. "But we have to work together if we are all to survive. So, I have a proposition to make."

Julia ordered a cab to the Ducie Arms which was located near the new prison at Strangeways with its distinctive tower that loomed menacingly across the city. On arrival, Isabel's servant showed her up the stairs from the side entrance, to the studio on the top floor. It was a converted attic with a large dormer window looking out over the adjoining rooftops and the prison beyond.

As she entered the room, Isabel Dacre jumped up immediately to greet her. "Oh, Miss Benson, I am delighted that you could come and visit us. Let me introduce you to my other guests. Miss Benson, this is Mrs Cordelia Bramwell, Miss Sarah Seymour and Miss Rose Crocket."

Julia shook each hand politely.

"And last, but by no means least, our source of

inspiration and encouragement, Mr Benjamin Preston."

Mr Preston shook Julia's hand, bowing slightly. He was tall, well-built, and handsome with a mischievous smile. "What Isabel means is that unfortunately, unlike these ladies, I have absolutely no artistic talent."

"Don't be silly, Benjamin. Now do sit down, Julia, and I will get you a drink. I have just made some hot punch."

Julia sat and Isabel brought her the drink.

"Miss Benson is from Dublin," Isabel said to the others. "I met her at the Institute last week where I acted as go-between, for her and an anonymous admirer. Is that not so, Miss Benson?"

Julia blushed, but responded confidently. "I am sorry to disappoint you, Miss Dacre – the admirer merely wanted to commission a portrait of his mother."

"His mother? How terribly disappointing. Still, it is an introduction of sorts."

"Miss Dacre, I am afraid that I am really not interested in the gentleman, or his mother. I have enough on my plate just now. The second letter, however, had more interesting news. A painting that I sent here by courier to the Academy of Fine Art has been accepted for the autumn exhibition by the selection committee, which is in a few weeks' time, I believe."

"Oh, how wonderful! Isn't that right, ladies? Another lady exhibitor! Soon we shall outshine the gentlemen."

"What is the subject matter of your painting, Miss Benson?" asked Rose, a quietly spoken young lady with plaited coils of hair framing each side of her face.

"It is a scene on the docks in Dublin, of a young couple about to leave their home and country, fleeing from the Great Famine that gripped the country in the forties – and

149

the continuing poor harvests which have been the source of a constant stream of emigration since. It is called *Farewell to Ireland.*"

"My aunt, who lives in Kildare, tells me that unlike here in England there is no rent control in your country," Rose responded, "and that the landlords, many of them living in England, show little mercy to those who cannot meet their dues. At least young Parnell is cutting quite a figure in parliament these days representing their case. In fact, I was only saying yesterday, Ireland seems to be constantly in the news."

"Yes, indeed, that is so. But my painting is really concerned with the impact on the women and children. To be forced to leave your home, your family and the country where you grew up is tragic. So many emigrants have died in the process.

"It's not only the Irish who are suffering, Miss Benson!" exclaimed Preston earnestly. "We too have suffered from the effects of poor harvests. There's many a Lancashire family starving. In fact, with increased competition from abroad and some factories on short hours, times are hard for many folks!"

"Oh, we are getting too serious altogether," interrupted Isabel. "We came here to talk about art, not politics. Now, Julia, what do you think about Mr Madox Brown's painting, *The Last of England*, painted a few years ago? It explores similar themes, I think."

Chapter 12

The Reverend Nicholas Weatherspoon's voice resonated in the high, Gothic-vaulted space as he denounced the evils of drink to the congregation of St Clement's. Julia had heard enough. She surreptitiously rubbed together her gloved hands – she was freezing. She seemed to be permanently cold here in Manchester. Edward, along with everything else, was careful with the coal. During the day it was warmer to walk the streets than sit in the sparsely furnished room. Julia, looking around absentmindedly, noticed a better-off class of people than those that lived around Shakespeare Street. The church was a walk away on Dillon Street and drew its congregation from the leafier suburbs of Victoria Park. Well-upholstered matrons and their shiny-suited husbands were accompanied by unnaturally tidy-looking children, their hair ribboned and ringleted, dressed in stiff Sunday clothes. A strong smell of carbolic soap, mixed with expensive eau de cologne, filled the air and made Julia feel queasy. She recognised a few of Harriet's neighbours. Which one of them was Mrs Wilson, she wondered? Julia had mentioned the name casually to Harriet, but she claimed not to know her.

Outside, it had stopped raining, and at the end of the service the congregation poured into the adjoining church hall for refreshments. Edward fetched two tin cups of hot black tea for Julia and Harriet. He was dressed in his Sunday best, a black dress coat and trousers, a starched neckcloth, and a silk top hat that had seen better times. Looking decidedly uncomfortable, he ran his finger around the rim of his collar. He had taken to growing his whiskers in dundrearies, a fashion made popular by the Queen's late husband Prince Albert.

Harriet's gown of aubergine satin was visibly strained over her extended stomach, Julia noted. She looked tired and wan – "dawny" as Molly always described her. Harriet was struggling, no matter how brave a face she was putting on.

Julia would have to go home soon, just for a fortnight or so – she needed to sort things out in Westland Row – but she would return. She and Edward had reached an understanding. She would move to Manchester and they would rent out the upper rooms in Westland Row. Julia had struggled with the notion but when an opportunity presented itself to her, she finally grasped the nettle. Harriet and Julia had spent an enjoyable evening drinking tea and eating cake with their fellow tenant Mrs Hunt and her two daughters, Grace and Dora. The generous Lancashire woman had told Julia that Grace had got a job in a convent in Liverpool, overseeing the making of vestments for the Catholic priests. In a month's time she was going to stay with relatives there. Julia had called in to Mrs Hunt following their visit for a quiet chat and they had hatched a plan that suited them both. Julia could have Grace's bed in the room she shared with her sister. It was not perfect, but at least she would have somewhere she could get away from Edward. She could not leave her sister to go through the birth alone. Julia shivered at the prospect, once more remembering her mother's frequent miscarriages. The thought of her sister and a new baby in Shakespeare Street was unbearable. Julia had argued that they could not remain there indefinitely and that if they worked together with the resources they had – they could afford to lease somewhere more suitable. She pointed out that, even when Edward qualified, it would take several years to establish a practice. Harriet was not strong enough to continue at the factory and, despite her initial hopes, music lessons were not going to be an option, as very few of their social circle had the luxury of owning a piano. Julia, on the other hand, could do piecework, hand-tinting for local photographers, illustrations for advertisements. She could also try and establish herself here as a portrait painter. And because she was more extrovert than her shy sister, hopefully they could start to build a social network of potential clients for Edward.

Edward for his part was to treat her with respect, allowing her to keep a portion of her own earnings. He had agreed, when they moved eventually, to give her own bedroom and another room that she could use as a studio. But, for now, that day was still in the distant future. Julia had resigned herself for the next year or two to living in squalor in Shakespeare Street and, despite the separate room, in distastefully close proximity to Edward. She had suggested this course of action in the knowledge that when it became too much she could always escape back to Dublin for a few days at least. Despite her misgivings, she knew it was her duty to look after her younger sister. It was what Mama and Papa would have expected. There was also the comforting fact that over the last week she and Harriet had become close again. Closer than they had been since their father's death.

Julia's thoughts were abruptly interrupted.

"Mrs Sutcliffe, this is my husband Edward whom you know, and this is my sister Miss Julia Benson – she is over from Dublin on a visit."

"Oh, nice to meet you," said a thin-faced woman with wispy grey hair drawn back from a dour face. "Did you enjoy the Reverend's sermon? He is such a moral beacon to us all, don't you think? And drink is such a problem, especially – if you will excuse me for saying – with your countrymen."

"Indeed, Mrs Sutcliffe, poverty and hunger are enough to drive any man to drink, don't you think?" Julia retorted.

"Well, it was lovely talking to you, Mrs Sutcliffe, please excuse us," said Harriet abruptly, pulling her sister away.

Edward followed them, his face thunderous. "Julia, please, mind your manners – we have to live with these people."

"Look, there is Mrs Hunt and her daughters," said Harriet, trying to diffuse the situation.

Ann Hunt approached, her soft, round face and kindly brown eyes beaming in welcoming smiles. "Julia, you look so well today, my dear!"

"Miss Benson, your sister showed me some of your drawings yesterday, the portraits that you did of your mama and papa," said Grace. "You also paint beautifully, I believe."

She was the eldest and smaller of the two daughters, fine-boned and neat in manner and style, fair-haired with hazel eyes. Her younger sister Dora, in contrast, was taller, awkward, and eager like a young colt. Julia could not envision her having the patience to stay still long enough to sew a hankie, let alone a mantle.

"Well, Grace, I paint as well as my sister plays the piano," said Julia, laughing.

"Oh Harriet, we didn't know you played the piano!" Dora said enthusiastically. "You must ask the Reverend if you could use the piano here in the hall. We could have a recital."

"Ah, did I hear that we have a musician in our midst?" A large-boned young woman, dark-haired, handsome, in her thirties, was standing close by. She put out her gloved hand to Harriet. "Mrs Williams, I believe? My name is Mrs Emily Wilson. I am a neighbour of yours, from just around the corner in Granville Street."

Startled, Julia stared at her as Harriet shook her hand.

"Mrs Wilson, this is my husband Edward, my sister Julia and my daughters Grace and Dora."

"Delighted to meet you all, I am sure," said the stylishly dressed woman as she shook hands with each of them.

"Mrs Wilson, not only is Harriet a musician but Julia is a portrait painter," said Dora then.

"Oh, really, Miss Benson, how fortuitous! My brother has recently left for America and he has asked me to get a likeness drawn to send over to him. I can't think why."

She bestowed on Edward an arch flirtatious look and, to Julia's surprise, he responded with an admiring glance. Mrs Wilson looked once more at Julia.

"Would you be interested in the commission?"

"I should like that very much, Mrs Wilson, but I am returning to Dublin next week to attend to some business," she replied, sensing Harriet stiffen.

"I am sure you can both come to some arrangement," said Edward with uncharacteristic sociability.

"Why don't you call in to my house – here is my card," said Mrs Wilson. "I work from home, piecework – I do embroidery. Maybe on Monday morning? Say eleven, does that suit?"

"Yes," Julia smiled, "that would be fine. See you on Monday."

The woman turned to leave, and Julia watched her as she left the hall. She didn't waste any time, she thought. But as she finished her tea, the queasiness she had experienced earlier and that anxious feeling returned, and she felt a little faint.

"Do you know, Harriet, I don't believe I have ever seen that woman before," said Mrs Hunt, who seemed perturbed. "I hope I am not going senile."

"Oh, don't worry, Mama," said Dora, laughing. "We shan't be able to tell when you do."

Mrs Wilson showed Julia into a sparsely furnished room on the first floor. In the corner reeded baskets held upright bales of material. And hanging from the ceiling were fishermen's nets packed with more fabric, folded and tied with ribbon. A large wooden table was in the centre of the room with piles of white chemises stacked neatly at one end. At the other end was an assortment of cotton reels, boxes, and pincushions – and in the centre of the table an embroidered cotton chemise was stretched on a tambour frame.

Mrs Wilson looked less formal today in her workday dress of navy cotton print, patterned with a small red-and-blue flowered motif. Her hair was in a loose knot held in place with a large black ribbon.

She gestured to her guest to sit beside the stove.

"A cup of tea, Miss Benson?"

"Yes, that we would be lovely, thank you." Julia sat, shifting uncomfortably in her seat. She waited to see what the woman had to say. She held out her hands to feel the warmth emanating from the stove.

Mrs Wilson placed a foldout card table in front of Julia and then busied herself arranging china cups on it and making tea.

After a few minutes' silence, she said in a business-like manner, "Mr Drennan, has been in touch with you, I believe, Miss Benson. He is extremely worried about Mr O'Keefe, who I believe is a good friend of yours."

"Yes, that is so."

Mrs Wilson placed a plate of biscuits on the table and then sat and poured the tea.

Julia noticed that she had beautiful hands, long-fingered and, unusually for a needlewoman, well-manicured nails.

"Miss Benson, I know this must all seem rather strange to you," Mrs Wilson said as she proffered the plate of biscuits. "But we are all on the same side, you know. The side of Irish nationalism. My own two brothers were involved in the Clerkenwell explosions and are still doing time in the New Bailey in Salford."

"But you are English?"

Mrs Wilson laughed. "I was raised here, certainly, but my family are originally from Sligo. We were forced to emigrate during the Great Famine of 1845. I was eight years old at the time. I remember our family being evicted for the want of a week's rent. My poor farther died from hunger on the road to Dublin, and my mother arrived in Liverpool with six young children, and only two shillings to her name. My two brothers and I survived, but the three youngest died of typhus which was rampant that first winter in the city."

"Oh, I am so sorry, Mrs Wilson," said Julia compassionately.

"Well, that was then. But now I have my health and plenty of work – although the hours are long, and my eyes are not as strong as they used to be. My husband was an engineer at the Gorton Foundry, but he was let go. He is now working up north. Unfortunately, we have not been blessed with children. But we have enough to eat, and a roof over our heads, thanks be to God. But I have never forgiven the British Government for allowing my family, along with millions of Irish, to die when they could have been saved by their intervention. It must never happen again." She looked directly at Julia. "Ireland must be responsible for its own destiny. For better or worse, Ireland must be free."

Julia shifted uneasily in her chair, and then said slowly and with emphasis, "Mrs Wilson, my meeting with Mr Drennan in Dublin was somewhat unexpected, and unfortunately brief. I did not get a chance to explain my situation properly to him." She paused. "You see, my family are staunchly Unionist – my sister, brother-in-law, and most of those with whom I socialise in Dublin support the British Government's rule in Ireland. It was my grandfather who made me see things from another perspective. Although I have sympathy with – and have indeed supported the Fenian cause in the past – it has been very much support at a distance. I have never been directly involved with the organisation – ever – nor do I want to be. In fact, if I might say so, I abhor violence in any form."

"I understand, Miss Benson – we all abhor violence, and none of us choose to get involved in it. Situations, however, seek us out and we have to either face them or their consequences, so to speak."

Julia's newfound sympathy for Mrs Wilson evaporated instantly.

"I will not be told what to do, Mrs Wilson. Not by you, or the Irish Republican Brotherhood, or anyone else for that matter."

"Miss Benson, I do not mean to alarm you, or make you feel uncomfortable in any way and I am sorry if my words offended you. I am merely talking about my own situation, not yours."

"I am sorry if I was rude. I must admit that I am a little anxious about recent events." Julia sat up straighter in the chair. "So, Mrs Wilson, let us cut to the chase. What has happened to Donal O'Keefe, and why does Mr Drennan need my help?"

"It seems Donal left New York, sailing for Liverpool and intending to return home to Dublin. On the ship he became friendly with a certain Frank Millen, a military man, and member of Clan na Gael. Millen is a bit of a loose cannon by all accounts. He worked as a journalist for the *New York Herald*, and spent time covering the recent rebel insurrection in Cuba. He was on his way to England to reconnoitre potential sites to dynamite. We believe that he enlisted Donal's help because of his useful connections in both Dublin and Manchester with the IRB. As you know, Clan na Gael member Jeremiah O'Donovan Rossa is exiled in the United States and is a prime mover in the policy of physical force republicanism. Millen's trip was paid for out of O'Donovan Rossa's 'skirmishing fund' set up by him for this purpose. Devoy who Donal was supposed to be reporting to, was only made aware of Millen's plans through a spy he had employed to keep an eye on O'Donovan Rossa."

Julia looked at the other woman in disbelief.

"I know – they all work for the one cause – when will they get sense? Anyway, this spy – let's call him O'Connor, although that is not his real name – turns out to be working for the British Government. However, Donal who is working with this man is unaware of this and as a result is in grave danger."

Julia's initial expression of disbelief had turned to one of alarm. Her hand trembling, she put her cup and saucer down on the card table, her tea spilling in the saucer.

"Why don't you tell him?"

"Because we don't know where he is. Once O'Connor realised Devoy had blown his cover, they all seemed to disappear. We were hoping that you might be able to find him for us."

"And how exactly do you think I can do that?"

"Well, are you close to any of his family who might

know where he is?"

"I have not been in contact with his brother Eoin for some time." Julia thought grimly of their last meeting. "But the last time we met, he had not heard from him either, not since Donal left New York. I could write to him, I suppose."

"Well, that would be a start. Does Donal know you are here?"

"No, I don't suppose he does."

"How about putting a notice in the *Manchester Chronicle*?"

"Saying what precisely?"

"Well, you are an artist – could you say that you are taking commissions for portraits?"

"It is unusual for artists to advertise in that way – if one is serious about one's reputation. Commissions are usually earned by recommendation. But maybe I could advertise drawing classes."

"Yes, well, why don't we try both?"

"We?"

Julia got up from her chair.

"I will have to think about what you have said and decide what to do."

"Very well, Miss Benson, but don't leave it too long – we cannot afford to dilly-dally – Donal is in grave danger."

***

6 Shakespeare Street,
Ardwick Green,
Manchester
14th September 1876

Dear Eoin,

I hope that you are keeping well, and that Lydia is practising her drawing diligently. Since we last met in July, my circumstances have changed somewhat, and I thought it prudent to advise you of recent events.

As you can see from the address, I am currently in Manchester visiting my sister and brother-in-law. However, before I left Dublin, and as you had correctly surmised, I discovered that Stephen Spendlove, a clerk my brother-in-law uses to oversee our books, was intercepting my letters from D. He had been instructed to do so by Edward, who shares your concerns about D's activities. Unfortunately, he subsequently burnt the letters, so I am none the wiser of their contents. I was wondering if you had subsequently heard from D. And if so, could you pass my new address to him and ask him to contact me?

For the foreseeable future, I will be in Manchester. My sister is due to go into confinement in a few months, and I wish to be here to support her during her ordeal. Somewhat fortuitously, I recently had a painting 'Farewell to Ireland' accepted by the Manchester City Art Gallery for their autumn exhibition. This good fortune has encouraged me to establish contact with other art galleries here in England with a view to selling and promoting my work. I believe there is a better market here for portraits than exists presently in Dublin.

Yours sincerely,

Julia Benson

Julia read the letter carefully before closing the envelope and affixing the stamp. She did not want to mislead Eoin, but she did not want to worry him unnecessarily with Drennan's concerns, which might, for all she knew, be totally unfounded. Although the anxiety she felt about Donal, at this stage, was all-consuming. She was afraid that Donal might have given up on her for failing to respond to his letters. But she would like to think that despite this, he still cared about her. Still, if what Drennan said was true – and why should he lie – he had been sent by John Devoy after all – then Donal was potentially in danger and, like it or not, she would have to try and help him in any way she could.

She put on her bonnet and pelisse and headed out of the house towards the post office on Stockport Road. From there she intended walking to the Steam Shipping office in Piccadilly to buy a ticket to Dublin for the following week.

Chapter 13

It was raining when she finally reached Westland Row and she was exhausted from the journey. But she was so pleased to be home and looked forward to the thought of sleeping in her own bed. Although after the first night in Shakespeare Street, Harriet had borrowed a hair mattress from the Hunts, she still felt that she had not slept properly for the entire fortnight. As usual, Molly welcomed her home like the prodigal daughter, hot bath ready for her, with warm towels and lemon soap from Sweny's Chemists. Leaning her chin on her knees, she had soaked luxuriously in the scented water in front of a roaring fire.

For dinner Molly had made her favourite dishes: lamb stew, followed by a ginger pudding, oozing with honey and covered in melting cream. Julia had devoured both at the kitchen table in front of the range as, despite Molly's protests, she had insisted on joining them for supper – it seemed foolish to dine alone upstairs. In between mouthfuls, Molly talked ten to the dozen and filled her in on all the local news and gossip, while Padraic attempted to interrupt with news from the studio. But each time he tried to speak Molly said, "Wait awhile, Padraic!" to which he responded, "Sorry, missus," and she continued relentlessly with her flow.

But when Julia described the desperate situation in Manchester, big tears fell down Molly's fat cheeks.

"The poor wee bairn," she said. "Thank God your mother didn't live to see the day."

Julia waited for the right opportunity to tell them about the plan she had agreed with Edward. When she finally broached the subject they were shocked initially, but they saw that it was the only way.

"Ye'll have no shortage of tenants for the first and second floor," said Padraic.

"Ah, Miss Julia, it will surely break your heart, to see strangers living here," said Molly.

"It will, Molly, but needs must." Julia, who until then had maintained a brave face, wiped the tears welling in her eyes with the edge of her handkerchief. "Anyway, the plan is that with the extra income Harriet and Edward will eventually lease a bigger house in Manchester. I will pay a portion of the rent to help meet with the expenses, but I will have my own room, a large room that I can paint in, and I will sleep in a small box room. When I am here in Dublin, I can sleep in the rear attic bedroom, the one across from yours that we use as a store." She looked sadly at their forlorn faces. "This will be hard on you both. But the last fortnight has proved that you can run the place on your own."

Julia paused to let them take all this in, then continued reassuringly. "I will be over every second week until we get everything sorted out. Initially, there will be a lot of work to be done. Padraic. We might get your nephew, young Ned, to help Billy with the moving, and Molly you and Tilly might need help afterwards to give the place a thorough cleaning – we can probably also stretch to getting a young one in from the parish to help for a few weeks. Meanwhile I will have to clear out my studio which will take me at least a week."

A lull fell in the conversation as the old couple realised that this was the end of an era.

"Unfortunately, once upstairs is let we will have to let Tilly and Billy go," Julia went on. "This is one of the harder aspects of all of this. We have grown so used to them over the last few years, and them to us. I will certainly miss Billy's cheeky smile and Tilly's way of looking at you when she's cross. But those two are young and strong, and I will try and help them both get other suitable positions."

But before they had an opportunity to become maudlin, Julia said brightly, "I brought ye back a present from Manchester."

She then went up to her room and returned a few minutes later with a bottle of Scotch whisky. "Well, it's not exactly from Manchester, but sure it was the thought that counts."

She poured out a nip for each of them and then raised her glass.

"To new beginnings, and old friends!"

"God bless us and save us!" Molly raised her glass.

"*Sláinte,*" said Padraic as he downed the contents of his and held it out for another.

The following morning Julia set about re-organising the

photographic studio. Padraic had already brought in her easel, together with her latest painting, *A Family in Need*. She was between appointments, the next being at twelve o'clock. Sadly, she listened to sounds of Padraic and young Ned moving her mother's bed out of her old bedroom on the second floor. A cart was waiting in the yard to take the redundant furniture up to the poorhouse. Most of it was not even worth selling. The parlour furniture, dining-room table and chairs on the first floor had come from her grandfather's house on Dame Street, and they would be stored in an outhouse in the yard until they could be shipped to Manchester as soon as Edward and Harriet moved to a bigger house.

Julia heard the doorbell ring, and a minute later Molly's head popped around the door.

"Mr O'Keefe for you, Miss Julia."

Julia held her breath,

"Mr *Eoin* O'Keefe," Molly clarified, giving Julia a withering look.

"Eoin, do come in!"

He was dressed for business, in an elegant overcoat with matching waistcoat and trousers and a burgundy silk necktie.

"Shall I ask Molly to take your coat?"

"No, thank you – I won't be staying long, I am on my way to the Four Courts."

They sat down.

"First, I want to apologise for my behaviour at our last meeting," he said. "I forgot my manners, Julia."

"Apology accepted," she said with a polite smile.

"Thank you. I got your note and was about to post my reply when I caught a glimpse of you in the window as I was passing. So, I decided, on the spur of the moment, to call in and deliver my reply to you in person. I hope it is not an inconvenient time?"

"No, not at all. I am not expecting my next appointment for another hour."

"Well, I still haven't heard from Donal," he said. "Although I have learned indirectly from a contact I have in the IRB that he is still lying low in Manchester."

"Are you able to get word to him?"

"No, my friend advises against it at the moment. Donal, it seems, is engaged in some mission or other, raising more money to free Fenians, no doubt. My friend strongly advises against any attempt whatsoever to try to contact him. It is an illegal organisation after all and, besides, he is supposedly working undercover."

"I really need to talk to him, Eoin."

"Well, it will have to wait I am afraid, Julia. He will contact me sooner or later I'm sure. Probably when he runs out of money." He paused. "Congratulations on having a painting accepted at the Manchester Art Gallery. That is quite an achievement. Is it one of those pretty flower paintings you do with Lydia?"

"No, not exactly, more what is described as genre painting or scenes from everyday life. Travelling to and from Manchester has made the effects of continuing evictions more real to me. The senseless waste of money going out of the country to absentee landlords in England who care nothing for their tenants' plight, when it could be put to better use here at home. Women and children are starving, conditions are so very poor for many of the Irish in Manchester – it's heart-breaking."

"Social inequality is always difficult to accept, Julia.

But that is the way of the world. Unfortunately, everyone cannot be equal, no matter what these damned Chartists say. Commerce and capital have given us industrial progress that was unthinkable a decade ago. The railways, steam engines, spinning machines, all manner of things."

"Yes, but with all of this progress, why are people still starving, in Ireland and in England as well? Why can the British government not control rents in Ireland and provide emergency sustenance for those who are not able to fend for themselves? Instead, they cart them off to rot in workhouses, or ship them off on famine ships to America, to die of disease, or starvation at sea, before they even get there."

"Why, indeed, a question that has plagued the government in recent years – it's called a free market economy. If we feed people this year, then they will not work to improve things for the next. The market must be allowed to dictate rents, the cost of labour – what is known as supply and demand. If we try and interfere with this natural order, the market will go into free fall and we will all perish." He said this carefully, kindly even, as if he were speaking to a child. "Anyway," he continued in a more light-hearted tone, "neither Donal, nor you, no matter how much you rail against it, are going to change the world."

He turned to look at the painting she had displayed on her easel, *A Family in Need*.

"This is a very fine painting, Julia. But maybe something a little more cheerful might sell better? Forgive me, I am a philistine as you already know!" He smiled at her. "When did you say your exhibition was?"

Julia bit her tongue and smiled back reluctantly. "October, it opens in October."

"Anyway, enough about art and economics. You are moving to Manchester."

"Oh, I will come back to Dublin, but for the foreseeable future I will be moving between here and there."

"Good, I would be sorry not to see you again."

Julia smiled abstractedly. She was agonising as to whether to tell Eoin of Donal's plight, but her instinct told her he would not be quite so accepting if he thought his younger brother was engaged in something far more serious than fundraising.

"Is there anything that I can do to help?"

"No, no, not at all," she said.

He took her hand in his and looked at her with kindness in his eyes.

"Because I would help, you know, in any way that I could."

Julia, confused, drew back her hand.

With that he turned and left the studio.

Chapter 14

Review Day, the City of Manchester
Art Gallery,

October 1876

Although she was apprehensive, there was no doubt in her mind that it was the best thing she had ever painted. *Farewell to Ireland* depicted a young couple on the quays with their meagre belongings around them. The husband, a figure of abject resignation, looked out from the picture directly at the viewer. His young wife seated on the ground beside him, tired and dejected, was leaning on him for support, the infant on her lap clinging to her.

The poignant emigration scene she had portrayed was of a family leaving Ireland to face an uncertain future in America, a scene reminiscent of the Famine of 1845-1849 when families, unable to pay their rent or buy food, were forced to flee the effects of successive poor potato harvests. At that time, the country's staple crop was attacked by a blight that had ravaged the entire country. But, in recent years, due to poor harvests and the continuing struggle for country folk to eke a living, the scene she had depicted was still a daily occurrence.

Standing some distance away from the work, beads of perspiration gathered on Julia's brow and feeling light-headed she steadied herself on her uncle's arm. Unused to such a tightly laced corset, she was finding it hard to breathe. She had borrowed the costume from Harriet for the occasion. Her uncle had insisted she was to dress appropriately – "None of your 'loose women's costumes'," he had said, referring to 'rational dress' favoured by the suffragists. He would hardly have intended any other connotations. But then she never could tell with her uncle.

She looked around the crowded room at the distinguished guests: local dignitaries, mill and factory owners, and the artists' families and friends. This was a private reception before the Academy's annual exhibition was opened the next day to the public. She wished that there were more friendly faces around to support her. Edward had refused to come – he did not approve of the art scene and would not let Harriet come either. Only for the fact that Harriet was so heavily pregnant Julia would have tried to talk her into defying him on this occasion. At least Uncle Charles had made the effort to be here to support her.

Putting these negative thoughts out of her head, she made a conscious effort to absorb the atmosphere. Outside dusk approached, but inside the salon sparkled. Gaslight from Waterford glass chandeliers danced off the edges of the gilt frames, particularly the larger paintings by successful academicians. The oily coal fumes from the fire were cut through with smells of white spirit and newly applied varnish. Some of the artists had only finished touching up their works minutes before the guests were admitted.

She felt the brush of taffeta and satin as determined ladies thrust by her like Bantam hens as they negotiated the crowded room. In the background a string quartet was playing the first Allegro from Mozart's, *Eine kleine Nachtmusik*. But its enchanting melody was drowned out by the sounds of the chattering crowd. The good and the great of Manchester were there this evening in all their finery – intending to see, and to be seen.

Mindful of her social duties, she turned to her uncle.

"I see Lady Derwent is wearing a gown similar to one worn recently by the Duchess of Manchester. I remember seeing it in the *Illustrated London News* last month."

"Pity though, the poor woman doesn't have the chest for it," replied Reverend Charles Benson, leaning in and twitching involuntarily. He then whispered theatrically behind one hand, "And look over there, my dear, at poor old Villiers with his wooden leg. They say that he has a touch of the tarbrush about him. Mother was a bit of a bolter. In fact, there is a question mark over his lineage, and because of this – and his spectacular losses at the horses, they call him Niagara Falls."

Julia laughed. "Poor man! Uncle Charles, you are being unkind, and you a man of the cloth. You should be ashamed of yourself! Although in Lady Derwent's case she deserves it – the old witch has just looked right through me even though I was introduced to her by Isabel Dacre at the Literary Society only last week."

Julia pulled her silk shawl around her shoulders. It was October and despite the large fires burning at either end of the exhibition hall, it was cool. She did not want to stand too close to her painting as she was afraid to hear the general response. But at the same time, she was anxious for critical approval – from the right people, of course. She glanced over at a group who were obviously engaged in heated discussion about her work. It was in quite a prominent position. Although paintings covered the walls from floor to ceiling, hers was at eye level. She had been amazed, considering its subject matter, that it had been accepted at all.

She took a deep breath and guided her uncle across the room, intending to study the painting dispassionately, as if seeing it with new eyes. As they reached their destination a smartly dressed attractive middle-aged man approached them.

"Miss Benson, how are you?" he said with a soft Scottish lilt.

"Mr Nicol, how nice to see you – what a lovely surprise! Let me introduce my uncle, the Reverend Charles Benson, who is visiting us from Dublin."

Charles shook Nicol's hand warmly.

"Uncle Charles, I am sure you have heard of Erskine Nicol. He has painted extensively in Ireland. We had the pleasure to meet a few years ago in Dublin when he gave me some private painting lessons. But, at that time, he was considerably less successful than he is now."

"She was a rather good pupil if I may say so, Reverend, if a little argumentative at times," he said with a wry smile.

"Oh, she was ever thus," replied the Reverend. "A woman who speaks her own mind."

Nicol turned to Julia. "This is a significant change from your previous work, Miss Benson. A new direction, I think. I am extremely impressed with it, and even more so with its underlying intent. It will be interesting to see how it is received this evening by the Manchester industrialists, who despite their own experiences of rags to riches with their fine clothes and fancy houses, for the most part, remain inured to the plight of others less fortunate. What's more, they are totally uncivilised when it comes to understanding the value of art."

Julia laughed. "I hope your opinion of Mancunians is mistaken, but you are very kind, sir, about my work. Yes, I must admit that I anticipate the reaction with some trepidation. Unfortunately, Mr Nicol, I do not have your comic turn, your ability to present this devastating situation cloaked in humour. Although," she turned to her uncle, "Mr Nicol feels as strongly as I do about the suffering this latest famine has caused, and the failure of the British Government to take any meaningful action to alleviate the situation."

"Indeed, sir," said the Reverend, "it is in a sorry state that our country finds itself. I must admit to being shocked at the plight of our people who have fled here. Julia and I walked through the tenements this afternoon in Ancoats where many of the Irish are living. I was horrified to see the level of poverty and disease and appalling living conditions. She showed me instances where there were up to thirty people sharing a room, in filthy courts and windowless tenements. Some were living in flooded basement cellars. Really these people are living hand to mouth in their own filth, with adults and children barely clothed. And the disease that these poor starving divils have brought with them from the ships is rampant. As a doctor and priest, I despair. I pray for their souls. The poor creatures!"

"Unfortunately, Reverend, the city fathers are struggling to accommodate the relentless onslaught. The municipal services are at breaking point and it is hard to see what is to be done – an even more worrying situation with the winter months ahead."

Nicol turned to Julia.

"Hopefully in some way your painting will at least move the hearts and minds of the people of Manchester to pity these poor devils and will encourage them to desist their current persecution and abuse."

"You never know," said Julia without conviction.

Nicol bowed his head and moved away as another couple approached.

"My dear Reverend Benson, how are you keeping?"

"Oh, Mr Montgomery, and Mrs Montgomery! You are looking quite lovely tonight, madam, if I may be so bold. How are you both?"

Julia privately winced at her uncle's gratuitous flattery. Mrs Montgomery looked anything but lovely – striking maybe, with her puce complexion, in a puce gown, and with her usual haughty demeanour.

"Allow me to introduce my talented niece, Miss Julia Benson. She is exhibiting tonight, a very fine painting even if I say so myself.'

"Indeed," said Mr Montgomery looking at Julia with a kindly but patronising eye. "I have just been discussing your work with Mr Muckley, Headmaster of the School of Art. We are both extremely impressed by the painting, Miss Benson."

"The figures, Miss Benson, are they drawn from life?" interposed his wife.

"Indeed, they were, ma'am. My younger sister and her husband who are living here in Manchester kindly modelled for me."

"Your younger – married sister – Miss Benson?"

"Yes, ma'am, my younger sister." Julia smiled, ignoring the jibe.

"Quite accomplished if I might say so," Montgomery continued. "Pleasant style – could remind one of Frith, one of Queen Victoria's favourite artists. Chap paints social scenes, you know, the races and such like. Who was your teacher, might I ask? It is hard to put a finger on your master's style."

"It is my own style, sir," said Julia, her chin tilted. "Although I have been fortunate due to my uncle's generosity to have been taught privately by several well-known artists – some indeed who are here in this room tonight."

Charles beamed at her affectionately. "It is I who am fortunate in having such a gifted niece, and one who shares my cultural interests. I am delighted to be here tonight to celebrate Julia's achievement."

Mrs Montgomery, turtle-necked, leaned forward. "The subject, my dear? Is it not a little unsuitable for a gentlewoman to be flaunting – if I may be so bold as to use the term – her opinions to the world?" Her tight smile failed to soften her intent.

Julia paused, and looked squarely at the woman.

"Although we are the gentler sex, ma'am, it must surely be appropriate – indeed almost a Christian duty – for those who can to highlight the suffering of women and children caused by the political neglect of our government."

"Really, Miss Benson, your intentions are commendable, but in this instance I think you are misguided. Indeed, matters relating to politics are best dealt with by our menfolk whose greater intellect I believe is better equipped than ours to deal with such matters. Come, Montgomery, I see Lady Derwent over there and I promised to …" She turned to find umbrage elsewhere, pulling her embarrassed husband behind her.

They were immediately swallowed by the crowd.

"Do not mind her, Julia. She is a most ungracious old hag, that woman. I have already heard several people commenting favourably on your work."

"Congratulations, Julia."

Julia turned at the familiar voice.

"Eoin, what on earth are you doing here?" she said, startled.

"Maybe it was the notice in the *Freeman's Journal*, and the *Manchester Chronicle* announcing to the world that you were exhibiting at the Institute. I thought you might have been desperate for people to see your work – or afraid that no one would turn up. So being here on business, visiting your brother-in-law amongst others, I thought I had better attend to boost numbers. But I can see from the crowd that my concerns were unwarranted."

"Oh, the advertisements for drawing lessons! I thought that if I mentioned the exhibition that it might give me some credibility." She turned to her uncle, flustered, her cheeks flushed, trying to cover her embarrassment. "Uncle Charles, may I introduce Eoin O'Keefe – he is a family friend from Dublin. I am not sure if you have met before?"

"Yes, of course, we are already acquainted. I remember your father well, and I think I met you first when you were a young feller – in Trinity, wasn't it?"

"Yes, that's right, Reverend, many years ago."

"So – you put an advertisement in the papers," Charles said, turning to Julia. "Good idea, my dear – nothing wrong with a bit of self-promotion."

"I don't know, Uncle Charles, if it was such a good idea. Edward was quite cross, said it wasn't seemly, or ladylike, to be drawing attention to myself."

"But you're an artist, my dear! What is your opinion on the matter, Mr O'Keefe?"

At that moment, Julia was startled as a young lad, scruffily dressed, bumped into her, and then scurried away.

He had pressed a note into her hand. Glancing at the two men, she saw that they were oblivious, having launched into an exchange about women artists.

Pretending to search for her handkerchief in her reticule, she surreptitiously unfurled the piece of paper on which was written:

Meet you on the terrace outside. D.

She was instantly energised, her heart thumping. He's here, she thought, is he insane? He *actually came* to my opening.

"Excuse me, Uncle Charles, Eoin, I need to go to the ladies' cloakroom. There is usually quite a long queue, so I might be a few minutes. Don't worry if I am delayed."

She made her way through the crowd.

As she passed the cloakroom, she glanced around to make sure no one was watching, then exited the hall through the full-height glass terrace doors, pulling her shawl around her against the chill of the evening air.

Out on the terrace, a young couple were engaged in a tête-à-tête. She moved towards the balustrade and looked out over the landscaped garden, but there was no sign of Donal. But then, lurking in the darkness, at the edge of the lawn she saw a shadowy figure. It was him – she was sure. She knew he would not approach with others present. She gave a few small coughs and hoped this would embarrass the couple into leaving. However, so intent were they on each other, they were oblivious to her presence.

She waited for ten long minutes, in silent communication

with the figure in the shadows, until eventually with a wave of his arm he was gone. Disappointed and dejected, she returned to the others.

"Ah, Julia, there you are. Eoin and I were starting to get worried about you. But you look a little pale, my dear – can I fetch you a glass of water?"

"Yes, please, Uncle. Yes, I do feel a little faint."

As soon as her uncle left her side, heading through the crowd towards the refreshments table, she turned to Eoin.

"He was here."

"Who?"

"Donal. In the garden. I placed the advertisement, hoping that he would try and contact me through the Institute. But he came here to the opening. He knew how important it was for me."

Suddenly, the sound of gunshot cracked through the air – one, two, three shots – then a resounding silence as time momentarily stood still. A woman screamed, and then another until the entire room was in an uproar. Midst the cries and confusion policemen armed with batons and guns rushed into the room and proceeded to bar the doors as people, panic-stricken, tried to leave.

The Reverend returned, holding the glass of water. "Someone's been shot outside in the garden."

"Oh my God, Donal!" cried Julia.

The Reverend, horrified, spasmed and dropped the glass so that it shattered at their feet.

"You idiot!" said Eoin, turning to Julia, glaring at her with hatred in his dark-brown eyes. "You vain and foolish woman!"

He stormed off to remonstrate with the policeman standing at the door.

180

∽◡◠

Part Two

Chapter 15

Strangeways Prison

October 1879

Donal watched as a black beetle emerged from underneath his foul-smelling chamber pot and walked brazenly across the red-and-black tiled floor.

Cold to the bone, he had been awake for hours. His chilblained feet were swollen and sore from the treadmill the day before. Drawing the thin, rough blanket about him provided little comfort. It felt scratchy against his neck and smelled rancid and slightly oily – the smell of some other man, some other prisoner.

Strangeways was quiet this morning and Donal savoured the temporary lull before the inmates were roused to perform their morning routine of slopping-out and cell chores.

The sounds of banshee-like wailing that had pierced his brain and kept him from sleeping during the night had stopped suddenly at about three o'clock. Probably because one of the screws had eventually got up off his arse and left his warm stove to deal with the tortured screamer. The episode had left him with a thudding headache.

He looked dispassionately at the marks he'd scratched with the end of his spoon in the soft plaster behind the door. A mark for each day, a block for each month. Three rows of twelve blocks – it was a depressing thought – he had been here three years. As he rubbed his temples, the peace was shattered by sounds of the prison belching to life. Daylight cast slanting shadows through the bars of his high-level window – he reckoned it was just after six. On cue, the warning bell went off. But before the morning circus commenced, he was startled by the sound of a warder's clattering keys and heavy boots climbing the stairs from the level below. He listened apprehensively as the footsteps approached along the steel platform, until eventually they stopped at his door.

"How are yeh doin' there, O'Keefe? It's fresh and well yeh're looking this morning," Feely Flanagan said sarcastically. "Did yeh sleep well?"

The warder's cherubic face was incompletely framed by the flap in the door, focusing on his eyes, nose and mouth. He had obviously false front teeth with thick and fulsome lips like a girl's. Donal imagined what it would be like to kiss them. He shivered, recoiling at the thought. Jesus, he was losing it!

"Flanagan," said Donal, "any news? Who was that kicking up a rumpus last night? What was wrong with the poor fellow?"

"He was looking for his mammy. They all do, you know, before they get the feel of the hangman's noose around their scrawny necks."

"God bless him. What did he do?"

"Well, he moidered his missus then cut her up into smithereens and fed her to his dog."

"God save us! Really?"

"No, yeh thick bastard, the last bit was a joke. But he did moider the missus." Flanagan stepped back as Donal came to the door, and patted his sweaty balding head with a square, fat hand. "Yeh've a visitor today. Yer lawyer, Trench – he got special permission, I believe, from the gov'nor. He's coming this afternoon to see yeh. I'll be bringing yeh and collecting yeh from the visiting cell." He lowered his voice to a whisper. "Mind yeh tell him to slip me a few bob. Twenty should do the trick."

"Jesus, you're a hard man, Flanagan."

"Well, look't, O'Keefe, yeh're in the wrong line of business – there's no money in Fenianism. Did ye hear we have a new house guest? Horatio Nelson, would you believe?"

"Is that another joke?"

"Yeh'd think so, wouldn't yeh? That's what it says on his papers. Horatio Nelson, from Middleton in County Cork. It's an alias, I bet. Yeh might catch a glimpse of him on your way to the treadmill. He's also doin' hard labour. I wouldn't get too friendly – he's a dangerous bastard – a dynamite expert, I believe."

With the sound of the rising bell below, accompanied by a screw bellowing, "*All out, all out!*" Flanagan made a hasty departure. The morning show was about to begin.

Donal started to roll away his mattress and fold his blanket. Thank God, at last he could empty the chamber pot and get rid of the stink. He placed his tin cup and plate, his 'brights', near the door ready for inspection at the line-up that took place on the landing, outside the cell door. He put on his prison uniform over his vest and long johns, motivated by the prospect of being warm at last as the comforting smell of the morning's watery porridge wafted up from the communal eating area below.

Donal met the new inmate sooner than he expected. As the prisoners, like an army of migrating ants, filed down the cascading steel staircases to breakfast, he picked out the Irishman immediately on the opposite landing. He looked normal enough, thought Donal – the ladies would consider him handsome, even in prison uniform. Tall, broad-shouldered, with a languorous gait, like a panther, controlled, ready to pounce. He looked a bit too pretty to be a serious player. He caught Donal watching him and grinned back. Donal nodded curtly in return.

Some hours later, the pains from the chilblains were forgotten. Donal's feet were now numb, and at this stage he was operating automatically. Drawing energy from some unknown inner source, he climbed the steps, twenty-four of them, set eight inches apart. Ratcheting noises of wood and steel were accompanied by groans from the men. There was an overpowering smell of sweat and machine oil. The room was like a scene from Dante's *Inferno*. No one spoke – words had no place here. The sixteen-foot wooden cylinders rotated to the power of the prisoners walking up the steps, encouraged by the frequent lash of a whip that scored the flesh of recalcitrant flaggers. Donal guessed the wheel revolved twice a minute. Every thirteenth revolution the bell rang. Every day he did fifteen quarter-hour sessions, which he reckoned was equivalent to a climb of 18,000 feet. You would think it would make you fit, thought Donal, but instead it only served to break you down. He was conscious that today at least he would get a reprieve, and God he needed it. But it came later than expected. It was not till he had been on and off the wheel for three hours that Flanagan punched him on the ear to get his attention, and then shackled his arms and legs for his meeting with Eoin in the visitors' cell.

Although they had not met for several months, it was obvious to Donal on seeing his brother's black expression that this was not going to be a pleasant visit. They embraced briefly then sat down on either side of the wooden table.

"Jesus, Donal, you look half dead! What in the name of God are you doing to yourself? How can anything be worth this?" Eoin paused, but no answer came. He changed tack. "What's more to the point, am I going to spend my whole bloody life sorting out the messes that you get yourself in?"

"Sorry, Eoin." Donal bent his head.

"Sorry doesn't cut mustard anymore, brother, I am afraid. The reason I am here is that I had a visit from Edward Jenkinson last week, a policeman from Dublin Castle responsible for tracking down Fenian dynamitards. He has promised if you cooperate with him, give him the names of the people you were working with, then he can get your sentence commuted to five years, get you out of hard labour immediately, and have certain privileges restored. Communal work, visitors, things like that."

"There will be none of that, Eoin."

"*You selfish bastard*," Eoin said slowly, teeth clenched, jaw tightened. "Do you realise that while you are in here playing the big fellah that others are suffering as a result?"

"Like who?" replied Donal defensively. "You and Bea

187

carry on as usual. Julia is fine. We write every week. She is well set up, travelling between Dublin and Manchester. I know she misses me, but she understands my duty to the cause."

"Well set up? You idiot, that's what she tells you. Do you not understand women at all, especially women like her? She tells you what she thinks you want to hear, but I would imagine her life is hell at the moment. Although her extreme stupidity and vanity in disregarding my instruction not to contact you undoubtedly led to your arrest, her motives were purely out of concern for you."

He got up from the hard chair and walked to the side of the room where he turned to look at his brother.

"Last week I was talking to Stephen Spendlove – he does the books for Edward, and he told me that things are difficult for them all. Presently they are living in a slum on Shakespeare Street. Julia is sharing a room with one of the other lodgers when she is there. There is very little money. Harriet has been unable to work since the child was born and Julia is doing all the housework. It's a far cry from what she was reared to do."

Donal looked at his brother, aghast. "But the paintings, commissions for portraits, the photography business in Dublin?"

"Putting on a good front for your benefit, brother. The photography business is barely surviving. That French operative is back running it for them – he drinks most of the profits as far as I can see – and they have rented out the rest of the house. But the income barely covers rent and living expenses here in Manchester."

"I had no idea … my poor love. I feel so helpless – what can I do, Eoin?"

"You could try and get yourself out of here, that would be a start. Talk to Jenkinson."

Donal rose to his feet. "You are asking me to betray my friends, and my country. *Never!*" His eyes locked with his brother's, his broken body taut with grim determination.

"Very well, Donal, there is nothing more I can do. I will pay that bastard Flanagan to bring you cigarettes, and some more books. You are not still reading that Danton, that French republican shite, are you? I'll get you something more realistic – maybe you should try reading *Hard Times* by Dickens – he based the town in which it is set, Coketown, on Manchester. Read about real life for a change." Suddenly, his bluster deflated, he looked sadly at his brother. "Donal, you look desperately thin. I hope you are eating. I don't want to be leaving with a coffin the next time."

He came and embraced him, feeling his bony ribs through the rough cotton prison uniform, and smelling the acrid smells emanating from his broken body.

"Things are getting worse at home," Eoin said, voice lowered. He wrapped his hands around the large clove-infused hot whiskey. The snug in the Shakespeare Inn was private, all brass and bees-waxed brown oak, but remote from the warm fire roaring in the public bar. "The country is in the grip of an agricultural depression, prices for farm produce have plummeted and American competition has not helped. All over the country, impoverished tenants of small holdings, are borrowing money from moneylenders, or 'gombeen men', at exorbitant rates that they cannot afford to repay. And, unfortunately, the land – if you can call it that, little more than cabbage plots in some instances – is being taken over by the bigger, better-off farmers who managed to put money by in the good times."

Edward nodded his head knowingly. "There is talk over here that this is no bad thing – it will lead to a consolidation of small holdings and to bigger farms that would be better able to cope with bad harvests in the future. Better for landlords anyway."

"Well, my brother's friends, the Nationalists, don't see it like that. Parnell is becoming a force to reckon with. Against all the odds, he has brokered a deal between Devoy and the American Fenians, and Michael Davitt in the IRB here, to combine forces to support Butt and the Home Rule Party. It's being called 'The New Departure', if you don't mind. Although, if only to manage our own affairs and normalise the market, I am beginning to think that even for Protestant landlords like us Home Rule might not be such a bad thing. Of more concern, Parnell has also been appointed president of the Land League – you know, the organisation founded by Davitt, dedicated it seems to me to the complete overthrow of the landlord system in Ireland. It's a worrying time for us all, with attacks and boycotting of landlords, and burnings being reported every day in the papers. Even my tenants in Wicklow are becoming agitated. I try to be fair – I am understanding to a point – if tenants are ill or have legitimate difficulties and are unable to pay rent. But I cannot afford to be seen as weak. I have a responsibility to my neighbours to preserve the status quo, or anarchy will prevail."

"From what I hear, Eoin, you have a reputation for being a reasonable man." Edward, awkward, coughed and rubbed his sideburns, shuffling in his seat. "That business with the will, Eoin, I never thanked you properly for your advice at the time."

"No need to, Edward. When I need a set of porcelain choppers in my dotage, I'll come to you."

"You will be looked after royally, I promise." He looked at Eoin, grim-faced. "The reason I wanted to talk to you is … it's just, well, things haven't panned out as I expected. We have struggled since we arrived here. The house is a slum – that's why I arranged to meet you here."

"Yes, well, I had heard that things were not easy for you here from Stephen. I met him up at the Law Courts. He told me that Julia is living with you full time since Harriet got ill."

"Yes, the birth took a lot out of her. Julia has been good to Harriet and the little one."

"And to you?"

"Well, we have our moments, but we have come to an understanding."

"She needs a firm hand alright. There is no denying that she is a beautiful woman, but she has wild streak in her. I think that in Donal's absence her living with you is a good solution. That Uncle Charles of theirs is for the birds. I tried to explain my concerns to the old fool and he just kept saying, 'God will look after his own'. I am afraid God is too busy on other fronts at the moment, or so it seems."

"I won't lie to you, Eoin, she's not been easy, a prickly pear if ever there was one. But that's not what I wanted to talk to you about. It's just that things are really getting desperate, financially. I need to move to a better location, to build a practice. I hate to ask but is there any way that you could help … for Julia's sake."

191

Eoin looked irritated at the request. "Edward, I have already been more than generous to you." He paused. "I have just come from Donal in Strangeways and there is no sign of him getting out of there anytime soon. Ghastly place, ever been there?"

"Yes, I do some work for the prison, emergencies mostly, and I look after the officers, give them a good rate."

"So you know how grim it is. Anyway, I told Donal of Julia's situation. I was trying to make him feel guilty. It didn't work unfortunately. That's the trouble with heroes," he said disparagingly. "They don't deal with the inconvenient truth of the social consequences of their actions. But in retrospect, it probably wasn't a good idea. I don't want him doing anything foolish. So, reluctantly, yes, I suppose I will help you. I will give you a loan – at five-per-cent interest, of course."

"Of course."

"How much? Would a thousand cover your expenses?"

"Yes, that is very generous of you, Eoin!"

"One condition."

"Anything," said Edward, trying to contain his elation.

"This is not to go beyond us – no one is to know."

"Understood."

Julia folded the letter from Donal, slipped it into the stack tied with fine red ribbon and placed it in the small trunk under the bed in her sister's bedroom where she kept a few possessions. She had brought over some clothes, although most of her gowns were still in Dublin. Her face, reflected in the mirror, looked drawn. Or was it just age catching up with her? Sitting at Harriet's dressing table, she took the rose face cream her sister had given her for Christmas and smoothed it onto her long neck using the small upward motions she had seen her mother use. It's a pity you cannot blur the ravages of age like you can in a portrait, or a photograph, she thought. She breathed in slowly, admonishing herself. She should be grateful for what she had. Donal was still alive, and Harriet's health was eventually starting to recover, although she hadn't regained enough strength to return to the mill after the birth. Finally, things seemed to have settled down. Still, she ached for Dublin, even after three years. Closing her eyes, she could almost smell the sea, and the heady mixture of seaweed and sewage that wafted up the Liffey on an easterly wind from Dublin Bay – or the whiff of hops from Guinness's brewery on a westerly one. But, more than this, she missed the sway and swagger of the place, of Dubliners, with their easy ways – their gushing praise that would lift the spirits of a heart of stone. In Dublin, thought Julia, happiness was an aspiration – to be constantly fuelled by small acts of kindness and grand theatrical gestures. But, most of all, she missed the cosseted comfort of the life they had lived there.

She still visited, of course, at least once every two months, but it wasn't the same. The house was now rented to strangers who walked its gracious rooms and fell asleep comforted by its timbery night-time creaks. Other people, she thought longingly, woke to the noise of the autumn arrival of the Brent geese on the dewy dawn-fields of Trinity College.

As the architects and solicitors moved in, Padraic and Molly had moved out. They finally asked if they could retire. They wished to live at the dairy with their daughter in the Strawberry Beds on the foothills of the Dublin Mountains. Julia had visited them last summer. Sally had sent the family's trap for her. It had been such a beautiful day. But she felt a moment of shame at the memory. Sally, Molly's daughter, who had been brought up with an aunt, had been so generous and welcoming, even though for all the years the faithful couple had served them Julia hardly knew the woman. Molly's daughter was a stranger to her, no more than a useful topic of conversation to be asked about in passing, a shadowy figure at the edges of their existence.

Julia pushed these maudlin thoughts aside, but they were swiftly replaced by others. Memories flooded back of that fateful exhibition three years ago and Donal's arrest – an event that still caused her stomach to drop with remorse and mortification at her foolish actions. That fateful evening was still the subject of recurring nightmares in which Eoin's cruel condemnation of her loomed large.

But the other disappointment, less important, but disheartening nonetheless, was the lukewarm reception in Manchester of her painting, *Farewell to Ireland.* On reflection, she had rationalised that the art-buying middle-class industrialists were hardly likely to sympathise with Ireland's social issues. Instead, she had to acknowledge that they preferred the tongue-in-cheek images of Irish poverty provided by Erskine Nicol. His cheeky chappies depicted as chancers and raconteurs were a more palatable representation of her countrymen. Not that she blamed him for trivialising Ireland's plight – in fact, she quite admired his style. It was just not her style.

There had been no portrait commissions either. You

couldn't ask a wealthy matron, or her pampered children, to sit for hours in their squalid living room. Cold and damp, Shakespeare Street was little more than a tenement. If only she had the use of camera, or a photographic studio, then posing would not be necessary. But Pierre was back at the helm in Westland Row and with his wages to be met there was little enough money to eat, let alone invest in a new business here. Anyway, even if there was money, Edward hadn't the interest and, to be honest, neither did she anymore. All her initial bravura and determination to make a go of things in Manchester had dissipated. She was physically worn down by the exhaustion of her daily domestic labours and overwhelmed by the desperation of it all. It took all her emotional energy to raise Harriet's spirits. And, if she was honest with herself, if it wasn't for the little one, Eileen, her ray of sunshine, whose innocent smile could lighten up the darkest corners of her soul, she feared she would not have had the strength to keep going.

She had to acknowledge, though, that there had been a few unexpected successes. After exhibiting *Farewell to Ireland,* the following year she had been elected an honorary member of the Royal Hibernian Academy. She was the first woman in Ireland to receive this honour and had anticipated the announcement to be accompanied by a fanfare of glory. At the very least, she had expected the news would be featured widely in all the papers – instead, it was mentioned only briefly in the small advertisements. It was as if the grey men in the academy were trying to slip the news in surreptitiously, under the blanket, as if it were not quite cricket. Her friends, of course, had made a fuss of her. The Gunns had held a dinner in her honour. Louisa and Hubert O'Grady, the playwright, were both there. Still, her nomination was a great honour and she still glowed at the success that it entailed. As well as the acknowledgement from her peers, the title also had a commercial value to her. She no longer needed to go through the selection committee for the annual show, to which she could now submit several works. Although, because of her circumstances, she had not been as productive as she would have liked. She had brought over a small table easel from Dublin and, usually, when the others were out for the day after Sunday service, she had managed to spend the day painting. Although Edward constantly moaned about the smell of white spirits, he was persuaded by the possibility of the extra income and had grudgingly acquiesced. She thought about her last work, *No Home to Go To* – a sad name that reflected these hard times.

To Edward's chagrin and constant taunting, she had made very little money. But she had shown paintings in the Liverpool and Birmingham galleries, one or two, not many really. A modest success, she thought wistfully.

Her thoughts were interrupted by the sound of Harriet's voice.

"Julia, come in here! Edward has some news!"

Julia joined her sister and brother-in-law in the living room. Harriet was sitting in the armchair with the child on her knee. Edward was standing with his back to the window. He was smiling, a rare occurrence these days. He had papers in his hand.

"I have just come from my attorney. Some good news for a change. Firstly, today I received notification from the College of Surgeons that my application to become a

Licentiate Dental Surgeon has been approved. Secondly, I have just signed a new lease on a house on Stockport Road – we will be moving there next week."

"Oh Edward," said Harriet, barely able to contain her delight, "you are absolutely wonderful! Eileen, don't you have the best, cleverest papa in the whole world?"

The small child beamed at her mother's joy.

"That's great news, Edward, I am very pleased for you all," said Julia. She paused, her eyes lowered, "I suppose you will have no more need of me so." Her heart lifted at the possibility.

"Julia, please don't say that!" said Harriet. "I know things haven't been easy. But, to be honest, we need you more than ever, to keep the house running smoothly while I work as Edward's assistant in the surgery, and to help with the little one of course. It will be a while before we can afford domestic help."

"Ah, yes, I see. We'd better start sorting things out so." Julia put her head down to hide her tears from Harriet, as the likelihood of moving home receded further and further into the distance.

Chapter 16

The Literary Society,
Manchester Institute, Mosely Street
1886

"The British should acknowledge the Irish as they truly are, as a separate, ancient civilisation, with a unique heritage," said Isabel valiantly.

She and Julia were standing in the reception area outside the main assembly room, drinking tea, after listening to a rather dreary talk about Maria Edgeworth's novel *Castle Rackrent*.

"If only people thought as you do," said Julia. "Although we are certainly respected in literary and artistic circles. In London, Georges Bernard Shaw has become a giant on the literary scene, and parliamentary reporting at *The Times* and the *Morning Post* has certainly, in recent years, been in the hands of the Irish. There is no doubt that we are influential."

"Yes, and there is also a certain cachet about being Irish – you seem to be able to navigate effortlessly the ranks of the British class system. Even though the popular press presents you as a nation of indolent peasants, within intellectual circles your wit is admired, and there is whiff of danger and scandal about you. They like to think of you as the recalcitrant children of the British Isles, wilful but entertaining at the same time."

"But it is not enough, Isabel, that we are a source of amusement – we need them to respect our need for political self-determination."

"What about your painting, Julia?" asked Isabel, trying to divert her friend. "How is that going?"

"Well, being an Irish artist in Britain carries similar challenges. Despite the success of the late Daniel Maclise and his wonderful paintings in the Houses of Parliament, and the esteem with which John Butler Yeats is held, unfortunately it's hard to get the same level of interest in Irish art here in Manchester from the mill and factory owners."

"Well, Julia, you are not alone in that regard, you know – it's difficult for us all. Most Mancunians cannot afford to buy paintings, and the ones who can don't value their own artists and go to the London Galleries to spend their money. Even our so-called Academy of Fine Art selects London artists over and above local ones for the annual exhibition. John Partington was quoted recently in the newspapers as saying that Manchester's industrialists were not interested in the arts, just obsessed with making money."

"Sorry, Isabel," said Julia. "I am on my high horse today. It is just that I am finding it all such a struggle. I thought that moving to Stockport Road would solve all my problems. The new house is much nicer, there is more space for us all, and now I have a studio at least. Harriet is in better health and is helping Edward in his practice. But I find it hard – I do miss Dublin."

"Why don't you go back? You still have the house in Westland Row."

"It's not that easy. The house is rented, and I am still needed here. Although I don't earn much, I do contribute. I supervise Eileen's lessons in the morning and, although we now have a housemaid, I also do all the cooking. It's a dilemma I constantly struggle with."

"Then there is Donal, of course," said Isabel kindly. "I admire your loyalty, but you have wasted too much of your life already on that man. I am afraid to say it, Julia, but he is a lost cause."

"You are probably right, but then so am I – a lost cause, I mean. I am forty-eight this year, Isabel. Where has time gone?"

"Well, despite your decrepitude you are still able to draw admiring male glances. In fact, to your left, a gentleman with light-brown hair wearing a fawn-coloured coat and yellow necktie, has glanced over at you several times. A handsome man, charming if I am not mistaken from the glint in his eye."

Julia looked over. Although she had not seen him for a few years, she recognised him instantly. She felt her hands sweating as she gripped the handle of her reticule. Prompted by her startled gaze, the man moved over to her side.

"Miss Benson, what a pleasure. I did not know you were a member of the Literary Society."

"Mr Drennan, the pleasure is mutual," she said with a wooden smile. "May I introduce Isabel Dacre?"

"We were just lamenting the fact that although the Irish are welcome for their wit and joie de vivre in England, their culture is not taken as seriously as it should be," said Isabel as Julia, flustered, fidgeted with her bag.

"Ah, ancient patrimony and all of that. I am a practical

man myself. I am more interested in liberty and freedom, for our people to have bread on the table, and to have security of tenure on their land."

"Have the Land Acts not gone a long way to giving some of that protection, Mr Drennan?" asked Isabel.

"Well, let's say they are a small step in the right direction, but we will only be truly free when the fruits of our toil are not exported to absentee landlords who have no interest in improving the living conditions of Irish people."

"Mr Parnell is exerting a huge influence over here, is he not?" Isabel said.

"Indeed he is, but it's too slow. It's taking too long," Drennan replied amiably.

Julia looked warily at Drennan.

"What can be done, Mr Drennan, to support the cause," asked Isabel, "that does not involve violence and destruction? We are all still reeling from the after-effects of the Clan na Gael bombings during the last few years in London. The Tower of London, the House of Commons, railway stations – where is it all going to end?"

"The violence is indeed deplorable," he said, with a grim smile. "That is why it is important to promote a positive image of our country, to try to counteract in some way the damage to our international reputation caused by these outrages. In fact, I am trying to raise interest amongst the business community in having an Irish section in the exhibition planned next year for the Queen's Jubilee here in Manchester. My intention is to promote our crafts and industries, and to showcase our products to our British neighbours. Hopefully, we can attract some investment from British industrialists and get some of that cash extracted by absentee landlords reinvested back home. As a matter of fact, I believe that there is to be an extensive Fine Art Section in the exhibition, with one room dedicated to local artists."

"Well, that is splendid news, Mr Drennan – is it not, Julia?"

But Julia did not get a chance to answer her. Isabel was bustled away by Grace Hunt to meet a shared acquaintance, leaving Julia alone with Drennan.

"Mr Drennan, I admire your industry in promoting Irish manufactures, but I can't help thinking back to our last meeting."

"Yes, indeed, Miss Benson, I remember it well. I did try to warn you. And how is our … friend?"

Julia paused. Choosing her words carefully, she lowered her voice to a whisper. "I have been extremely worried about him for some time. Although his letters are censored, he writes as often as he can. He is unwell, he caught pneumonia – again – and is currently in the prison sick bay. I am concerned about his welfare."

"His situation is not a surprise to me. Ten years at hard labour is enough to grind down the strongest man. It is opportune that I meet you here today. You see, your Mr O'Keefe is very highly regarded and has not been forgotten by his friends. John Devoy was very taken with him, as was General Millen, the American military strategist O'Keefe was working with. Maybe there is something that we can do. There is a guard in the prison, a man named Flanagan, who is sympathetic, I believe – particularly when his palms are greased. Flanagan lives near the prison, but his wife is from your parish and still attends church there every week with her parents. Do you think you could contact her? I believe she works as a quilter in Broughton Mills."

"Why would I do such a thing?"

"Do you want your 'friend' to die in prison, or do you want him to live? It's as simple as that." Drennan's easy smile was gone, his cold eyes looking into hers. "We are going to attempt to free another of the Brothers who is also detained there. So, there is a possibility of also helping Mr O'Keefe at the same time. However, the window of opportunity is limited."

"Mr Drennan, did you come here today with the sole intention of meeting me?"

"I am afraid I did, Miss Benson."

"Who is the other man?"

"A Mr Nelson, Horatio Nelson."

"Is that an alias?"

"No, his mother was from Cork – she obviously had a sense of humour."

Drennan, unsmiling, handed Julia a *carte de visite*. It was blank with no image. A date and a coded message were written on the back.

"Give this to Flanagan directly. No one else."

Julia looked around and slipped it into her reticule. When she looked up, she saw Drennan's back as he left the room.

"Ah, there you are, Isabel!"

The two women resumed their conversation easily.

After a few minutes, Julia asked, "Tell me, do you know a Mrs Flanagan? I believe she is an excellent quilter, and I was thinking of asking her to make one for Harriet, for her new bedroom."

"Yes, I do, but not very well. Her husband is a prison officer at Strangeways and is regular customer at my mother's pub. In fact, he can be found propping up the bar there most evenings. No wonder his wife quilts." She smiled mischievously.

"This is where Papa's patients wait before Mama calls them in for their appointment, Uncle Charles. And this is the surgery." The chubby, fair-haired child showed the Reverend Charles Benson and her Aunt Julia into a large room brightly lit by a south-facing window draped with red damask curtains. In the centre was a black, cast-iron reclining chair with claw feet and red-velvet upholstery – it had all manner of winches and handles and was elongated with a reclining head and footrest. "Look, Uncle Charles, it can go up and down if you press this peddle. Papa lets me sit in it sometimes when he has no patients."

Beside the chair, a red glass spittoon was set out on a small table covered with a white cloth, and on the adjacent wall was a small mahogany cabinet with a large enamel bowl. A floor-to-ceiling glass-fronted, mahogany display cabinet on the opposite wall was filled with blue glass jars of chemicals, marked *Ethanol, Nitrous Oxide, Laudanum* and *Ether*.

"What on earth is this contraption?" asked the Reverend, pointing to a wheeled pulley suspended from the ceiling and attached to the floor with a treadle pump.

"Oh, it's a drill, to make holes in your teeth," said the child.

"It looks like an instrument of torture." The Reverend twitched uncontrollably at the thought.

"Well, some of the people who come here do make the most dreadful noise. Papa got the room made soundproof, so that you cannot hear the noisy ones when they scream. He said last week a man was screaming so much that he had to stuff his ears with cotton wool. But we couldn't hear a thing."

"Oh Eileen! That is not kind – the poor man was probably in dreadful pain. He had an abscess and he refused to take the painkiller your father offered him."

"Well, Papa said he made a terrible racket," said Eileen.

"As you can see, Uncle Charles, Eileen has a mind of her own."

"Just like her Aunt Julia," said Charles, laughing.

"Eileen, why don't you run upstairs and ask Florrie to make your mother a cup of tea. She is doing your father's books in the front room. I will bring Uncle Charles up shortly. I just have some business to discuss with him."

"Very well, Auntie."

With that she ran out of the room and they could hear her small, determined body bounding up the stairs.

"*Walk like a lady, don't run!*" Julia shouted after her.

Charles leaned against the dentist's chair. "Well, my dear, how are you bearing up? I do miss your company, you know. It's so dreary to have to go to all of these art exhibitions without you." He smiled and then said thoughtfully, "That offer is still open, you know, to be my housekeeper."

"I didn't believe you meant it then, and I don't believe you mean it now, not for a second," Julia retorted, laughing. "You would go into a decline without Kitty to fuss over you. Although I have thought about it often enough, that and being a governess. But lately I have come to realise that it's not about choosing freedom but negotiating commitment. And although my situation here is far from being satisfactory, it's the best of a bad lot. I also

205

have certain obligations that I cannot easily dismiss."

"And who is thinking of you, Julia – who is committed to your happiness?"

"Who amongst us is really happy, Uncle Charles? Happiness seems such a selfish thing. Being committed to something, even if your contribution is small, has to be worth something."

The Reverend sat down on the surgical chair which was in a lowered position and swung up his long legs to rest them on the foot cushion.

"How is it here with Edward?"

She shrugged. "It is bearable. But I still curse Papa for making me so beholden to him."

"Indeed, but it has worked out for the best. Things always reach equilibrium of their own accord. I am a firm believer in letting fate take its course. Do you ever see Donal's brother, that O'Keefe fellow?"

"No, and I don't mind if I never see him again," said Julia irritably.

"Ah, because of what he said all those years ago the night Donal was arrested."

"Yes, that and other things subsequently."

"He came to see me, you know, after your father died. He was concerned for your welfare. Offered to find you a position as a governess. I told him I had already failed in that regard."

"A governess. Is that what he thinks of me? How dare he! The man's arrogance knows no bounds."

"Well, my dear, I think that you can probably tell him that in person. Although I do hope you won't." Charles smiled kindly at Julia. "I believe Edward has invited him for Sunday lunch tomorrow in honour of my visit."

"Sunday lunch!" said Julia, horrified. "He never discussed that with me! I must talk to Harriet."

With that, she stormed out of the room, enraged, leaving Charles relaxing in the surgical chair, staring longingly at the bottle of laudanum.

***

Edward had not come in till late the night before, and that morning he had left the house directly after returning from Sunday service at St Clement's, so Julia did not get a chance to speak to him and was still seething. He had only just returned and had gone straight to his bedroom. She had tried to talk to Harriet, but her sister did not really see what her problem was. Eoin was a colleague of Edward's and he had been incredibly good to them, helping to resolve issues regarding their lease in Stockport Road. What was one extra for dinner? They were putting on a show for Uncle Charles anyway.

Julia thought with exasperation that the Reverend was not helping matters. She had been waiting on him hand and foot all morning. Thank God, he was resting now in the front room. He claimed he had a migraine. The guests were due to arrive shortly, and Julia was still in the kitchen with Florrie. Harriet had helped prepare the meal but had gone up stairs to make herself look respectable, and to cajole Eileen into wearing the tartan dress she had made her for Easter.

Julia straightened her cap. There was nothing for it but to try to get through the afternoon as best she could. She had changed her gown earlier and was wearing a long apron to protect it. Florrie would answer the door when he arrived and would show him up to the front room. It would give her some breathing space to tidy herself before the meal. The onion soup was ready, and the lamb was cooked and had been set to rest on top of the range, where some lamb's kidneys were also braising in red wine. Julia had made an apple tart and custard for the dessert, to be followed by some of the madeleines she had made yesterday for Uncle Charles.

The doorbell rang. Where was Florrie? Damn the girl, thought Julia. She had heard her go out to the privy ten minutes before.

"*Harriet, would you get the door please?*" shouted Julia up the stairs.

"*Julia, sorry, I am not quite dressed!*"

The bell rang again, more insistent this time.

"*Damn, damn, damn!*" Julia ran up the basement stairs to the hall and opened the door, conscious that she was red-faced from the heat of the range and still wearing her cap.

Eoin was on the doorstep.

"What a lovely surprise, Julia," he said, smiling, "and how well –"

"Eoin, do come in. I am so sorry no one was available to answer the door. Let me take your coat and hat. Uncle Charles is in the drawing room – I'll take you in." She took his hat and cloak and hung them on the hall stand.

When they reached the drawing-room door, she stood back to let him go ahead of her, but he turned and said sheepishly, "Julia, our last meeting was not on good terms. I spoke harshly and in anger. I deeply regret what I said."

"There is no need to apologise. That was a long time ago and I have forgotten it entirely. Now come in and say hello to Uncle Charles." Julia smiled unconvincingly and opened the door for their guest.

After a glass of red wine, Julia was feeling slightly lightheaded. The meal had been a disaster. The lamb was overcooked, and the pastry in the apple tart that they were currently eating was soggy.

"How is your brother bearing up? I believe that he has pneumonia again," said Edward.

"Yes, his chest is not good. That's why I am over here this week. I received permission to bring a specialist physician into Strangeways to attend to him. Conditions in the sick bay are pretty basic as you could imagine, but he seemed a little better today."

"Is there no chance of a reprieve?" asked Harriet.

"Not even a remote one, I am afraid. The continued violence and intimidation against landlords at home by the Land League mean that the government is increasingly concerned about the Irish situation. This is also being fuelled by a general fear of revolutionary activity across Europe since the assassination of Tsar Alexander in St Petersburg. The shock waves have reached us here in England, I am afraid. There are all kinds of wild rumours and conspiracy theories of plots to assassinate various members of the Royal family, though, I personally think that this is highly unlikely. But after the murder in the Phoenix Park in Dublin three years ago, of the Chief Secretary for Ireland, Lord Frederick Cavendish and the permanent under-secretary, Thomas Henry Burke, people are understandably nervous." He paused. "I think a moral line was crossed by the Fenians with those assassinations, which let's face it were brutal murders. The subsequent bombings on the London underground, Scotland Yard and Whitehall have all contributed to a state of perceived anarchy caused by the Americans in Clan na Gael. And despite their head man Alexander O'Sullivan breaking off links with the IRB, because of their opposition to the terror campaign, no one quite believes that the two organisations are not inextricably linked. Consequently, no one is particularly sympathetic to Donal's case, I am afraid. His only hope is an amnesty if Home Rule is passed. But who knows how many more years that could take? I hope he is still alive to see it."

Julia, shocked to hear Donal's prospects framed so brutally, thought she was going to faint.

"Well, Julia," said Charles, valiantly trying to change the subject, "how is the planning going for this art exhibition for the Queen's Jubilee here in Manchester?"

"Yes, I was talking about it on Friday at the literary society with Isabel Dacre." Julia tried to regain her composure. "We are both hoping to be invited to submit works by the selection committee."

"Have you got a painting prepared, or do you intend to make a new work?" enquired Eoin politely.

"Well, yes, I have just had a painting accepted for this year's RHA exhibition in Dublin that I was hoping to submit for the Jubilee Exhibition. It's called *A Family's Despair* – I had intended it to capture the impact and helplessness of those who are committed to, but not directly involved in, the cause."

"Don't tell me you are seeing sense finally, Julia?" Edward said sarcastically.

"My political views haven't changed," she retorted.

"Regardless of Parnell's constitutional advantage, the recent failure of Gladstone's Home Rule Bill proved that British landlords would have to be dragged kicking and screaming to accept Irish independence and the potential threat to their Irish income."

"I am relieved to hear that you are not getting softer in your old age, Julia," Eoin said without thinking, but he regretted it immediately when he saw the look on her face.

She rose abruptly and rang the bell for Florrie who entered and started collecting the dessert plates.

"Oh, I was wondering was there a second helping of pudding?" asked Charles. "Although the pastry is a little soggy, it is still rather a good tart."

"Certainly, Uncle Charles," said Julia through gritted teeth and cut him another slice.

"It is difficult enough for us here, Julia," Edward said, "trying to build the dental practice and to curry favour with the local community. Whatever you do, please don't attract any more unwelcome attention to us."

Eoin, grim-faced, interjected, "I think Julia's painting, *Farewell to Ireland*, struck the right note. Making a point, highlighting the hardships faced at home, without unduly annoying our Unionist colleagues."

"Thank you, Eoin, for your vote of confidence," said Julia archly.

As Uncle Charles ate his pudding, she remained silent and, while the others chatted, she ignored both men.

Chapter 17

With the gloaming, a black, smoky fog had descended on Manchester. Across the city in Cotham Street Police Station, in a small office in the shadow of the looming walls of Strangeways prison, two men sat either side of a mahogany desk. The oil lamp was burning, and the fire Dodd had lit earlier was now smouldering. They had no more coal. Thank God, thought Dodd, with his back to the fire – he was roasting. Hodge, permanently cold, wrapped his bony fingers around an enamelled cup.

"And the plan of action?" asked Dodd.

"Nowt, for the time being – we are instructed to wait. The informer will be in contact with Jenkinson nearer the time."

"Did the boss give you any hint as to this man's identity?"

"No," said Hodge. "He referred to him only as Albert, although he said that was not his real name."

"And what's Jenkinson role in all of this?"

"The boss said that we report directly to Jenkinson in

Whitehall – he was brought in from Dublin to track the Fenians. He in turn reports directly to Henry Matthews, the Home Secretary and the Prime Minister Lord Salisbury. Jenkinson also works with the Irish Bureau, a Special Branch unit within CID. Since the bastards blew up Scotland Yard, they are onto them like a ton of bricks. You mun make no mistake, he said that this here development is a threat to national security."

Hodge put the cup down and leaned back in his chair, his arms behind his head. He appeared to be thinking things through. He was small-boned, of less than average height and balding, but had a profuse black moustache that sprouted out from under his aquiline nose. His mannerisms were precise, with long well-manicured nails. Flicking through the file on his desk, his very preciseness made Dodd feel like a hairy mammoth, larger and clumsier than usual.

Dodd squirmed in the seat, his trousers straining at his thighs. Under his heavy frock coat he was sweating profusely. But it would be unthinkable to admit this to Hodge.

"All this cloak and dagger stuff, it's unsettling really – bloody Fenians – they have a lot to answer for," said Dodd to break the silence.

"Well, we don't want another Clerkenwell here in Manchester, now do we?"

"Lord, no," replied Dodd. "A cousin o' mine delivered her baby three months ahead of her time. As well as knocking a crater in t'prison wall, it blew down her house, together with the entire street. There were as many babies born, due t'shock as people kilt. A sight I am not soon to forget."

213

"Well, the bombs they are using now are more sophisticated. In Clerkenwell it was gunpowder packed into a barrel. Recent explosions, by that O'Donovan Rossa fellow, have packed dynamite into metal cartridges, or boxes, fused by clockwork devices, or detonated remotely by a pistol shot."

"And the prisoner we are keeping dibs on, the one we arrested with dynamite at his lodgings, Horatio Nelson – bloody comedians these Irish – what 'ole did he crawl outa?"

"He was one of O'Donovan Rossa's men scouting out the terrain for potential sites. O'Donovan Rossa and Devoy have fallen out according to our sources. Always the same with the Irish – if they're not fighting with us, they are fighting with each other."

"Well, sir, it beats rounding up prostitutes and drunkards, I suppose."

"Indeed, but not a word, Dodd – to keep this under wraps is a matter of honour for us. Show the London Peelers a thing or two."

"Very good, sir. Have we any contacts in the prison amongst the screws?"

"A man called Flanagan – he's working with Albert, hand in glove, says the boss."

"Looks like we have it covered so, sir."

"You'd think so, but we can't afford to be cocky with these Irish bastards – you mun keep yer eyes and ears open, and more to the point, Dodd, your gob shut."

On the other side o' the twenty-foot-high wall, the prisoners were settling in for the long night ahead. In the prison sick bay, a guard was seated on a wooden chair by the door. He was snoring gently. Donal slipped his book out from under the lumpen pillow. Unlike the cells, there was an oil lamp here at night that shed enough light that he could just about read. There were only two other patients. One an elderly man who had suffered a mild stroke and slept most of the day. A second, the infamous Horatio Nelson, had been admitted that afternoon with a head injury after an incident with Flanagan. Flanagan had hit him with his truncheon after Nelson had kicked him in the bollocks. Donal had heard the guard warning the matron that she was to accept no truck from him. As the matron, who was built like an Aberdeen Angus, was no Florence Nightingale, Donal thought that the warning was probably unnecessary. Nelson had been sedated and had not moved for most of the afternoon.

Donal's eyes were closing. He was finding it difficult to concentrate on the book, a tedious novel by Trollope that Eoin had brought in for him when he had visited that afternoon with the physician. Donal's breathing was still laboured and he was as weak as a kitten. He had fainted earlier in the day, collapsing on the floor when the doctor got him out of bed for the first time since he had succumbed to this latest bout.

"We meet at last."

"Jesus, Nelson, what the hell are you playing at?" Donal thought he was going to have a heart attack when he saw Nelson crouched beside his bed.

"Don't worry, O'Keefe. Yer man's in the Land of Nod, dreaming of plump nursery maids and pints of Somerset cider."

"But he'll wake."

"He won't. Flanagan arranged to slip a sleeping draft

into his tea. He won't wake till morning. So, we have all night to chat and get to know one another." Nelson spoke with a soft Cork accent. "Move over there." He got into the bed beside Donal. "There's no point in me being frozen – now is there?"

"What the hell are you playing at? What do you want with me? Look, I'm recovering from pneumonia, I'm very weak."

"You're no longer infectious, according to Flanagan. Do you think I'd be here sharing the bed with the likes of you, if I thought you had anything contagious? Relax, will you?"

The two men lay on their backs in the narrow bed, unmoving and staring at the ceiling.

Nelson spoke quietly, a little above a whisper. "I'm here to talk to you. Flanagan has told me that the Brothers are coming to get me out. But they don't want another fiasco like Clerkenwell. It seems they are taking you at the same time."

"Me, what do they want with me after all this time? Who on earth is arranging this?"

"O'Donovan Rossa wants me, and I believe Drennan suggested you for your local knowledge. Millen is co-ordinating the event."

"But how will they do it?"

"Well, that's why I'm here, knucklehead. Two heads are better than one and we have all night to come up with a plan. We have to set up a conduit for messages, and Millen wants that to be through a third party – someone other than Flanagan. He has already had one of his men making an approach to a friend of yours."

"A friend of mine? Who? I don't have any friends in this city."

216

"Well, it seems you have one at least who is willing to help you. A Miss Benson, Julia Benson."

"Julia. You cannot be serious." Donal became agitated and tried to climb out of the bed.

Nelson grabbed him from behind around the throat and forcefully pulled him back, one hand covering his mouth.

"Easy there, boy, easy."

Donal relaxed, and Nelson released his grip.

Donal turned to glare at the Corkman.

"There is no way I would allow her to put herself in any danger."

"I think you're too late, my friend – anyway the decision is not yours to make. I am depending on the lovely Julia as well. I hear she is a good-looking woman but no spring chicken."

217

❦

Chapter 18

Stockport Road
Manchester

Julia folded the pound notes and put them in a small satin pouch that she hid at the bottom of the drawer where she kept her stockings. She had been pleasantly surprised when she had gone to Newton's Gallery that morning and learnt of the unexpected sale of her painting. She had given Mr Newton the work a year ago as a display piece. But, instead of leaving some of her earnings as credit for future framing, she had taken all the money. When she returned home, she refrained from announcing the sale to the family in her usual valedictory fashion. Ordinarily, with the windfall she would treat Harriet and Eileen to some small luxury that Edward's constant scrimping would not allow. The last sale had paid for a weekend in Blackpool for them all. These small acts of defiance represented her attempts at financial independence. She thought back with fury to a few years ago when she had tried to persuade him to give her an allowance from the income from Westland Row, now that his own situation had improved. She would never forget her humiliation during the encounter and his condescending attitude. He had emphasised the fact that she was living there because of his generosity – that she had made a mess of affairs in Westland Row – and that her financial mismanagement had brought great hardship on the family. He reinforced her obligations to Harriet and the hurt she would feel if Julia were to throw their generosity in their faces and "go her own way", as he put it. Despite reasoned argument, he was adamant – he was her financial and moral guardian, a position that had been thrust unwillingly upon him by her father and was his duty, no matter how difficult or unpleasant he found it, to maintain in her best interests. She was, he reminded her, a vulnerable spinster without sufficient means to support herself – a burden which was his duty to shoulder.

Julia had left the encounter feeling trapped and worthless, feelings that had remained with her ever since.

"Julia, did you not hear me calling you? Could you do Eileen's ringlets? She fidgets so much – I just don't have the patience – and I have to help Edward in the surgery in ten minutes."

Julia had been looking forward to a few hours painting in her studio, a rather grandiose name for the small attic box room.

"Very well, Harriet," she replied with forbearance. "Harriet, by the way, do you know of a Mrs Susannah Flanagan – she attends service at St Clement's Church? I understand her parents live in the neighbourhood."

"Yes, I do, of course – they are patients of Edward's – she's a fine needlewoman and makes the most beautiful quilts. Her husband is a prison officer if my memory serves me rightly."

"Could you introduce me to her on Sunday, do you think?"

Harriet's small figure stiffened noticeably.

"Why, Julia?"

"Well, I am quite interested in learning how to quilt. I thought that it would be something to do on long winter evenings."

"Do you think I am a complete idiot, Julia? You hate even sewing on a button. You always got Molly to do your mending. What is the real reason you want to contact this woman?"

Julia cursed inwardly – she should have thought through her approach more carefully. Ever since she was a small child, she had been unable to lie to her sister.

"Harriet, I need to get a note to Donal. I have been told that Flanagan would be a willing messenger."

"Why don't you just write to Donal as you usually do?"

"Well, his letters are read by the prison staff."

"But you are hardly likely to be writing explicit missives at this stage."

Julia was stung at Harriet's response. However, it was not unexpected – her sister who was normally understanding, left her usual generosity at the door when Donal's name was mentioned.

"I need to pass him a private message from someone else."

"Julia, I am sorry – but no. I will not introduce you to Mrs Flanagan. Really, Julia, please think about what you are doing! As I have said a million times, you are wasting your life on Donal. He is never going to be released. The bombings are a disgrace. How many people were killed on the London Underground? What about their families, mothers, children? How can you condone such violence? The whole city of London is in a state of constant fear. Many of our English friends have withdrawn from us lately. It's bad enough being associated with the drunken Irish louts that roam the streets of this city, but it's intolerable when our attempts at building a life here are being sabotaged from within the family. Julia, it's difficult to separate your views from ours, particularly as you never fail to share them, whether people want to hear them or not. Do you know that last week the Ponsonbys moved to a dentist off Piccadilly? Think about us, Julia – for once – instead of getting involved in this foolishness."

Stung, Julia responded heatedly, "Firstly, Harriet, Clan na Gael are responsible for the bombings, the American Fenians – not the IRB. As you know, the IRB are still committed to the ceasefire. Secondly, the bombings had nothing to do with Donal. Although he was initially impressed with the Clan, he now realises that our only hope of success is with Parnell as our leader. Harriet, politics aside, Donal will not last another winter. The treadmill and the conditions that he endures are horrendous."

"So, what are you suggesting? That an attempt will be made to rescue him by the Brothers? You saw what happened at Clerkenwell. If he is mad enough to attempt an escape, and it fails, which it will, he will end up with a hangman's noose around his neck, and this time you might very well be joining him!"

With that she strode out of the bedroom, slamming the door, and Julia heard her determined footsteps heading down the stairs towards Edward.

Julia started counting – she got to a hundred before

Edward came bounding up the stairs and barged in her door.

"It is polite to knock, you know, before you enter a lady's bedroom."

"Harriet just told me about your insane plans!" His eyes were bulging with hatred like a strangled animal's. "You ungrateful bitch! Have you no shame? I cannot believe that you could be so selfish and recklessly wilful. This time you have gone too far, Julia. You will not contact Mrs Flanagan – I absolutely forbid it. And if I hear that you have, make no mistake you will live to regret it!" He banged his fist down on her mother's old dressing table so that the silver brushes hopped off the polished mahogany surface, and a china bon-bon dish that held her earrings fell and smashed into smithereens over the oil-clothed floor.

Julia did not go down to dinner. She told Florrie she had a migraine and asked for a plate of cold cuts from yesterday's Sunday roast to be sent up to her room. Lying on her bed, her head was throbbing. Although the heavy brocade curtains were closed, she could still hear sounds from the street below, and the whistle and clickety-clack of a steam train in the distance. She could not face sitting across the table from Edward, and she was furious with Harriet. She was feeling teary and more than a little sorry for herself. Her life was intolerable. She was the chattel she had always feared she would become, with no life of her own, living in other people's shadows: Harriet's, Edward's and even to a certain extent Donal's. She longed to go home where at least she had her own identity – where her life as an artist was taken seriously – where she had friends, where she was someone. Harriet did not need her as much now that Eileen was older, and anyway it would serve her right, she thought bitterly. If she left, her little sister might appreciate how much she did for her.

But what depressed her so thoroughly was that she knew in her heart she could not leave Donal in this state. She had finally steeled herself to accept the fact that she would have to try and help him escape. What choice did she have? But how would she contact Flanagan now? After the scene earlier, Edward and Harriet would watch her like a hawk. And there would be practical difficulties in contacting Mrs Flanagan if she had no one to make the introduction. Also, since their rise in social status with their move to Stockport Road, Julia rarely left the house unaccompanied. Edward insisted that Florrie go with her, even if she was only going to the butcher's shop a few doors away. It was ridiculous, thought Julia indignantly. Manchester was not Dublin – there were so many women working here that it was common to see them out on their own. But not upper-middle-class women, such as themselves, argued Edward. They had a position to maintain. Julia thought sadly how quickly he had forgotten his friends in Shakespeare Street – Harriet too – they had both made excuses every time that she had suggested the Hunts come and visit them in the new house.

Maybe she should try and contact Flanagan directly. She dismissed the thought as foolish, but then she remembered something Isabel had said. An idea dawned on her, and she smiled to herself – a plan, a crazy possibility began to emerge.

A few hours later, as the clock struck half past ten, the household had wound down for the night. There were no sounds, other than the usual timbery creaks. Edward was probably still in the front room. He had probably imbibed a few glasses of the port that Eoin had brought yesterday and was dozing in front of the fire. She knew Harriet took a draft to help her sleep and had, likely, conked out as soon as her head hit the pillow. The child would be well asleep at this stage. And Florrie, who did not need any medicinal help, was usually exhausted from her day's work. Julia had heard her trudging up the stairs to her attic room over an hour ago.

As soundlessly as possible, Julia rose from her bed, took off her nightgown and pulled on her dressing gown. She opened the door and tip-toed down the three flights of stairs to the basement. Through the kitchen was a scullery where they did the washing. Out of the wickerwork basket of soiled clothes, she took a pair of Edward's trousers and a shirt – and from the pegs on the wall she grabbed a jacket and coat that he used for gardening. She took off her dressing gown and pulled the clothes on. She then took a fine-knit woollen stocking out of her dressing-gown pocket and fitted it over her head, stuffing the hair pinned on top under it as neatly as she could. From a shelf overhead, she took down an old, felt, man's hat with a wide brim and pulled it down tightly over her stockinged head. A pair of thick socks and Florrie's brown leather boots completed the outfit. In the small, cracked mirror on the wall she could only get a glimpse of how she looked. It would have to do.

She threw her dressing gown into the laundry basket. Then, opening the door slowly, she slipped out into the night.

Her heart was pounding. What if she met someone she

knew – or Edward discovered she was missing? Breathing deeply, she tried to calm her nerves and concentrate on the task ahead. She had read the previous week in the *Illustrated London News* about the independent young women who dressed up in men's clothes to go unaccompanied to the theatre, or the opera. She had remarked to her sister on their bravery, but Harriet had been horrified. Imagine what Edward would think, she had said. Indeed, what would the ould straight-arse think if he could see her now, Julia thought with some amusement. But she needed to concentrate – she had business to do.

It was so strange being out at night, alone, walking the streets. The moon was nearly full and glowed through the oily night air, accentuating the biblical effect of the city's night-time sky. As once darkness fell, the black-smoke plumes were transformed into fiery-red fumes emanating from the mouths of the chimneys. They looked like ancient beacons, portals from the gods of an angry underworld. Awed by the sight, she breathed in deeply but, constrained by the bindings she had used to flatten her breasts, she coughed and spluttered as coke and coaldust caught the back of her throat.

She walked briskly, along the dusty pavements, head lowered, between the light and the shadows, staying on the line of the gas lamps. Stockport Road was quiet, apart from a couple of nightsoil men. It was Monday night after all. The men were back at work in the mills today after their Sunday off. The odd straggler and a dog walker passed by without even looking at her. She met no one's eyes.

Two prostitutes, poor creatures, only a few years older

225

than Eileen, hailed her on the corner of Ardwick Green. "Anything stirring, young sir, that we can help you with?" She looked up, but a policeman was approaching, and the two young girls scarpered away giggling, until they were swallowed into the murky darkness.

At Piccadilly Station, by the light of oil lamps, men were loading wooden crates onto a cart headed for the printing works. In the distance, she could see Begley's Mill on nightshift at full throttle, the sound of steam-loom pistons carried on the night air, the glass in the windows shivering with their action. It looked like a giant magic lantern glowing and vibrating in the dark.

Julia began to relax – she had never felt so alive and aware of all her senses.

"Evening, sir," said another policeman on his beat, not even giving her a second glance.

She passed a few lads on their way home from a late shift, laughing and larking about.

Florrie's feet were bigger than hers and, despite the thick socks, the boots were beginning to chaff. But she kept going.

It took her over an hour to walk across the city towards Strangeways' tower, a bastion of control on the city's skyline. Not a familiar spewing chimney, thought Julia, but a threatening presence. Eventually she reached the Ducie Arms, nestled in the shadows of the looming prison walls.

The pub looked quiet enough. Oil lamps were burning inside, and the large glass windows were steamed up with condensation. She had been there many times to visit Isabel, but it looked different at night, slightly seedy.

As she stood outside the bar, a horse-drawn carriage

drew up, the horses skittish, anxious to get home, their breath steaming in the cold night air. The driver hopped down from his seat and opened the door, as two smartly dressed women got out and headed to the side entrance that led to rooms above. Julia's heart stopped – she could hardly breathe with terror as Isabel turned suddenly to look at her. Her friend's face frowned as if in recognition, then puzzled and conscious she was staring, she turned away. Julia paused, catching her breath. Well, if Isabel had not recognised her, no one else was likely to.

Tentatively she opened the brass-handled door.

In the noisy bar, men jostled and joked, smoked and spat. She paused. No one paid her any heed, but the smell of sweaty bodies, tobacco, and sour ale almost made her gag. At the edge of the crowded room two young men were playing cards. She approached them and, in an attempt to deepen her voice, which came out more squeakily than she intended, she asked if either of the gentlemen knew a Mr Feely Flanagan.

"Sure, doesn't everyone know Flanagan? He's the one up at the bar, sitting alone, nursing his porter."

"Thank you," Julia said with a nod.

She pushed her way through the crowd till she was standing beside Flanagan at the bar. She took a pound note out of her pocket and put it down on the counter beside him.

He turned and looked at her. "Are ye buying me a drink, sonny?"

"Indeed and I might, Mr Flanagan," she said, lowering her voice. "But first can we go outside and talk?"

He looked at her and the blurry bloodshot eyes focused. He pocketed the note, then called to the barman.

"The snug, Freddie, is it free?"

"The one at the back is – just for ten minutes, mind – Mr Shouldice is due in shortly."

Flanagan inclined his head and led the way, indicating she should follow.

In the snug, he looked at her closely. "You're older than I first thought."

She acknowledged this remark with a shrug but, not knowing what to say, said nothing.

"Well, what's this all about?" he asked.

"My name is Mark Benson," she said, noticing his yellowed false teeth behind his fulsome lips. "I am a friend of Donal O'Keefe's. Drennan sent me – he told me to give you this."

He looked at the card she gave him and its coded message. "What's it with these fellas and their bloody ciphers! Anything else to give me?" he said menacingly. "Did he give yeh a few bob to wet my whistle?" Suddenly, he grabbed her tightly by the collar.

Choking, she managed to gasp, "No, I don't have much money – this is all I have." She pulled another pound out of her pocket and slipped it on the table.

Picking the note up, he released her.

"It will have to do, but away with yeh – yeh're only drawing attention to me in here."

Julia, with relief, turned to leave.

"Next time tell Drennan to send me a real man. I am not a fancier of lady-boys."

Julia hastily left the premises, nearly knocking down a man with a pint in his hand who turned to hit her but she dodged his sprawling fist.

Terrified by the encounter with Flanagan and despite

the throbbing blisters on her feet, she walked and ran intermittently, all the way home.

When she reached the house on Stockport Road, she cut down the laneway to the back and opened the garden gate. She had left the scullery door open. As it opened to her touch, she felt a sigh of relief. She was home.

But out of nowhere, she was grabbed from the back – one hand covered her mouth, an arm held her neck and pulled her back into the garden.

"You filthy bitch, you have gone too far this time!"

She bit his hand as hard as she could, feeling the taste of blood seep from his salty flesh and he instantly released her. She spun around to face Edward.

"Have you no shame? Look at you – you are nothing more than a slut – a whore in men's clothing. Where have you been?"

Julia, still in shock, said nothing. She turned to try to get back through the door. But he pulled her back, yanking her so hard that she fell into the shrubbery. Leaning over her, he grabbed her by the shirt collar and pulled her to him so that she could see his eyes next to hers, and in his eyes was not just hate and anger but something else. She felt fear liquefy her body.

"Where have you been, you whore! Did you meet Flanagan?"

"No, I did not get to meet Flanagan," she instinctively lied. "But they are going to get Donal out. Then I will be out of your hair for good!"

He pulled her collar again in anger, and with it the shirt ripped open, leaving her bound breasts exposed.

Above, a window opened.

"What's that racket going on!"

"Nothing to worry about, Florrie – I just caught a fox at the bins – go back to bed!"

The window snapped shut.

Seizing the moment, Julia broke away, clutching the torn shirt around her. She ran through the kitchen up the three flights of stairs to her bedroom, locking the door securely behind her.

She lay awake for most of the night, terrified that he might try to get into her room. Until eventually she fell into a restless sleep, writhing, tying her bed linen in knots. Her mind continuously re-enacting what had just happened and trying to figure out how she could escape from Stockport Road.

When she woke in the early hours of the morning, she was determined to leave. She reasoned that currently her entire fortune amounted to five shillings, but it was enough to get a passage to Dublin. Uncle Charles would take her in. Although she knew that she would have to make difficult choices. She also reached a new determination to force Edward to give her some of the income from Westland Row. She realised that the only person who might be willing, indeed able, to help her to achieve this was Eoin. She got out of the bed, lit a candle and sat down at her dressing table to write him a letter.

At five o'clock she heard Florrie trundling down the stairs from the attic above, heading down to the kitchen to light the range before the family rose. Julia dressed quickly. She wrapped cotton bandages around her blistered feet and hid Edward's soiled and ripped clothes at the bottom of the wardrobe.

She left the house, heading towards the post-box on

Stockport Road, just a short distance away. The shops were still closed, shutters drawn except for Kennedy's bakery. Sweet, yeasty smells emanated from the little shop, a hive of industry, with oil lamps blazing and the windows steamed up from the heat from the ovens.

As she reached the red post-box, she heard footsteps running behind her. Just as she was about to post the letter, Edward grabbed it from her hand like a predatory seagull.

"I'll take that." He looked at the address. "Eoin? He won't take any heed of you. He wouldn't believe you. He thinks even less of you than I do. Now let's go home like a good woman. And Julia," he grabbed her firmly by the elbow, "no word of this to your sister. She's not to be upset. She has enough on her plate right now. Did she not tell you that she's with child again? At her age it is an increased risk, and with all the trouble last time we'll need you here for a while more at least."

Julia's heart sank, realising the implications of what he had said.

"And about last night. Your behaviour was totally unacceptable from a respectable Christian woman. I will be watching you like a hawk. If I hear of any more involvement with Flanagan or the Brothers, I will take a whip to you myself to make you see sense, mark my words. But be in no doubt, in the long term I want you gone. I do not wish your immoral behaviour to be corrupting my wife, or my daughter. But right now, I don't want Harriet upset, not at all."

Julia walked beside him, desolate, and they both returned to Stockport Road.

Chapter 19

"Julia, we thought you were not going to be able to make it. I met your brother-in-law – he told me you were indisposed and confined to the house," said Isabel.

"Yes, I was resigned to not coming tonight, but I managed to escape," Julia said, smiling, carefully choosing her words, and thinking about the row she had just had with Edward about coming here to the Literary Society at the Manchester Institute for the evening. In the end, thankfully, Harriet had intervened on her behalf.

"It is such a treat," said Isabel, "is it not, to hear Elizabeth Gaskell speak? She is one of our own. I believe she lives just around the corner from you. Have you read *Mary Barton*? You know it's based on Manchester?"

"Yes, I read it before I came over, to get an idea of the city."

"And was it as bad as you thought?"

"Worse," said Julia, laughing.

"I know you don't mean that," said her friend. "Did

you hear that I have been asked to help Mr Ford Madox Brown with his commission to decorate the dome of the main exhibition hall for the Jubilee Exhibition? I don't know the details of what is expected of me yet. But by all accounts, the exhibition is going to be bigger than anything we have ever seen before in this city. They are starting to build it already up at Belle Vue. There is to be an Irish Section. Remember your Mr Drennan telling us about it? I believe he is one of its promoters. But most importantly there are to be thirteen galleries for Fine Art, with one dedicated to local artists. It's an amazing opportunity for us all. Have you something to submit?"

"Yes, a painting that's being exhibited in Dublin at the moment, but as it is inherently political it is unlikely to be sold. It's called *A Family's Despair* – I must show it to you and see what you think. It's of a husband and wife reading a letter and learning for the first time that their son has been arrested. I am trying to capture the price of violence, and the grief and suffering that the families of those who have sacrificed their lives to the cause must endure. They are victims too. It's my way of making sense of last year's events. I cannot tell you how upset I am at the bombings. To think that innocent people were killed. I do not condone violence at all. I feel sick to the pit of my stomach when I even think about it."

"I know, Julia, we all do."

"You would not believe the number of my friends, other artists, who have politely ignored me since Dynamite Saturday, those attacks on the Tower of London and the House of Commons. People are now suspicious of anyone with an Irish accent. Even though a quarter of the city's population must be Irish, or of Irish descent. I

233

have never been so conscious of being Irish, but for all of the wrong reasons."

"Surely that's a bit harsh, Miss Benson."

The two women jumped apart, startled.

"Mr Drennan, it's very rude to eavesdrop, you know," said Isabel coyly.

"I am sorry if I startled you. I was waiting patiently to intervene, but you were both so engrossed in conversation and I couldn't help overhearing. If I might be so bold, you are both looking very well this evening."

"Why, thank you, Mr Drennan," said Isabel coquettishly.

Julia was not in the mood for Drennan. She was still suffering from aches and pains from her fall and felt emotionally drained after the earlier scene with Edward.

"Will you both excuse me? I need to go to the ladies' cloakroom to powder my nose," she said.

Julia left Isabel, knowing that her friend would be delighted with the opportunity to flirt with the dashing Drennan. But, on leaving the cloakroom, as she approached the anteroom entrance, he was waiting for her.

"Are you avoiding me, Miss Benson?"

"You flatter yourself, Mr Drennan."

"I just wanted to say well done on delivering the message. By all accounts, you looked very fetching as a boy. I didn't know you had it in you. Mr Flanagan was very taken with you. He was asking for a formal introduction."

Julia, flushed with anger, moved to leave.

"Julia, I'm sorry – I am joking. The Brothers were extremely impressed with your actions, your bravery. It has been a great help. So much so that I have another task for you."

"Absolutely not, Mr Drennan!"

"Julia," he said abruptly, "don't raise your voice – you will draw attention to us." He put his hand on her arm and moved closer. "I am afraid you have to. Donal will not last, we have to get him out – *now*. What we need you to do is quite simple. I am going to give you a message and map inscribed in cipher on tissue paper. What I want you to do is bake an apple tart and insert the tissue between two sheets of baking parchment and place it under the pastry base. Make sure to dress the pastry over the plate. I want you to take the tart on Sunday to the prison."

"But Donal is not allowed visitors?"

"No, but Horatio Nelson is. Look, we are going to be called in five minutes to go into the lecture."

Before Julia had time to protest further, taking her right hand in both of his, he slipped her a small, folded sheet about the size of a playing card. "Now, Miss Benson, unfortunately I must go and find my seat."

In Stockport Road, two days later, Edward was still fuming following the row with Julia. He opened a small bottle of laudanum and took a tablet to settle his nerves. As luck would have it, his next patient was Feely Flanagan. He had been a patient of Edward's since Shakespeare Street when he had negotiated a deal with Strangeways to give the prison staff a reduced fee. He had fitted the vain officer with a set of three china teeth after Flanagan's own had been knocked out in an incident with a recalcitrant prisoner a few years before. Since then, because of the heaviness of the teeth, he suffered with bleeding gums which required constant cleaning and treating with spirits.

Harriet showed him in.

235

"Flanagan, good to see you, come in and sit down. How are the teeth?"

"Well, I am gettin' used to them, although I still feel like an ould goat lookin' over a gate. But they are not slipping as much, and the gums have settled down."

"Let's have a look." He turned the ratchet and raised the chair, adjusting the head and footrests until Flanagan was prone.

Edward carefully removed the three china teeth set in a gold plate and fixed with gold wire to his good teeth, recoiling from the foul smell of decayed food trapped beneath. Then he pulled across the dental mirror to give himself a better view of his gum and prodded gently until it drew a little blood. Better to give Flanagan a reason for a return visit.

"Still quite a bit of bleeding there. Now rinse out your mouth, there's a good man." He handed him a glass of spirits and the red glass spittoon. After he had used it, Edward refitted the teeth. He then adjusted the ratchets on the chair until Flanagan was once again in sitting position. Flanagan rubbed his jaw.

"I'll just write a script for some more spirits to rinse out your mouth."

"Right," Flanagan mumbled.

As he wrote, Edward asked, "How are things in Strangeways?"

"Well, I was attacked a few weeks ago by Horatio Nelson, the infamous Clan na Gael dynamitard. The boyo was arrested at Liverpool a few years ago with letters of introduction on him from O'Donovan Rossa, and the names and addresses of known Fenian sympathisers. The eejit was overheard talking about 'infernal machines' and plotting incidents in a local hostelry. The bold Dodd and Hodge arrested him after finding traces of dynamite at his lodgings. Word on the street has it, the Irish Bureau tipped them off. It was quite a coup at the time. Last week the bastard took me unawares, and I am still recovering."

"I am sorry to hear that – your job is indeed a difficult one. But it is reassuring to know you are finding these blackguards. We are all on tenterhooks not knowing when or where the next atrocity will occur. The sooner they are all locked up safely behind bars the better. At least they are well secured in Strangeways. There has never been an escape, I believe, since it opened?"

"No, it's impenetrable. Despite manys have tried, none have succeeded. And your family, Williams, how are they?"

"Well, thank you for asking. My wife is expecting another child. We are rather pleased about it."

"Congratulations! That's great news, a new wee bairn." He paused. "I believe you have a Miss Benson staying with you – a portrait painter I have been told?"

Edward froze. He knew Julia had headed off to meet Flanagan that night, but she had told him she did not actually get to meet him. What if she had lied?

"Yes, we do – my wife's sister. She's a bit of a handful, I must admit, a difficult woman – has a mind of her own."

"Attractive though, I have heard."

"Yes, she is one of those women who makes men do things that they normally wouldn't," Edward retorted with exasperation, then instantly regretted his outburst.

"That's women for yeh, Williams." He looked at him as if he wanted to hear more.

Edward, however, folded the script and put it in an

envelope, his mouth tight-lipped. He handed it to Flanagan.

"A firm hand is what she needs," said Flanagan.

"Indeed, Flanagan."

"If yeh ever need someone to talk some sense into her, give her a bit of a scare I mean, I'm yer man."

"Flanagan, I don't know what you have heard. But be very sure – Julia's political views are not those of the rest of the family. Donal O'Keefe is a friend of hers. He is in Strangeways, as I'm sure you know. I have my hands full trying to keep her away from him."

"Williams, we all know that you're a staunch supporter of Her Majesty's government."

"I should hope I am!"

"Thanks," said Flanagan, waving the envelope. "I will be in touch."

Later that afternoon, Harriet was instructing Julia about the surgery and giving her a demonstration of how the chair was adjusted.

"Please God, Julia, you will only have to help Edward for a month or two during my confinement. I know that this will be difficult for you, but can you try not to kill one another and keep the peace, at least for my sake?" She put her hand on her sister's arm. "I am relying on you to keep things going. I hope that I won't be as bad as last time but it's best to be prepared."

"Harriet, of course, I will behave. I'll bite my tongue and bow and scrape and be ever so biddable," she said bitterly. You will find me so boring that you will be begging me to act normally."

"If only it would be true." Harriet smiled sadly.

"Anyway, please try for me. The anaesthetics are here. We use laudanum for women and children always. But if patients are in terrible pain Edward gives them an injection of cocaine. It is important to sterilise the syringes with phenol, and for added safety Edward insists that they are boiled monthly. If he needs to put patients to sleep, say after an extraction, or if they have had their teeth ground down to make them level, or a filling, we use ether. You wouldn't believe it but there have been a number of deaths recently caused by chloroform, where patients have actually turned black. Although we sometimes have no alternative but to use it, as some big men prove difficult to sedate. On one occasion, one of the prison officers chased poor Edward around the surgery, yelling at him and being quite abusive. Fortunately, the poor man remembered nothing afterwards. This is the famous American drill. It is operated by this foot pump, but you won't have to use it. Although Edward might need you to operate the treadle."

"Harriet, I cannot wait. I don't know how I am going to bear the excitement."

"Oh Julia, it won't be that bad! But that's probably enough training for one day. Come on, let's go upstairs and have a nice cup of tea. Eileen is due home from her elocution lesson shortly."

"Hold on a minute, what's your hurry, Mrs O'Reilly?"

In Strangeways prison, two burly guards, one arm under each of her elbows, dragged the woman from the advancing visitors' queue to a table at the side of the anteroom. She was about thirty, unkempt, wearing a creased and greasy pink gown, and over this a burgundy

239

velvet pelisse. She had blond curly hair and too much rouge. Julia's mother would have described her as blowzy. She had been chatting to another visitor, a darker-haired woman, more refined, attractive.

Julia thought she recognised her. There was something familiar about her, but she could not quite remember from where. Alarmed, she watched as the two guards manhandled the blonde woman then, passing her large handbag to another guard, asked her to go into a cubicle to be searched.

"Now, Mrs Reilly, we can do this the easy way, or the hard way," said a female attendant who came and dragged the woman away protesting.

"Yes have no right, why are yes picking on me? Is it because ye can see I'm a poor and weak creature? Why don't ye give yer woman a work-over?"

With horror Julia saw the woman was pointing at her.

"Take no heed, missus," said the guard monitoring the queue to Julia. "Now what's the name of the prisoner you are visiting?"

"A Mr Nelson."

"Horatio, no less. What's a nice lady like yourself doing involved with the likes of him?"

"I am from the St Clement's Prisoners Relief Association," said Julia primly. "I was given the prisoner's name by the committee. Another lady was to accompany me, but she called off sick at the last minute. I didn't want to disappoint the prisoner."

"Ah, yes, you do good work, you ladies. The scum in here don't deserve it. Still, you'll get your rewards in heaven, no doubt. Been here before?"

"No."

"Well, be careful, missus, especially as you're on your own – they can sometimes be rough, and crude with it. What have you got there?"

Julia lifted the tea towel over her basket.

"It's an apple tart."

"You're Irish?"

"Yes, my brother-in-law Mr Edward Williams is the prison dentist."

"Don't know him, thank God!" He smiled, revealing several missing teeth. "I've no truck with dentists, as you can see. Sorry, missus, for the interrogation, but we have to be careful with your countrymen, cos of those damn Fenians. In you go. Sit down at window number three and the prisoner will be called."

Julia sat down on a wooden chair opposite the window, one of a line of barred openings, with her basket on her knee. She did not have to wait long.

"Miss Benson, nice of you to visit." Nelson sat down, his face pressed close to the barred opening. "Drennan didn't tell me what a pleasure it would be," he said softly. "O'Keefe's a lucky man."

He was handsome, thought Julia, with fair wavy hair and pale grey eyes that smiled knowingly at her, but by God did he seem to know it!

"Mr Nelson, I am glad you are enjoying this, but I am not," she murmured. "Can we stick to the matter in hand? How is Donal, is he any better?"

"Well, he's out of the sick bay at least, but he's still very poorly. The sooner you lot get us out of here the better."

"You are mistaken, Mr Nelson. I am not part of anyone's lot, as you call them. I am only here to help

Donal. Drennan told me to give you the apple tart – there's instructions and a map under the pastry case."

The blonde woman from the queue entered the room and proceeded to engage the guard near the door in heated conversation, chastising him about being searched. As the two argued, the darker-haired woman who had been chatting to the blonde in the queue walked over to the row of windows and, reaching Nelson, with her back to the distracted guard, she brazenly lifted her skirt and pulled out a small pistol from a black lacy garter, which she then shoved through the bars. Nelson took it and swiftly slipped it under his shirt. In what seemed like a seamless move she then sat down on the seat next to Julia to wait for her visitor.

A prisoner sat down.

"Who the fuck are you?" said the prisoner.

"You know who I am, I am the mother of your child, you bastard!" she shouted.

"Guard, I don't know this woman!" the prisoner called to the guard.

"Jesus, guard, may God forgive him!" She started sobbing loudly. "You bastard, you took advantage of a poor Catholic girl!"

"I'll have to ask you to leave, ma'am."

The blonde woman who had been arguing with the guard walked over to stand beside her friend who was still shouting.

"I'll make you acknowledge my poor wee bairn if it's the last thing I do!"

The other woman said, "Come on, Mary, he's not worth it." She took her arm and pulled her out of the room, leaving the prisoner looking totally baffled.

But as she passed Nelson, Mary gave him a huge wink.

Julia, gobsmacked by the scene, turned to Nelson.

"Oh my God, I cannot believe what they just did!"

"That was Gráinne and Emily – Jesus, but they make a great double act."

Julia, horrified, stuttered, "Mr Nelson, I must go – the apple tart …"

"Just give the basket to the guard, Miss Benson – he will search it and hand it over to me this side. Thanks for coming. See you soon, hopefully."

Julia, shaken, got up and gave the basket to the guard.

"This is an apple tart from St Clement's Prisoners Relief Association, for Mr Nelson."

"Very good, missus." He took the tart and returned the basket to her. "You didn't stay long, missus. Mind you, I don't blame you with all these bloody histrionics – it's been better here today than the Grand Pavilion. Better off staying home next time and just saying a few prayers for 'im."

"Next time, maybe I will. Good day, sir."

⌒⌒⌒

Chapter 20

The keys turned in the lock. Donal looked up anxiously. He had heard the six o'clock bell ring about ten minutes ago. The screws were having their supper and it was unusual to have a visitor at this time.

"Nelson!" said Donal. "What the ...?"

"Quick, get the fuck up and dressed. We don't have much time." He was waving a pistol about wildly in one hand, gesticulating for Donal to hurry.

"Jesus, Nelson, where in the name of God did you get the gun?"

"Look, we've no time to chat – just get the hell up."

Donal swung his legs slowly over the side of his mattress. He reached for his prison uniform, gingerly pulling on the trousers and jacket.

"For Christ's sake, O'Keefe, can you not move faster than that!"

"I am going as quickly as I can."

"They are waiting for us outside the wall. We have to

get down to the yard."

"How did you get out of your cell?"

"I bribed Flanagan to bring me some cigarettes as he went down for his tea, and then overpowered him. You should have seen his surprise when he realised that this was for real after our last playacting. I gagged his mouth, handcuffed his hands behind his back and locked him in my cell. He's not a happy man. I broke his false teeth – they were fierce annoying, with his big girl's lips. I was looking forward to smashing them for ages. Look, put an arm around my shoulders and lean on me. We gotta go, now!"

"But, Nelson, I'll never get out of here – if they catch me, I'll hang."

"Jesus, O'Keefe, no fucking melodrama!" Nelson shoved the pistol hard into his ribs, "For the love of God, *move*! I'll kill you if I have to. So you're leaving here dead or alive!"

The two men hobbled across the landing. No one was around and it was eerily quiet. The screws were in their canteen off the main refectory space. The smell of boiled pigs' trotters and cabbage rising up from below permeated the space. They descended the stairs awkwardly, Donal leaning against Nelson, until they were in the refectory space on the ground floor.

"Where to now, genius?" said Donal, catching his breath. He felt cold and clammy even though he could feel his heart pounding.

"Over here, there's a service corridor that leads to a door onto the exercise yard. The boys bribed one of the porters to leave it open for us. Come on, we don't have much time."

They stumbled and ran along the endless corridor until eventually they reached the heavy steel door that led to the yard. Donal held his breath in terror as Nelson eased open the heavy black bolts top and bottom. The deadlocks had been left unlocked as promised.

Once out in the yard, Donal could feel the sulphurous cold night air hit him like a sledgehammer as it cut through the flesh in his lungs. Weak as a kitten, he leant against the prison wall for support, surveying the twenty-foot-high walls surrounding the exercise yard in dismay.

"How the hell are we going to get out of here? What about the watchtower, won't they be able to see us?"

"British propaganda – it's not a watchtower, it's a ventilation tower."

Nelson put two fingers in his mouth and whistled three sharp notes. Three whistles responded. Nelson whistled the same sequence again, then waited.

A sound of a rock being thrown was heard hitting the other side of the wall.

"Shite," said Nelson, whispering. "Come on, men, did none of ye ever throw a sliotar?"

The rock was thrown again and failed a second time to go over the wall. Donal thought he was going to pass out, but on the third attempt it made it. There was a rope tied around the rock. Nelson drew a silver watch out of his pocket and checked the time. "We only have five minutes." He ran over to the weighted rope, to which he could see a rope ladder attached, and pulled it down, until the rungs reached the base of the wall. He then stopped and whistled again. This time four times. Four whistles responded.

"Go on – you go first."

"I don't know whether I have the strength," said Donal.

"You better have the bloody strength! Get up there or I'll put some lead in your arse," said Nelson, once more waving the gun. "I am not leaving you behind to blather about me."

Donal put his foot on the first rung of the ladder, which was counterweighted by men pulling ropes on the other side. Slowly he climbed the rungs, stumbling halfway, but managing to catch his foothold again.

Nelson watched him nervously. "Go on, you bastard!"

Donal looked down, and once more thought he was going to faint. He breathed in deeply and somehow managed to draw strength from somewhere to get to the top, where a figure dressed in black, with extended arms, pulled him up the last few feet to lie across the top of the wall. Nelson climbed up behind him until the three men were perched on top of the wall.

"Mind the glass," said an Irish voice.

Donal looked down – his hands and knees were bleeding from the shards of glass embedded in the wall. Below in the street he could see four men. They had dropped the ropes and were intent on positioning an extended ladder which swayed as its end approached them. Once in position the stranger descended first and indicated to Donal to swing his legs around and put his foot on the ladder as he provided a protective cradle around him. They descended slowly. Once they hit the ground another dark figure bundled Donal into a waiting cab and someone inside wrapped a blanket around him. He watched as Nelson shimmied down effortlessly after him.

"Goodbye, brother – hang in there!" said Nelson gleefully, as he jumped on a bicycle leaning against the wall and cycled off, disappearing into the dark night.

"Let's go!" shouted one of the men as he banged the cab door closed. The horses neighed as the driver's whip startled them, and they proceeded to move at speed down the narrow road that ran along the prison perimeter. Donal, looking out of the window, noticed faces silhouetted by candlelight pressed to glass windows in the houses on the other side of the street. Men with pistols had closed either end of the road where they held up carts and carriages – several terrified people stood watching the drama unfold. But as the driver shouted, they jumped aside to let the carriage pass.

Donal passed out.

When he woke sometime later, Donal was not sure how much time had passed. He was in a small bedroom. Someone had removed his prison uniform and he was wearing a long linen nightshirt. His hands and legs were bandaged. It was daytime – he must have slept through the night. Daylight cast speckled shadows on the woollen blanket, and he could hear the shouts of costermongers from the street outside.

"Ah, you are awake, Mr O'Keefe. My name is Emily, Mrs Emily Wilson." A tall dark-haired young woman with a smiling face had entered the room.

He tried to focus but his vision was blurred.

"Congratulations! You have the dubious achievement of being one of the first men to escape from Strangeways prison. How are you feeling? You are very weak, Mr O'Keefe. You had a terrible, raging fever. You've been out of it for two days. You've been sayin' terrible things – when you're better, I'll tell you what, but I wouldn't want to embarrass you in your present state."

"Oh, I'm so sorry," he said weakly. "Where am I?"

"Oh, I couldn't be telling you that, but you're in a safe place. Mr Nelson was here this morning asking for you."

"Is he here?"

"No, but he's not far away. I'll get a message to him and tell him you are ready to receive visitors. Would you like a bit of a wash, to freshen up?"

He attempted to pull the sheets around him with his bandaged hands.

"Don't worry," she said, pulling the soiled sheets down to reveal his partially bandaged, pale, hairy legs, "there is nothing you have that I haven't seen before. Come on now. Let's get you sorted."

The next time he woke, it was some time in the morning. He seemed to have slept for days. He had some hazy memory of a doctor visiting and applying leeches. His arm was still bandaged but the dressings on his hands, knees and feet had been removed. Rubbing his hands together, he could feel that the bumpy lacerations were healing. Elsewhere in the house, he could hear the soothing murmur of women's voices, and outside the clackety-clack of horses' hooves on cobblestones.

With effort, he sat up in the bed, his breathing still strained. He felt as weak as a kitten. A sudden fit of coughing splattered droplets of phlegm on the bedspread.

"Jesus, O'Keefe, I thought for a while there that I'd wasted my time gettin' you out of Strangeways only for you to die in a more comfortable bed."

"Nelson, where am I?"

"Heaven, boy!"

"It seems like I've been asleep for a week."

"Well, for three days anyways. How are you feeling?"

"A good deal better, thank God, but I am still feeling pretty weak."

"The doctor says you should be up and about in a week or so, provided you get plenty of rest and take the medication. He's calling back to see you on Friday."

"Nelson, I cannot believe what we did. What you did. To have escaped from that hellhole. But I have also been lying awake here wondering, what now?"

"Well, you didn't think that we got you out of there for the good of your health, did you? We have work to do, O'Keefe – that's why I need you to concentrate on getting better."

"What work – what do you mean?"

"All in good time, O'Keefe," said the Corkman mysteriously. "Meanwhile there is a certain lady who is looking to see you – the lovely Miss Benson."

"Julia? Is she here?"

"No – but if the doctor gives you the all-clear on Friday, we will arrange for a visit. But tomorrow we will have another visitor, a Mr Drennan, the man who masterminded our escape – he has something to discuss with the two of us."

The following day at about eleven Emily helped Donal wash and shave and provided him with a crisp linen shirt and a serviceable woollen jacket. The trousers, those of a bigger man than he, were loose around the waist, and he tied the leather belt tightly to cut the slack. But when

Emily showed him his reflection in a looking glass, he was shocked. He looked so thin and wasted.

She left him for a minute then returned with a bath chair.

"What's that for?"

"It's for you. You are probably too weak to walk any distance just yet."

"Nonsense." He got up from where he was seated at the side of the bed and tried to walk towards the door but only managed two steps before collapsing back onto the bed.

"Well, maybe I need it for a few days, just until I get my strength back."

She wheeled him into the hall and then into a back room. He had not realised he was on the ground floor. They entered a parlour where a fire was burning in the grate and Emily positioned him alongside a chaise longue and a wing-backed chair.

Nelson entered with another man, whom Donal had never met before, of medium height, cleanshaven, tanned with light-brown hair. He was neatly dressed in well-tailored dark-brown coat and matching trousers, a crisp, white, round-edged collar and a puce-coloured satin tie.

"Ah, O'Keefe," said Nelson, "it's fresh and well yeh're lookin this morning, and Emily as handsome as ever."

"Away with you, Nelson," said Emily. "Don't tire Donal out now – he's been very ill. Can I get you both a cup of tea?"

"I wouldn't say no, sweetheart," said Nelson.

Drennan smiled and nodded.

"O'Keefe, this is Colm Drennan. The brains behind our operation."

"Pleased to meet you," said Donal. The two men

shook hands. "I suppose I should thank you for getting me out of there – but I am still trying to figure out why. Nelson assures me you are going to enlighten me."

"Well, it's complicated. You are probably not up to speed with recent events. Parnell has been using the fact that he holds the balance of power in the House of Commons to persuade Gladstone to introduce a Home Rule Bill. Unfortunately, not all his colleagues were enamoured with the idea and it split the Liberal party, and ultimately defeated the government. Now Lord Salisbury and the Conservatives are back in power. This has been a crushing defeat for us. Although the boys here in the IRB are still with Parnell and plan to hold true to the truce, our friends in America are less patient and are becoming agitated. The situation is further complicated by the fact that the boys in America can't agree amongst themselves, and since you have been out of circulation there are now four mutually hostile, nationalist groups there: the Fenian Brotherhood, headed by Patrick Cassidy, the United Irishmen by O'Donovan Rossa (who organised the London bombings) and two branches of the Clan na Gael, one headed by Alexander O'Sullivan, and a breakaway group headed by Devoy. Although, officially anyway, they are all committed to support the political route, behind closed doors O'Sullivan, in Clan na Gael, is secretly planning to go back to war. General Millen, their military strategist, is planning some fireworks for the Queen's Jubilee. Although events are centred in London, the planned Exhibition of Arts and Industries here in Manchester has provided us with an unexpected local opportunity to take part in the celebrations, so to speak. You spent some time with Millen on the steamship from the States some years ago. You made an impression, and he remembered that you knew Manchester and thought you could provide local knowledge."

"Well, I cannot say the respect was mutual – he seemed full of guff to me. All talk and no action, not someone I trusted anyway. He was with a sliveen called Cullivan who, I suspect, ratted on me to the police in Manchester. Anyway, that's history – what about Devoy and the Fenians in America – are they involved in this?"

"No, it's a Clan initiative."

"As you know my loyalty is to Davitt and the IRB here," responded Donal with passion. "Although Parnell has suffered a setback, we, or should I say they, still believe the political route is the only way. To have even got a bill to the House of Commons looking for Irish freedom was an incredible achievement, more than has been achieved by the countless battles over the past hundred years."

"That may be so. But some would say that the dynamite activities persuaded Gladstone that ultimately freedom for Ireland was inevitable. As an oppressed nation Ireland could never match British military prowess. But, with the dynamite campaign, we have struck the fear of God across Britain where it hurts them most, not in some remote battlefield, but in their own back yards. But now with the change in government, it will be years before Parnell gets an opportunity to introduce another Home Rule Bill – and with the Unionists in the north of Ireland becoming mobilised against a United Ireland, the possibility is looking even more remote. We are talking about political targets here, O'Keefe – no one will get hurt."

"People always get hurt."

"And what about our own people dying of starvation and disease?" said Drennan angrily. "Our problem is we are too soft. Look at France and Russia. Where else in the world would a nation stand by idly, and watch, while thousands of their people die en masse from starvation – while their harvests are exported to another country – and they not raise a hand to their oppressors! Only in Holy Catholic Ireland, the Land of Saints and Scholars!" He paused. "We need you, O'Keefe. I am only a blow-in. I don't know the lie of the land here in Manchester, and Nelson here is all brawn and no brain."

"Thanks, Drennan," said Nelson, peeved.

"And Devoy and the IRB?" asked Donal.

"They are not to know. This is being run by Millen – he keeps a tight ship."

"I am sorry, Drennan, but my time in prison has made me think about what is important to me. I am not a young man anymore. Too much time has passed. It's time I sorted out my own life. I have responsibilities to my family."

"This is not an invitation, O'Keefe. It's payback."

"I really do not want to get –"

"Involved? But you are already. O'Keefe, listen to me. The lovely Julia is now implicated, helping to assist a prisoner's escape. How long would she get for that? Mind you, she'd look good in a prison uniform. But they'd chop off her lovely red hair." He paused then faced Donal with a menacing expression. "If you walk, O'Keefe, there will be consequences. Be under no illusions – the Clan has a long memory. And if you were rearrested you would be hung, I'd say. Wouldn't you agree, Nelson?"

"Bloody sure!"

"Where would the lovely Julia be then, O'Keefe? Think about it. But don't take too long – we have work to do. I'll be back tomorrow. *Slán!*"

"It's in all of the papers. 'Daring Escape by Fenian Prisoners.' The *Manchester Star's* article is entitled, 'The Luck of the Irish'." Harriet, still in bed, put down the newspaper and looked in horror at her sister who was seated at the dressing table. "Julia, I beg of you, tell me that you had nothing to do with this!"

"You overestimate my abilities and my opportunity to be involved in such adventures. For me to even go to the butcher's these days unchaperoned is a step towards female emancipation."

"Nonsense, Julia, Edward is just concerned for you. But how do you think they got the gun? The paper seems to think that there was some inside involvement, that one of the guards was bribed, or blackmailed, into helping them."

"Who knows? But at least Donal is out of that hellhole. He was at death's door by all accounts – hopefully now he will get the medical attention he needs."

"Julia, have you thought about what you would do if he tries to contact you."

"I have been thinking of nothing else."

"But you cannot, you simply cannot, get involved," Harriet said, alarmed at her sister's words. "Julia, we have so much to lose. We have only just got our lives back on track, and some semblance of security. With the little one on the way, I beg you, please do not get involved."

"How can you ask me this, Harriet? Seriously? I must

see him. I have been ill with worry for the last six months, thinking that the next time I would see him would be in a morgue." She paused, appealing to her sister's better nature. "Harriet, my life went on hold after Donal was arrested all those years ago, an event for which I still feel responsible. Since then, I have been living in a suspended state, beholden to you and Edward. Do you know what it feels like to live in the shadows of the lives of others, not to feel truly loved?"

"But we love you, Julia."

"Do you, Harriet? Do you really?" said Julia wearily. "Do you love me, or is it that you need me? If you loved me, would you have allowed Edward to take my birth right, my income and to hold me to you with ties of dependence and obligation?"

"Julia, that is totally unfair of you! How can you drag that up again, after all these years? Those were Papa's wishes. And typical of you to see things purely from your own perspective. I have given you a home and shared my family with you. Papa was right – you are impossible. So, what will happen now? Will you see him?" Harriet was white with fury.

"Yes, of course I will, and if you want me to stay until after you have had the baby, you will say nothing to Edward. Otherwise, I will leave, and go home to Uncle Charles. I have had enough."

"But Julia!" Harriet, trying to control her rage, softened her voice and pleaded with her sister. "Be sensible. You have not seen Donal for ten years. You have both changed, you have both got older. You are now a middle-aged woman. Donal has spent most of that time in prison. By all accounts he is broken and not the man you fell in love with all those years ago. To continue to commit yourself to someone under these circumstances is foolhardy."

"Do you think that I have not thought of all this?" Julia looked at her face in the mirror, smoothing the crow's feet at her temples, noting her hair peppered with grey. "Yes, you are right in what you say. But inside, Harriet, I am the same person. I feel the same, I feel the same about Donal. I still feel my pulse race when I think about him. I feel the same desire."

"Oh, for God's sake, Julia! This is not a Jane Austen novel. You will become his nurse, not his lover. You will be swapping one set of dependencies for another."

"Harriet, have you no heart? Does Edward not stir passion in your soul?"

"Absolutely not. He is a good man. We are comfortable together – happy, what with the new baby arriving," she patted her expanding waistline, "and Eileen, as you know, is the light of my life."

"Well, I suppose that's it in a nutshell, Harriet. Donal is the light of mine."

⌒∽⊃⌒∼

Chapter 21

Dodd twiddled with the buttons on his jacket – he must get the missus to let out the one at his waist – it was getting too tight for comfort. He took his watch out of his pocket – where was Hodge? He was always on time, and he had said that it was urgent. He must be getting a right bollocking from them upstairs. The newspapers and reams of paperwork on his normally pristine desk represented the gravity of the situation, and the scale of the official response to yesterday's events. Afraid even to look at them, he sat straight-backed in the chair and tried to relax.

Eventually Hodge came in, red-faced and flustered, sat down at his desk and started nervously fingering his tufted moustache, beads of sweat glistened on his shiny pate.

"Bad day, Dodd – bad day. I've just met with the Superintendent and the head of the CID from London – the Governor of Strangeways was there too. The Super was livid. He's had Jenkinson from the Irish bureau in Whitehall breathing fire down his neck. This is extremely embarrassing for the government – Strangeways was supposed to be bloody airtight. How the hell could this have happened? The Queen has even sent a letter to Lord Salisbury, asking what the police in Manchester were doing to let those dangerous villains escape."

"Have you any more of t' details, inspector?" asked Dodd anxiously.

"No, very little. They think it was a Clan na Gael initiative – our spies in the IRB had no knowledge of it. The two men were not really that important, by all accounts. They had both been in prison for several years. If anything, they were out of the mainstream, and what's even more baffling is that O'Keefe is a basket case – he's recovering from pneumonia. It's all a bit of a mystery."

"How did the' do it?"

"Well, as you have undoubtedly read in the papers at this stage, Nelson overcame that fool Flanagan and snatched his keys. He had a gun, which turned out to be fake. CID think it was smuggled in with the officer's linen by some Fenian sympathisers. That's the problem in this city, the bloody Irish are everywhere."

"I sometimes wonder if my own wife isn't a Fenian sympathiser, inspector – her mother's family were –"

"I don't want to know, Dodd."

"Sorry, inspector. So, what mun we do?"

"Well, the Superintendent has ordered a search of all known Fenian sympathisers in the city. Jenkinson's spies are watching the railway stations and the ports. I must go up to Whitehall tomorrow, to be briefed by him about some new development. But, before I go, I wanted to warn you that I have given your name to Albert, Jenkinson's spy. Just in case he needs to contact you. If he does, send me a telegram immediately."

"Yes, sir," said Dodd.

"And one other thing, Dodd. I want you to follow – discreetly, of course – a Miss Julia Benson. She visited Nelson a few days before the escape, said she was from St Clement's Prisoners Relief Association. See if you can check her out. She is an artist, quite vocal in her political opinions, I have been told. But, Dodd …" He paused.

"Yes, sir."

"As I have said, be discreet."

"Isabel, I cannot tell you how much I appreciate your visit today. I know how busy you are with the commission. How is it going? I believe you are working day and night."

"Yes, it's been an experience I am not likely to forget, ever!" She laughed.

"Here, let me take your coat and bonnet," said Julia, thinking her friend did indeed look tired and wan. "Come into the parlour and tell me what it has been like working with the great Ford Madox Brown. He's in our parish, you know – I was introduced to him recently – he seems quite a nice gentleman."

Julia led her into the parlour and rang a handbell for Florrie to bring in some tea.

"To be honest, it's been a nightmare," Isabel said. "Mr Brown is painting figures for panels on the underside of the dome which is the centrepiece of the main exhibition hall. The dome itself is 150 feet high and 90 feet wide. The panels are huge, eight pieces, each 36 feet long by 18 feet deep. They are intended to represent Manchester's industries: Wool, Corn, Shipping, Commerce, Coal, Iron, Weaving and Spinning. The problem was that there was no prepared canvas available anywhere in the country of that size within the time frame. Eventually he found a floor-cloth manufacturer in Dundee who supplied sail cloth, but it was so rough that a coach painter from Altrincham had to prime and prepare it first. And because of the huge sizes of the pieces, Mr Brown had to convert his stable and carriage house into a studio to undertake the work. Of course, he could not do it alone within the time required, so he invited Bruce Wallis of the academy, Knewstub an assistant, and three other ladies as well as myself to help. Together we make quite a merry team. But it's exhausting work climbing up and down those ladders, and it's so hard to judge perspectives at that size. To give you an idea of how difficult it is, the wings of the angels in the curved corners are 12-foot long. I'll never offer to do something like this again. I am so looking forward to seeing it completed and getting back to my normal life again."

"That sounds so exciting, Isabel. I am almost embarrassed to show you my poor little studio – it's more of a nest really!" Julia laughed. "While we are waiting for Florrie to make the tea, let's go and look at the painting, it won't take a minute."

They reached the second floor and entered the room. It was north-facing with one window. The opposite wall was fitted out with shelves, stacked tidily with books and jars of brushes, pencils and boxes of paints. At the end of the shelves, a small wardrobe with the doors removed held stacks of canvases, and on the other wall was a small worktable adjacent to the easel.

Isabel's eyes were drawn to the painting on the easel which was positioned facing the window to catch the best of the poor light.

"It's called *A Family's Despair – A Letter from H. M.'s Prison*," said Julia. "In Dublin everyone was trying to pin it on a specific arrest. But, to be honest, it isn't any one in particular. The painting is just trying to capture the helplessness and desperation of the families of rebels who are living in constant fear of what is to come."

The painting depicted a man, sitting at a kitchen table with a letter in his hands, staring ahead. His expression was one of utter desperation. The woman seated beside him, was distraught, her head bent over the table crying into her hands, hiding her tears. Nearby, a gun leaned against the wall and a small child, oblivious to unfolding events, played on the floor. On the wall behind them, subtly highlighted and beautifully painted in miniature, was a poster of the Manchester Martyrs. The three men were painted within a trefoil with St Patrick on one side and Erin on the other and surrounded by other nationalist imagery such as harps, an Irish wolfhound, and a Celtic cross.

"Uncle Charles just brought it back from Dublin for me. To be honest, I didn't expect it to sell at the RHA. I am afraid it got mixed reviews. The critic from the *Freeman's Journal* said, it was decidedly clever, though not of a high order of merit. I also submitted it to the selection committee in this year's Fine Art exhibition here in Manchester, but it was rejected. To be honest, I was not surprised. But I was hoping to submit it to the Jubilee Exhibition. What do you think?"

Isabel, standing back as far as it was possible in the cramped space, silently considered the work.

"I agree with the *Freeman's Journal*, in that it is clever," she said, after what seemed like an age, "but I think they were unkind about its merit. I think it is very nicely painted. Who modelled for you?"

"Well, as you know, I can't afford the luxury of models. The male figure is based on Edward. I sketched him in the evenings reading his newspaper. He wasn't very pleased, but as Harriet usually sits with him, he couldn't complain. And the woman is Florrie. I suppose in some way it reflects my own feelings of helplessness."

"Julia, God knows you have had more trouble than most," said Isabel kindly, "and I understand where you are coming from, or at least I think that I do. There is no doubt that it is a fine painting. But I would be very surprised if it is accepted by the selection committee. They will probably be advised by the Academy, and you know how conservative they are! Even though they have reluctantly accepted that women are capable of painting more than flowers and fairies, a painting like this with such obvious political implications would be a step too far. Why even the gentlemen would not attempt something quite so radical. When you consider the Manchester artists who have experimented with Impressionism are only now, reluctantly, ten years on, being given their due regard by the critics. I am sorry, Julia, but you must know yourself that this is not going to be accepted under any circumstances. I mean, their Royal Highnesses, the Prince and Princess of Wales, are to attend. This event is meant to be a celebration – no one will brook this type of political criticism."

Julia sighed. "I know, Isabel, I thought as much. Thank you for your honesty, but I wanted to show it to you anyway. I will probably still submit it though on principle."

Isabel placed her hand on Julia's arm.

"It's an incredible achievement, Julia," she said kindly. "Particularly since I know that Edward forbids you to attend life drawing classes. Your figure drawing is very skilful. I am impressed."

"Well, I have had more practice than you think. I used to organise classes with a model in Dublin myself, in my days of freedom."

Isabel looked at Julia sadly.

"Such a pity you couldn't join us on our trip to Rome – you would have enjoyed it so much. The light there, Julia! I don't know how you can even paint in this gloomy room. I have a new studio in South King Street that I am sharing with Mary Monkhouse. Anytime you want to join us you would be more than welcome."

"Thank you, Isabel. Now we'd better go back downstairs – our tea will be getting cold."

Isabel smiled. "Julia, why can't you just paint flowers and fairies like other women!"

$\backsim \!\! \propto \!\! \curvearrowright$

Chapter 22

12th April 1887

"Julia, one of my patients, who is downstairs in the surgery, saw your cards in the hall and asked if you could paint his sister's portrait. He wants it as a birthday present. She's incapacitated though, and you would have to go to his house. Could you come down and talk to him? He said he had met you before at the Literary Society."

"Certainly," Julia replied curtly to Edward – when Harriet wasn't around, they didn't bother much with social niceties.

She followed him down to the surgery.

"Mr Drennan, this is my sister-in-law, Miss Julia Benson."

"Miss Benson, lovely to meet you again."

"Mr Drennan, what a surprise! I didn't realise you were a patient here." Julia's pulse was racing in anticipation of news of Donal and, smiling, she forced herself to overcome her usual dislike of the man.

"No, this is my first visit, and following the thorough check-up I have just had, I reckon I am in safe hands. Has Mr Williams told you of my predicament?"

"Yes, he has indeed. I am so sorry to hear of your sister's ill health. But what a lovely present for her, and what a delightful opportunity for me to meet her."

"Yes, I think you will enjoy her company. She's very well read, a great fan of Emily Bronte's poems. I think that you would get on famously. It will also keep her amused – lately I am spending so much time at committee meetings organising the Jubilee Exhibition that she is quite cross with me."

"I am sure you do her a disservice – she surely knows it's such a good cause," said Edward. "Maybe you could discuss terms with Mr Drennan when you have had a chance to think about what is involved, Julia."

Julia smiled thinly at Edward's patronising tone.

"Yes, that would be a sensible approach, Miss Benson. But in the meantime, may I send my sister's companion, a Miss O'Reilly, around tomorrow to bring you to our home? We live in Granville Street."

"Ah, yes, I know where that is – an acquaintance of mine used to live there, although it is many years since I met her. I think she moved on."

"Really, I don't know many of the neighbours. I travel a great deal on business, you know. Could we say ten o'clock in the morning?"

"Perfect."

"Well then, I will take my leave of you both. Good day, Miss Benson, and you too, Mr Williams."

He picked up his coat, hat and silver-topped cane and left.

"Well dressed, must have a few bob – told me that he was a gas engineer."

"Really," said Julia sarcastically.

Julia had dressed carefully. After considering various outfits, she chose the dark-blue wool costume with the black lace trimming that she kept for special occasions. She knew it set off her hair, which she had washed and styled into a loose chignon, a style she knew he liked. Her make-up was artfully applied, a touch of black crayon to enhance her eyes, tinted beeswax on her lips and the faintest dusting of rouge. Thinking her décolleté was a little low for daytime, she pulled a black lace scarf around her neck and pinned it in place with a blue Wedgwood cameo brooch belonging to her mother.

She had hardly slept the night before. Was she mistaken to think she was being summoned to meet Donal? Perhaps Drennan wanted to see her for another purpose? Or just to give her some news of Donal, good or bad? But his demeanour has not suggested any bad news. There was no tension about him, and her every instinct told her that she was at last to see Donal again, after all these years. And, if she did, how would it be? Would his time in prison have damaged him profoundly? Would he still want her after all this time? Would her feelings be the same when she saw him in the flesh – no longer the vibrant hero of her dreams, but broken, aged, a victim of his life's harsh reality?

She applied a little more powder under her eyes to hide the shadows.

There was a knock on Julia's door and Florrie stuck her head in.

267

"Miss Gráinne O'Reilly for you, Miss Julia – says she has an appointment."

Just then the clock struck ten. She was punctual.

"Thank you, Florrie. Yes, Gráinne is taking me around to meet her mistress in Granville Street. I'll get my pelisse and my sketchbook – tell her I'll be down in a minute."

When Julia saw the woman, she was momentarily taken aback – it was the blonde woman who had caused all the fuss when she had visited Nelson in Strangeways.

Grainne grinned and winked as they shook hands. "Pleased to meet you, Miss Benson."

The exuberant Gráinne chatted away to Julia as they walked to Granville Street.

"It was such a lark, Miss Benson – did you see your man's face when Emily told him he was the father of her child?"

"You should both be on the stage, Gráinne. I must admit you fooled me."

Another surprise awaited Julia as Gráinne's accomplice answered the door. She now recognised her. It was Emily Wilson.

"How lovely to see you again, Miss Benson."

"Gráinne and I were just discussing last week in Strangeways, Mrs Wilson. That was quite a performance."

"Well, it was all for a good cause – and I hope it hasn't given you a bad impression of me," she said, her eyes twinkling.

"No, not at all," replied Julia, thinking about her own recent exploits with some embarrassment.

"There is someone here who is very anxious to meet you," said Emily, smiling, as Gráinne took Julia's cloak and bonnet. "Could you get Miss Benson some tea, please, Gráinne?"

She showed Julia into the parlour and invited her to take a seat.

"I'll go and see if Mr O'Keefe is ready."

So, it was to be. Julia sat, suddenly feeling faint.

Emily left, and Julia waited, almost overwhelmed with tension.

"Julia, my darling!"

After what seemed like an age, Donal was standing at the door, leaning on a walking stick for support. Tears were running down his drawn and haggard face. Aged beyond his years, his once thick brown, wavy hair had greyed and thinned, and his eyes were shadowed, smudged purple, and sunken in his skull. He hobbled into the room to greet her.

She embraced his scrawny frame, feeling the bony ribs of his chest. Until, afraid she was going to crush him, she released him, and he stumbled into the chair beside her. Leaning over, he took her hand – she could see the shame in his eyes as he tried to gauge her reaction to his appearance as he absorbed hers.

"How well you look, Julia, you have not aged a bit, only mellowed. In fact, you look more beautiful than ever. You must be shocked at the state of me, a bag of rags and bones." He was smiling, but she could see that he was anxiously awaiting her response.

"You are so frail, my darling! I am shocked, I cannot deny it. But to see you after all these years – you have no idea how this has eased my heart. A day has not passed that I have not thought about you, my love, and how much I regret my foolish actions."

"Hush, Julia, it was nothing to do with you. I was being followed. If not there at the gallery, they would have got me somewhere else. Manchester is a hotbed of spies willing to sell their souls for a shilling. Let's not dwell on the past. It is so good to see you again, my love."

"Oh Donal, I cannot believe that you are here beside me, that at last you are free!"

He let her hand go abruptly and turned away from her.

"Except I am not free. Drennan has plans for me – for us."

"Drennan," said Julia distastefully. "I dislike and distrust that man."

"I am not sure that I trust anyone anymore." Donal looked out of the window, his eyes dull and unfocused.

"What plans, my darling?" She took his hands in hers again, forcing him to look at her.

"Drennan seems to be acting on instruction from O'Sullivan who I have been told is increasingly frustrated by Parnell's lack of success. The man who was released with me, Nelson, a dynamite expert, is also Clan na Gael. And according to Drennan, their boss O'Sullivan is planning an initiative, a dynamite attack to take place here in Manchester, but I don't have the details yet."

"Donal, tell him to go to hell! Tell him that you will have nothing to do with their evil actions!" Julia jumped up and paced around the floor.

"It's not as simple as that, my darling. I am a wanted felon – if I were recaptured, I would most certainly be hanged. The embarrassment caused by our escape from Strangeways to the government will have to be assuaged by the authorities. And if I don't cooperate with their plans, I fear Clan na Gael may execute me themselves – what other choice would they have? I know them and could identify them."

"Oh, my love! What are you going to do?"

"Well, Julia, I am damned if I do, and damned if I don't. I need time to think about this."

"Tea!" Emily barged into the room laden with a tray.

Julia was fairly sure she had been listening at the door."

Chapter 23

18th April

It had been unseasonably hot weather followed by two days of heavy rain, and a black gritty smog clung over the city. In the Salutations Public House, a tavern close to the university on Oxford Road normally habituated by impoverished students, two men sat in the snug. They were huddled together deep in conversation, drinking the tavern's finest whiskey, being attended to, obsequiously, by Briggs the ferret-faced and pockmarked barman.

After inspecting them carefully, Briggs had considered they represented the evening's best chance of a good tip. Both men were middle-aged. One was smartly dressed, cleanshaven, a city type with a satin top hat that he had refused to give to the barman but had kept beside him, and a coat that was cut in a fine, dark-grey material. He had a stiff, white, linen collar and a sapphire-blue silk tie fixed with a gold pin. Although to Brigg's ear, which was well tuned in these matters, his clothes didn't really match his accent, which wasn't quite as la-di-da as his appearance suggested. His companion, conservative, and without the style of the other man, was unquestionably middle-class, had long sideburns but he hadn't heard him speak. A quiet cove, thought Briggs.

"Is your honour alright fer everything? Is there owt else I can get ye? Some pigs' trotters mebe, or a few jellied eels?"

"We are fine, my good man – all we want is some privacy."

"Certainly, sir, your honour."

Jenkinson took out a small ebony pipe and proceeded to fill it with tobacco from a silver box with a crest emblazoned on the front. He did not offer any to Albert although he knew the other man smoked.

"Difficult times, Albert. I do not know what the world is coming to. I believe our new Prime Minister, Lord Salisbury, has lost the plot. He's scheming quietly with Parnell on the side, promising to support Home Rule, to maintain the Irish M.P.'s support and his own control in the House of Commons. Whilst he has also let it be known amongst his conservative peers that he considers it his honour and duty as an Englishman to protect the union between the two countries at all cost. Churchill is stirring up Unionist support in the North which is helpful. But there is no doubt Parnell is in a particularly powerful position right now. Hopefully, this won't last long, it looks like there is a concerted campaign under way to discredit him."

"Organised by Salisbury no doubt."

"That wouldn't be for me to say, Albert."

"The recent series of articles in *The Times*, quoting letters written by Parnell and others, alleges the Irish party and Parnell are inextricably linked with the outrages taking place in Ireland in the land war, the Phoenix Park murders, and the dynamite campaign. Although Parnell has denied these as forgeries." Albert paused to wait for a reaction from Jenkinson, but the other man remained silent, his mouth set in a grim line. "I suppose it's only to be expected – of course he would – but it's not going to do him any good. Where there's smoke there's fire, and all of that. Unless he takes them to court, but that could take months to resolve. How are things going here with the local men?"

"Hodge and Dodd are working out quite well. They make a good team. He's dogged, Hodge, I'll give him that – and Dodd does what he's told, he's not a blabber. Not like that old woman Flanagan." Jenkinson drew on his pipe, in short sharp intakes, then savoured the fumes.

"So, have they learnt anything about Nelson's whereabouts?"

Jenkinson exhaled a plume of smoke slowly. "Well, they have made some progress. After following Miss Benson for two weeks to the milliner's, chemist's and various art venues, he eventually struck lucky. She visited a house in Granville Street a few days ago, rented by a Mrs Emily Wilson, a known Fenian sympathiser. A neighbour told Dodd that from her bedroom window she had seen a stranger heading out to the privy in the back garden very early one morning, said he was using crutches. Could be O'Keefe. Dodd has been watching the comings and goings at the house and Nelson finally visited last week. He thought he had him trailed but he lost him in Victoria Station. He's a slippery fellow. So, for now, Albert, you should maintain a low profile but stay linked in with Hodge. I'll be in touch nearer the time." With that he got up and gathered his hat and walking stick. "Good evening to you, Albert."

"The bill?"

"Fix it up, will you, there's a good man? I'll add it to what I owe you."

∽つ☾∼

Chapter 24

"Emily, could you get us something to drink, please? If you don't have anything stronger, tea will do."

Drennan sat down in the wing-backed chair opposite Donal who was sitting upright on the chaise longue. Freshly shaved, he had put on a bit of weight over the past few weeks and he'd lost the hollowed-out skeletal look. But the clothes that belonged to Emily's absent husband were too big for him, accentuating his emaciated frame.

"Emily's cooking is doing you good, O'Keefe – you're looking a great deal better than the last time I saw you," Drennan observed matter-of-factly.

The door opened, and Nelson strolled into the room.

"Afternoon, men," he said with his Yankee-infused Cork accent.

"Would you look at what the dog dragged in! Where have yeh been holing up?" asked Drennan.

"I am stayin' with a friend, boss."

"What friend?"

"A lady-friend, yeh don't know her."

"Listen, Nelson. I would rather you stay put here – half the city is looking for the two of you. It's too dangerous for you to be cavorting around Manchester with some doxy."

"I'd be the lucky man to be cavorting, boss. Anyway, after all that time incarcerated, I need a bit of female diversion. Isn't that right, O'Keefe?"

Donal shot him an exasperated look.

"Nelson, if you're caught again, you're on your own! You can go hang yourself," remonstrated Drennan.

"Never mind my domestic arrangements, boss – what's the plan?"

Drennan, elbows on the armrests, steepled his hands, tapping his fingertips. "I was down at Belle Vue today inspecting the progress of the exhibition buildings – my 'company' has taken a stand. The whole complex is breath-taking. Basically, it's two enormous glass-and-steel structures divided by a grand avenue, with a covered porch linking the two that serves as a set-down space for carriages. To give you an idea of the scale of the place, the smaller structure is 330 feet long by 210 feet wide. One pavilion is exhibiting 'Machinery at Rest' and 'Machinery in Motion'. The second pavilion, which is probably the main public space, houses Chemical Industries, Industrial Design, the Irish Section – where I have a booth – and the refreshment and dining rooms, and also the Fine Arts exhibition galleries. In the centre of this pavilion is an ornamental fountain crowned by an enormous glass dome. Beyond that are the Botanical Gardens with its lakes, bandstands and a Fairy Fountain which will be lit up at night. But the main public attraction is beyond that again – a reconstruction of Olde Manchester and Salford, which has cobbled streets and alleys complete with Roman gateways and a miniature version of Manchester Cathedral."

"So, is this where will we place the Infernal Machine, to get maximum impact?" said Nelson.

"Well, there would be some poetic justice in the 'Little People' blowing up mini-Manchester," Drennan said wryly. "But for maximum impact, the Irish Section which is adjacent to the dome in the centre would be preferable."

"Ford Madox Brown and Isabel Dacre have spent months working on murals for the base of that dome," said Donal, appalled.

"Go 'way!" replied Drennan ironically. "I am afraid we're an uncouth lot here, O'Keefe. Michelangelo himself could have painted them for all I care."

"What about all the visitors?" said Donal, horrified as the full implications of what Drennan was outlining begin to dawn on him.

"We cannot be thinking of that – we have to look at the bigger picture."

"But setting off the dynamite in the Irish Section! These are our own people, damn it!"

"Look, O'Keefe, if it wasn't for Dynamite Saturday, Gladstone would never have agreed to support Home Rule. We can never take on the British by traditional military means – look at what happened in '78 for Jaysus' sake. The Brits know that in this war there are no winners – only losers – and they will be the losers if voters vote with their feet."

"What about Parnell? I know he has suffered setbacks but look at the progress he has made!"

"Well, since you have both been on holidays," Drennan retorted sarcastically, "the Brits, Salisbury's lot, are hell bent on his destruction. The pity is, our charismatic leader hasn't seen it coming, or maybe he thinks he's unassailable. They say that they have letters linking Parnell to the Phoenix Park murders, dynamitards, and Land League atrocities. Parnell has sworn that they are forgeries. But by the time he has proved it in court, the damage will be done. There is also the not inconsequential matter of his living with Mrs Kitty O'Shea, a married woman whom he's had three children by – although one of them died early. It is only a matter of time until that little gem of information is known publicly. They hope to damage his reputation irrevocably. When that happens – and no doubt it will – we will be back where we started, with no hope of Ireland's independence. It would probably take another generation for someone of his calibre to emerge. Let's face it, no one since Daniel O'Connell has been able to unite the various Irish factions like Parnell."

"But the IRB are still supporting Parnell's truce, so are the Clan, although I know they are getting impatient. So, on whose instructions are you acting?" asked Donal.

"The Clan are officially supporting the truce, but our leader O'Sullivan is getting impatient, so this operation is being run under cover by General Millen, the Clan's military strategist, who reports directly to O'Sullivan."

"So basically, this is an unauthorised cell, unauthorised by the joint military councils that is," Donal replied angrily. He got up and started pacing agitatedly around the room.

"I would prefer to call it an initiative."

"Drennan, I will have nothing to do with killing innocent people," said Donal through gritted teeth.

Drennan jumped up swiftly, grabbed Donal in an armlock from behind and thrust a Webley revolver into his cheek.

"O'Keefe, listen carefully, it's this, or you can say your prayers. Why the hell do you think we invested the energy to spring you from Strangeways? There's no choice here. Do your service for your country like a man."

There was a knock and Drennan released Donal and hastily returned the gun to his pocket.

Emily's head appeared around the door. "Miss Benson to see Donal."

"Jaysus, Emily, not now! Get rid of her," said Nelson.

"No need to raise alarm," said Drennan calmly, smoothing his hair and straightening his tie. "Show her in." He turned to Donal. "Look, O'Keefe, think about what I said. If all goes well, we'll have you on a steamer heading for New York within a few days, with a few bob in your pocket and a clean passport. You can start a new life. Your lady friend can follow you out. Now not a word to the lady, O'Keefe, or we will deal with her as well – if we have to."

The two men got up to leave as Julia entered the room.

"Miss Benson, what a pleasure," said Nelson, bowing slightly at her. "You wouldn't happen to have brought an apple tart with yeh for the invalid? Jesus, but you make lovely pastry, it melts in yer mouth. It's as good as me mammy's."

"Surely you can come up with something more original than that!" said Julia. "You need some new lines, Mr Nelson."

"Ah, a sharp tongue and a cold heart. O'Keefe, be careful!" He bowed his head slightly and, smiling, bid goodbye.

Drennan, unsmiling, nodded at Julia and followed, closing the door behind them both.

"What a pair of blackguards!" said Julia.

Donal put his finger to his lips, and then nodded towards the door.

"Ah, sorry." Julia sat down on the edge of the seat that Drennan had vacated.

"Well, how are you, my darling?"

"I've been better. I wasn't invited to exhibit my painting, *A Family's Despair,* by the Jubilee exhibition selection committee."

"Oh, I am sorry to hear that, Julia," he said, getting up awkwardly and pulling her up and into his arms.

Donal breathed slowly, inhaling her floral and peppery scent, as he tried to calm down after his interchange with Drennan.

"What's worse," she said, "poor old Newton, trying to cheer me up, put the painting in his gallery window and all of our friends and neighbours have been giving out all week about its subject matter."

"That's disappointing after all your hard work. Your bravery is an inspiration to me. But you must be strong – these are difficult times. But it won't always be so hard, you know." He tried to distract her. "And the other artists, your colleagues?"

Julia left his arms and paced the room.

"Well, Isabel was asked – but only one small portrait was accepted – and so were Houghton Hague, Frederick Shields, and of course John Partington – they wouldn't

281

dare leave him out. But we were promised a whole section of local artists. There only seems to be a handful, even though there are thirteen galleries! Partington is right, it just shows how little they think of local artists. What chance have I, being a woman – and Irish?"

Donal limped over to her and, holding her close, whispered in her ear. "Julia, shush, you have to listen carefully to me and keep quiet. I don't have much time. They are planning to blow up the opening of the Jubilee Exhibition when the Prince and Princess of Wales are there."

"Oh my God!" She jerked her head back and gazed at him in horror.

He pulled her close to him again and whispered, "Drennan is one of the organisers of the Irish section. He is telling everyone that he owns a gas engineering company. The dynamite is on its way as we speak. It's being brought over by two men from New York, to be delivered in time for the opening ceremony. Nelson and I have to receive the shipment, then plant it in the dome where the explosion will have the most impact."

"Donal," she whispered, "that is appalling – the exhibition will be full of innocent men, women and children who could be killed."

"Shush, my darling. You must help me get out of here. I want you to send a telegram to Eoin today. Tell him I need his help urgently."

She nodded and he released her.

"I am so sorry, dearest," he said, his voice returning to normal, "but I have a pounding headache that has come on all of a sudden, and I am very tired. Would you mind if we called it a day? I must get some rest."

After much deliberation, the telegram was brief.

D. NEEDS YOUR HELP URGENTLY. COME SOONEST. JULIA.

Leaving the Post Office, she headed back to Stockport Road. Her head was in a turmoil and her heart was racing as she considered how dangerous Donal's predicament was and the fact that they both might be leaving England suddenly. All other concerns vanished. Nelson and Drennan were basically thugs and would stop at nothing in pursuit of their political agenda. Julia wondered with renewed alarm whether they were armed.

She approached the black door and green shuttered windows of Number 42 and, climbing the steps, saw Eileen peeping through the drawing-room lace curtains. The child promptly opened the door to her.

"Oh, there you are, Auntie Julia. Mama has been looking for you for ages. She has one of her headaches. She asked me to look out for you."

"I am sure she did nothing of the sort. Eileen, you know you are not allowed peep out of the curtains – it's not a very ladylike activity. Have you practised the Mozart piece on the new piano your father bought you? If you don't, he might give it to the poor children in the workhouse who might make better use of it." She instantly regretted her mean-minded comment and relented, "I suppose it is very hot, darling, to be playing the piano."

"Absolutely, Auntie, I just don't have the energy," Eileen said dramatically, holding her hand up to her forehead. "But some iced lemonade might revive me."

"Oh, off you go then and find Florrie. I'll go to your mother shortly, once I have taken off my hat and fixed my hair."

Eileen's chubby arms hugged her aunt around her

neck and Julia breathed in the reassuring smells of Pear's soap, and the lemon juice her mother used to lighten her hair.

The child released her aunt peremptorily then scuttled happily down the stairs to the kitchen to find Florrie.

Once divested of her straw bonnet, Julia sat down in the chair for several minutes composing herself before the inevitable confrontation with her sister.

When she eventually went upstairs, she found Harriet lying on a chaise longue in her bedroom.

"Oh Julia, there you are. I'm afraid I have been feeling rather unwell," Harriet said wearily, stroking her swollen belly. "This little one is very agitated."

Harriet's age was making this pregnancy even more difficult. Julia noted that her sister was looking dawny, her freckles visible under her heavily powdered skin and her ginger hair clinging limply around her face. Julia was reminded, and not for the first time, of their mother.

She sat in an armchair close to the chaise longue.

"Harriet, I have just come from Donal."

With that, Harriet's lethargy evaporated instantly, and she sat bolt upright.

"I do not believe it. As if your perverse behaviour, allowing that obnoxious painting to be placed in Newton's window, was not enough to bear! Modelled on Edward, to make it worse! But your continued involvement with Donal is beyond endurance. You are putting yourself, not to mention the rest of us, in grave danger. It is stupidity personified. It is only a matter of time before Donal is caught again. If Edward knew you were visiting him, I do not know what he would do. You are only here as far as Edward is concerned – living with us – on sufferance. I am sorry to have to say it but, unfortunately, it's true. I know you've been very good to Eileen and me – in fact, I don't know what I would have done without you after she was born. But I simply cannot bear the awful atmosphere in the house any longer, the constant bad feeling between you and Edward. If you must know, I have been so upset by it all recently that I even suggested to him that you return to Westland Row and look after the tenants, or maybe find a job as a governess. But, to Edward's credit, he would not hear of it. He is willing to put up with you, to keep Eileen and me happy, and is anxious that you will be here for the birth of the new baby. However, I am warning you, Julia, don't test his patience too far."

"Or what, Harriet? What will he do? Send me to the workhouse?"

"Don't be foolish, Julia – but he might insist you take up Charles's offer and become his housekeeper."

"Unlikely. I think it would cost him too much to replace me here."

"There you go again! He is a good man, Julia – he works hard and we are all very lucky. I just cannot understand why you can't see that. Why do you persist in disrespecting the hand that feeds you?"

Julia sighed. There was no point in going over historic gripes again. Nor had she confided to her sister about Edward's brutal attack, and his behaviour since. It would have destroyed their marriage, and she could not do that to her sister. Anyway, it was too late now, too much time had passed. Since then, she had made it her business to avoid him as much as possible. She had caught him looking at her, the odd time, in that strange leering way he had – but in front of Harriet and the servants they were invariably polite to one another. However, lately things had got worse following Donal's escape. The atmosphere was charged. They were like trapped animals, on tenterhooks, and this tension that pervaded the house was affecting them all.

"Julia, I want you to promise me that you have no foolish plans to go off and marry Donal. You know that would not be the answer either – it wouldn't do."

"Harriet, if I choose to marry Donal I will, and neither Edward nor you can stop me. He cannot lock me up for ever."

"Oh Julia, don't be so dramatic! He has never locked you up. He is simply exercising his right to provide guidance as your moral guardian and head of the household."

Julia ignored her homily. "I cannot promise you, Harriet. I haven't thought that far ahead. Seeing Donal after all these years has been a shock – for us both. I feel I am only getting to know him again. Although the feelings are still there, the physical feelings, I mean."

"For God's sake, Julia, that's just ridiculous nonsense! Read romantic novels if you want some passion! You .have been apart for years and you are both middle-aged at this stage!" She almost spat this out. "Apart from the 'passion' as you call it, how would you both live? He is a wanted felon – surely even you cannot want a life on the run, constantly in fear of his being apprehended? What sort of life would that be?"

"Well, Harriet, what I want is rather academic at this stage. I have not decided yet, and he hasn't asked me to marry him. Not recently anyway."

"It's only a matter of time."

Julia looked curiously at her sister. "How can you be so sure? Particularly after all you have just said."

"Oh, for God's sake, you are practically throwing yourself at him!"

"That's a little unfair, don't you think? We have been promised to one another for many years now."

Harriet's anger evaporated suddenly, leaving her once more limp and wilting. "Julia, it's just that I couldn't bear to lose you, not now."

She turned her head away, but not before Julia saw uncharacteristic tears filling her eyes, falling in feathery traces down her powdered face.

Somewhat reluctantly, Julia relented. "I am not going anywhere, not today anyway," she said half-jokingly as she thought of her uncertain future. "Oh, by the way ... Donal told me Eoin is arriving any day soon."

"Really? Edward didn't mention it. They normally meet up when he is over."

The following afternoon Julia was still upset after the events of the day before but was confident that once Eoin arrived he would somehow foil Drennan's plan and extricate Donal from his control. And, as she reasoned that a speedy departure for Donal and herself was likely, she resolved to put certain of her affairs in order.

Running late for her meeting with Isabel at the Ducie Arm's, she hailed a cab on Stockport Road. But just as the driver was helping her into the carriage, she noticed someone just outside the house, leaning against a lamppost reading a newspaper. He looked like he was waiting for someone. Dressed in a serviceable brown coat and a soft, black, wide-brimmed hat, Julia thought he looked somewhat incongruous, awkward even. As if he sensed her staring at him, the man looked at her and, with an alarmed expression on his face, in a jolting reaction doffed his hat.

The world is full of lunatics, thought Julia as she sat back into the seat, closing her eyes, trying to still her pounding heart.

At the Ducie Arms Isabel answered the side door in a fluster.

"Sorry, Julia, my mother has asked me to make sandwiches in the bar as she is short-staffed today. Would you mind coming into one of the snugs? I'll lock it from the public side, and we can have a chat in private. Unfortunately, I will have to take you through the public bar to get to it. Don't tell Harriet, she would be scandalised. Although there are not many people here at this time of the afternoon. The shifts haven't changed in Strangeways yet – then it will be bedlam. Just follow me."

Julia smiled to herself. If Isabel only knew about her previous visit!

As they crossed the room, the door to another snug opened. A well-dressed man, suited, cleanshaven and middle-aged, stepped out, leaving his two companions in Julia's direct line of vision. One had his head bent down so she couldn't see his face, but he was wearing the Strangeways uniform – and the other, she noted, aghast – was Edward. She felt fear exploding in the pit of her stomach, and for a moment she thought she was going to faint. Then she moved swiftly away, following Isabel as she headed towards the far side of the half empty bar.

As Julia entered the snug she turned, but the three

men were already leaving and approaching the door. Trying to appear detached, she asked, "Who are they, Isabel? That group of men over there?"

"Who? Oh, them! They meet every week or so. My mother calls them the Three Musketeers – very secretive, up to no good I'll bet. The man with the sideburns usually has a scarf covering his face – I always thought he must be deformed or badly scarred. The other gentleman comes from London, I've seen him on the London train on my way to the Royal Academy. The third man is Flanagan, he's one of our best customers. Works at Strangeways, a prison warder. Not very well liked by anyone, I hear. Likes men – so my mother told me – you know what I mean? Anyway, we get an odd lot in here. So, let's just close the door and pretend they don't exist. Sandwiches, Julia? Cheese and pickle, will that do? There is not a lot of call for cucumber sandwiches in the Ducie Arms!"

"There's nowt I likes more than a bit of pickle," mimicked Julia, slightly hysterical after her shock at seeing Edward. "And to be honest, Isabel, it's the reason I am visiting you. I am in a bit of a pickle myself. I might have to go away for a while."

"Oh, I'm sorry to hear that! Is it to do with Donal's escape?" She put her hand up. "Don't tell me if you don't want to."

"Well, yes and no. As you know, over the last few years things have not really worked out for me in Manchester. Maybe what has happened with Donal is a wake-up call for me to face the fact that I need to take control of my life, once and for all. Edward only keeps me to work as an unpaid servant and to stand in as his assistant in the surgery when Harriet is unable to work. I seem to have very little time or energy left for painting. Although I get a few portrait commissions, for children mainly, I am wasting my time here. Whereas at home I have some level of recognition from the Royal Hibernian Academy and a circle of friends who will support me in my work. Here it is all such an uphill struggle. I thought that *A Family's Despair* would change all of that, establish my reputation, be a new start. But its rejection has proved to be the final nail in the coffin."

"Oh, you shouldn't take it so badly!" said Isabel.

"I didn't, though I was deflated. But then, because he felt sorry for me after I was refused by the selection committee, Newton kindly hung it in his gallery window. And, since then, I have received nothing but sneering comments from people I thought were my friends, and from neighbours and fellow parishioners. My association with Donal is also known. Although, God knows how, not from me certainly."

Julia paused, her blue eyes sad and her shoulders drooped in defeat.

"Saying I don't support violence is never enough, it seems. Nobody believes me – the Irish here are all tarred with the one brush. Sometimes, when I am out shopping, I even try to make my accent more English – I'm becoming quite a good mimic!"

"What about Harriet? Does she not need you?"

"Well, I think that even she has had enough of me at this stage. And, believe me, I am sorry that I have caused her so much distress. I hope to return for the birth, and I might see if Molly, our old nanny, could send one of her daughters over to stay with her for a few months. It is

Eileen that I will miss most. I have minded her since she was a baby – she has been like my own child. Of course, I will miss Harriet but I feel I have put my life on hold for hers for long enough."

"It's the spinster's lot, I am afraid," her friend responded sympathetically.

Julia chose her words carefully – she did not want to involve her friend in what was going on, any more than was strictly necessary. "Yes, it is – although I hate that word. Whatever happens with Donal, I'd be better off in Ireland – though his escape to Ireland is looking unlikely. According to the papers, the Irish office in Whitehall have a dedicated team trying to track himself and Nelson down. Edward thinks it's only a matter of time before he's caught again."

"Julia, let's hope it doesn't come to that – but I am so sorry you will be leaving. I, for one, will miss you terribly."

"We will still keep in touch, and hopefully you can come over and visit me. Now enough about my problems. How are the murals going for the dome? Is Mr Madox Brown happy? I cannot wait to see them. Will you be going to the opening?"

Her friend's eyes lit up with excitement. "Julia, wait till you see them! They are utterly amazing – it took at least twenty men to hoist them into position. I will send you season tickets for all the family, I was given twenty in part-payment for the work. The building is incredible – it's as good as the Crystal Palace any day!"

***

As Julia approached Newton's Gallery, she noticed with relief that the painting was no longer in the window. It had been replaced with a pleasant landscape of Belle Vue Gardens. It had been a terrible mistake. Friends who had seen the painting had described it as "interesting", or "unusual". Some people had just been downright rude. Like Mrs Birtwistle the postmistress who told her it was an abomination, and the vicar's wife who had chilled her to the core by saying it was an affront to her god-fearing countrymen and a disgrace to her sex. Finally, after a thundering row with Edward that morning, when she was afraid that Harriet, visibly distressed, was going to give birth prematurely then and there at breakfast table, she had come to Newton to ask him to take the picture down. She was relieved that he had already done so.

As she walked through the door, she was comforted by the faint whiff of turpentine, and the brass bells that chimed her arrival. It was like being back in her grandfather's shop in Dame Street. Every wall here in the gallery on Oxford Street was covered in chromolithographic prints of famous works of art. Others were stacked, unframed, in display stands. Turner, Constable, Whistler were all represented. But the window was reserved for original paintings by local artists: landscapes, history paintings, genre paintings. To have your work displayed in Newton's window was considered by art aficionados as one of the Manchester art world's highest accolades.

It was rumoured that the Jew was once a well-known artist from some far-flung country in Eastern Europe. And that in the back of the shop was a secret studio where the one-handed septuagenarian made tortured but unsuccessful attempts to rekindle the talent that others had brutally taken away. A black leather glove with pinned-back fingers covered the stump. It was also suggested that Newton was probably not even his real name, but some anglicised version of a name too complex for British tongues to pronounce.

"We are all foreigners in this town – it is one of Manchester's great strengths, but also one of its weaknesses," he had once said to her.

She had asked him then about his past. But he had been evasive and, with his usual politesse, he had adroitly avoided answering her.

On his head he always wore a satin kippah – and dressed head to toe in black. Julia thought he looked like Rembrandt himself, the darkness of his garb a foil to his long grey hair. But also, because everything about him was tremulous and shimmering. His luminous eyes were watery and his lips moist. It was as if he were physically defined by silvery highlights.

Julia liked and admired the old man, whose kindness to struggling artists was legendary in the city. He never judged, and you were never quite sure whether he valued your work or not. His gentle nod and melodious "*Hmm*" indicated mild approval no matter what the subject matter. Importantly, especially for Julia, he operated an honour payment system for framing and artist's supplies.

The old man brought Julia to the back of the shop where they examined the offending work.

"Honestly, Mr Newton, why do you think it was rejected? And what has caused such a bad reaction? Please, I would really value your opinion. I have received only well-intentioned platitudes or distressing insults from everyone else."

293

"Miss Benson, I do not like, as you know, commenting on the artistic endeavours of others. Who am I to judge? To paint, for some artists, is to bare their soul to the world. Although many consider it an expression of ego, for others painting can be an altruistic act and I suspect that you are one of them. For you, my dear, it seems almost a compulsion to speak the truth no matter how difficult it is to hear. Indeed, I have noticed that your paintings over the last number of years have increasingly reflected your frustration at the social injustices suffered by the poor and weak in this city."

"How very astute of you, Mr Newton. You are right – sometimes, as a woman, I feel like a caged bird, and to paint is the only way that my voice can be heard. It is my poor attempt to influence public opinion."

He nodded sadly then carefully considered the painting, his luminous eyes mournful, lost in his own private thoughts as though the image evoked painful memories of his own. Crossing the long spindly fingers of his good hand over his black-gloved stump and bowing his head for a moment that seemed like an age, he was silent. Then he turned, looked at her and sighed wearily.

"Although technically your painting is not remarkable, it is nevertheless accomplished, Miss Benson."

Julia was momentarily taken aback by his directness.

"But what distinguishes this painting, in my humble opinion and if I may be so bold as to say, is the subject matter. It is very brave, very brave indeed. Particularly so because you are of the fairer sex. But, unfortunately, in my experience, people condemn what they do not understand. In this painting you are asking people to identify with the parents of someone who has presumably killed other parents' children. And, in the face of their own fear, because of recent events and atrocities carried out by some of your countrymen, it is for many people here in Manchester, I suspect, a step too far."

"I see. Yes, you are probably right, Mr Newton. But do you see that that was not my intention? My intention was to highlight the human impact of violence."

"I think it is the poster of the Manchester Martyrs with all of its nationalist associations that nails your political sympathies to the mast, so to speak."

"Well, yes, I do support the Irish cause, but by political means."

"Yes, my dear – I suspected that – and you know that – but your viewer judges what is presented before them, and that ambiguity I believe is the source of your problems."

Julia was crestfallen. "So, instead of this painting creating my reputation amongst the Manchester art world, it has probably achieved the opposite. It has destroyed it."

The weight of sadness in Newton's eyes answered her question more succinctly than any words could convey.

Chapter 25

Elsewhere in the city the hot spell was accentuating underlying tensions and the cause of frayed tempers. Inspector Hodge ran a finger around the inside of his collar. The new starch his wife was using was irritating the red and scaly skin on the back of his neck. That damn fool Dodd was late. Where was the fat bastard? He was supposed to meet him here at three. Hodge had just been berated by Jenkinson on the telephone apparatus that had been fitted in the operations office last week – a luxury that was a sure sign of Whitehall's increasing nervousness. Hodge took his watch out of his pocket and shook it – even the bloody watch had stopped.

"Inspector, sorry I am late." Dodd's red face appeared around the door.

"Come in, sergeant, and sit down. I haven't got all day."

Dodd sat down, his scant black hair sticking to his head, and beads of perspiration glistening on his forehead.

"The city is completely clogged up wit' traffic for t'exhibition. Builders and suppliers' carts are everywhere, inspector. An't weather is –"

"Nor have I time to discuss the weather, Dodd. Let's get down to business. Where the hell is Nelson? Why has it taken you so long to track him down? Jenkinson has just been on the phone giving me an earful. Lord Salisbury is like an Antichrist."

"Well, there has been some progress, sir. There was a delivery today at Granville Street. A young lad on a bike arrived around eleven o'clock with two baskets covered in cloths, looked like groceries. Except t' baskets were so heavy that when he stopped, th' poor lad could barely balance his bike. Very wobbly he was. He went straight up t' path to the front door, bold as brass, and two men came out to help him carry in baskets, they were that heavy."

"Must be the dynamite," said Hodge.

"That's what I thought meself, sir."

"And the men were?"

"Well, Drennan and O'Keefe, sir. O'Keefe seems to have made a good recovery. Still has a limp though."

"Good work, Dodd. *Mm*, things are moving along, it seems. According to Jenkinson the plan is to detonate an infernal machine the day that the Prince and Princess of Wales officially open the exhibition on the 3rd of May."

"God between Their Majesties and all harm. Do you know how they are going t' do it, sir?"

"Not just yet, Dodd, all in good time."

A crack of thunder of unusual intensity reverberated in the sky outside, causing both men to stiffen momentarily in fear.

297

"Cor, that gave me a fright, sir. I thought the pesky blighters had us rumbled."

Relaxing, Hodge looked at his watch.

"Seems to have fixed my watch at least. Now, Dodd, off you go – that's good news but we still need to find Nelson urgently."

The thunder was followed by torrential rain. Umbrellas were useless in the downpour. Black sooty water flowed through the city streets, cascading into the already swollen River Irwell. It collected in inky ponds that stained the ends of women's skirts and blackened the dirty feet of street urchins. And everywhere, across the city, piles of cinders from fireplaces and factory fires turned into molten, tar-like mud.

At the tea rooms off Piccadilly, the windows were steamed up. It was packed and several ladies caught without umbrellas were crowded in the doorway, waiting for the rain to stop.

"You got here before me," said the tall dark-haired woman wearing a distinctive navy-and-cream-striped costume. She had pushed her way through the throng at the door and approached the conservatively dressed, middle-aged man who was already seated.

"Yes, I just managed to escape the downpour. I see that you, unfortunately, did not."

"The cab left me at the door – even still, my boots are soaked through and the ends of my skirts are destroyed. I had an umbrella for all the good it did me." She straightened her bonnet, and the hovering serving girl obligingly took her wet cape away. "I am so looking forward to a nice hot cup of tea!"

She sat down and arranged her skirts, her bustle thrusting her forwards in the chair like the prow of a ship. With a click of his fingers, he called back the serving girl who had been distracted by another customer. She took their order.

"So, any developments?" he enquired.

"Yes, the material arrived this morning, and they have come up with a plan, of sorts." She paused and tilted her head to one side. "No, actually, it's quite a good plan. I think it will do nicely. There is one thing I am worried about though."

"What's that?"

"O'Keefe. You see Drennan and Nelson are committed, they are invested so to speak. O'Keefe on the other hand is a loose cannon. I know we needed someone to represent local interests. But you know his links with the IRB are tenuous."

They sat back as the girl set out the china cups, teapot and various accoutrements on the linen tablecloth. She poured the tea, but they waited to resume their conversation until she returned with a plate of iced buns.

The woman sighed. "Well, it's just that I feel he's beginning to waver, even though Drennan outlined in no uncertain terms the consequences of his not cooperating. Your Miss Benson called yesterday. She should have been kept away – she might convince him to do a runner."

He pulled at his dundrearies. "Well, firstly she's not my anything," he said grumpily, "but she could be useful. Can you not use your considerable charms to persuade him to stay?"

"No, although I must admit I did try." She smiled archly. "He is quite a looker. But he's a bit too refined for the likes of me. I prefer my men to have a certain animal magnetism. Anyway, he resisted I am afraid. Not like some. It's a good thing, Albert, that you are not quite so scrupulous."

"No, indeed," he said with a tight smile, then as he lifted a pink iced bun to his thin lips he inhaled sharply as, under the table, he felt her hand firmly grasp the inner side of his thigh.

In the corner of the member's lounge in the Athenaeum in Mosley Street, Edward recognised Eoin sitting in a high-backed, green velvet chair reading *The Times*.

"Eoin, what a pleasant surprise!" Edward shook the other man's hand firmly. What brings you to Manchester?"

"The same as the other thousand or so visitors. I have come over for the opening ceremony of the Exhibition. It has got great coverage in the Irish papers. I am visiting with Thomas Deane, an architect who is involved in the design of the Irish Section. He is considering a similar initiative for Dublin. He thought it might be a way of funding an extension to the National Gallery which is cramped for space."

"I didn't realise you were that interested in art? I thought that was your younger brother's vice. Well, one of them anyway."

Eoin smiled. "Well, I am Deane's legal adviser, so I thought I'd better show support. Good for business. Why don't you join me for a few minutes?"

Edward sat down beside Eoin, pulled out his pipe and started to fill it from a leather pouch in his pocket.

"Any news of Donal's whereabouts?"

"No, Edward, no news. I know he's impossible, but I

am extremely worried about him. My sister has a path worn to St Andrew's church with all the time she spends there praying for his safety. If only she knew that he's beyond prayers at this stage."

"It's not looking good, I have to admit."

"How is Julia holding up?"

"Don't mention that woman, the trouble she has caused. In her latest attempt to discredit my family, she has publicly displayed a painting with barely veiled Fenian sympathies. She was even misguided enough to submit it to the Jubilee Exhibition for consideration."

"That's not like Julia," said Eoin thoughtfully. "She always deplored violence."

"Well, that's certainly not the message she's conveying recently. I have lost several patients because of it. I must admit I am at my wits' end with her. Only for the fact that Harriet needs her more than ever with her confinement approaching, I would send her packing."

"And then there is also her money," said Eoin provocatively.

Chapter 26

The library on Plymouth Grove was, on the face of it, an odd place to arrange to meet. But it was the only place that Julia could think of. She knew she wouldn't get a chance to talk privately to Eoin in the house on Stockport Road, and if they were to meet publicly they would run the risk of bumping into one of Harriet's or Edward's acquaintances. At least, with Harriet laid up, Edward could no longer afford to send Florrie with her everywhere she went.

When she arrived at the library at nine o'clock, shortly after it had opened, there were no other readers, and the librarian Miss Featherstone was busy cataloguing new books at the desk. At the rear of the library was the reference section where taller shelves and full-height screen walls formed a private alcove that surrounded a table with chairs. It was a place for readers to study the larger books.

Eoin was already there looking at an atlas but stood up when he saw her.

He kissed her affectionately on the cheek. "Julia, I came as soon as I could. Tell me what has happened. Do you know where he is?"

"Thank you, for coming so quickly. Yes, he is alive, and his health is improving, but he is in terrible danger."

"Thank God he is alive. I have been worried sick about my little brother. Your telegram was a relief of sorts. I have heard nothing at all from him after his escape, and I was beginning to panic. So, what kind of mess is he in now?"

They sat down and Julia described the events of the past few months – how she met Drennan through the Literary Association and how he had promised to help Donal escape if she in turn smuggled a message to Flanagan. She described her night-time visit to the Ducie Arms. But, for some reason she did not fully understand – shame possibly that it was in some way her own fault – she omitted to tell him of Edward's brutal attack. She described the visit to Strangeways and the mock fight between the two women. Although her description of these events amused him, she could see that he was shocked by it all.

"I am beginning to think that it was a mistake to get involved. But I was at my wits' end and did not know what to do. I thought that Donal wouldn't survive another winter doing hard labour. He had already told me that he had talked with you and that there was no legal solution possible. As usual, I am afraid my actions were misjudged."

She bowed her head and tried to fight back the tears.

Eoin put his hand over hers.

"No, Julia, I have been harsh with you in the past – but

I was wrong. It is Donal who is responsible for his own situation, not you, or me, or anyone else for that matter. But you said that now he is in danger – what danger?"

Julia described her last visit to the house in Granville Street.

"Who else is in the house?"

"Well, the woman who rents the house is a Miss Emily Wilson – she's an embroiderer who does piecework at home. Her husband is an engineer working up north. Although I have never met him. There are also two men from Clan na Gael there: Colm Drennan – he reports to a General Millen, Sullivan's military strategist who is masterminding the operation – and Nelson, Donal's fellow escapee. But Nelson is not actually staying in the house – he comes and goes. Drennan seems to be the brains of the operation."

"Was Donal able to tell you what they plan to do?"

"Yes, it's horrific – it doesn't bear thinking about – they are planning a dynamite attack at the opening ceremony of the Jubilee Exhibition."

"*Are you serious?*"

"Deadly serious, unfortunately. Donal obviously does not want to have hand, act, nor part in it. But he is a prisoner there. He is really upset but, more than that, Eoin, he seemed frightened. And Eoin, I must admit, I am frightened too."

He reached out and held her shoulders firmly, forcing her to look into his eyes.

"Julia, don't worry. I am here now and I think it's time I extricated my brother from this mess once and for all. For all of our sakes."

Julia tried to hold back the tears. "I just hope it's not too late."

"Look, you must trust me. But first I need to talk to some contacts I have and check out the lie of the land."

He released her and they both sat down at the reference table. Julia picked up the atlas he had been looking at, but her hands were trembling, and she put it down hoping he wouldn't notice.

"By the way, after I arrived, I met Edward yesterday at the club. He has invited me to dinner tonight. I believe you are having a guest."

"Yes, a patient of his, I believe." Taking her cue from him, she breathed in, smiled and tried to act normally.

"I should tell you he suspects that you are in contact with Donal, but he is not sure."

"Really? I have been followed by someone recently. I wondered if Edward was paying someone to check up on me."

"Are you sure you are not imagining it?"

"Absolutely not."

"Did this man follow you to Donal's location?"

"No, I am fairly sure he didn't. I managed to lose him that day in Piccadilly Station."

My word, we do mean to impress tonight, Julia thought as she surveyed the dining room.

Harriet had supervised the laying of the table with their mother's flamboyant Waterford glass epergne filled with white roses as the centrepiece. Light from the chandelier, also of Waterford glass, reflected on the impressive array of Benson silver, and her grandmother's china dinner service.

Julia had been in the kitchen, adding the final touches to the rhubarb tart, lemon pudding and cheesecakes.

Thinking back to the last dinner Eoin had attended in Stockport Road, which had been a disaster, Julia was thankful that Harriet had borrowed their neighbour's cook for the evening. It had been her sister's idea – a peace offering of sorts – so that Julia could have a night off. Well, most of the night anyway. She had been asked to do pudding as Mrs Dobbins claimed she was a plain cook with warm hands, and as a result she couldn't handle pastry in those 'forin flans' as she called them. That was her excuse anyway.

Julia smoothed down her hair which she had set in a loose knot at the top of her head. Her gown of mint-green silk was edged in a cream antique lace. It was not new, or of the latest fashion, but she knew the fitted style showed off her figure. Despite the constant fear in the pit of her stomach, she had made more of an effort than usual with her appearance. It was not every day they entertained, she reasoned with herself, and it was a distraction.

Edward occasionally invited one of his patients or prospective patients to dinner, in an attempt to lure them from a rival surgery in Stockport Road. This one was a married lady who lived a secluded life as her husband was working away from home. Julia hadn't yet met her.

Just then she heard the company rising from their seats in the drawing room.

Then Edward entered the room with Emily Wilson on his arm.

Dumbfounded at seeing her, Julia tried to control her shock.

"Julia, there you are," said Edward. "Mrs Wilson has reminded me that you have met before."

"Yes, of course, how lovely to see you again, Mrs

Wilson, and what a surprise!"

Harriet, following behind with Eoin on her arm, quipped without much enthusiasm, "Yes, it is a surprise. Edward thought Mrs Wilson might like to meet Eoin as they have so much in common."

"Really, and how is that?" Julia enquired, eyebrows raised and with a brittle smile that did not reach her eyes.

"Oh ruins, you know, Julia," said Harriet. "They both go off tramping around the countryside to look at ruins of old castles and churches. We were just talking about it."

"Really, Eoin, I never realised you had that interest."

"There is a lot about me that you don't know, Julia," he teased.

"You'd be surprised at the interesting facts that you find out about people when you are their dentist," said Edward earnestly.

"Actually, my interest in ruins, as you so charmingly call it, Harriet, is how I met Thomas Deane, the architect, and the client with whom I am attending the exhibition. We are both members of the Royal Dublin Society and great fans of Ruskin and the Gothic Style."

"Our grandfather was also a member of the Royal Dublin Society – you know he supplied them with art materials," said Harriet. "Anyway, let's sit down. Edward, you sit at the head of the table. Mrs Wilson can sit beside you on one side, and Julia on the other. Eoin, if you sit to the left of me and, Eileen, you can sit beside me where I can keep an eye on you."

"Yes, Mama."

Eileen was in a state of high excitement as she was allowed, on this occasion, to join the adults in an attempt to make up the numbers, on the strict instruction that she was there to be seen and not heard. Julia had curled her blond hair into fat ringlets with the curling iron and helped her to embellish her slightly tired Sunday dress with a new satin ribbon.

After the men were served wine, Florrie, all dressed up in a spruce white apron and cap for the occasion, brought in the first course of Julienne Soup, laying the tureen beside Edward who then passed it around to the guests.

"Well, Eoin, how are things in Dublin?" Edward enquired solicitously.

"No one can talk about anything other than Parnell at the moment, I'm afraid. People are shocked at the content of his letters printed in *The Times* newspaper. And because he has repeatedly claimed that they are forgeries, they don't understand why he doesn't sue the paper for libel. I am afraid that the damage to his reputation could destroy the Irish party, and all the political momentum we have gained over the last five years. The fact that Parnell has consistently denied links to terrorist activities has underpinned his extraordinary popularity both here and at home. Particularly as O'Sullivan of Clan na Gael is straining at the bit to resume physical action and only looking for an excuse to do so."

"How about the IRB here?" asked Edward.

"They are standing strong behind Parnell."

"So, a bombing that was attributed to the IRB and Clan na Gael would destroy that alliance, and Parnell's credibility?" asked Julia, alarmed, catching Eoin's eye.

"It would destroy everything, Julia," Eoin replied solemnly. "We would lose the hard-fought political advantage, not to mention the hearts and minds of our people. We would not see Home Rule for another fifty years at least."

"Let us hope that Parnell can prove that the letters are forgeries – and that there are no rogue Clan na Gael initiatives," said Mrs Wilson smugly.

"Yes, indeed," Eoin replied.

"Well, I for one would be glad to see the back of Parnell," Edward responded pompously. "Let's face it, Ireland has neither the critical mass in terms of population, nor the natural resources to support industrial growth to the same level as Britain. We will always be dependent on her. As you all know, I am still strictly Unionist, as my father was before me."

"Yes, indeed," said Mrs Wilson, "and Mr Parnell is such a hypocrite don't you think, with his philandering with that Mrs O'Shea?"

"Exactly," said Edward brusquely. "Though it's not really a subject for polite conversation, I think." He glared at his guest and nodded his head at Eileen.

"What does philandering mean, Papa?"

"Stamp-collecting, dearest, eat your soup," her mother interjected. Then, looking up, she said to her husband, "I'm fed up with Irish politics. It's all we ever seem to hear about these days. Can we talk about something else?"

"But your husband is so knowledgeable about these matters – politics, I mean," said Mrs Wilson, leaning over and exposing her generous cleavage to Edward while squeezing him affectionately on the arm.

"It's a pleasure to see a woman interested in politics, Mrs Wilson," said Eoin, as Edward appeared to freeze with embarrassment. "Don't tell me you are interested in sport too?"

"Well, I am, actually," she said, eyes sparkling at Eoin, "especially field games."

"Where did you say your husband was working, Mrs Wilson?" Harriet enquired frostily.

"Oh, he's in a mill up north. He's an engineer, you know. I miss him terribly."

"So, who is going to the opening of the Jubilee Exhibition next week?" said Eoin, in a rather obvious attempt to change the subject.

"Oh, I expect we will all be there, in some capacity or another," said Julia absentmindedly. A chill ran over her body, at the painful reminder of the potential cataclysm that was unfolding.

Florrie had cleared the soup plates and now began to serve the second course, laying a platter of curried eggs on the table.

Julia jumped up from the table, afraid she was going to get sick.

"Please excuse me, I am feeling rather unwell."

"It must be the curried eggs, they always make me vomit," said Eileen helpfully.

Her mother, horrified, kicked her daughter under the table.

Julia returned in time for dessert and accepted all the compliments about her cooking skills graciously. But after the plates were cleared and Harriet rose to retire to the drawing room, leaving the men to smoke cigars and drink port, Julia excused herself, claiming she still felt unwell.

Eoin jumped up to open the door for the women, and as Julia approached he took her hands in both of his and said solicitously, "I do hope you will feel better soon, Julia.

If you feel up to it, could I avail of your expert knowledge next Monday? Over the weekend, I must visit the construction site of the exhibition pavilion with my architect. Although by all accounts the building work is finished – they are just assembling the exhibits and fitting signage – the final snagging that sort of thing. So could we take a jaunt to the Manchester City Gallery on Monday? There is a painting there by an artist that I am thinking of investing in, and I would really value your opinion."

"Of course, Eoin, I would enjoy that very much."

"Say about noon, and we can get some lunch."

"Perfect."

Edward frowned, signalling his disapproval. Julia ignored him completely.

∽∾ᔆᔆ∽∾

Chapter 27

Looking out onto the busy street from the drawing room on the following Monday, Julia was waiting for the carriage to arrive. Through the open window she could hear the chorus of the city's bells as they struck noon. They sounded like an orchestra of petulant musicians warming up before the main event, which in this case came thirty minutes later, when the louder, dourer notes of the knocking-off bells marked the lunch break for the mill hands. Across the road, in anticipation of the Royal visit the next day, she could see that her neighbours had already tied red-and-gold bunting across the first-floor windows.

The meeting with Eoin would at least offer some temporary relief for her inner turmoil as since the dinner party she was torn between feeling she had a responsibility to pass on the knowledge she had acquired to the authorities, against the certainty that it would be at the cost of Donal's life. To justify her current position, she tried to tell herself that there was still time to avert the crisis, and that Eoin provided the only glimmer of hope to salvage what seemed, on the face of it, a catastrophic situation.

To make things worse, breakfast that morning had been preceded by one of Edward's more tiresome, and often repeated, lectures on the evils of female vanity. The homily was prompted by the fact that he had just received the bill from the dressmaker's for costumes that Harriet had insisted on, for herself, Julia and little Eileen for their visit to the exhibition the next day. Isabel, as promised, had sent season tickets for the whole family, including the opening. By all accounts, it was going to be the main social event of the year and would involve several visits. For Julia, the purchases were more of a necessity than a luxury as most of her clothes were dated and worn. But justifying her actions as an act of defiance, she had changed before meeting Eoin into the new costume – a navy merino woollen dress, pelisse, and matching bonnet which she had decorated with pheasants' feathers that picked up the tones of her auburn hair.

Julia was already at the door, as Eoin climbed down from the brougham to greet her. She was hoping to avoid social introductions, and the possibility of another meeting with Edward. It was cooler today, the recent thunderstorm having cleared the heaviness from the air with a light northerly breeze tainted, barely perceptibly, by a sulphurous odour from the nearby dyeworks.

"Julia," Eoin opened the carriage door for her, "ravishing as usual."

"Enough of the fulsome compliments – you will turn an old woman's head."

"I think you know you can still manage to turn heads, Julia," he smiled.

He shouted an instruction to the driver, which she did not hear. Sitting beside the driver was a man with his coat collar turned up and a cap pulled down over his ears. Julia caught a glimpse of a pockmarked face. He seemed vaguely familiar.

As the horses set off at a pace, Eoin leaned back in the seat facing her. He looked tired.

"What did you think of our unexpected dinner guest – Mrs Wilson? I remembered you told me the name and I put two and two together. Mind you, your reaction also gave the game away."

"Well, I was flabbergasted to be honest – how on earth did Edward meet her?"

"I have no idea – I didn't know he had it in him."

"Really, Eoin, he's my sister's husband. I don't want to know."

"Sorry, Julia. Anyway, apart from that, apologies for my silence, I know you must be worried sick, but I have spent the last two days staking out Granville Street. At a discreet distance, of course. I have been watching the comings and goings at the house. And interestingly, there was a man in a brown coat with a black felt hat also engaged in the same activity. Odd-looking character. He saw me, I saw him, but it didn't seem to faze him. He just continued in his vigil."

"That's the man who was following me. Tall, stocky man."

"Yes, that's him. Looks like a bit of a dunce, I reckon he's from the local constabulary, doing detective work. Anyway, Drennan and Nelson are only there in the morning. Mrs Wilson seems to leave the house at three o'clock in the afternoon, leaving Donal alone for about an hour. That's the window of opportunity for me to break into the house and help him escape."

"When?" asked Julia.

"We have no choice – we are running out of time – we have to do it today."

"Oh my God, are you serious? Is it safe?"

"We will soon find out. Just in case I borrowed this." With that he drew a pistol out of his inner coat pocket. Stephen has one too."

Julia then realised where she had seen that familiar pockmarked face before.

"Stephen Spendlove?"

"The very one. He's being paid to help me. I was always afraid that this day would come when I would have to take the law into my own hands and rescue my brother. To be honest, Drennan has done most of the dirty work for me."

"Eoin, why am I here?" she asked nervously.

"Well, you will probably find this boring after your recent adventures," he said ironically,   "but I reckoned we will need to get away fast. I did not think you would want him to go without you."

"And what happens when you have got him?"

"Well, we will drive immediately to Holyhead and you can get the next ship to Dublin. Before we leave the country, we can send a telegram to the police in Manchester advising them of the plot. When we get to Dublin you can head for a cottage that our family owns in Tinahealy. It's in a remote part of Wicklow."

"I know, I heard about it, many years ago," she said softly.

"Ah, I see."

"What if they are watching the ports?"

"Well, that's where you come in. We will take his wheelchair. I have forged papers with me for an Anglican minister and his nurse. There is a nurse's uniform in the bags – you can change in the carriage."

"Eoin, I don't mean to sound petulant, but you didn't even consult me on this plan?"

"No, there wasn't time. Come on now, I'm relying on your good sense – no drama – be a good woman and let's get this over with."

"But what about Edward and Harriet?" she said, exasperated. "When I do not return Edward will inform the police."

"Don't worry about Edward – I will deal with him."

The brougham stopped a few doors up from the house in Granville Street, and Eoin got out of the carriage. Stephen, dressed like a costermonger in his cap and breeches, jumped down from the back. He knuckled his forehead at Julia, "Miss Benson." But, without waiting for a response, he hastily followed Eoin as he headed down a narrow alleyway that appeared to connect to a lane at the back of the houses.

Julia sat back in the carriage, hoping no one would recognise her. There were two small children playing in the cobbled street. One of them, a boy of about five or six years old, climbed up onto the step and peeped in the window.

"Spare a few pennies, missus?"

Julia reached into her purse and threw a few coins as far as she could, and the two youngsters scurried after them.

She thought about recent events, trying to calm her

rising panic. She seemed to be trapped in a vortex of anxious days – and nights filled with terrifying dreams. Last night they were so vivid that she woke up in a cold sweat with searing images of dead children covered with blood, their bones broken and exposed, lying on shards of glass amongst the debris of a giant imaginary glasshouse. Eoin did not seem to appreciate that her concern for Donal was overshadowed by this all-consuming dread of the carnage that would ensue because of Drennan's planned explosion. She was also aware that she was being, irrevocably, stitched into the fabric of this unfolding drama.

Trying to push these thoughts out of her head, she thought again of the dinner party, which had been so bizarre, with the entrance of the lascivious Mrs Wilson. Her connection with Edward seemed so random. But was it random? Or was it in some way linked to Donal's situation? Then she remembered a connection that had not occurred to her before.

Her thoughts were interrupted by the sound of breaking glass, and a door slamming. Shortly after, the front door opened, and the two men came out. Eoin strode over and got into the carriage.

"What's happened?"

"We were too late, they have gone. The whole house has been cleared out."

"What about Mrs Wilson?"

"She obviously got a better offer."

"Oh my God, what are we going to do? The opening ceremony is tomorrow. Eoin, it's too late to find him – we will have to go to the police!" As Eoin got in the carriage she continued. "But there is something that just occurred to me. Edward's connection with Mrs Wilson. It isn't just a coincidence. I mean, it cannot be. A few days ago when I was visiting my friend Isabel in the Ducie Arms, he was there in the public house. He was there with Flanagan, the prison officer, and a well-dressed gentleman from London. Flanagan was the man I had to deliver the message to for Drennan when he was trying to arrange to free Donal and Nelson. Is it possible that Edward is also connected in some way to Drennan? How can that possibly be? Why would he be? It doesn't make sense."

"No, not at the moment," said Eoin grimly. "It surely doesn't. But let's go and find out." He pulled open the hatch and shouted to the driver. "Stockport Road, and don't spare the horses!"

When they arrived at Stockport Road it was after four o'clock and the last patient had gone. Edward was in his surgery doing paperwork. Harriet, at this time, was usually upstairs in her bedroom resting, and Julia knew Eileen was in Devon visiting cousins, relatives of Edward's. Julia knocked on the surgery door.

"Julia, I didn't expect to see you this afternoon. What do you want?" Edward greeted her in his usual peremptory manner, until he saw Eoin and Stephen behind her. "Ah, Eoin and Stephen too, what a surprise. I didn't know you were in Manchester, Stephen."

"Edward, we just want a quick word, this shouldn't take long." Although Eoin's tone was polite, he was obviously in no form for small talk.

Stephen closed the door, locking it behind him. "We don't want to be disturbed, Mr Williams," he said.

"That's really not necessary," said Edward. "Come in and sit down."

318

He pulled over two visitors' chairs for Eoin and Julia and left Stephen standing.

"What's the problem? Is it Donal? Has he been recaptured?"

"No, he hasn't. But this does concern Donal. Without beating about the bush, Edward, could you tell me how you came to meet Mrs Wilson?"

Edward, startled, replied, "As I told you before, she visited me some time ago with an impacted wisdom tooth. She wasn't happy with the service from that charlatan Rigby down the road. He's not even a registered dentist, you know."

"Edward, this is important. I am going to repeat the question, and this time I want an honest answer. What is your relationship to Mrs Wilson?"

"Eoin," Edward said, looking nervously at Julia, "this is hardly appropriate."

Julia could see beads of sweat beginning to trickle down his pallid face.

"Tell me – are you having an affair with Mrs Wilson?" Eoin demanded.

"No! Now let's stop this at once – right now, do you hear me!" Edward said angrily. "You have no right to come in here making libellous accusations." He jumped up and opened the door. "I won't have it. I would like you both to leave – *now*. Stephen, I am extremely disappointed in you – and as for you, Julia, I will deal with you later." He looked with unconcealed hatred at her.

"No, Edward, we won't be going just yet," said Eoin, pulling the pistol from his coat pocket. He slammed the door and pushed Edward who stumbled, shocked, back into the room. "Edward, there are a few things that are not adding up here. Maybe you should consider your position carefully."

"Or what? You will shoot me! What will that achieve? Two O'Keefes convicted felons?"

"*Mm*, you are right, killing you would achieve little," said Eoin calmly. "Stephen, lock the door again, please. Julia," he said, waving the gun at the shelves, "which of these concoctions will relax our friend and make him more forthcoming and cooperative?"

"Eoin, you cannot be serious!" said Julia, terrified.

"Julia, which of them – please? Laudanum is too mild – morphine could make him unreliable, is that not so? How about ethanol? Taken intravenously that loosens the tongue by all accounts. Look, that bottle up there." He pointed to the array of colourful apothecary's demijohns clearly marked with their contents. "Make up an injection for our friend, there's a good woman."

"But, Eoin –"

"You don't want me to shoot him, do you? But believe me, I will – if I have to. First his leg, then his groin and then his heart, until he tells me what I want to know. Stephen, help Edward up onto his dentist's chair, there's a good man. I believe those are restraining straps – strap him in good and tight. It's for his own good."

"Eoin, you are really scaring me," pleaded Julia. "Please stop this – Edward will tell us what you want."

Eoin turned to him once again, "Edward?"

"I've told you all I know, Eoin. Mrs Wilson is just a patient. I think she's mixed up with the Fenians, but I don't know anything about it." He turned to Julia. "You will never see your sister again after this stunt. I am warning you one last time. For the love of God, let me go!"

Eoin placed the gun at Edward's temple and pushed him to the chair, which was in a prone position, pushing him to sit down then to lie back on it.

Stephen looked at Eoin who nodded, indicating that he should strap him in.

"Calm down, there's a good chap," said Eoin.

Stephen proceeded to buckle the wide leather restraining straps. One across his torso, a brace at each hand and one around his knees and ankles.

"The room is soundproof, is it not? That's what you told me last week."

Edward looked terrified – Julia could see a wet stain spreading down the front of his trousers.

"Eoin, please don't do this," she pleaded.

"Do it. Go on, woman! Do it, or I'll have to shoot him."

She took down the bottle of ethanol, filled a syringe and approached Edward who was lying in a state of shock on the chair.

Her hands shaking like a leaf, she pulled up his shirtsleeve and after an initial unsuccessful attempt, managed to inject Edward into a vein as she had been taught by Harriet several months before.

Edward looked pleadingly at his sister-in-law, but she avoided looking directly at him.

"Now, Julia, sit over there." Eoin waved the gun, indicating the seat. "How long before this takes affect?"

"About three minutes," she replied.

"Well, let's start with Mrs Wilson again, Edward – you met her how?"

Edward's eyes bulging with terror as he stuttered, "We

started having an affair – she threw herself at me."

"So hard to resist a woman's charms," said Eoin.

"No, really, Harriet was not well, and she was not interested in –"

"Spare me the marital details."

"And then, she started blackmailing me. She instructed me to have Julia followed, or accompanied, at all times. It was she who made the initial suggestion to get Julia to bring the note to Flanagan as a way of implicating her and using her as a bargaining tool to get Donal to play his part. I tried to prevent her involvement and to stop her meeting Flanagan. But, as you know, she is a stubborn bitch. The stress of it all! I was becoming involved with Fenians. It was like living my worst nightmare. And this harridan, this vixen, was only making it worse with her constant harping on about the Irish cause and her bloody nationalistic paintings." He shot a look of pure venom at his sister-in-law.

Julia flinched under the enormity of his hatred.

"But then Flanagan offered me a way out. He was secretly also working for the Irish Bureau, reporting to an undercover unit that was tracking Drennan and his antics. They still are."

"Where is my brother?"

"He is in Mrs Wilson's house in Granville Street."

"Not any longer, they moved him. Where have they moved him to, Edward?"

"I don't know."

"Where, Edward? Now which leg would you prefer, the right or the left?"

"Eoin, have mercy, I don't know! I swear to God I really don't know!"

Edward was becoming increasingly agitated. He started whimpering and tears rolled down his face.

"You won't tell Harriet? The new baby – Harriet is my life."

"Your source of income, you mean."

"Well, what about your role in that?" he spat at Eoin, but his words were starting to slur. "Does my sister-in-law know about your involvement in those particular arrangements?"

"We won't talk about that now, will we?" Eoin said menacingly.

Julia looked at Eoin questioningly, taken aback by Edward's words.

But Edward had fallen back comatose in the chair.

"What does he mean, Eoin?"

"Later, Julia – right now we have to get out of here. Look, you go up and pack a bag. When you are ready to go, tell your sister that you are running off with Donal. She will understand that. Try and buy some time for us before she comes looking for Edward. When he wakes up, he will probably inform his contacts in the police, so we don't have much time. Be as quick as you can."

She stood in a state of total shock, staring at him blankly.

"*Now, Julia!*"

When she knocked on Harriet's door a few minutes later she found her sister reading a book, unaware of the drama that had unfolded two floors below. But Harriet noted her sister's grave expression.

"Julia, what is it?"

"I have to go, Harriet. I am so sorry. I have to go immediately. Donal needs me."

323

"But what about me, what about the baby?" Harriet said, clutching her belly. "Julia, please don't leave me on my own."

"Don't make this harder for me than it already is. I don't have a choice. I will be back hopefully before the baby is born. You have Edward, Eileen and Florrie to look after you." She went over to the bed and kissed her stunned sister on the cheek.

As she left the room, almost as an afterthought she said, "Oh, Edward has an emergency extraction to do, and he asks that you don't disturb him for an hour or so. Goodbye, Harriet."

Chapter 28

As the carriage departed from Stockport Road, Julia realised her whole life had just been turned upside down. That knowledge, as well as her fear for the potential carnage at the exhibition and Donal's safety, was gnawing at the pit of her stomach. She went over what had just happened, trying to make sense of it all. Her head was turned away from Eoin, whose violence to Edward and her part in it had frightened and shaken her to the core.

The brougham stopped and started. It was about half past six at this stage and still light. From the window of the carriage, she watched as factory and millworkers poured onto the streets, the tired and grimy workers released like termites into the red-bricked labyrinth of the city. But as the boisterous gaggles of men and women headed for home, despite their fatigue there was an energy in their gait and in the banter that passed between them, in anticipation of the holiday ahead.

In contrast to the shabbiness of the workers, the streets

they passed through were decorated with buntings and pennants hanging between buildings in preparation for the royal visit. From windows hung swathes of blue silk banners with gold fringes with messages of welcome and loyalty to the Queen and the royal visitors. Shop-owners vied with one another with flower-framed fealties – and teams of carpenters were in the process of building viewing platforms for spectators along the royal route.

Julia felt as if they were caught up in some uncanny medieval pageant, a strange dream sequence, a continuation of the nightmare experience she had just had in the surgery.

Eoin's driver dropped Stephen off to a cousin's house in Ancoats, where most of the destitute Irish lived. The royal procession would not be passing through here, thought Julia. There were no banners or bunting in this corner of the city.

The carriage stopped at the end of the court, an incongruous name for the arrangement of back-to-back houses over cellars that faced onto a yard. Some of the windows had no glass, and a sheet of oilcloth was the only thing that protected the occupants from the elements. Washing hung between the windows, mostly shifts and grey, tattered undergarments. But in one window, grimy lace curtains framed a statue of the Virgin Mary. The pathetic scene made more poignant by the sound of children playing barefoot in black mud, the liquefied ash-piles from the recent rain, whilst dodging between their ankles, chickens and scrawny dogs scavenged for putrid scraps to survive.

Stephen jumped down from the back of the carriage, doffed his cap at Eoin and Julia and disappeared wordlessly into the tenement enclave.

"So where are you taking me to now?" asked Julia wearily, inured to the sight before her.

"Well, I have rented a house near Victoria Park. My housekeeper Mrs Appleby will make you comfortable. I told her to prepare for visitors. I just was not sure who, and how many," Eoin said ruefully. "While you are there, I will be staying at my club."

Julia nodded abstractedly.

"I am sorry to have exposed you to the episode with Edward in the surgery, Julia. If I could have avoided it, I would have. There was simply no other way. But" he said, smiling at her kindly, "I cannot think of any other woman who would have risen so admirably to the challenge." He paused. "However, although that dramatic episode was enlightening, we still don't know where Donal is. The opening is in less than twenty-four hours – how on earth are we going to find him?" He looked out of the window, deep in thought. Then he turned to Julia. "But if Flanagan is acting as a double agent, working as a spy for Drennan and the Irish office, it looks like Drennan's posse is being set up and someone is pulling the strings. I think you hit the nail on the head, Julia, at dinner on Friday – a bombing attributed to the IRB and Clan na Gael would ruin Parnell and the Irish party's credibility and destroy any prospect of Home Rule. In fact, it could turn British society en masse against the millions of Irish who are living here. I do not believe that the IRB would have any part in a plan that would be the death knell of the current detente. Donal, the gobshite, has been chosen specifically by Drennan's gang because he is not an active, or important member, of the IRB – but technically he is still a member. That's why he was rescued – he's the nominated local representative, singing to the tune of the American boyos."

"But who could possibly be orchestrating this?"

"I don't know, but I intend to find out."

"Eoin, why is Stephen here? I know he still does the books for Edward in Dublin, but I have not seen sight nor sound of him since he was spying on me all of those years ago."

"Well, after you told me about what Edward was up to, I paid Stephen a visit. Stephen, as you discovered, is a mercenary and at that time I needed someone like him to carry out detective work in divorce cases and the like. So, he has been doing bits and pieces for me to supplement his work in Trinity ever since. I thought I might need assistance when I got your telegram. So, I brought him along – and I am glad I did."

"And what was Edward insinuating about your involvement in Harriet's financial arrangements?"

"Oh, he was rambling, some old gripe he had about some legal work I did for him in the past. Anyway, that's not important now."

It seemed to Julia that he avoided her gaze.

"As soon as we get to my house you can freshen up and have something to eat after this appalling day," he said. "We need to figure out what to do next."

Julia looked completely deflated and exhausted. Eoin took her hand and kissed it and put his arm around her in a brotherly fashion. But she turned awkwardly as he did so and their faces and lips almost touched. His hand ended up resting on her breast. She didn't have the strength to pull away – and he, drawn to her, magnetised, kissed her briefly, fully, on the lips. A second passed, both caught in a trance, signalling wordlessly their desire, their senses pulsating. Until he, breaking the bond abruptly, pulled away.

"I am so sorry, Julia. That should not have happened."

He turned to look out of the window, and they passed the rest of the journey in silence, both drained and bone-weary, distracted by what had come to pass and trying to calm and rationalise their inner demons.

The Italianate-style house in Daisy Bank Road on the outskirts of Victoria Park was large and detached. The housekeeper opened the door with a stiff, slightly disapproving smile.

"Good evening, Mrs Appleby. Miss Benson was planning to travel to Dublin, but her companion has been taken ill suddenly and she finds herself having to stay in Manchester for a few days. I have assured her that you will do everything possible to make her stay here as comfortable as possible."

"Certainly, sir."

The woman, taking in Julia's apparent respectability, reappraised her reading of the situation and adopted a kindlier tone.

"Miss Benson, you look done in, if I mun be so bold t' say. If you would like t'come upstairs I can bring you up a jug of hot water to freshen up. I'll get Peters to make you a nice cup of tea and unpack yer case for yeh."

"That sounds excellent, Mrs Appleby, if it is not too much trouble."

"Thank you, Mrs Appleby," said Eoin. "I will be staying at the Athenaeum. But I will be back after dinner to talk to Miss Benson."

"Very well, Mr O'Keefe."

"Julia, I will see you later so." He lifted his hat, bowed slightly and left.

Several hours later, after dining at his club, Eoin directed Gus to return to Stockport Road. He had a few loose ends he wished to tidy up. As the carriage approached the house, at the far side of the road, as Eoin had anticipated, Julia's stalker was waiting. He was standing under a broken gas lamp smoking a pipe. Eoin opened the hatch and shouted to Gus. "Drive to the end of the terrace then slow down, don't stop. I am going to jump out and I want you to double back and wait for me just outside Number 38."

After he jumped from the moving carriage, Eoin crossed the road to the opposite side then walked back briskly to the figure under the gas lamp.

"Good evening, sir," said Eoin. "Could I trouble you for a light?"

The man took a box of matches out of his pocket and offered them to Eoin who took a cigarette from a silver case. After lighting the cigarette, he inhaled deeply and blew the smoke out of his rounded mouth in a plume which he watched evaporate into the darkness. The man was stocky, six-foot tall, dark-haired with a swarthy complexion. But his eyes belied his brutish physique – they were brown and gentle, and he was unable to hold Eoin's gaze before lowering them to the ground.

"Been here long?"

"Waitin' for somun'," the man mumbled.

"Who exactly?"

"None of yer business, sir," he said, pulling back his shoulders and sticking out his belly.

Eoin pointed the pistol, still in his pocket, into the man's side.

"Who? Or I will shoot."

The man stiffened in fright. "I am waitin' for t' man who does for t' gentleman in Number 42," he said, alarmed.

"Oh, Mr Williams' man?"

"Yes, sir."

"Mr Williams' doesn't have a man. He does for himself. But he does have a sister-in-law, a Miss Benson who tells me that you have been following her for the last number of weeks. Why?"

"There is some mistake sir. I ain't been followin' no one. I must have the numbers mixed up – mebe it were Number 43."

"If you don't tell me what you are doing, I am going to raise the alarm and call the police."

"Don't do that, sir!"

"Why not?"

"Because I'm a policeman."

"I don't believe you. Who do you report to?"

"Inspector Hodge, sir."

"Well, let's go and see this Inspector Hodge then, and see if we can find out what this is all about."

Eoin beckoned to Gus who was parked fifty yards down the road, and he pulled up to where the two men stood. Both got into the carriage.

In Cotham Street Dodd showed Eoin into Hodge's office.

"Inspector, good evening, the Right Honourable Eoin Trench is my name – solicitor. I must apologise. I accosted your officer." His introduction was delivered in his best Oxford English accent.

"My client, Miss Julia Benson, has complained that your Constable Dodd here has been following her and has been doing so for several weeks. In fact, I have just caught him lurking suspiciously outside her house in Stockport Road. But, before I make an official complaint, I thought I would give you an opportunity to explain exactly what is going on here."

Hodge, alert, took in Eoin's elegant apparel and haughty demeanour and carefully considered his words.

"Have you been representing Miss Benson for long, Mr Trench?"

"No, only recently since these events began to occur."

"Mr Trench, I am not sure whether you are aware that your client is a close friend of a Mr Donal O'Keefe, a convicted Fenian, a criminal who escaped from Strangeways prison a few weeks ago. We are currently pursuing a line of investigation and have some leads, but nothing definitive. We were hoping Miss Benson with her connections might lead us to O'Keefe and the other members of the gang. Security is on high alert because of the Prince and Princess of Wales' visit to the exhibition opening tomorrow. For these few days before and after the opening we are being aided by police officers from adjoining counties. Every undesirable is being watched closely. So, please Mr Trench, offer our apologies to Miss Benson but explain to her that our actions are in the interests of her own safety." He paused. "But you should also be aware, Mr Trench, that your client Miss Benson is known to be a Fenian sympathiser. There was a painting in Newton's windows last week that I believe upset a lot of people."

Eoin looked startled. "What you have said comes as a

surprise to me, Inspector Hodge. I was not aware of my client's political leanings." He paused and appeared to consider what Hodge had just told him. "Are the two things connected, inspector? The opening of the exhibition and Donal O'Keefe's escape."

"I believe they could be, Mr Trench."

"So, you think that they are up to something?"

"We think it's a strong possibility."

"Well, that puts a different complexion on the matter entirely."

"Precisely."

"Well, thank you very much for your honesty, inspector. And apologies to you, Constable Dodd, for any misunderstanding. I will have to consider taking further instructions from the lady."

As Eoin and Dodd left the room, Hodge pulled out a worn copy of Debrett's from his drawer to verify Trench's credentials. Then looking at the black contraption on his desk, he sighed before lifting the mouthpiece and tapping on it twice.

In a loud and formal voice, he said, "Get me Jenkinson in Whitehall immediately."

Eoin's second visit of the evening was to Drennan. He had figured that if Drennan was an exhibitor he would, at some stage, have to visit and inspect his stand at the pavilion. Finding the location was easy enough, as an indexed plan was available through the organiser's office. At his club, he had been briefed by Stephen who, earlier in the day, had visited the site at Belle Vue gardens armed with forged identification provided by Eoin. A client of Eoin's from Dublin, an artist, provided a useful, if costly, service forging documents. Posing as a reporter from the *Limerick Leader*, Stephen had been searched and vetted before finally being allowed to enter the compound. He had told Eoin that the place was like Bedlam, with contractors everywhere, installing signage, and fine-tuning the machinery. Half of Manchester's citizenry was employed at the venue in some capacity or another, and groups of people were receiving instruction on how to proceed the next day. Stephen told Eoin how he had sat on a public bench in the Irish Section and had spent the morning pretending to write his impressions of unfolding events in his notebook, with a clear and uninterrupted view of the stand of Drennan and Sons Gas Installation Engineers.

Eventually, Drennan arrived about noon, and had spent the afternoon instructing his employees, organising trade literature, and arranging the company's display of cast-iron ovens. When he left, Stephen had followed him at a discreet distance to a well-appointed residence on Plymouth Grove.

Eoin realised that he was taking a considerable risk in attempting to face Drennan down. But he had no choice. If he could not prevent Donal from committing this atrocity, his brother would face certain death. He could feel the blood pumping through his veins, giving him the strength to continue in a situation from which he would normally run a mile. He knew he should have waited for Stephen who had gone back to collect another gun from his cousin in Ancoats, but time was running out. As he got out of the carriage on Plymouth Grove, he had instructed Gus to wait in the vehicle just up the road from Drennan's house.

Eoin paused briefly behind the cover of a tree where he had a clear view of the house. Light flickered in the window of a first-floor reception room. He watched as a single figure rose from a chair. Elsewhere the house was in darkness. Please God he was alone.

Eoin opened the gate and, as he climbed the entrance steps and knocked briskly on the door, he wondered was Donal even there at all.

A footman answered and Eoin presented his card, expressing a desire to talk to Drennan. It was his own card this time, bearing the name O'Keefe. The footman returned and let him in, taking his coat and hat before showing him up the stairs and into the drawing room where Drennan was seated in a wing chair wearing an elaborate oriental brocade jacket and smoking an elegant ivory pipe.

"Ah Eoin, at last I get to meet the Unionist branch of the O'Keefe family." He remained seated and did not attempt to shake his guest's hand. "You don't mind if I don't get up? Please, take a seat."

"Drennan, as you have surmised, this is not a social visit. I know of your plans. I have come from Edward Williams. I believe that my brother is staying with you at the moment."

"Yes and no – he is not here – but yes, he is doing a small job for us tomorrow. I thought you would be pleased that at least he has some prospect of being a free man. Provided of course that there are no surprises between now and tomorrow."

"There is no point in telling you that your plan is misguided. But there is something that I think that you should know. I believe that you have been set up and encouraged to carry out this dynamite attack to deliberately collapse the ceasefire. Your operation will be foiled, and you will be captured, at the last-minute no doubt, by the police. But the damage will have been done."

"What an interesting idea! Your interpretation of events is enlightening, Mr O'Keefe, and forewarned is certainly forearmed. But, regardless, unless they have detailed knowledge of how we plan to execute this – and I am confident that they don't – it is too late at this stage for the authorities to stop us."

He got up from the armchair and went to stand at the window, inhaling the pipe, and blowing out slow sharp breaths so that the smoke created a cloud of condensation on the window. Then he turned slowly towards Eoin, his previous sangfroid vanished, and his face distorted with anger.

"You idiot, O'Keefe! You have been followed here! That gobshite Dodd is crouched in the bushes outside!"

The two men stiffened as the front doorbell broke the silence and voices could be heard in the hallway below. Eoin thrust his hand to his pocket but, before he could reach the Webley, Drennan was pointing a pistol at him.

"What exactly did you hope to achieve by your visit tonight, O'Keefe?" Drennan did not take his eye, or gun, off Eoin for a minute.

The door opened suddenly, and three men entered – whiskery Inspector Hodge, and two armed police detectives with guns drawn.

"Just in time, Inspector – this man forced his way into my house, and I was just trying to persuade him to leave."

"Drop your gun and stand aside please, sir – we have him now."

"You are under arrest, Mr Trench," said Hodge. "Or should I say Trench-O'Keeffe."

"For what precisely?"

"Assaulting a police officer, and conspiring with an illegal organisation," Hodge said.

"I am a solicitor, as no doubt you are aware," Eoin said.

"Yes, but even so a few nights in Strangeways might make you see things differently," he replied curtly.

"My brother, do you know where he is?" said Eoin, desperation staring to creep into his voice.

Hodge ignored him. He looked out through the front curtain, signalling to Dodd, still crouched in the bushes, that they were finished. "Sorry for the subterfuge, Mr Drennan, and for entering from the back lane – we didn't want to alarm your neighbours."

"No problem, inspector."

"Detective Hardy, leave as you came – through the back lane – and take him to the station, charge him. Make sure all the paperwork is in order."

"You won't get away with this, inspector!" said Eoin furiously.

After handcuffing Eoin, the two detectives marched him to the door.

As Eoin passed Drennan he stopped and said menacingly, "If any harm befalls my brother, I will kill you with my own hands."

"Enjoy Strangeways, O'Keefe."

Glaring at Drennan, Hardy led Eoin away.

When Hardy and the other detective left, Hodge turned to Drennan.

337

"Mr Drennan, it appears that you know Mr Donal O'Keefe."

"Dublin is a small town, inspector, and Donal O'Keefe is notorious, as you can imagine. Of course I know both brothers. I have done business in the past with Eoin O'Keefe, who I have always believed, until now, was a committed Union man. For some strange reason he was under the misguided impression that I might be able to tell him where his brother is."

"And do you know, sir? Because if you do, and we were to find out subsequently, it could be a serious matter indeed – perverting the course of justice at the very least."

"I can assure you, inspector – I have no idea where he is. I have my hands full with the exhibition tomorrow, all the final arrangements. I have only just got back from Belle Vue. And I am very tired – it's been a long day, as you can imagine. So, if you don't mind …"

"*Mm*," mused Hodge, then changing the subject swiftly, said, "How are the arrangements going for tomorrow? I understand that you are on the organising committee for the Irish Section."

"Yes, it will be great to do something positive here in Manchester for our country's reputation, instead of us all being tarred with the Fenians' brush."

"Indeed. I hope our officers there are being helpful. And thank you for tonight, Mr Drennan. We cannot be too careful with our Royal visitors. Better be safe than sorry. Sorry to disturb you, sir. Good night."

"Absolutely right. Good night, inspector."

Drennan sat back down in his wing chair and relit his pipe.

By ten o'clock Eoin had still not returned as he had promised earlier. Exhausted from the day's events, Julia rang the bell and told Mrs Appleby she planned to retire for the evening and that if Mr O'Keefe called to tell him she would see him in the morning.

She spent a restless night tossing and turning. The very quietness of the street, in contrast to the constant clatter of wheels and hooves on Stockport Road, unsettled her. Thoughts of Donal haunted her dreams in a sequence of disjointed events where he became Eoin and Eoin became him. She woke up bathed in a cold sweat, feeling an overwhelming sense of foreboding, which weighed on her chest, making her breathless. She was trapped in a prison of circumstances from which there was no escape.

Several hours later the dawn eventually broke, piercing the heavy woollen curtains, and shedding bands of light on the damask bed cover. And as she bathed her face in the ice-cold water left for her on the dresser the night before, she steeled herself to do what must be done and to face the day with a new resolve.

In the breakfast room she pushed away the plate of coddled eggs prepared by the cook. Instead, she drank the strong coffee and ate buttered toast to calm her nauseous stomach.

"Miss Benson, Mr Stephen Spendlove to see you – he says it's urgent. Will I tell him to come back later?"

"No, Mrs Appleby, I think you had better send him in."

A few minutes later Stephen, as mole-like as ever,

339

entered, hat in hand. She noticed he was now bald. He looked nervous as she stood up to receive him.

"Miss Benson."

"Stephen, it's been a long time."

"Yes, we didn't get a chance to talk properly yesterday. I wanted to say to you that I still regret what happened all those years ago." He lowered his head contritely. "But I was only acting on Mr Williams' instructions."

"Despite the fact that you knew it was wrong. You do know right from wrong, Stephen?"

"Of course, I do, Miss Benson. It's just that my wife had glandular fever at the time, and I needed the money for doctors and medicine."

Julia was not in the mood to listen to his sob stories.

"You should have refused. I am sure there were other ways that you could have earned extra money."

"It's easy for you to say, Miss Benson. People like us don't always have a choice. The line between right and wrong can be blurred in the face of want – and doing what's best for your family. I couldn't afford to refuse Mr Williams. I do regret it though." He paused, then continued. "I cannot change what you think about me, Miss Benson. But I came to you because I didn't know who else to trust, and I am worried about Mr O'Keefe."

"Donal?"

"No, Mr Eoin. Last night I went back to Ancoats to collect something and I spent the night with my family. Later Mr O'Keefe's driver, my cousin Gus, left him off first to Stockport Road, where he met a man who he subsequently went with to the police station in Cotham Street. He stayed there about half an hour and then asked Gus to take him to a house on Plymouth Grove, near the hospital. Gus waited outside for Mr Eoin as instructed, but he never came out. After a few hours, all the lights went out in the house and Gus got concerned. So, he called at the door, but the footman said there must have been some mistake as there had been no visitors all evening. Gus knew he was lying, but there was nothing he could do. So, Gus returned back to the stables at Mr O'Keefe's club with the carriage, and when Mr Eoin hadn't returned by daybreak, he was very worried and called to me first thing this morning."

"Oh my God!" said Harriet in alarm.

She went over to the sideboard, poured Stephen a cup of coffee and indicated that he should sit beside her.

"I'd rather stand if you don't mind," said Stephen, looking uncomfortable, but accepting the coffee.

"The opening is today, Stephen. We still don't know where Donal is, Eoin has now also disappeared and if we don't find them or do something, in five hours Drennan and his gang are going to dynamite the Royal party, kill thousands of innocent bystanders and destroy Parnell and Home Rule for Ireland – forever." Julia, hysterical with the enormity of the situation, looked at Stephen in helpless horror.

"What should we do, Miss Benson?"

Julia began to hyperventilate and started to pace in an agitated manner around the room.

"Miss Benson, calm down."

"Don't you dare tell me to calm down!" She tried to breathe in and out slowly, her head bent, leaning against the table for support.

Stephen waited patiently, saying nothing.

"We should go directly to the police," she said eventually.

Stephen rubbed the back of his neck.

"If we do that, they will arrest Mr Donal, and he will hang."

"Yes, you are right. But we may end up having to – think of all of those people!" She sat down at the table and put her hands to her head, rubbing her temples. "Alright, alright. What do we know?" she asked, desperately, trying to gather her thoughts. "Or what do we think we know. Let's start with last night. Who was the man that Eoin met at Stockport Road?"

"Gus said he was –"

"Is Gus with you?

"Yes, he's outside."

"Then bring him in – he can tell me himself."

Stephen left the room and a few minutes later returned with Gus.

His cousin, a young man in his thirties, was taller and stockier than Stephen, with fine black hair, olive-skinned, without the pockmarks but with the same thin facial features.

"Tell Miss Benson what you told me about the man Mr O'Keefe met in Stockport Road."

"Well, missus, he was tall, well built, wearing a black hat. It had a soft brim, like the jarvies wear in Ireland. He had on him a brown coat."

"The man who is following me!" said Julia excitedly. "Sorry – continue Gus."

"Yes, missus. By the way he was standing, kind of unnaturally upright, I'd say he was a peeler."

"A policeman?"

"Yes, missus, a policeman, not in his uniform. Then I drove himself and Mr O'Keefe to the station at Cotham

Street, where Mr O'Keefe stayed about half an hour or so. Then he left alone, and we drove to Plymouth Grove."

"If I might interrupt here, Miss Benson," said Stephen. "Yesterday afternoon Mr O'Keefe instructed me to follow Mr Drennan to see where he was staying, and to see could we track Donal. He gave us each fake press passes for the exhibition as reporters, from the *Limerick Leader* no less. Gus and I visited the exhibition to get the lie of the land, and that afternoon when he left, I followed Drennan to a house in Plymouth Grove. This is the house that Gus dropped him off at last night."

"So, what happened to Eoin? Please God he is safe!"

"We have only five hours till the opening, missus," said Gus. "Then all hell will break loose. Half of Manchester will be there. My family already have their children all made up for the day's celebration. My nephew even had a Union Jack. I confiscated it, of course."

"Oh my God! Oh my God! Concentrate, Julia, concentrate!" Her panic was rising again. "If we only have five hours, at this stage, there is no point trying to find Eoin or Donal. We had better use what resources we have, to stop the attack. Surely between the three of us we can do that?"

Gus and Stephen looked dubiously at one another.

"We must go to the opening, and head to Drennan's stand – he is sure to be there supervising the action – and confront him. Together, we could force him to abandon whatever crazy plan he has. I must be able to do something, even if it's only to cause a distraction." She was thinking of Mrs Wilson's theatrical performance in Strangeways.

343

"If we are to have any chance at all, we will need to be armed," said Stephen, still sounding unconvinced. "Do we have any guns? I have a pistol I got from one of my other cousins. That was all I could get. But we will need at least one other gun." Stephen looked at Gus.

"Our kind are not likely to own up to having a gun in this city, and less likely to lend them," said Gus.

"Edward has a gun – he keeps it in his study in the rolltop desk," said Julia reluctantly. "But the desk is locked, and he carries the key with him."

"Shouldn't be a problem persuading Edward to lend it to us – we've already softened his cough after yesterday," said Stephen, smirking.

"Oh dear, that means going back to Stockport Road," Julia said, dismayed. "But assuming that we get the gun, how are we going to stop the attack? Let's think this through." She paused. "Will they use dynamite, or these bombs they can throw by hand into a crowd that explode on impact?"

"I doubt that they will be throwing anything, missus. If they exposed themselves in any way, they would be lynched by the mob."

"Right, so they will place the dynamite somewhere. They have to put it in something, do they not? A box or a container of some sort."

"They have used cases, even large handbags in the past," said Gus. "The permutations are endless. They could place it anywhere, at any time."

"Well, Miss Benson," said Stephen, "if the security I had to get through yesterday was anything to go by, that will not be easy. I was bodily searched. Hard to see anyone bringing in anything that wasn't inspected thoroughly. I've never seen so many policemen and security men in one place before. And in any case, if they did manage to bring some in, they would still have to ignite it. One of them would have to be there."

"Eoin was intrigued that Drennan went to so much trouble to get Donal involved, so presumably he will be there," said Julia.

"He was also concerned that this might be a set-up. And if that is the case then we cannot trust anyone, even the police," Stephen said.

"So, if we can get to Donal and prevent him, or whoever, from activating the device, that is probably our best chance?"

"It would seem so, Miss Benson."

"If throwing a device at the actual ceremony is unlikely, then where would they place the explosives?" Julia got up again and paced the room. "Well, the Irish Section has to be an obvious choice. Drennan has had access there for the past two weeks, and it would also be appropriately symbolic."

"He'd hardly shit in his own back yard!" said Gus.

"No need for that language, Gus," said Julia. "But I think you are right. Is there a focal point in the exhibition hall? Yes, the dome, it has to be the dome – the papers have been full of it. The murals by Ford Madox Brown, the famous artist."

"Never heard of him, missus, but I'll take your word for it," said Gus.

"We will need season tickets to get in, but my friend Isabel helped paint the murals and she gave me passes for all the family. I was supposed to review the art exhibition."

"Well, they'll be of no use," said Stephen. "Only reserved seat-holders, that's people attending the ceremony, and press will be let in while the Royals are in the building. We will have to use the forged press passes again. Eoin was not planning on you being there, so you might have to doctor the name on his. But what about another gun?"

Julia steeled herself. "Alright, we will have to revisit Edward to see if we can persuade him to lend us his gun."

An hour later Julia and Stephen entered the surgery from the basement steps. A note was pinned on the outer door with a brass tack, '*Closed – Mr Williams will not receive patients today due to the celebrations for the Royal visit.*' Inside, the inner door to the surgery was closed. Edward was presumably doing paperwork.

Without knocking, Julia entered the room, followed by Stephen.

"*You! What the hell are you doing here!*" Edward shouted, red-faced and livid, veins protruding visibly at his temples. "*You have a bloody nerve! Leave immediately, or I will raise the alarm for the police!*"

"We won't detain you long, Edward. We need your gun," said Julia.

"Are you stark, staring, mad, woman? Why in God's name would I give you my gun?"

"Well, it is purely precautionary – but what we want it for is no concern of yours."

At the same time, Gus entered the room with his gun extended and moved to hold it at Edward's head.

"I believe it's in your desk – give Miss Benson the key," Gus said gruffly.

Alarmed by the stranger, Edward turned to Julia and hissed, "Do you know what you have done, you bitch! Your sister has miscarried. She collapsed in the surgery yesterday when she saw what you did to me. Doctor Maplin was here most of the night. You will leave this house and never, *ever*, darken our doorstep again! Do you hear me?"

Julia stared blankly as what he was saying sank in.

"Harriet, oh my poor darling!"

"*The key*," said Gus, taking control. "We don't have time for this. Miss Benson take the key and go up to the study. Now!"

Julia, steeling herself, opened the drawer, took the key out and ran out of the room. She ran up the stairs to the ground floor and entered the study which was behind the drawing room. She could hear Florrie moving about and talking in Harriet's bedroom above.

Thinking of Harriet, tears were running down her face as she opened the familiar roll-topped desk. It had come from Westland Row. Memories of her father seated, writing letters, flooded her mind. What would he think of her now? But this was not the time for retrospection, or regrets. She would have to deal with Harriet later.

The desk had the usual cubbyholes stuffed with correspondence. There was no sign of the gun. But she knew there was a hidden compartment. Papa had shown it to her as a child. She pressed the panel, and a secret shelf was revealed, and there was the gun. Alongside it was a rolled parchment tied with a thin blue satin ribbon. Julia took it out and briefly examined it. On the side was scrawled, *The last will and testament of Mark Benson.* What was this? A copy of his will? Julia stuffed the parchment into one of her coat pockets, and the gun in the other.

Back in the surgery, she nodded to indicate she had achieved her mission.

"I wouldn't raise the alarm if I were you, Edward," Gus said. "You haven't told Harriet about Mrs Wilson yet, have you?"

"You bastards! Just get out – and take that whore with you!"

As Eoin opened eyes it took a minute for them to adjust to the light streaming through the small, barred window of the prison cell. He had a piercing headache from the clatter Flanagan had given him by way of greeting when he arrived the night before at Strangeways. His back was also aching, from lying on the thin mattress on the hard floor – sleep had been impossible.

As the hatch in the door slid open, a black uniformed arm passed him a white-enamel bowl of watery porridge.

"Breakfast, O'Keefe," said the voice. "Welcome to Strangeways."

As he took the bowl the familiar thick lips of Flanagan were framed in the hatch opening.

"Begod, but we'll have the whole of the damn O'Keefe family in here sooner or later."

"You won't get away with this. I want to see my solicitor."

"But aren't you the clever fellah! *You* are a solicitor – why would yeh want to be throwing away good money hiring someone else?"

"Call the warden. I demand my legal rights."

"I'll pass on yer message. But I wouldn't hould yer breath, sunshine."

Not far from Drennan's house, in another rented house on Victoria Road, Drennan and Nelson were being served a hearty breakfast of bacon, cold meat, poached eggs and Manchester sausages by Drennan's housekeeper.

Emily Wilson poured coffee for the men.

"Donal, are you not eating anything?" Nelson asked.

"No, and I don't see how you can eat anything with this mass murder that you propose hanging over you!" Donal replied, trying to suppress his anger.

"You'll need your strength, man," said Nelson. "An army doesn't march on an empty stomach."

Donal pushed his plate away and got up abruptly from the table. He had been trying, unsuccessfully, for the last thirty minutes to convince them that the plan was crazy. That they didn't have a chance. Security at the exhibition had been organised by the city authorities with military precision.

Nelson read from the morning's *Manchester Courier*, "'*The volunteers lining the route will be a hundred strong from the following corps – the Manchester Artillery, Manchester Rifles, Lancashire, Salford, Oldham and Rochdale Rifles.'*" He looked over the top of the paper at Drennan. "Jesus, there'll be more soldiers there than visitors." He continued reading. "'*The royal couple will arrive at half past one at Chester Road where they will be received by a welcoming committee. After passing through Old Manchester and Salford –*' that's the model village – '*they will lunch at the Palm House Dining Room. When luncheon is finished, after a short retirement, they will form a procession and proceed by the Grand Avenue, under the dome, and then by the Northern*"

Avenue of the east nave to the dais in front of the orchestra
where the opening ceremony will take place. Immediately after
this has concluded, the Prince and Princess with their suite,
and the executive committee, will enter the art galleries by the
eastern door. They will leave by the north-western one, through
the Silk Section and across the north transept into the Irish
Section –' where we will have a special welcoming
committee for them."

"Nelson, we do exactly what was agreed. No
improvisations! Not unless strictly necessary."

"Grand boss."

"Alright. Let's go over the plan one more time," said
Drennan. "At about ten o'clock, I will enter the pavilion
at the Talbot Road railway entrance, at the front of the
building, and proceed straight to my stand – as all
exhibitors must – and wait there, all day basically – until
after the Prince and Princess have left the building. You
and O'Keefe in the wheelchair will come in through the
cripple's special entrance at Chester Road, which is at the
rear of the building, at half past ten. You will proceed
through the Flower Sculptures Hall that links into the
back of the dome. From the dome there is level access
through the Cotton exhibits to the Irish Section. Off this
area, are the 2nd class refreshment and dining rooms, and
a 3rd class café – presumably for us Irish peasants. The
café is our target. Nelson, when you hear the clapping at
the end of the ceremony, at approximately four o'clock,
you will wheel O'Keefe into the café. A young lad, a
sympathiser of the cause, will be working there clearing
tables – he will be expecting you. His name is Ned, a
ginger chap like yourself from Cork. O'Keefe will need to
use the lavatory. Needless to say, there are no lavatories

inside for 2nd and 3rd class visitors – they have to use the ones in the gardens. O'Keefe will become agitated, he's afraid he won't make it in time, and the lad will offer to help. The nearest public lavatory can be reached through the café store, to another, outdoor café behind. Unfortunately, it won't be possible for O'Keefe to take the wheelchair through the narrow store without help as there are four steps. So, the lad and Nelson will offer to help you to the privy, and once outside you will all three make a getaway. Leaving the chair behind you in the kitchen store packed with dynamite. An alarm clock will mechanically trigger a primed pistol to fire at the glass capsule containing a chemical, which will detonate the atlas powder within ten minutes."

"What time will it go off?"

"I have timed it for five o'clock, just after the opening ceremony finishes, as the royal couple are touring through the galleries."

"Where will you be when all of this is going on?" asked Nelson suspiciously.

"I will be at my stand supervising events until your exit. When you don't return after ten minutes, I will express concern and go to find you, and then scarper too. O'Keefe, you are very quiet."

"What's left to say?"

"Let us be clear, O'Keefe – there will be no heroics from you. Your dear brother is in Strangeways as we speak, so unfortunately he is not around to help you. The police are ready to arrest your Miss Benson. I believe she and your brother were involved in roughing up poor Albert in a misguided attempt to try and find out where you are."

"Albert?"

"Sorry, I mean Edward – we call him Albert because of his sideburns, his dundrearies like Prince Albert, our little joke. Isn't that right, Nelson? Yes, your sweetheart's brother-in-law has been an informer for years. Didn't you know? How do you think you were arrested at the Mosley Institute that night?"

Donal stared at Drennan in disbelief.

"Where is Julia?" he demanded after a few seconds' stunned silence, thumping his fist on the table.

"No need to get upset, old man. Albert ended up throwing her out of the house with your brother. Foolish woman. She's on her own now. Although, not quite – there was another sliveen with her, according to Albert, a spotty fellow, bald as a coot. Your brother's sidekick."

"Stephen Spendlove?"

"Yes, that's the man."

◦◦◦◦

Chapter 29

Later that morning, having entered at the Botanical Gardens entrance designated for wheelchair users and the physically infirm, Nelson pushed Donal through the Flower Sculpture Gallery, a lush display of exotic tropical plants. Scents of orchids pervaded the warm humid air, with the gentle sound of the spray irrigation system in the background. Intended to be a calm, naturalistic introduction to the frenzy of the world of industrialisation, instead it made Donal feel queasy. Over his knees was a tartan rug, for effect mostly. To add to the pathos, Drennan had insisted that he wore a Royal Irish Fusiliers uniform. But what was causing Donal most concern was the ticking of the alarm clock that he could feel under his buttocks.

"Jesus, O'Keefe you weigh a ton in this bloody chair. There will be no more apple tarts for you from now on. Otherwise, you'll be as fat as that bastard Flanagan. Let's hope that Drennan hasn't done a runner and is already here."

Donal knew Nelson was nervous but was too distraught to engage with his blather. In his mind he went over, endlessly, different options of how events might play out.

"There you are, men!" Drennan was in flying form when, after what seemed like an age, they finally reached the stand where he was engaging in lively banter with one of his fellow exhibitors. "These are two cousins of mine from home," he said to the man. "I hired them as attendants for the week. I thought that poor old Donal's war wounds might persuade a few matrons to try out our ovens," he quipped. Then, turning his back on his fellow exhibitor, moving aside and lowering his voice, he said, "All ye need to know about gas ovens, lads, if any of the women ask ye, is that they make the lightest sponges. But avoid any questions about pastry. Pastry is a bugger."

Drennan was wearing the obligatory morning suit, as was Nelson. But whereas Nelson's morning suit looked like it had seen better days, with trousers slightly too short, Drennan's was immaculate, and well fitted in fine wool cloth. A red, white and blue silk handkerchief embellished his pocket, and his tie was in matching red satin.

"Jesus, Drennan, but you are a hypocritical bastard," said Nelson, unimpressed.

Outside the protected realm of the pavilions, the whole city was a carnival. People were lining the decorated streets, already in position on stands that had been built at every vantage point along the Royal route. Picnics had been brought for the occasion – bread and pies in cloth-covered baskets, with bottles of beer for the men, and cordial for the children. Those who were walking were heading with purpose to their designated viewing point. In thirty minutes' time the royal party's procession was due to start out from Manchester Central Station to Belle Vue.

There were no cabs to be had – anyone with four wheels and a horse had offered their services for hire at exorbitant rates weeks before. Gus was to meet them inside – he was to tail Drennan for the day. Julia and Stephen decided to walk. Reluctantly, she allowed Stephen to take her by the arm. They made an incongruous couple, thought Julia, trying not to look at the dandruff on his collar, or his shabby suit. As agreed, he was carrying the hatbox that contained a miniature camera that Uncle Charles had sent her for Christmas. She herself was dressed in a serviceable, dark-green unstructured coat, a black dress, and matching bonnet. It was one of her looser costumes. The hemline of the skirt was shorter than was fashionable – suffragist style – exposing sensible boots. And she was wearing bloomers underneath. She was not sure what lay ahead that day.

Like everyone else in Manchester, Julia had watched the construction of the buildings, towering over the city's skyline. For the last six months there seemed to have been a constant stream of carts and horse-drawn vans between the railway stations and Belle Vue. All classes of vehicles carrying materials clogged up the traffic in the main thoroughfares of the city. Up close, she could not help being impressed by the sheer scale of the glass-and-steel structures – these cathedrals to industry were an incredible feat of engineering. But most Mancunians would have to wait another day for this experience.

Today there were only the carriages of the gentry, and

rich industrialists and professionals in their phaetons and Broughams. The opening ceremony was a strictly controlled event, confined to committee members, exhibitors, reserved seat ticket holders and the press. There would be no riffraff. Or none that the organisers knew about, Julia thought grimly.

Julia and Stephen joined the queue for reserved ticket holders at the Talbot Road entrance, where black top-hatted men held the arms of their wives, middle-class matrons bustled and bonneted in their Sunday best. She noticed a uniformed soldier with his sweetheart who was also waiting patiently. Amongst only a handful of children, two young girls, hair ringleted and curled, happily waved small paper Union Jack flags, whilst their brothers, their hair slicked with spit, maintained an unnatural restraint like restless puppies on a short leash.

The atmosphere was festive, everyone was in good spirits in anticipation of the day ahead. At this stage Julia had given up trying to make small talk to Stephen, and just smiled vapidly at the throngs of people around her. She felt as though she was in another world, afraid that at any moment she was going to burst into tears. Without thinking, she squeezed Stephen's arm and then, alarmed she was giving him the wrong message, apologised profusely.

They queued for an hour, or so. Julia found the wait interminable. She watched as policemen in their uniform walked up and down the line of people, their boots polished to a tee, their faces expressionless, only occasionally smiling at the antics of the children, or the sight of a pretty girl.

It was twelve o'clock when the doors were eventually

opened, and the queue started to move. An endless stream of carriages also started to arrive, driving up beside them to discharge their passengers under the entrance canopy, before heading to the designated carriage park near the Trafford Arms.

She wondered where Donal was, and if Drennan and his cronies were already inside. Or, if not, how they would arrive – probably by carriage, she thought.

Security at the door was thorough. Julia started to sweat profusely. When they reached the head of the queue, she presented her ticket and her handbag was then checked by one of two policemen at the door. She thought she would faint as she felt the pressure of Edward's pistol fixed in a thick band of elastic garter to her outer thigh. He asked for, then looked closely at her press pass which she had doctored the evening before

"I am a photographer, officer, Miss Julia Benson. I am working for the *Art Journal*."

He looked her up and down, taking in her suffragist's costume, and, with a slight cynical smile, he waved her through.

She waited for Stephen. The two policemen looked at the hatbox with raised eyebrows.

"And what have we got here then?"

"It's mine," said Julia, smiling with as much confidence as she could muster. "This is a miniature camera – I intend to take photographs of the paintings of the dome for the *Journal*. They are by my friends Isabel Dacre, and Ford Madox Brown the artist. I am sure you have heard of Mr Madox Brown. The camera is only in patent at the moment. As you can imagine, I am so excited to use it today for the first time on such a special

357

occasion. Look, would you like me to show it to you?" From the hatbox she took out the miniature camera. It was called Marion's Metal Miniature and came in a walnut box that contained the lens, slides and a box of plates. The box also acted as a stand. Mr Newton had helped her to fix a carrying strap to transport it in a hatbox a few weeks earlier, and the previous evening Stephen and Gus had fitted a false bottom, under which was concealed the other gun.

The officers carefully examined the camera, then called over a sergeant standing nearby and explained what she had just told them.

Julia's heart was beating rapidly, but she continued to smile as convincingly as she could.

"There's no photographs t' be taken of any t'exhibits without the permission of t'Executive Council," he said officiously, but she could see he was intrigued by the device. He examined the camera carefully. "And none whatsoever of t' royal party and t'opening ceremony. Although there will be a few photographers at stands takin' portraits of visitors. But nowt has been said by anyone concerning pictures of t'building." He looked at Julia with a twinkle in his eye. "I am a bit of a photography buff myself," he informed her knowingly. "And I've heard about Mr Marion's cameras, very clever, very clever indeed." He scribbled a note on a yellow form and handed it to her. "Here, give this to them as asks what you are about. But only the dome, mind, nowt else. Off you go, ma'am, and good luck with the photographs." He waved Julia and Stephen along.

Julia, not believing her luck, grabbed onto Stephen for support as they climbed the steps from the foyer and entered the main exhibition building directly under the dome.

Despite the fact that her heart was still beating rapidly, she looked around the space in awe. As a young woman, she had been to the Great Dublin Exhibition in 1853 but this building seemed to be half as high again.

A spectacular fountain gushed at least thirty feet in the air. Four cast-iron fluted columns supported the glass dome overhead. And between these were the spandrel panels, beautifully decorated by Ford Madox Brown and Isabel. Momentarily she forgot her fear, lost in rapt admiration, until a familiar voice interrupted.

"Julia, how wonderful! I am so pleased you could come!"

Julia's heart sank suddenly as she lowered her gaze, to be met by Isabel's. She had known her friend would be here, but she had hoped that she might avoid her in the crowds.

Isabel looked strangely at Stephen, waiting to be introduced.

"Isabel, lovely to see you and thank you so much for the tickets! Unfortunately, Edward and Harriet couldn't come, so my friend Stephen who is visiting from Dublin came instead. He also kindly offered to carry my camera for me." She said this in a slightly patronising manner, signifying Stephen was there on sufferance, only to be of service. "I am going to take photographs of your panels and send them to the *Art Journal*. It was meant to be a surprise for you." Julia was conscious that she had done nothing but lie through her teeth all morning.

"Oh, how thoughtful of you! Madox Brown will be delighted. He's here today somewhere. Unfortunately, the poor man has a chest infection, after all those long nights spent in his draughty stables getting this finished." She continued in her usual animated fashion. "Do you know, Julia, I just saw your Mr Drennan – he was on his way to the Irish Section. He was quite charming as usual. He had his two cousins with him, one of them a soldier from the Royal Irish Fusiliers. The poor man was in a wheelchair – he was injured in Egypt according to Drennan and was in full uniform. Still looked rather unwell, I thought. They are acting as attendants on Drennan's stand, trying to sell gas ovens he tells me."

"Oh, we must say hello," Julia managed to respond.

"Well, I must go and take my seat. Good luck with the photographs. Cheerio!"

Julia looked at Stephen, the fear on his face reflecting what she knew was on hers. A voice bellowed over the microphones of the public-address system.

"Will all reserved ticketholders please proceed immediately to their seats. There is no access to the stands at this time. Ladies and gentlemen, take your seats, please!"

Julia tried to smile calmly even though her heart was racing. She turned to Stephen.

"If they are at the stand, then they must not be planning to attend the opening ceremony. Damn! The attendants will make us leave until after the royal tour of the exhibition is completed if we don't have seats."

Stephen rubbed his neck anxiously and then said in a lowered voice, "There is an open-air café behind the Northern Gallery where there is a small room for the press. Gus and I were there yesterday. Follow me – we'll say we need to pick up a telegram urgently. There may be other reporters there, but when everyone has left for

360

the ceremony, we will lock ourselves in. If we are questioned, we can say you feel faint, and when the clock strikes four, when the formalities are due to finish while everyone is still at the Eastern end of the pavilion, we will confront Drennan. Please God we won't be too late."

Donal, to distract himself, looked around the Irish Section. The decorations in this part of the pavilion had been inspired by Celtic interlace. Donal vaguely remembered Eoin telling him that his client, the architect Tom Deane, had designed them. There seemed to be various displays demonstrating Ireland's progress in civil, mechanical, and engineering works. Just opposite them were models of dry and wet docks in Dublin and Belfast. Across the hall the railway companies also had stands, as did the Dartry Waterworks. But in different circumstances, the display that would have interested him most were Howard Grubb's astronomical instruments. The company were famous for supplying these all over the world. He thought ironically how these would have also fascinated Julia.

He sat, as instructed, in Drennan's booth surrounded by large domestic cast-iron ovens decorated with copper pots and pans, and china jugs filled with unlikely bunches of rapidly wilting bluebells. He moved slightly in the chair – the gun in the holster under the heavy military jacket was sitting uncomfortably on his chest. Drennan had provided them both with guns shortly after they arrived, smuggled in some weeks earlier during the construction of a false fireplace that formed part of the display. He looked around him, trying to take in the lie of the land. He could just about see the roof of Grubb's iron-

and-wood observatory with the revolving dome that he had read about in the papers.

Despite the visual distractions, the hour during the ceremony passed slowly. Donal's breath caught at the top of his throat. He was painfully aware of the ticking time-bomb under his arse. It seemed to pervade his whole body, so that his heart seemed to be in tune with its metallic beat. He thought of what had led to today's events, and of Julia, Eoin, and poor Bea in Dublin. He had let them all down, he had been a burden on them for years. And in all honesty, he felt he had achieved very little. No matter what happened today, he must make it up to Julia. Drennan's claims of Edward's treatment of her as an unpaid skivvy had sickened him. He had trusted him to keep her safe. He thought sadly how she had given up her life for him.

He breathed in deeply and resolved to do the right thing for once.

The drone of interminable speeches went on and on, interspersed with music which could be heard clearly from the Eastern end of the gallery where the ceremony was taking place. Eventually they heard the clatter of seats scraping as people stood up when the Royal couple left the dais and headed towards the art galleries to start the first leg of their tour of the exhibition. Donal started gesticulating to Nelson that he needed to use the lavatory.

Nelson, leaving Drennan and his ovens in the main exhibition area, entered the empty café, pushing Donal in the wheelchair. As promised, Ned was there waiting for them, wearing a long white spotlessly clean apron. The young lad, freckle-faced and ginger-haired, eagerly led the two men to the store off the cafe area. They passed through a room filled with cartons of Typhoo tea, bottles of Camp coffee and boxes of Garibaldi biscuits. From the store there were four steps to a passage that lead to a door into the open-air cafe.

"We will leave the chair here," said Nelson. "Up you get, O'Keefe. Is the device still ticking?"

Donal got up slowly, pulling out his gun and pointing it directly at Nelson.

"Sorry, old chum, we are not leaving the chair here. Slight change of plan, I'm afraid."

"O'Keefe, for Christ's sake, don't be an ass! Put the gun away!"

Ned put his hands in the air, eyes round and mouth wide open, a look of terror on his face.

"Nelson, I have never been more serious in my life. Now give me your gun and lift the chair down the stairs."

Nelson, eyes locked with Donal's, reached under his jacket and reluctantly handed him his gun.

"Ned, you can go back to the café like a good man – thank you for your help. Nelson and I are going for a walk."

Not hanging around, Ned turned and scarpered back to the café as fast as his skinny legs would carry him.

At the back of the western nave of the Northern Gallery, in the small press room, Stephen and Julia were standing with their backs pressed to the wall on either side of the window, so that no one looking in would see them. As an extra precaution, they had locked the door. Julia was getting restless. Her back was sore from standing for so long.

"Miss Benson, are you alright?"

"Yes, Stephen. Although I never thought I would end up in a situation like this, hiding like a common criminal!"

Ignoring her comment, he replied, "Judging from the time, I would say the ceremony is over. The music has stopped anyway. Everyone is supposed to stay in their seats until the Royal party has completed the exhibition tour. We need to get back to Drennan. We should take the route through the Flower Gallery as that's the only way Mr Donal in his wheelchair can leave the building. Do you have your gun ready?"

"Look the other way, Stephen."

After making sure his head was turned, Julia bent down, and hooching up her skirt withdrew the gun from her garter.

"If anything happens to me today, Stephen – could you tell Harriet I am sorry – truly sorry."

"Any message for Edward?"

"He can go to hell!"

"Nice, Miss Benson. Nice."

Julia smiled to herself. "And Stephen?"

"Yes."

"I am sorry for being so unforgiving earlier, I should have shown more compassion for your circumstances."

"That's alright, Miss Benson. Now come on, we both have families to go home to. Let's go and get this over with."

Julia and Stephen left the open-air café, as Donal and Nelson were entering from the kitchen store, missing one another by seconds.

Heading through the flower gallery, Julia and Stephen walked back under the dome and into the Irish Section.

Drennan was still there chatting to one of the other exhibitors. There was no sign of Donal.

They approached the dapper Drennan and Julia asked brusquely, "Where is Donal? We know what you are planning to do."

"Miss Benson, your manners if you please – and this is?"

"It doesn't matter who I am," said Stephen, taking his pistol from his pocket and pointing it at Drennan.

"I am sorry to say that you are too late," he said, unperturbed. "Such a pity to have missed him. Mr O'Keefe will be devastated."

"Where is he?" Julia asked, thin-lipped.

"I believe he has already left the building."

Drennan looked at his watch. "And you should too, you know, and quickly. I think we have just about fifteen minutes. Cheerio!"

Julia and Stephen watched in horror as he walked briskly away from the stand and down the gallery. They looked at each other blankly and automatically Stephen raised the gun, aiming at Drennan's back. But just as he did Drennan turned his head and, with a quizzical look and condescending manner, smiled and lifted his hat.

Julia put her hand firmly on Stephen's arm so that he lowered the gun.

All around them other attendees were watching what was happening with alarm. The Royal couple were still in the art galleries but would be here any minute. One of the exhibitors that Drennan had been chatting to started shouting at Julia and Stephen.

"Ye feckin' eejits, would ye have a bit of sense! Get out of here now, before half of the British army comes around that corner and makes minced meat of ye!"

365

"Missus, you should know better – are ye Fenians? There's a door from the café over there that leads through a store to outside!" shouted another Irish voice.

Julia and Stephen panicked, and ran towards the café door. The sound of the pipers accompanying the royal tour was getting closer and closer.

They ran across the café, knocking into the chairs and tables in their haste to leave. They ran through the door, through the store and down the steps. The door outside was unlocked and they passed through to the open-air café from where they had just come.

Julia stopped suddenly and turned to Stephen. "We cannot just leave – the dynamite is about to go off – we need to raise the alarm."

Stephen looked at her, then almost reluctantly said, "Yes, of course, you are right – we will go back to the dome and inform the police."

They entered the flower gallery from the open-air café to return to the dome. But, as they did, they saw through the glass two distant figures in the garden – two men. One in a wheelchair, the other in a soldier's uniform pushing him down the long path towards the bridge to the island in the middle of the ornamental lake.

Julia reckoned that they were several minutes away from them.

As the figures crossed the bridge, as if in slow motion, the man got out of the wheelchair and pushed it into the lake. As it hit the water the wheelchair exploded with a large bang that cracked under the ceiling of low cloud and reverberated across the sky. A plume of black smoke billowed out, encasing the figures on the island, and hiding them from view.

With the explosion, soldiers and policemen en masse ran out of the exhibition pavilion and started running towards the island and the escaping fugitives. After a few minutes, the cloud subsided, and two figures could be seen running around the far side of the island, through the flower beds towards the side exit to the gardens.

Donal was running with difficulty, trying to keep up with Nelson. They were both heading for the staff exit from the gardens at the back of dining rooms. Donal's gun was in his hand, but he had taken the precaution of throwing Nelson's gun into the lake. But Nelson did not need any persuasion – at this stage they were both running for their lives.

When they reached the gate, they slowed down. There was a young guard at the single door to Chester Road, but other than that the road was quiet. A couple of hours earlier the Royal couple had entered, a hundred yards or so up the road, at the Royal Entrance. But now the queues to enter the exhibition, once the Royal couple had left, were at the front of the building.

"Shoot him, O'Keefe – it's our only chance."

"No, I have other plans – you will have to trust me on this one, Nelson."

Nelson looked in disbelief, as Donal grabbed him from behind and pointed the gun at his head.

"Guard, I need your help! You just heard the explosion. Get me a carriage please, urgently, I need to take this Fenian suspect to the police station as soon as possible." Donal, dressed in his officer's uniform, flashed the gun briefly at the guard.

"Right, sir," the guard said, saluting the officer.

The guard whistled, calling one of the hansom cabs parked up the road.

As the cab drew up, the two men climbed into the carriage – Donal with the gun still pointed at Nelson's head.

"Cotham Street Police Station driver – *now*."

The carriage pulled off, leaving the flustered guard behind on the pavement wondering what had just happened. Minutes later soldiers in pursuit of the fugitives poured out of the exit – too late, as the carriage disappeared down Chester Road.

Julia and Stephen watched with other attendees as crowds started to gather in the gardens.

"What is happening?" people asked.

"Has there been a dynamite attack?"

"What was the explosion on the lake? Was it the Fenians?"

Suddenly, alarm bells sounded, rattling the glass in the pavilion, but they stopped after a few seconds.

A disembodied voice was heard over the public-address system. "*Ladies and gentlemen, please, there is nothing to be alarmed about. There has been an incident on the ornamental island on the lake. We think the fireworks, planned for later, have gone off accidentally.*"

People nodded knowingly, throwing their eyes up to heaven.

The voice continued, "*The Royal couple Their Majesties the Prince and Princess of Wales have now left the building and we would like you to enjoy the rest of the day. You are cordially invited to enter the exhibition, which has now been officially opened. Thank you, and good afternoon.*"

Julia looked at Stephen, tears running down her face.

He took her hands in his. "They got away, Miss Benson, they got away, and no one was hurt. We can go home."

Without really understanding why, Julia felt desolate as she followed Stephen to face the long walk back to Daisy Bank Road.

Chapter 30

By the time Julia got back to the house in Daisy Bank Road, it was dark. Stephen bade her goodbye at the gate and she climbed up the short flight of steps and knocked on the door. As Peters opened the door, she stumbled into the hall, exhaustion finally catching up with her.

"Well, look at the state you're in!"

"Molly! What are you doing here?" said Julia, completely taken aback.

"Mr Eoin sent me a telegram, said you needed me, and Miss O'Keefe kindly organised a ticket, and here I am. And not before time, be the looks of yeh. What in the name of God has happened?"

Peters took Julia's coat and bonnet, then with a nod from Molly scuttled off.

Molly looked scathingly at Julia's costume. "Still wearing those quare clothes, I see."

"Where is Mrs Appleby?" said Julia anxiously.

"Don't worry about her, she must have hollow legs

that one. She took to the bed after a half bottle of whiskey but not before I'd weaselled out of her about the strange comings and goings in this house. Poor divil, she is scared out of her wits, I can tell you. Doesn't know what her master's involved in at all. She was jabbering about the Queen's visit, and this exhibition, and there's talk downstairs of people following other people, like somethin' from those detective books. I didn't say it, mind, but it sounds to me ye are all involved with those godforsaken Fenians agin!"

Molly bundled Julia into the drawing room and sat her on a chair in front of the fire, wrapping a Foxford blanket around her shoulders. And, as she left to instruct the housemaid to take hot water up to the bedroom and to make tea, Julia stared into the fire, completely drained of all energy.

When Molly returned with the tea, she watched Julia drink the hot liquid as she jabbered on with the gossip from her daughter's dairy, and Westland Row. Julia nodded and smiled but she felt as if everything was happening in slow motion, in a world she was not part of, seeing through a haze.

She was aware of Molly subsequently taking her upstairs to her bedroom, undressing her, and giving out about the state of her undergarments – how her linen had been badly mended – and how she'd be ashamed if Mrs 'fancy pants' Appleby were to see them. She put Julia's nightgown and dressing gown on her and sat her by the fire.

Julia eventually began to regain her self-possession as Molly filled a basin for her with hot water and coaxed her to put her feet in it. And Julia soaked her blistered feet, feeling the warm water coax the blood back through her veins. Molly, using a soft cloth, washed her hands, neck, and face as gently as if she were a child. Then she dried her feet tenderly in a warm, dry towel.

At the other woman's touch, Julia burst into tears, her body racked with despair.

"There, there, let it all go – soonest gone, soonest mended," said Molly, helping her to her feet and guiding her to sit at the end of the bed, her arms around her, "Nothing's that important. Not Ireland, nor any man."

She looked at her closely as she said this, and Julia sobbed even more. Until, eventually spent, the sobbing gave way to a hiccoughing whimper.

"Molly, I am so sorry – I've got you all wet."

"*Shh*, Miss Julia. Are yeh alright, pet? Is it – is it Mr Donal? Are they going to hang him, is that it?"

"I don't know. I don't know anything anymore."

"And Mr Eoin, what's the story with him? He's got quare considerate lately – that was very thoughtful of him to bring me over."

Julia looked like she was going to start sobbing again and Molly looked at her anxiously, folding her once more into her ample bosom.

"There's none of 'em good enough for yeh, yeh know. Come on now. Let's get yeh into bed. We can talk tomorrow. For now, yeh're no use to God nor man, yer all done in."

Over in Cotham Street, the two men sat around the table waiting for the phone to ring. Jenkinson had his arms crossed and was sitting upright with a pained expression on his face.

Hodge was pinching tufts of his sprouting moustache between his fingers. Neither man was in the mood for conversation.

The phone rang, echoing in the windowless office.

Hodge picked it up. "Yes, Jones, put him through." He handed the earpiece to Jenkinson.

"Good evening, sir. No, sir … absolutely, sir … you are right, it is not a good evening. Well, events played out unexpectedly today, sir. O'Keefe and Nelson handed themselves in here this evening. O'Keefe claims he was set up by Drennan and others in 'high places', and Nelson is backing him up. We thought under the circumstances to play down any Fenian involvement until we get our story straight. O'Keefe's brother is here too, we arrested him yesterday for assaulting a police officer. But he is a very slippery character. He's a solicitor it seems, not to be trifled with. Seems his mother is some sort of distant cousin of Lord Burlington's. Very well, sir."

Jenkinson handed the phone back to Hodge who replaced it on the receiver.

Ours not to reason why, thought Hodge, as he tried to understand the recent, disturbing turn of events. How the hell, he wondered, am I supposed to explain this to Dodd?

The following morning Eoin had still not returned. Julia had given Molly a sanitised version of events. She told her about Donal escaping and how he had got involved with the Americans, a bad lot, and that Eoin had tried to help him, and had ended up being arrested. Julia spent most of the day reading the newspapers about the exhibition and the events of the previous day. She

373

couldn't understand why there was no mention of the explosion and Donal's dramatic escape. She was also concerned about Eoin not returning.

She asked Mrs Appleby to arrange for a boy to drop a note to Stephen in Ancoats. But before she had even finished the note, Mrs Appleby showed Stephen into the drawing room.

Julia shook Stephen's hand warmly. "Any news, Stephen?"

Whilst wringing his soft hat, he explained. "I've just come from Cotham Street Police Station. Mr Donal and Mr Eoin are both there. Mr Eoin spent the last two nights in Strangeways, but he's got some fancy brief, I mean solicitor, from London. They tried to hold him under the charge of assaulting a police officer. But they couldn't make the second charge stick of him being a member of an illegal organisation. His brief has arranged bail, so he will be released later. Mr Eoin has friends in high places," he said knowingly. "Anyway, I didn't get to talk to Mr Eoin, but he sent me a note saying to make sure that you are alright, and not to worry about Donal – he's handed himself in, and Eoin and his brief are trying to broker a deal for him."

"He won't be hanged?" asked Julia anxiously.

"It's too soon to say, I am afraid – we will just have to wait and pray."

Julia tried to control her welling tears. "But, Stephen, why was there nothing about it in the papers?"

"No idea, Miss Julia, very strange indeed."

Molly and Mrs Appleby spent most of the afternoon in the kitchen gossiping – and drinking whiskey, Julia suspected. But Molly had also washed, ironed, mended and darned every scrap of clothing Julia had with her.

Julia, in anticipation of Eoin's return, was not able to relax and spent most of the day in the drawing room, ostensibly reading a book from Eoin's library about medieval buildings in the Lake District and trying not to look out of the window. She was not allowing herself to think about the future, as when she did she felt a dull depression as she considered the potential outcomes to her present situation. Until finally at ten o'clock, when he still had not returned, Molly insisted she go to bed.

Tossing and turning, she couldn't sleep. Sometime in the early hours of the morning, her throat was parched. A dog barked in the distance, but apart from that the house was unusually quiet. She guessed it was about three in the morning. She took her dressing gown from the armoire where Molly had hung it so carefully the evening before and, lighting a candle, she made her way down to the scullery in the basement to search for some of the cook's homemade lemonade.

But, as she approached the kitchen, she noticed a light under the door. She thought it must be Mrs Appleby but instead she found Eoin sitting at the kitchen table, his back bent, and his head in his hands. A glass of ale was in front of him, untouched. He looked up as she entered.

"Julia."

"Eoin, at last! I was worried sick about you." She stopped in her tracks. His face was bloodied and bruised, one eye swollen purple, and blood had seeped through the back of his shirt. You are injured! My God, are you alright?"

"Just a few cuts and bruises – Flanagan got his revenge," he said, forcing a smile.

"Let me look at these for you."

She got water from the scullery and filled a pot, placing it on the range which was still burning. She searched the scullery presses for lint and clean cloths and finally returned to him with a basin of warm water.

She stared to gently wipe his face. She sensed his embarrassment at her proximity and the intimacy of her actions, but he did not look at her. Trying to appear detached, although her heart was beating, she helped him to take off his shirt, and she carefully wiped the congealed blood off the still raw lacerations.

He winced but stayed silent, his breathing laboured. She noticed his skin was sallow and covered with fine black hairs, not like Donal's. Dressing the deepest cuts first, she wet lint with some extract of lead which she had found amongst the medicines. She then covered these with some greased lint, fixing the dressing with plasters, and finally she wrapped cotton bandages around his chest. He lifted his head as she did so – she could feel his breath on her cheek.

"Thank you, Julia," he said quietly, his eyes looking anxiously into hers.

"It is I who must thank you, Eoin," she said, taking a deep breath and trying to quell her racing pulse. "For letting me stay here – for Molly."

"It was nothing," he replied, the hooded brown eyes half closed once more. "I thought, no matter what happened you would need her."

He then proceeded in a matter-of-fact way to relay the previous day's events. He told her of his visit to Cotham Street police station and then to Drennan's house, and his two nights in Strangeways.

She in turn told him about the unexpected turn of events at Belle Vue and Donal's escape.

"What has happened to Donal?" she asked.

"Well, he is in Cotham Street Police Station as I am sure Stephen told you. He handed himself and Nelson in. It was the only honourable way out. It sounds to me as if Jenkinson set up Drennan, using Flanagan and your brother-in-law Edward as informers."

"I wonder if Jenkinson was the man I saw with Edward and Flanagan at the Ducie Arms."

"Very probably. It seems Jenkinson justified the whole business saying that pre-emptive strikes such as this were the only way to oust the Fenians."

"What a tangled web of deception! You wouldn't believe it, even if you read it in the papers!"

"No, I don't believe you would," said Eoin thoughtfully.

Chapter 31

The next day, some miles from the smoke-plumed skies of Manchester, in the charming seaside town of Formby – in one of the town's superior boarding houses – a gentleman and his female companion were eating a late breakfast.

"Sugar?"

"No, thank you. I'm sweet enough as it is," she replied.

The woman, dark-haired and attractive, buttered a teacake and ate it enthusiastically, butter trickling down her chin, and licking her lips when she finished.

Drennan wearily handed her a napkin.

"You might need this."

The breakfast room was empty – it was still early in the season – other than old Mrs Caldicott who was stone deaf. She was staring vacantly out of the bay window, past the lifeboat station and out across the glittering sea to where steamships could be seen in the distance coming to and from the busy port of Liverpool. The sea was surprisingly calm after the storm that had raged for hours the previous night. As a result, Drennan had slept badly. He swallowed a mouthful of coffee. Looks like we are stuck here in Formby for the next few days, he thought gloomily, at least until the dust settles. They are probably watching the ports.

"I'm sorry, Mr Stewart, this man just pushed right passed me!"

Drennan jumped up from his seat, his knife in his hand.

The maid bustled officiously behind Eoin who now stood face to face with Drennan.

"Lovely view, Drennan. Mrs Wilson, so nice to meet you again. My brother sends his regards. He is one of your many admirers, I believe."

Emily scowled.

"Mind if I join you?" Without waiting for a response, he sat down and waved the maid away.

She hesitated briefly but Drennan nodded to her in acquiescence.

"How did you find us?" said Drennan.

"Relatively easily. Gus, a colleague of mine has been tailing you since you left Belle Vue. Stephen and Gus are outside just in case we need them." He nodded towards the door. "But we might as well be civilised about this." Eoin's face was expressionless. He looked at Drennan lazily, under his hooded eyes. "As you may, or may not be aware, my brother is in Strangeways with the prospect of the hangman's noose hanging over his head."

"Good enough for him!" said Drennan angrily, "If it wasn't for his bloody heroics, we would all be halfway across the Atlantic Ocean at this stage."

"Possibly, but as you know Donal believed that your

plan was a travesty – on all fronts – the needless deaths and the political repercussions. Home Rule would have been permanently off the political agenda."

"Will ye never learn? Violence is the only language that the Brits understand, despite Parnell's lily-livered approach and high falutin' rhetoric!"

"We must beg to differ on that score, but something Miss Benson told Stephen has been bothering me, and that was Edward Williams' connection with Jenkinson and Flanagan. As I previously suggested, before we were so rudely interrupted, is it possible that you were being set up? Or were you also working for the British government?"

"Listen, you bastard, I would die for Ireland if I had to."

Emily stiffened as Mrs Caldecott, who had picked up her ear trumpet, was staring over at their table.

"Gentlemen, can ye calm down please!" Emily glared at Drennan, then turned to Eoin, "Mr O'Keefe, I nursed your brother, and I am very fond of him. I know you must think very little of me, but you know we all prostitute ourselves in one way or another. I do what I do best and believe me I have just cause to hate the British. We both do." She put her hand on Drennan's sleeve. "We only made the connections between Edward and Jenkinson after the event, when I visited Edward to tell him I was in the family way and to persuade him to pay me a stipend to support my child – 'our child'. Such an upright gentleman, if I might be so bold as to say so," she said provocatively. "I knew we would have to make a hasty retreat and I needed a little extra cash. He had told Harriet everything, so at that stage blackmail was no longer an option. Unfortunately, I had to tell him a little white lie."

She smirked at Drennan whose face was still thunderous. "He reluctantly agreed to pay me an amount of money after I told him the Brothers have their own ways of dealing with philanderers and informers. But he was in quite a state. He told me he was in fear of his life that British government spies were going to kill him because he knew too much. He was particularly terrified of Jenkinson whom he described as a cold heartless bastard."

Drennan, who had been quiet as Emily talked, interrupted.

"O'Keefe, it is in no-one's interests that this fiasco is exposed. Despite Donal's defection – because have no doubts that is how the Brothers will see this. Yes, we were set up. Although the Brothers would never admit this. The real duplicity, however, is at a level above Jenkinson. I was informed after the Belle Vue debacle through one of our contacts in Whitehall that Jenkinson reports to Lord Salisbury. He also told me that Salisbury has had General Millen, Clan na Gael's military strategist, in his back pocket for several years. It was he who orchestrated the plot, to set us up, supply us with dynamite and point us towards the Jubilee celebrations. They had hoped for the Queen, but she sent her son and daughter-in-law instead."

"Why would they do this? Why take these enormous risks?" asked Eoin.

"To discredit Parnell, of course, and the Irish party. To return Salisbury to a position of power within the government, so that he is not relying on their vote."

"Is there any way of proving this?"

"Well, the Brothers will be dealing with General Millen. Maybe if he was arrested and put on trial in England, then the British people might get more than they bargained for, maybe even bring down the whole bloody government."

"Could you arrange that? For Millen to be arrested, I mean?"

"I will have to talk to the Americans, but yes it should be possible. Fortunately, Jenkinson and the Irish Office operate mostly outside of official police circles. So yes, we could arrange to have him picked up. But that might take time."

"Time is something I don't have," Eoin said defiantly.

❧

Chapter 32

She had never been inside a police station before. Molly had insisted on coming with her, and for once she was grateful for the older woman's support.

The policeman at the front desk had lifted a flap in the front counter and brought her down a narrow staircase to the basement, where he left her sitting in a small room with only a high-level barred window. The room was simply furnished with a desk and two chairs. An overwhelming smell of bleach made her nauseous. She took a hanky out of her handbag and breathed in its comforting lavender smell.

After about ten minutes, Donal entered. Although he was bruised and beaten, he looked as if he had been cleaned up for the visit which had been organised by Eoin's solicitor.

Julia jumped up and ran over to him.

"It's alright, it's alright, I look worse than I feel."

"Donal, I didn't know what had happened to you,

whether you were dead or alive. Thank God you're alive!"

"Just about, I think," he said, smiling. "I had no idea you were there at Belle Vue until Eoin told me. My God, you are a brave woman. You'll have to join those suffragist women, put all of that dering-do to better use than this!"

"Maybe I will," she said sadly. "What's going to happen, will you be sent back to jail?"

"For a while anyway, until they have extracted every bit of useful information from me. But Eoin is confident he can get me out – for good this time." He let her go and took her hands in his. "I have had enough, Julia – I have given up enough of my life for this. My time in Strangeways has made me see sense. I have made my contribution, made my sacrifices for Ireland, I have no more to give. When I get out of here, we can go to America and start a new life. At least now I have property there – I never got a chance to sell it. A house on a farm on the outskirts of Chicago. I can get a job in a local attorney's office. Eoin has several contacts there. Julia, my darling, we can be together at last."

"Until the next knock on the door, in the middle of the night. You know the Brothers will never forgive you." She moved away, then turned to face him, her eyes filled with tears. "Donal, I don't know if I can do this anymore – to start again. Chicago is a long way away."

"What will you be leaving? More to the point, who will you be leaving – Harriet, Edward? Just think, a new life. And you can paint away to your heart's content. Julia, my dearest, I love you so much, you mean everything to me."

She looked into his tearful eyes, then looked away.

"Look," said Donal, a note of desperation creeping into his voice, "you don't need to promise anything now, just think about it."

The bedroom in Daisy Bank Road was light and airy as morning sun filled the room. A lovely room, looking out onto a well-manicured garden, thought Julia. It reminded her of her mother's bedroom in Westland Row.

Molly had woken her at nine and had asked the housemaid, Peters, to bring her warm water to wash.

Julia then dressed slowly and carefully. During the night she had stayed awake for several hours thinking things through, until finally she had come to a decision. She then fell into a deep satisfying sleep. She knew what she must do. She would stay in Daisy Bank Road until Eoin returned. She felt that this was the least she could do, to thank him for all he had done for her. Stephen had sent her a note saying that Eoin was in Liverpool but would return to be charged later in the week before the Manchester Assizes, for assaulting a police officer. The note also said that Donal and Nelson were still in the cell in Cotham Street Police Station being interrogated pending a preliminary hearing before the district judge.

She tried not to think about Donal, or Eoin – the sadness of it all was too much to bear. She wiped away tears that were falling down her cheeks. Forcing herself to sit up straight and adjusting her hair, she thought she would probably ask Gus to take herself and Molly in the carriage to the shipping company in Piccadilly to buy a ticket to Dublin, and then back to Stockport Road to make her peace with Harriet.

"Miss Benson, sorry to disturb you," said Peters, "you have visitors. It's very early, I told them you haven't even had breakfast yet, but one of them says she is your sister."

"Oh," said Julia, alarmed, hastily drying her eyes. "Thank you, Peters, I will come down immediately."

Julia opened the door of the breakfast room, a small bright room at the back of the house also overlooking the garden.

Harriet was standing by the round table which was laid for breakfast. Beside her, seated, was Kitty, Uncle Charles' housekeeper.

"Kitty, what on earth are you doing here?"

"Miss Julia," said the kindly, round-faced woman, tears in her eyes, "I am sorry to say I have bad news for you. Your uncle died two days ago. He made me promise I would come over here and tell you myself."

Julia broke down. Big loud sobs racked her body as she stood shaking with grief, tears running down her face. Silently Kitty stood up and put her arms around her.

"There, there, Miss Julia, it were for the best – he's gone to the good Lord, he was in terrible pain. You know, his condition had got much worse."

Julia eventually stopped crying and looked at the older woman, noting her swollen and red-rimmed eyes.

"Poor Kitty, you were so good to him. I am just so sad that I wasn't there for him in the end."

"Don't worry, Miss, he knew you had your own problems."

Kitty looked at Harriet who stood, pale-faced and expressionless.

Julia went over to her sister and embraced her.

"Harriet, I am so sorry, you must be so upset too – he

was like a second father to us both."

Harriet squeezed Julia peremptorily then disengaged herself.

"Julia, we have to talk. Kitty's news has brought other things to light. You see –"

"Miss Julia," interrupted Kitty, "on his deathbed the Reverend asked me to come here to put things right, events that he regretted being involved in, after his brother, your father died ... to do with the will."

"The will?" said Julia. "What had he to do with the will?" The memory of the document she had found, although only a few days ago, was like a blur in the long distant past. She had put it in her carpet bag in her room for safe keeping and, with everything that had happened over the last few days had promptly forgotten about it, assuming it was a copy of the will that they had found in the bank all of those years ago.

"Well, it seems that a second will was written when your father was delusional – at the end when he was wandering in his mind. And they made the Reverend witness it. They both said it was for your own good. But the Reverend always regretted it."

"Who made him?" asked Julia, fearful of the answer.

"Maybe I should explain," said Harriet.

"Yes, Harriet, maybe you should," said Kitty.

"When Father was dying," said Harriet, "Edward came up with the idea that a new will be drawn up that made me the principle beneficiary, as I was engaged to him at the time. Edward felt that he would be the right person to provide financial and moral guidance in Father's absence. Until you married Donal – then you would regain your share."

"Moral guidance, what on earth do you mean?"

"Well, at the time, Julia, you were throwing what little money we had away on fancy cameras and hiring French photographers. Edward was afraid that if you had control of our inheritance that we would have little left by the time Father's affairs were put in order."

"You were so wilful and headstrong, Miss Julia, they was all worried about you," said Kitty. "And you were mixed up with that queer arty crowd."

"Not to mention the Fenians," Harriet added.

"You mean to tell me that you persuaded our demented father to sign a will that disinherited me? That during all these years I have been living as an unpaid servant in your house when I could have been independent!"

"Don't be foolish, Julia – there is no such thing as an independent woman," Harriet said caustically.

Julia sat down, suddenly winded.

Her sister walked over and knelt in front of her, taking both her hands in hers.

"I am so sorry, Julia – I should not have agreed to it. At the time it seemed like the right thing to do. Donal was tied up with the IRB and was not in a position to settle down."

Julia shook off Harriet's hands and stood up again with her back to her sister while she tried to collect her thoughts.

"Donal knew about this?" she asked quietly.

"Well, I talked to Donal. I explained to him about the financial risks you were taking and that I was worried that we would both end up in the workhouse."

"Donal! Oh my God!"

"He felt it was a short-term measure, just until you married. But then he was arrested. As I said, it was in your best interests."

Julia turned to face her sister.

"I cannot take it all in. I feel utterly betrayed by you all. And Eoin?" She paused. "Did he know?"

"Of course. He drew up the will and gave it to that fool Octavius Roe to administer."

Julia suddenly felt small and worthless.

"When Kitty came to Stockport Road looking for you, I spoke to Edward – for the first time, since I found out about Mrs Wilson. After Eoin and you intimidated Edward, he told me everything – how he had been blackmailed by the Fenians. That was why I miscarried." She wiped a tear from her freckled cheek. "Anyway, later he discovered the original will was missing from his desk. I suppose you have it?"

Julia nodded. "I haven't had the chance to read it," she said, almost in a whisper, looking at her younger sister, taking in her unspoken grief at the loss of the child but unable to feel any sympathy.

"You would have found out soon enough. Anyway, you will get your inheritance back shortly. I have asked Edward to arrange the necessary paperwork. I suppose you will marry Donal now that he is to be released."

"Donal is to be released?"

"Yes," said Harriet. "Haven't you heard? Eoin has done some deal with the police, I believe – I don't know the details."

Julia stood up.

"I would like you both to go now, if you don't mind." She gave Kitty a hug.

389

"And Miss Julia, I forgot to say, your uncle left you some Bank of Ireland shares worth about five hundred pounds. But he left the house and the rest of his savings to me. He was a good man. We lived as man and wife, you know." The older woman looked down at the floor, embarrassed.

Julia smiled at her. "You looked after him very well, Kitty, it is only what you deserve."

Kitty left the room, but Harriet paused at the door.

"You had everything, Julia, you know, looks, talent – but you were always so wilful and self-righteous. As I have said before, it was difficult being your younger sister."

She closed the door behind her.

~~~

Chapter 33

It was a clear day – the sun was still high in the sky as the steamship left the docks in Liverpool and started the journey to Kingstown. Molly was in the lounge gossiping with a woman she had met that she knew from the Coombe. Julia looked out across the steel-blue sea. There was a cold easterly wind with the tide pulling in the opposite direction. A bit of a coddle today, she could almost hear Uncle Charles say. She pulled the ribbons of her bonnet tighter to keep it firmly in position. Dispassionately, she looked around. The deck passengers on the return journey were mostly good-humoured, they were going home. Still, there were a few green faces to be seen. One poor man, his head over the rails was emptying the contents of his stomach with great gusto into the Irish Sea.

She wondered how Donal had reacted to her note sent early that morning. She tried not to think about it, any of it. Her brain was numb.

"Julia."

She turned suddenly, her heart racing.

"*Eoin!* What on earth are you doing here?"

"Stephen told me you were going home. I wanted to see you – talk to you."

"I thought you were in Liverpool."

"Formby, actually. It's a long story. But I wanted to explain."

He stood looking down at her, hat in hand, not as smartly dressed as usual, his hair slightly greasy, his brown eyes sad and mournful.

"You heard about the will," he said matter-of-factly.

"Yes, Eoin." She looked directly at him, anger filling her, till she finally exploded. "How could you? I trusted you."

"At that time, I don't think you actually did. But, yes, it was unfortunately necessary."

"In what circumstances is it 'unfortunately' necessary to falsify a will?"

"It was in your best interests. A woman – to be left alone with no male guidance – it was not right. Besides, I felt I needed to look after Donal's interests."

"Was I a mere chattel, to be parsed and parcelled amongst you?"

"Julia, in retrospect it was probably not the right solution," he attempted to reason, "and then events unfolded unexpectedly."

"Do you know that Edward made my life a total misery, that he used and abused me. *He abused me, Eoin!*" she shouted, the pent-up anger suddenly released.

The other passengers on deck stared horrified at the couple who, unseeing, were in a world of their own.

He moved closer to her.

"He didn't lay a hand on you?" His face was white and strained in anger.

"Yes, he did, several times, as I don't like to recall."

Eoin's head sank. "Can you ever forgive me?"

"No, Eoin, I don't think I can." She paused, her eyes locked with his, her resolve unwavering. "What about Donal? What has happened – he told me you have come to some arrangement with the authorities for his release? What was that all about?"

"Well, as you rightly surmised, they were being set up – by Lord Salisbury's agent, Jenkinson. Salisbury hired a General Millen, an American military mercenary, who works for Clan na Gael, to supply Drennan with dynamite. Millen masterminded the dynamite attack at the opening ceremony of the exhibition. The intention was to discredit Parnell and the Irish party."

"What was Drennan's part?"

"Drennan, ironically enough, was politically motivated. He was unaware until the last minute that he was being managed."

Julia tried to gather her thoughts and to make sense of it all.

"So why wasn't news of the explosion in all of the papers?"

"Well, that is why you have not seen me for the last few days. I have been busy. Edward and Flanagan, as we found out that day in the surgery, were double informers spying on you and Donal for Drennan, but also for Jenkinson. I pointed out to Jenkinson that it would be in no-one's interest to have this dirty business exposed in the courts. I threatened to go to *The Times* newspaper with

393

my story about how the government instigated a plot to blow up the Prince and Princess of Wales at the opening of the Jubilee Exhibition in Manchester. That seemed to set the cat amongst the pigeons. After a flurry of phone calls between Whitehall and Manchester Police Headquarters, Lord Salisbury agreed to drop the charges, and to give Donal an early release. Unfortunately, Nelson will have to finish his sentence but he will have privileges reinstated."

Julia turned away from him, leaned against the railings and looked out to sea.

"And the matter of the will?"

"We will lodge the original will in the courts as only recently coming to light." He paused. "Will you marry Donal?" he asked almost uninterestedly, looking down at his hands.

"No," she said sadly but firmly.

He lifted his eyes and turned, taking her hands in his. "Then, will you marry me? I am not a sentimental man, Julia, but I have loved you since I first set eyes on you in your father's shop all those years ago. Unfortunately, you were only ever interested in my romantic younger brother." He paused and then continued simply, "I know we are both no longer young, but I have been overwhelmed by my feelings for you – you have bewitched me, and I cannot get you out of my mind." He smiled. "Julia, you would do me the greatest honour if you would agree to be my wife. I love you – with all my heart. I love you, Julia."

He embraced her and kissed her passionately on the mouth. Her body succumbed to his, as every nerve screamed silently in response. But after a few minutes she found the strength to pull away.

"I cannot marry you, Eoin, not now, not ever. I will not

be dependent on you, or anyone else for that matter, ever again."

She turned away, so he could not see her tears, and walked blindly towards the door of the first-class lounge.

∽◡◠∽

Epilogue

Getting off the Number 30 tram at Dollymount, she walked out across the wooden bridge towards the Island. Three well-dressed widows passed her by, gossiping, oblivious to their little dog straining at the leash, as a large brown rat ran across the wooden planks behind them. They paused, staring at her strange costume, and wondering at the fact that she was there alone.

When she eventually reached the end of the path, she turned left and walked along the deserted beach looking out to sea. Today, under a grey sky, the summit of the Hill of Howth was hidden from view under the mantle of a single, low lying, gossamer cloud.

She stopped and closed her eyes, remembering what it felt like, what she had known. She thought about love, and longing – and letting go. Sometimes she did not think of him for days, then unbid, a certain place, an inflection in a stranger's voice and the memories flooded back – like now. If she closed her eyes, she could almost touch him, feel his face, smell his breath on hers. Was it all for nothing? Only time would tell. But for now, Parnell was dead – brought to an early grave – worn down by the libel case, fighting against those lying articles in *The Times*. It turned out in the end they had been penned by a British government spy. But the fact he was shunned by his friends and colleagues – after news was made public that he was living with the married Kitty O'Shea and had several children by her – that was what put the final nails in his coffin. Home Rule was once again a dream, for another time, for other people.

She willed her mind to the present, opened her lips to savour the taste of salt on her tongue, and breathed in deeply the familiar smells of drying seaweed. Rain was on the way.

Suddenly, the sun emerged from the clouds illuminating the land and sea, and across the bay at the end of the South Bull Wall its rays caught the mirror on the Poolbeg Lighthouse which sparkled with refracted light like a thousand shards of glass. She could feel beads of perspiration on her skin. It was getting warmer and the first of the sea pinks were starting to appear. It would be summer soon, and in a few weeks she was planning to join Louisa, Isabel and a group of friends to paint in Italy. Looking around, she thought it was not a remarkable scene, nor a particularly beautiful one. But she was here. She took out her watercolours and decided to paint it anyway.

The End

Printed in Great Britain
by Amazon

62562367R00234